A Second Glance

Cara D. Smith

Warning

This is a work of fiction. Names, characters, businesses, places, events, and incidents are either the products of the author's imagination or used in a fictitious manner. Any resemblance to actual persons, living or dead, or actual events is purely coincidental.

A Second Glance—Copyright 2021 by Cara D. Smith
Cover design by Cara D. Smith & Shannon Evans
Editing by Evident Ink

ALL RIGHTS RESERVED. This publication contains material protected under International and Federal Copyright Laws and Treaties. Any unauthorized reprint or use of this material is prohibited. No part of this publication may be reproduced or transmitted in any form or by any means, electronic or mechanical, including photocopying, recording, or by any information storage and retrieval system without express written permission from the author/publisher.
For permission, contact the author via the address below.

Rooks Road Publishing
P.O. Box 191
St. Paul, KS 66771

Or

cara@caradsmith.com

The following story contains mature themes, strong language, and sexual situations. It is intended for mature readers.

Dedication

For Steven and Isaac

&

For two others I will not name here, but you know who you are. You both had a hand in shaping Heidi.

One more time, for the people in the back!
The following story contains mature themes, strong language,
and sexual situations. It was written for a mature audience.

Chapter 1	1
Chapter 2	5
Chapter 3	12
Chapter 4	20
Chapter 5	29
Chapter 6	36
Chapter 7	45
Chapter 8	52
Chapter 9	57
Chapter 10	60
Chapter 11	67
Chapter 12	72
Chapter 13	80
Chapter 14	89
Chapter 15	95
Chapter 16	98
Chapter 17	105
Chapter 18	111
Chapter 19	114
Chapter 20	124
Chapter 21	127
Chapter 22	135
Chapter 23	138
Chapter 24	146
Chapter 25	152
Chapter 26	156
Chapter 27	159
Chapter 28	164
Chapter 29	173
Chapter 30	177
Chapter 31	185
Chapter 32	188
Chapter 33	195
Chapter 34	200
Chapter 35	203
Chapter 36	208
Chapter 37	214
Chapter 38	219
Chapter 39	225
Epilogue	231

The story you are about to read includes references to past abuse and trauma that might be difficult for some readers. There is a happily ever after for the character in question.

Past trauma is the reason I write. I found healing in the pages of books when I was not looking for it. It was not easy, but I did it. I hope you can too. Our paths may be different but you don't have to walk alone.

If you are currently in a bad situation please seek help.

Call:

1.800.799.SAFE (7233)

TTY 1.800.787.3224

Text

"START" to 88788

Or visit thehotline.org to chat online.

Chapter 1
Heidi

One more corner and I'm home free. Life will be easier later if I back this trailer in now, but doing so will wreak havoc on my anxiety. I could do it. I know how. But it's not worth it. I'm one turn and parking away from saying I made the trip with no mishaps. My brother will kill me if I return his truck and trailer with so much as a scratch in the clear coat.

Fortunately, this doesn't look like the sort of neighborhood where door dings or hit-and-runs will be a problem. And if something *does* happen, someone will knock on the door and politely exchange insurance information if they don't insist upon calling the cops to report themself for their crimes.

Exactly the sort of neighborhood my ex and his crew loved to prey upon. Half these homes probably aren't locked. Everyone here is too honest.

I flip my signal on and hold my breath. It's a short trailer, but the road is narrow, thanks to the cars parked on both curbs. All the same, I manage it.

"Yes! Thank you!" It's about time things start going my way.

My good fortune and good mood are short lived. There's a small crowd in the yard next to the house that is my new home according to the numbers neatly stenciled on the mailbox. *Great. I live next to* those *people.* They probably play their music too loud, get belligerently drunk, and then fight with each other, yelling over the music to do so. Someone will sit in their truck and rev the shitty engine for twenty minutes for no reason at all. Their offspring will run around like heathens while one or two of the parents sit there, sucking back booze and yelling at them to stop *"or else,"* but never get off their asses to back it up. They don't seem like the type of people to inhabit an upscale neighborhood like this, but they're an invasive species.

Or worse.

They could be the sort of people who invite you to join them and refuse to take no for an answer, even when you clearly do not want anything to do with them. One of them takes pity on you and shows you around, insisting you make yourself at home. The food is mediocre at best, but they're convinced it's the best thing you'll ever eat. The conversation is awkward because you hate being the center of attention, and everyone wants to talk about you. And you're miserable until you can find a polite excuse to leave.

I hope they're the drink-to-belligerence sort. Those people might be loud, but they smile and wave when you turn them down. Maybe bring you a beer if they see you outside. They're too busy doing their own thing to worry about being polite.

I creep closer to the curb in front of my house and stop. Once I'm sure the truck is in park and the parking brake is set, I let my head fall back against the headrest. I hate this. I hate moving. I hate new jobs. I hate people. I hate all of this. Every last thing about this situation. It all fucking blows.

But this is my life, and it's better than the alternatives. I could be dead. Or in jail.

My almost-pep-talk complete, I slide out of the truck and carefully close the door so as not to draw the attention of the gang next door. Like a woman on a mission, I hurry to the front door, watching them from the corner of my eye the whole way. Once the door is safely closed between them and me, curiosity gets the best of me. I dash to the nearest window with a view of the neighboring yard and watch them through the grill smoke drifting in the breeze.

Two kids—a boy and a girl—play on one of those fort things with a slide and a swing set attached. I wanted one of those so bad when I was little. The neighbors had one, but Mom and Dad didn't allow Thomas and me to make friends with the neighbor kids. We might let it slip that Dad frequently gambled away his paychecks and there'd been nothing on the table for the last meal. Maybe even the one before that.

The girl is the older of the two. She is carefully pushing the boy on a swing while he shrieks like a pterodactyl. I suppose some people would call that laughter and find it endearing. It's just annoying. With any luck, if either of them lives next door, it'll be her. She, at least, looks old enough to be tolerable. The wide age gap and difference in coloring lead me to believe they probably aren't related, at least not closely. She's got long, dark hair and a bit of a tan. At least, she's tan compared to the boy's pale complexion. They're far enough away; it's hard to determine if his hair is a bleached-out red or blond.

The adults are seated in a loose group around a patio table, watching the children play and sipping their drinks while they chat. This is the tell. They're *that* group. The ones who will passive-aggressively strong arm me into joining them later. *Just fucking great.*

One of the men, the only redhead in the group, rises and walks to a massive grill positioned away from the house and the table to protect them all from heatstroke since it's already hotter than Satan's armpit outside. He must be my neighbor because guys don't touch another guy's grill. I hope this guy spends a lot of time in his yard. I can see the definition in his arms from here. Broad shoulders taper down to a narrow waist. Yeah, looking at him every day would *not* be a hardship. But I hope that kid isn't his.

More smoke billows out when he opens the lid, and I watch him turn whatever he's cooking while my stomach growls. I haven't made it to a grocery store yet, and I don't want to unhook from the trailer, so I probably won't. My stomach is just going to have to get over it. *Won't be the first time.*

Unless I want to sleep on the floor tonight, I need to stop being a voyeur and get busy. It might be worth it to stand here and watch them for a while longer. It's all so *normal.* I've never had a backyard barbecue of my own. The ones I attended under protest don't count. I was only there to distract the nice people while someone slipped in a side window and robbed them blind. My friends weren't the type to barbecue. They preferred boosting cars and petty theft to grilling steaks and potatoes. All their hobbies were best kept away from prying eyes.

My mood deteriorates further after dredging up the past. I made mistakes. I'm paying for them. It's time to put it all behind me. After a trip to the bathroom to check my resting bitch face, I stomp back out to the trailer to get this shit over with.

***

Called it. I've made it inside with a grand total of two boxes when the group next door makes first contact. I pretend to rearrange boxes while stealing glances at the woman who either volunteered or was elected for this chore. Or maybe she just drew the short fucking straw.

This one is tallish, with golden blond curls that people pay small fortunes to duplicate with chemicals. Her long legs make quick work of the distance—too quickly for my liking. *That just means she'll leave faster.*

"Hi!" she calls from a few yards out to warn me of her approach. I do appreciate that. I hate it when people sneak up on me.

Undeterred by my lack of response, or my resting bitch face, she blithely continues on. "My name's Tara. I'm sure you've noticed my friends and I have the grill going. We'd love it if you'd join us."

At least she is smart enough not to state the obvious—that I'm new here. I take a deep breath to mentally prepare myself and force my face to smile. Half of me expects the skin to crack like old, dry-rotted rubber, but it doesn't. "I appreciate the offer, but I'll have to pass." Hopefully, if I speak her language, she'll understand the first time, and there won't be a repeat visit. "I've got a lot of work to get done tonight."

She looks past me to the jumble of things waiting to go inside. "Is anyone coming to help you?"

3

"Tomorrow," I lie. Someone is coming tomorrow, but only to exchange his truck and trailer for my shitty car. Thomas made it clear that he's too busy to help other than letting me borrow his stuff. *Too busy, or just done helping?* I don't want to think about the bridges I've burned right now.

"You know, there are ten of us. Well, nine . . ." One hand caresses her very pregnant belly in that annoyingly endearing habit all expectant mothers develop. "My doctor has me on a weight restriction, so I'm not much help right now. The others can get all this inside in a hot minute, though."

Did not see that one coming. The offer is tempting, if unexpected. But I don't want to owe anyone else anything. Not even a favor. "Oh, no. It's alright, really. I don't want to interrupt your party."

"It's no trouble at all!" she insists and waves over her shoulder toward the house she came from. "We just moved Chris in next door last week. We're pretty good at it now."

So my neighbor is new here too. Good. He'll be too busy settling himself in to try to help me. "Thank you, but I can manage."

She takes one more look at my things in the trailer and raises an eyebrow at me, but she smiles in a way that speaks of understanding. "Well, if you change your mind, you know where to find us. And we've got plenty of food if you're hungry."

"I'll keep that in mind," I promise, holding in a sigh of relief that she's backing off so easily. "Thank you." I really do mean it this time. I almost regret turning her down. I think I could like her—in another life.

Chapter 2
Heidi

I'm out of boxes I can reach to carry in. To get to the rest, I have to carry in the furniture, which I do *not* want the gang next door to see me struggling with. I can probably get the bed frame inside, maybe the mattress if I like roll it on its sides, but the rest . . . I'll have to work on Thomas when he gets here tomorrow. But I can at least carry in the couch cushions and sleep on those tonight. Steeling my resolve and straightening my spine, I step outside once more only to freeze mid-step.

There's a kid on my lawn. Shitting.

My brain knows what my eyes are seeing, but it's not making sense. There's a kid shitting on my lawn. *There's a kid shitting on my lawn!* What the hell do I do? This is why I hate kids!

A deep voice booms through the quiet evening, sending chills zipping up and down my spine. "Keaton! No!"

Keaton's head whips toward Chris's house, but he doesn't move. Pounding footsteps act as a warning for the redhead who comes charging into view seconds later and picks the little shitter up only to hold him out at arm's length and take off running again without a backward glance. Leaving me staring at a pile of shit that is grotesquely impressive in size in relation to the small human who created it.

"I've got it," a resigned, feminine voice calls from next door. It's not Tara, though. A few seconds later, my yard is invaded again by a new woman carrying a sack and dragging a garden hose. *I'm starting to understand why old people get pissed off about people on their lawns.*

She's one of those unfortunate souls who stopped growing somewhere in middle school—if it took that long. Like the last one clearly would be if she weren't knocked up, this one is skinny as a toothpick turned sideways. As she draws near, it becomes evident that her tiny body is all muscle. But she's got a killer smile, and I'd do sketchy shit for her dark curls—big, bouncy barrel curls that fall to the middle of her back. I almost like her already. *Damn it.* The smile is a trap.

"I'm so sorry about that," she tells me, bypassing the landmine and coming toward me. Her smile shifts into a sly, mischievous grin. "Kind of a shitty way to welcome you to the neighborhood."

My laugh is involuntary but well-earned on her part. That was good.

"I'm Fern." She offers me her hand, and I'm not at all surprised by the callouses when I take it. She looks like a woman who knows how to work, even if she simultaneously looks like a Pinterest Mom—one of those women who bakes cookies and does crafts all day. And she has to be a mom; only a mother would jump in to clean up that kind of mess with such resolved calm. She's probably president of the PTA. If it weren't for the unapologetically dropped curse word, I'd think she teaches Sunday school too. She just has that wholesome look about her, like she has her shit together.

"Heidi," I reply, my mind still reeling from the absurdity. "You don't live there, do you?" With any luck, Red wasn't Chris, this is Red's wife, and they and their spawn live miles away. But no . . . Grills don't lie. Red and Chris have to be one and the same.

She waves a hand in the opposite direction of the house next door, drawing my attention to the huge rock on her third finger. "No, my husband and I live a few blocks away. Two of the others live nearby as well."

I pinch the bridge of my nose and pray that some genetic fluke gave her a redheaded child because that was one little detail my brain did pick up on. The boy was a redhead. Maybe Chris is her brother, and the red hair skipped her. Stranger things have happened. "Good, so you'll be going home later and taking the kid with you." The words slip out through clenched teeth before I can stop them, but it's too late to take them back. *Not sure I want to.*

"Oh!" She hesitates, her pretty face puckering into a scowl of confusion. "No . . . Keaton isn't mine. He lives next door."

Well, shit. Literally. "Oh. Wonderful." I don't try to mask my sarcasm. A kid defecated in my front yard. I'm entitled to be upset.

Her lips twitch, struggling to hold back a smile. I can't imagine what she's found to be amused about, but it makes her look extra adorable, which just isn't fair. I'd look like a stroke survivor struggling to make my mouth work if I made that face.

"I'll get this all cleaned up," she says. "It was nice to meet you." And fuck if she doesn't sound sincere. I don't want to like her. I don't want to like any of them!

Liking people never works for me. *It's not like Dean and the gang will show up and clean them out this time.*

"You too," I sigh. I don't know what to make of this woman. Most people get pissed off when you're rude and sarcastic, but she answers it with polite amusement and goes about her business.

I watch her for a moment, fighting back a gag and wondering why any woman would willingly get knocked up when things like that are part of daily life after kids. It's not my problem, though, so I get back to work.

Fern is spraying the contaminated patch of grass to wash away what she couldn't scoop up when I hurry by carrying my headboard. It's not that heavy, but it's awkward. Every step I take, I knock my shins into it. When I come back out after the footboard, she's standing at the back of the trailer looking in.

"You look like you could use a hand," she says casually.

She might sound casual, but I know better. This is the second contact. The point of no return. She's the one who won't take *'no'* for an answer. I'm not at all surprised that it's her.

"I've got it," I lie. She's right. I need help. But not theirs.

She shoots me a sidelong look and grins. "I'm sure you do, but unless you have a secret identity and jump out of phone booths wearing Lycra and a cape, you're not getting that sofa inside by yourself, honey. I get the drive to be independent, but sometimes you have to accept a hand when it's offered. There are five strong guys next door that can have all your furniture inside in a jiffy, and they'll even put it just where you want it. The girls and I can help you with the rest of the boxes while they do that."

Fuck. How do I say no to that? Again. It's a perfectly reasonable offer, but I don't want to give these people more of an in than they've already found. It's a weak excuse, but maybe it'll work . . . "I can't afford—"

She cuts me off with a soft chuckle that embarrasses the hell out of me. "It's called being a good neighbor. You don't have to pay us. After all, Chris's kid shit in your yard. It's kinda the least we can do."

She surprises another laugh out of me. *Why is it so hard to tell her to kick rocks?* I had no problem turning Tara down. For some stupid reason, I *want* to tell Fern yes just to spend more time with her. I know better than to get close to strangers but—no. That's in the past. There's no reason I *have* to keep my distance. I can accept their help this once, and then I don't have to convince Thomas to help me tomorrow. "I don't like asking for help," I confess.

Fern shrugs a shoulder. "I get it. Trust me. But you don't have to ask. We're offering."

"Alright," I relent, accepting the wisdom of her words. But only because they're offering. And because I don't want to beg my brother.

Smiling again, she beckons for me to join her and leads me across the yard, directly to Red, who is blushing furiously. "Chris," she begins, confirming what I already know, "this is Heidi."

That blush is cute. He's probably cute even when his face is *not* redder than his hair. But there's something very guarded about him. In my experience, guys as buff as he appears to be—if his arms are any indication of the rest of him—exude a lot more confidence than he is putting off just now.

For a second, he's too embarrassed to react, but he finally ducks his head and offers me a hand. "I'm so fu—" He stops mid-word and tries again, "I'm so sorry about that. It won't happen again, I swear. He's just . . . he's potty trained but very curious about why our neighbor's dog doesn't have to use the toilet and . . ." Wincing, he shakes his head. "I'll shut up now."

The urge to smile is strong, but I bite my cheek to hold it back. I can't let my attraction to this guy make a complete fool of me. I have to live next to him and his kid. I don't want him thinking he can charm his way out of everything.

Fern doesn't hold back her smile this time. A tall, dark-headed guy with eyes the color of the Caribbean stops on her other side and slings an arm around her waist, resting his hand on her hip. The sun glints off the screen of the top-of-the-line smartwatch on his wrist. She glances up at him and lays a hand on his chest. "Heidi, now that you've met Chris, this is my husband, Mason."

Oh shit, we're going to do the introduction thing. I break out in a panic sweat. There are too many of them; I'll never remember all their names. *Calm the fuck down, idiot.* I don't *need* to remember anything about them. Not their names. Not who is with who. Not who lives where. And definitely not their movements. It doesn't matter. I'm not a lookout anymore.

Still, they're nice enough to help me. The least I can do is try to remember who is who. Because I *want* to. Not because someone is expecting me to.

I somehow manage a deep breath and shake the huge hand he offers me. *Mason, dark hair, blue eyes.* I can do this. I just have to mentally catalog names and remarkable features. And there are a *lot* of remarkable features here, especially where the men are concerned, but that's probably just personal preference making me biased. If I didn't know better, I'd swear I stumbled onto a movie set. I've never seen this many fine-ass men in one place unless I was watching television. *Is it wrong to just stand here and drool?*

Mason smiles, which should be criminal. *Those two smiles should not be in the same room, much less the same relationship.* "Nice to meet you."

"You too," I mumble.

Fern points to the blond guy—the only blond guy—who would be tall if Mason wasn't around. He's sitting next to Tara and has a hand on her shoulder. The casual comfortability says they're together. "That's Gabe, and I believe you've met his wife, Tara."

Tara beams, and Gabe and I exchange nods.

Fern's finger swivels to the girl on the other side of Tara. "This is Trista, and her boyfriend, Ryan."

They're both dark-headed with brown eyes. Trista has to be shorter than Fern. She's *tiny*. Fern is short and svelte, but Trista is a different class of small. All the same, it's obvious she has her fair share of muscle. *What do these people do for a living?*

They must be fitness junkies. I bet they all met at the gym. The fitness trackers or smart watches they're all wearing fit that theory.

The word for Ryan is *wow*. His face could easily grace the pages of magazines, but there's this sense of darkness around him that makes me want to take a step back. It's hard to judge with him sitting, but he's probably on the tall side of average, but broad. His pierced eyebrow and the small fortune worth of ink decorating his arms sets him apart from the other two guys with dark hair. He nods and lifts a finger while his girlfriend offers me a shy smile.

Next up is a tall blond chick with an enviable resting bitch face, a model's figure, and perfectly straight hair. She's probably as tall as Ryan, if not taller. I've noticed a trend, so she must be Chris's significant other since she's the only one not seated next to a guy. *Damn. Doesn't mean I can't appreciate the scenery, though.* But something about the way she's sitting makes me question that. She's not as comfortable here as the others are. Instead of relaxing into her seat, she's somewhat stiff, like she's ready to spring to her feet at a moment's notice. Could be that she just doesn't like to sit still, though. There's no giant rock on her hand, but Trista and the last girl aren't wearing one, either. "This is Noel." A smile erases her RBF. There is no 'and' at the end of her introduction.

My foolish heart does a hopeful little flip. *Don't be an idiot.* The *last* thing I need is another guy manipulating my life.

"Her husband is still being a stubborn ass and refuses to let bygones be bygones," Tara tells me, rolling her eyes. There's a story there, but it's none of my fucking business. That doesn't stop my curiosity from driving me crazy, but I keep my mouth shut. I'm better off not caring.

Noel sighs but doesn't contradict the other woman.

Fern shrugs at me as if to say *she's not wrong* and carries on. "And, last but not least, Austin and his girlfriend, Jamaica."

Austin and Mason have to be brothers. They look too much alike to be anything else. His eyes aren't as blue, though, and he's probably not quite as tall. He's sprawled in his chair like he doesn't have a care in the world, but his leg bounces with restless energy.

Jamaica's hair and light brown skin are easily distinguishable from the other ladies, even the tan ones. Her shoes are on the ground in front of her, and her legs are curled beneath her. She smiles brightly and waves. "Nice to meet you," she says with an accent that reminds me of a trip with my grandparents to the island she's named for.

"In addition to Keaton, my stepdaughter, Ronni, is meandering around here somewhere," Fern adds, piquing my curiosity. There's a lot of love in her voice when she says the words *'stepdaughter.'* I'm not familiar with the sentiment coming from a stepparent. Lord knows I got none from my stepdad, though he insisted we call him Dad and pretended he loved us like his own.

"She's supervising Keaton while he gets dressed," Chris interjects. "They'll be right down."

Mason and Fern nod their approval simultaneously. "Alright, everyone," Fern calls, getting their attention again. "Heidi has thrown in the towel. Let's get her unloaded."

"Awww," Austin groans, throwing his head backward and somehow sinking farther into his seat.

So much for everyone being happy to help . . . I scramble to tell him not to worry about it, but Fern scoffs.

"Don't pretend you don't like to show off for Jam," she teases him.

He pops to his feet, a wide smile that screams mischief firmly in place. "Damn, you caught me."

These people are weird.

Still giggling, Fern turns to me. "Why don't you go back your truck into the drive?"

My already overactive anxiety shoots through the roof. "Um, I'm not sure if I can."

Ryan and Fern both hold out their hands. "I can do it, if you'd like," Fern says.

"*You* can?" Ryan asks, raising his pierced eyebrow and only that one. He's on his feet now, like everyone else, and I'm pleased to note I was right about his height. Dean taught me well.

However, he also taught me that bodies don't lie, and this man's says he knows how to use it. His every move carries the grace of a trained fighter. It's good to know, but people like him typically don't lash out at unsuspecting victims. Still, I'm wary of him. I never expected Dean to snap and beat the shit out of me, either.

"My grandpa taught me to drive in a *semi*," Fern says. "Because if I can drive that, I can drive anything."

Holy fucking shit. This woman really *is* a badass. All the same, I'm not giving up Thomas's keys. "My brother will kill me if his truck has so much as a scratch when he comes for it tomorrow," I tell her, shaking my head.

Fern smiles and reaches over to pat my arm. "Ryan here restores old cars as a hobby, just him and Trista from start to finish."

"Except the upholstery," he interjects.

"I'm learning!" Trista cries.

"I know, Pixie Stix," he says fondly, raising her hand to his lips to kiss it.

Fern shrugs like it's no big thing if she backs it into a pole or something. "If I damage it, I'll pay to fix it. And Ryan can do the work unless your brother would prefer to find his own body man."

My head is spinning with the influx of information. I've learned way more than I ever wanted to know about any of these people in the last ten minutes. How can she so casually talk about paying to fix a truck? But I know the answer to that. The rock on her hand told me, paired with the watch her husband is wearing, the fact that they live in this neighborhood, and the cheapest vehicle in front of this house is parked in the driveway like it belongs here. She's fucking loaded. It's not a huge leap to assume they *all* are.

My heart twinges with regret. Sure, they're all nice enough now, but if they ever find out that my ex-boyfriend and all his buddies are serving time for burglary, they'll hate me.

I was right about this neighborhood. I shouldn't be here. But they sure as hell don't act like the rich assholes my ex kissed up to, hoping for handouts and pocketing things when they weren't looking. They're out here, sweating their asses off like the common folk, willing to get their hands dirty to help me. *I'm going to regret this.*

No matter how reasonable Fern's logic seemed earlier, they're going to want something for this. And they're going to shun me when they learn the truth. Still, I reach into my pocket and hand over the keys. They won't back down now, and they'll be done sooner if they don't have to carry things as far. The sooner I can get them out of my life, the better.

And . . . maybe I'm a teeny bit curious about them now in the same way my grandmother was enthralled with those daytime TV dramas before she died.

Chapter 3
Chris

Fern strides across the yard full of the same determined enthusiasm with which she tackles everything, leaving us to follow. Despite Austin's grumbling, none of us really mind. Watching Heidi struggle with what little she's carried in was driving us all nuts on some level. It was never acknowledged out loud, but glances and grimaces said it all.

There might be some guys in the world who could sit by and watch *anyone*, not just a woman, struggle with something that would be mindlessly easy for them, but it's not us. It doesn't matter that we don't know her. It's just the thing to do.

It doesn't help that she's so thin a gentle breeze might knock her over. *Maybe she's sick?* That only makes me more determined to help, and not only with moving her in. Something about Heidi unsettles me, putting every instinct on high alert. Not just the protective ones, either. I shove my hands in the pockets of my jeans to keep them from obeying the voice in the back of my head, screaming for me to touch her.

"Where do you think you're going?" Gabe's question to Tara carries back to me, where I'm trailing along behind the pack with a reluctant Heidi at my side.

Tara brings one hand up to cradle her stomach. So far, the only complications with her pregnancy have been severe morning sickness early on, but her doctor is acting in an abundance of caution as her due date creeps closer. It's making her crazy, but I think it's more worry for the child than the restrictions chafing. "I know I can't help carry, but I can stay inside and help Heidi tell everyone where to put things."

"Why don't you go keep an eye on Keaton and Ronni and the grill?" I ask her once we've all stopped in Heidi's yard to wait for Fern to get the truck maneuvered into place. The extra cars on the curb aren't giving her much space to work, but she's doing great.

Ronni is responsible, but I'll feel better with an adult close at hand since the rest of us are leaving the yard. And it'll probably be time to put the steaks on the grill before we get back. The potatoes will be done soon.

Tara glances over her shoulder and smiles at me. "Okay. I can do that." She peels off and goes back to my place, easing the small knot of tension in my shoulders.

"Thank you!" I call after her.

She turns around to walk backward and blows me a kiss. "You bet."

I have the best friends on the planet. How many other people would willingly watch a kid that isn't theirs? But they all love Keat almost as much as I do. And I love them all the more for it.

"You guys really don't have to do this," Heidi says in a small voice.

I turn to look at her, only to find her shrunk in on herself, trying to be smaller. Invisible. Kind of the way Fern used to do before she and Mason were a thing. It fucking shreds me, but I can't put my finger on why. "We *want* to," I say.

Forgetting myself, I reach to pat her shoulder like I would Trista or Fern but stop with my hand hovering in midair when she flinches away from my touch. I yank my hand away and hold both up where she can see them clearly. Whatever else this woman is going through, someone hurt her at some point in her life. Ryan and I get a lot of women like her at our gym, The Bar, mostly there for self-defense classes. *Maybe I'll gift her a membership as a housewarming gift.*

Ryan and I lock eyes, and he nods subtly, letting me know he caught it too. He pulls Mason, Austin, and Gabe aside and they put their heads together. I don't hear the words, but I'm sure he's warning them. They'll take care not to make her uncomfortable. *I have the best friends.*

Ryan holds up a closed fist when the back of the trailer is close enough to the little house, and the brake lights on the truck and trailer glow red. The truck shuts down, and Fern hops out. "I'm impressed, short shit," he tells her, patting her on the head when she gets close enough, initiating the little game they play now that he knows she has enough training to make him work not to get his ass kicked. He immediately winces, his eyes darting toward Heidi because he knows what's coming next.

Sure enough, Fern swings at him, a perfectly controlled motion that stops when her knuckles graze his cheek. She freezes, clearly thrown off that Ryan didn't move to defend himself.

He doesn't so much as flinch, let alone retaliate like he usually would, likely because of Heidi, but Fern doesn't know. Mason grabs her arm before she does anything else and shakes his head just a bit, and she tips her head in question. Mase shakes his head again, *later* he's saying in their unspoken method of communication. It all happens in the time between one blink and the next.

13

Heidi makes a little squeaking noise and steps to the side, putting me between them and her. "They're just playing," I murmur, keeping my voice low so I don't scare her any more than she already is. "Ryan could be a professional boxer if he really wanted to, and Fern is well-versed in Muay Thai. They like to pick on each other." Anyone else and I'd call it flirting, but they're both happy in their relationships. It's more like siblings tormenting each other because they can.

"They're done?" Heidi asks in a whisper that probably doesn't carry.

"They're done." Without turning around, I hold out my hand, letting her decide if she needs the comfort of a friendly touch to calm her stress. Looking at her would put too much pressure on her to decide. I don't want that. It's okay if she takes the offer; it's okay if she doesn't. Whatever she needs to be comfortable. But it takes every ounce of willpower I possess not to reach for her again. I want her in my arms. I want her to know she never has to be afraid again because I will keep her safe.

What the hell? I just met her. It's fine to not want to make the situation worse, but I shouldn't care quite this much.

She sidles out from behind me with her hands tucked into her pockets, and her head ducked low—not hanging, just low and wary. She glares around, hostile eyes daring anyone to comment, but Ryan has trained us better than that. In fact, the guys are already in the trailer, and the girls are acting as if nothing happened.

Nothing needs to be said unless she wants to talk about it. Ryan didn't mean to make her uncomfortable; picking on Fern is just a habit of his. But now we have a good idea of the depth of Heidi's fear. And I hate it.

I lean down so I can speak softly without my voice carrying to anyone but Heidi, all while keeping myself at a distance. "Ryan teaches self-defense classes." I pull out my wallet and extract a card, holding it lightly between two fingers and extending it to her. "We own the place. Come by sometime if you want to try the classes. My treat. Just tell whoever happens to be at the desk that you need to talk to me."

Ryan and I are both certified, but he's much better with battered women. He checks his anger at the door, picks up the patience of a saint, and somehow makes those women feel safe and secure in his studio. Logically, I know the best way to protect them is to teach them to protect themselves, but I struggle to push them to do what they need to when their past rears its ugly head. My odd reaction to Heidi will make it harder for me. Assuming she takes me up on the offer.

Her eyes, a dark blue that somehow looks dull and flat, narrow in suspicion. "Why would you do that?"

I shrug. "Housewarming present? Welcome to the neighborhood."

Never taking her eyes off me, she snatches the card from my fingers and slips it into the back pocket of her jeans. "Thanks."

Nodding, I walk away, giving her space to recover. If I stay, I might do something stupid like try to hug her.

"Heidi?" Fern calls from the doorway. "We're going to need you to tell us where you want things when you're ready."

From the corner of my eye, I watch Heidi scurry into the house, her shoulders bunched up around her ears, but her back is ramrod straight. *Good for her.* She's tough. She'll be alright in time.

I jump into the back of the trailer and grab a two-person dining table. It's not big or heavy, so I can manage it by myself. Inside Heidi's house, she's standing in the middle of her living room, eyes wide and one arm wrapped around her middle while she tells Ryan and Mason where to put her couch and the girls where boxes go. Gabe puts a chair down and goes back for another, but there's only one place for a table, so I wade through the controlled chaos toward the back of the house.

I toured this place the same day I visited my house, so I know my way around a bit. I decided it was too small and I didn't want to rent anymore. She doesn't have a dining room, which is kind of good because this dinky table would look out of place in a room by itself and she doesn't have another unless she's hiding it under boxes. There aren't that many boxes, though.

In the kitchen, I place the table in the only logical spot and return to the truck. The big stuff is all in already, so I grab a double stack of boxes labeled kitchen and go. On my way back out for more, I pass Ryan carrying the toolbox he keeps in his car. It's stocked more for fixing cars and things at the gym than household projects, but knowing him, he's probably got everything he could possibly need to fix anything anyone throws at him.

There are only four boxes left in the truck. I grab two more and go. Jam and Trista are waiting at the back of the trailers and surge in when I step out. Ten minutes, tops, and it's done. Mason closes the trailer up, and Fern jumps in the truck to drive it around the block and park it on the street again since it's technically too long for Heidi's little driveway.

I leave the boxes on the counter and go back up front in case they need me for something. Heidi's standing in the doorway of her new home, her eyes rimmed in red from tears she's fighting. She's stiff as a board from head to toe, and her eyes are bouncing around, landing on one of us and darting away. "Thank you," she murmurs.

"You're welcome," Jamaica tells her, stepping forward to ease an arm around Heidi's shoulders. Heidi allows it, and Jam gives her a little squeeze. Of all of us, Jamaica is probably best suited to comfort her. She's never said her ex hit her or anything, not to me anyway, but he sure as hell was a psychopath. "What else can we do to help?"

Heidi shakes her head. "You've done enough already."

"Are you sure?" Trista asks. She turns in a slow circle, taking in the room that's already getting that lived-in look because Noel unpacked a trash bag full of throw pillows and blankets and is busy arranging them on the couch and chairs. "I mean, I noticed you don't have a lot of things to assemble. Ryan and Mason will have your bed together in nothing flat if it's not already done, so if there's anything else . . ."

"That's really it." Heidi's lower lip trembles. She bites it to make it stop, then swipes at her nose with the back of her hand. "The rest is just unpacking boxes. I don't even have a TV to hook up."

Now that she's mentioned it, I haven't noticed *any* electronics. *Maybe they're in the cab of the truck.* I wouldn't leave them out there, though. Yeah, this is a nice neighborhood, but it's not exactly gated. "Do you have more boxes in the truck?"

She shakes her head. "This is everything I own. The cool stuff was my ex's."

Her ex's . . . so she's single. Recently single if she's just moving. Not that it matters. I have no business caring, and I won't be a rebound. But that odd feeling is back with a vengeance, filling my head and my heart with ideas about me and the girl next door.

"All done here," Mason says, stepping out of the larger of the two bedrooms. "Do you know where your bedding is?"

Noel grabs a full trash bag off the floor. "Got it."

"Do you even know how to make a bed?" Gabe asks Mason dryly. It would be a fair question, Fern was Mason's housekeeper for years and did things like that for him, but he also lived alone for a while before he met Ronni's mother.

Mason fixes his eyes on the bag, and they go wide. "Wait . . . You mean it doesn't just happen?"

Gabe rolls his eyes. "Smartass."

Mase grins and winks at Heidi. "A smart ass is a good ass, and good ass is hard to find."

There's a second of complete silence before the house practically shakes with laughter.

Noel wipes a tear from the corner of her eye and makes a shooing motion with her hands. "Alright boys, off you go. It's your night to cook. We'll finish up here and be right over."

***

"Ronni, would you go next door and let the ladies know dinner is ready?" Ryan asks our honorary niece while I pull the food off the grill.

Dinner turned into quite the production. I promised steak and potatoes, but Tara and Gabe showed up with a foil packet of asparagus for me to throw on the grill. Jamaica and Austin contributed homemade coleslaw. Trista and Ryan made fruit salad. And Fern and Mason brought a sheet cake that Austin keeps trying to hide from everyone else.

Ronni drops her jump rope and takes off across the yard. "Sure, Uncle Ryan!"

Heidi will probably be happy for a break. The girls are great, but they're probably a little much for her in large doses. However, with as little as she has, they'll have her completely unpacked in an evening if she stays back and tells them where she wants things. And if Madi had come tonight . . . She'd have everything organized by color in a heartbeat. *That does make it easy to find my favorite shirts, though.*

Giggles grab my attention as the girls troop across the yard. Heidi is sandwiched between Jamaica and Trista, but she's smiling—something I hadn't seen her do yet. That irritating urge to hug her surges to the front of my mind again. She has a killer smile.

Her smile is wrong, though. It doesn't have that pained, forced look to it like she's trying to hide misery. And it doesn't look like she's faking it because it's expected of her. I can't quite figure it out. It's almost like . . . Like it's been too long since she's had a reason to smile and mean it. Like smiling as an automatic reaction to a situation is foreign to her.

That's it. I'd bet anything. I've been there, but Keaton saved me. Hopefully, someone comes along to save her as well. The voice in the back of my head says that could be me, but I ignore it. Heidi is too young to be interested in me. Even if she was, she doesn't need my drama. And I don't need to give someone else the chance to hurt me. I'm one shitty breakup away from swearing off relationships for good.

It would be easy enough to do, though. Heidi's pretty—long, dirty blond hair, big blue eyes, and I've tried really hard not to notice the swell of her breasts under her baggy sweater or the curve of her hips, but I *am* a guy. If I'm right about her age, her eyes are awfully hard for someone so young. She's been through some shit, but I already knew that. Her reaction to Fern and Ryan roughhousing gave that away. *Haven't we all, though?*

Gabe was an alcoholic and—briefly—a drug addict. Tara was assaulted by his dealer. Mason lost his first love in childbirth. Fern lost her family in a car accident. Jamaica's psycho ex had a gun to Austin's back just a few months ago. Ryan found his college girlfriend dead from an overdose. Trista's mother was so controlling, she didn't even know what her favorite color was until she removed herself from that toxic situation. And Noel . . . well, I'm not sure about her, but I'm sure she's got her story. I'm sure girls know, but nothing has ever been said to me about it.

And then there's me, forced to choose between the woman I thought was the love of my life and the little life we accidentally created together. My whole future changed over morning coffee on a random Tuesday. *Lydia takes a sip of her coffee and puts her mug down calmly. "I'm pregnant."*

Her voice is still perfectly clear in my mind all these years later. I try to push the memory back and focus on what I'm doing, but it won't stop.

Lydia fidgets with her thumb ring, focusing on the little band like it holds the answers to the meaning of life to avoid looking at me. Something isn't right here. *I duck my head, trying to put myself in her line of sight, but she closes her pretty blue eyes. "I'll take care of it," she mutters.*

Her words open a pit in my stomach. I can't stand even the smell of my coffee right now. *"Take care of it? What are you talking about?"*

She rolls her eyes. "I'm having an abortion."

Ryan nudges me with his elbow, breaking me out of my own personal hellhole of a memory. "You okay, man?"

I shake my head, trying to fling the memories out of it. They never go away, though. I really thought forty weeks was enough time to change Lydia's mind, but that'll teach me to think. She held that abortion over my head as long as she could, then spent the rest of the pregnancy complaining that she should've done it. She said it as she walked into the hospital to give birth that cold December day. "Yeah, I'm good. Just . . . thinking."

"About?"

"Lydia." There's no use lying to Ryan about it. He was right there with me through it all. All of them were there. My parents, Tara, and Fern were fucking lifesavers when I was too tired to think, and he wouldn't sleep. Ryan was the rock our business needed. And all of them assured me that I wasn't a selfish asshole for choosing my kid.

But we ended that day. Our previously solid relationship was dashed to pieces because neither of us was willing to budge. We were over either way, though. I couldn't have stayed with her knowing that she could make that decision without consulting me.

Yes, the burden was hers, and it is her body, but it's not like she got knocked up by a random one-night stand who wouldn't take responsibility for the consequences. I was part of her life and willing to step up and be a father. To pay for everything and lessen that burden in whatever way I could.

Maybe there was no right answer in that situation. But it's too late to change anything. I'm happy with my life, and as hard as it is for me to accept, I hope she's happy with hers.

Ryan watches me, waiting for me to explain. He's good at getting answers out of people. He just watches and waits until the truth comes bubbling out.

"She would've liked this place, I think." The Lydia I met would have. I'm not so sure anymore.

He shrugs, his lips twitching into a sneer. He never cared for Lydia to begin with, but he never rubbed it in my face that he was right. "Who cares what she thinks?"

"I know." I sigh and look around the yard again, imagining her here. "But sometimes, I wonder what life would be like if she'd changed her mind." I wouldn't trade Keaton for the world, but what if Lydia had chosen us. Or if I had chosen her.

He snorts. "Miserable, because deep down, you'd always know she's not the woman you thought she was. But at least you'd be enjoying all that money you spent," he adds with another nudge to the ribs, referring to Lydia's boob job, liposuction, tummy tuck, and vaginal rejuvenation.

I shrug that off. I meant what I told her that morning over coffee. I didn't love her for her looks. And really, she didn't gain much weight at all. In fact, the doctor was worried because she wasn't gaining. But after she gave birth, she insisted her body was wrecked, and it was all my fault. I thought she was even more beautiful than the day I met her, even though my feelings for her were long gone. She's still the mother of my child. Some part of me will always appreciate her for the son she gave me. That will never change.

I give myself another shake to cast off the past and reach with the grill tongs for another potato.

"We got you, man," Ryan says, patting my shoulder instead of elbowing me again.

"Thanks," I whisper with another shake because the chill of the past just won't let go despite the heat of the grill and the lingering heat of the beautiful late September day.

He shrugs. "Figured it was coming sooner or later. You left a lot of history in that apartment."

"It needed to be left," I murmur. I'll miss it. So many of Keaton's firsts happened there. But there are just as many unhappy memories there that will only drag me down.

He salutes me with his beer. "I'll drink to that. You ready to eat?"

"Yeah."

He follows me to the table, and we take our seats. Someone brought out a chair from the dining room table so we'd have a seat for Heidi. Mason moves around the table, pouring wine for anyone who wants it from one of the bottles they brought from Fern's vineyard. I pass when he gets to me. I don't drink when Keaton is home. The wine is excellent, but what if something happens and I need to take Keaton to the hospital? One glass won't get me drunk, but it's not worth the risk.

The food goes 'round the table family style. Conversation flows as freely as the wine. Under the influence of good food and good friends, the leftover tension from the dredged up past melts away.

But with my mind unburdened, my thoughts—and my eyes—veer toward Heidi far too often.

Chapter 4
Heidi

My stomach rumbles. I fold my pillow around my head, covering my ears like it'll go away if I can't hear it. The hollow pain of hunger is sharp this morning, making it impossible to go back to sleep and ignore it. After the huge meal I ate last night, I don't know how I could possibly be hungry now, but I am. It's like a good meal set my stomach's expectations for life. And I have nothing to eat. *Suck it up.*

I've dealt with worse—whole weekends where I might not eat unless Thomas managed to find an odd job at a restaurant in exchange for food because Dad blew our grocery money. And then he screamed at us for it, like it was our fault. *It's only one meal. I'll be alright.*

The doorbell rings. *Thomas!* He's early, but I'm not complaining. I'll have my car back and can go shopping for some groceries.

I don't know why I'm so excited to see him. We haven't really talked in a while. The last time I saw him, he handed me his keys with a scowl and left. He'll either trade me keys and leave again, or he'll want to talk. And if he wants to talk, it's not going to be happy. But I hurry to the door in my pajamas, eager to make the trade and get this over with.

Someday, Thomas may love me again. That day isn't today, and it's going to take a lot of work. I'm not even sure if it's worth the effort. I'll only disappoint him again. I always do. It's probably better in the long run if I leave things the way they are. I don't want to hurt him again.

Stop it, you idiot. That's Dean talking, not you.

I snatch the keys off the shelf Fern hung for me last night before dinner and yank the door open, looking up into brown eyes, but they're not Thomas's. It's Chris, standing there in a pair of gym shorts and a sleeveless shirt that fits tight enough to hint at the muscle underneath.

With an undignified yelp, I slam the door in his face. I'm not wearing a bra! And my pajama shorts barely cover my butt. My hair is a mess, and I probably have lines on my face from sleeping. It's one thing to answer the door for Thomas looking like the hot mess I am with a little too much on display. He's my brother. He's not looking at *me*. He'll just mutter curses and tell me to put some clothes on. But the ridiculously handsome guy who lives next door? That's a problem.

It doesn't matter that girls like me aren't even a blip on his radar or that getting involved with someone in any capacity isn't on mine right now. I need armor to face him—or at least a bra and some denim. Pajamas leave me too vulnerable. "Just a second!" I yell through the door.

Hugging my chest to keep the bounce under control, I race back to my room and snag yesterday's bra off the top of the pile I left my dirty clothes in before I fell into bed in the small hours. I was too full and tired and something close to happy to care about the mess at the time.

Yanking my pajama shirt off, I drop it, reach behind me to grab one side of my bra, hook the stupid thing, and turn it around the right way so fast it's amazing I don't have carpet burn or something. I shove my arms through the straps and grab my box of clean clothes—one of the only things that didn't get unpacked before dinner last night. Dumping it on the bed, I grab some denim and jump into it. It's a pair of jeans that are a little big, but I can change them later. I just need something to go to the door in. The first shirt I grab goes over my head, and I wrestle my arms through the sleeves while I run back to the door.

I yank the door open again, already apologizing for whatever the hell that was. "Sorry. I thought you were someone else." That I have the urge to apologize at all is weird. It's not like I invited him over. Or want him here. But he was so nice last night. And he didn't treat me like a bomb about to go off when I spazzed out over Fern play punching the scary guy . . . what was his name again? Ryan. That's it. The one who moves like he was built to destroy the world. I can't believe he just stood there and let her swing at him. My dad would've—*stop it, you idiot. Don't think about that.*

Chris smiles. It's a nice smile, devoid of mockery and malice. I noticed that last night about all of them. I didn't have to search for a hidden meaning behind any of their expressions. It was nice, if bizarre. "No worries." He holds up a clear plastic container, the contents hidden by a haze of steam. "Should probably take the lid off for a bit before they get soggy, but Keat and I made you some muffins. I noticed you didn't have much in the kitchen last night and thought you might be hungry."

Movement catches my eye. Keaton peeks out from behind his dad's leg and smiles shyly. I must have a twitch or something because my mouth pulls into a smile.

I don't know what to say. I don't know what to *do*. For the first time in years, I don't have to worry about Dean swooping in to screw over any friends I make. But these people won't want to be my friends forever, so accepting their generosity now feels like I'm taking advantage of them. Years of experience, both before and after Dean, tell me that this is a no-win situation. Even if they don't expect anything in return for their kindness, they'll abandon me when they find out about my past. It doesn't matter how good they are; they won't want to associate with someone like me.

Some part of me wants these people to be exactly what they seem to be. I want to believe that they can accept my past and restore my faith in humanity. A dog can only be kicked so many times before it gives up, though. *I guess I haven't been kicked enough yet.* It's just hard to resist this level of nice.

Like the idiot I am, I smile back at him and reach for the container. The warmth feels good in my hands. Soothing somehow. My stomach rumbles again, betraying me. "Actually, I am. Thank you. Um . . ." Shit. Manners. I open the door a little wider and take a half-step back. "Would you like to come in?"

Even as I ask, I hope and pray he says no. It was different yesterday when there were so many other people here. Now, it's just us—and his kid—I don't have to *trust* them yet, but after hours of listening to them chatter and tease each other mercilessly last night, it's hard not to like them a little bit. They didn't pressure me to talk about myself or even to talk at all. They let me sit in their circle and take it all in like I belonged there with them. And the food *was* good. Those steaks might actually be the best thing I've ever eaten.

All the same, I don't know that I'll ever feel safe alone with a man again. This one doesn't move with the same deadly grace as his friend, but if you know what to look for, you can tell he knows how to use his body for violence. The ones that don't are probably more dangerous—you don't know to keep your guard up—but I'm not stupid enough to put myself in a compromising position with a man who might as well have a warning label.

Still smiling, Chris shakes his head, easing the knot of anxiety in my stomach. "I'm on my way to work. Just wanted to swing by and drop those off before we left. I would've made it all of an hour before I felt guilty and sent Fern to feed you."

Why does he care? I force a laugh like that last part is a joke. After last night, my laugh isn't as rusty as it used to be, but it's still a strange feeling. "You didn't have to do this," I say, raising the container, "*or* call Fern. My brother is supposed to bring my car and get his truck today. I'll go shopping after that."

Given the option of dealing with Chris or Fern, I'll take Chris. Fern might be the more dangerous of the two. Not even physically; she'll have me spilling all of my secrets, and then none of them will want to associate with me anymore. *I don't want to be a disappointment to anyone else.*

Chris takes a step back, stopping short when he bumps into Keaton. He stoops to pick the boy up, settling him on his hip. The kid hides his face in his father's neck. *You weren't shy last night when you were shitting in my yard* . . . "Well, at least you have muffins to hold you over until he gets here."

"I appreciate it."

"Any time." With a smile and a wave of his free hand, he turns and leaves. Watching him leave isn't a hardship. The man has a fantastic ass. It would be a crime not to enjoy the view.

***

The doorbell rings, interrupting my pointless dusting. I needed something to do to distract me from my grumbling stomach so I don't grab another muffin and call it lunch. Steeling myself, I force a smile and open the door. I saw him a few days ago, but I'm still amazed at how little Thomas has changed in the last year. Or has it been two? Same face unmarred by lines despite the burdens he's carried. His eyes, identical to mine in shape but not color, are a little harder than they were before. *My fault.* "Hey. How was the drive?"

It should be easy to smile. He's my big brother. I love him. He's done so much for me, but that only serves to remind me that I ran away and left him to deal with Dad's anger. And I went back to Dean every time Thomas helped me get away from him.

Thomas shrugs. He looks over my shoulder, into the living room, and raises his eyebrows. "What nice family did you steal all that from?"

I force myself not to react, not to let him know how deep that barb pierced my heart. *I deserve that.* Still, my eyes sting with tears that want to fall, but I am stronger than they are. "I didn't steal it. I bought it all. I never stole anything."

He tips his chin up, a smile tugging at the corners of his mouth. "Oh, that's right. I forgot. You were just the lookout or the distraction. Look over here at the pretty, harmless little girl while her boyfriend robs you blind!"

I deserve that too. I take a slow, deep breath to hide my pain. It's low, and it hurts, but he's right. It wasn't always that way—no. That's not right. It *was* always that way; I was just oblivious to it for years.

I step back and open the door wider, inviting him inside. He strolls on in and flops down in one of the chairs while I close the door behind him. I go to the couch, but I don't sit. I'm too restless.

"You know I didn't do it because I wanted to," I tell him, forcing the words out between teeth clenched in an effort to keep my frustration at bay.

"Could've fooled me. You went back five times in," he pauses to count on his fingers, "eight years."

"*You're not better than any of us, Heidi Decker. You're a criminal too. It doesn't matter that you never take anything. You're just as worthless as the rest of us as far as the world is concerned. No one loves you anymore—no one but me—and no one ever will because to them, you're nothing more than a lowlife thief.*"

I shake Dean's voice out of my head and run through the reminders my therapist gave me, trying to reprogram my brain. That's Dean. Not me. He was wrong. He said things like that to keep me weak, but I'm not. I was strong enough to survive when he put me in the hospital. I'm strong enough to fight my demons and make it out alive. But that bit is the hardest to cast off because, unlike all the other nasty shit he ever said to me, it might actually be true. "You don't know—"

"What it's like," Thomas finishes for me, rolling his eyes.

I guess that's fair too. I said it every time I left. It doesn't make it any less true, though. He *doesn't* know what it was like . . . Dad was abusive, sure, but he didn't play mind games like Dean did. "He convinced me that you and Mom hated me for running away."

Thomas's face hardens. Pointing at me, he sits upright but doesn't move to stand. "That's bullshit, and you know it!"

I grab the back of the couch in front of me to keep my hands from shaking. "Did I? You were awful the first time I called you after I left."

He passes a hand over his face and sags into the cushions behind him. His chest expands with a deep breath, and he lets it out slowly. "I'm sorry. I was angry you didn't ask me to go with you."

And you have no idea how hard it was to leave without you. But you were so much closer to freedom. "I wanted to." But Dean convinced me that Thomas would stop me or tell our parents. Some days, not telling him and letting him stop me is the biggest regret of my life. But there's nothing saying that staying wouldn't have been worse in the long run.

"I know."

Of course, he knows. We have some version of this conversation every time we talk, and every time I hope we'll finally resolve *something*—whatever it is he can't get over because there's more than just me leaving without him, or we'd be okay now. But I always end up feeling like we'll never leave it all behind us and move on. Like he'll never forgive me.

"I'm sorry, sis," he says softly. "I was just . . . you had a chance to make something of your life, and you blew it on him. That's the part that gets me. You jumped out of one bad situation into a new one. Honestly, I want to be mad at you about it all. I'm trying hard to, but I can't."

A lump clogs my throat. He's never said any of that before. This could be progress, but I don't know how to respond.

Before I can figure it out, he continues. "I've read the transcripts from the trial."

I wince. Taking the stand was the hardest thing I've ever done. Harder than running away from home or any of the times I called Thomas to save me—or the times I went back to Dean because Thomas said or did something that I felt confirmed all the lies Dean told me.

"I knew he was a manipulative asshole, but shit, sis . . ." His eyes, full of a familiar concern now that he's abandoned his anger, search my face. My knees threaten to buckle from relief at the familiarity of that look, the one he used to give me every time Mom and Dad fought. "Did he hurt you?"

"Only the once." That was all it took. He scared me plenty of times by threatening to hurt me if I didn't do what he said, but he had me convinced that it was my fault he was that way. That he wouldn't have to make those threats if I would just be good.

He scans my face again, making me wonder if he's looking for scars or shadows of old bruises, but there's nothing to see. There anyway. "What happened?" he asks, his voice sharp and demanding, the same tone he used on Mom when we'd find her crying.

I used to think it was fear in his voice, but I know better now. It's frustration. He wants to fix it, but he can't.

If he's seen the transcripts, he knows everything. There's no need to rehash every detail. It will only agitate him because he can't do anything about it. "You read."

He shakes his head. "No, I don't want to hear the script written for maximum effect. What happened?"

Walking around the couch, I finally sit, but I can't bring myself to look at him while I give him the answers he wants. Instead, I pick at a frayed spot in my jeans over my knee. I don't want to watch him pass judgment. He may have read the transcripts, but he obviously still has questions if he's asking me to relive it. And if this is what it takes to make things right between us, so be it.

"They got reckless." I tried to tell them it was too soon, but they were cocky after so many successful sprees. "Dean and I would usually scout out a neighborhood for weeks. We'd walk the streets every evening like we belonged there until we found an in with some locals and scored an invite to something. He was so good at it. He knew exactly what to say and do to get those people eating out of the palm of his hand. He'd make a map of which people lived where and make me memorize it so I could text him and tell him which houses were empty based on who was at the party. I'd show up alone and tell everyone he would be there later, send the text telling him which houses were safe, and watch to make sure no one went home."

"But someone left without you noticing?" Thomas asks softly. His leg bounces, the familiar tic proving how agitated he is though his voice gives nothing away.

Leaning forward to rest my elbows on my knees, I nod. "Yeah. I got distracted. Unfortunately, Dean and the others were in that house at the time. Dean got out, but the cops got Jack before he made it out of the neighborhood. He had a few thousand dollars' worth of diamonds on him. Dean lost his temper and . . ." My words are lost to a knot in my throat. Angry tears threaten to fall, but I fight them off. I won't give in.

"And put you in the hospital?" he finishes for me.

I nod again, swallow hard, and take a deep breath so I can speak. "Jack gave the cops names, and they picked us off one by one. They didn't really need me at that point, but they promised to get me off easy if I'd confess everything. They seemed to think it would make the case against Dean tighter. And . . . Well, the whole time Dean was . . . All I could think about was listening to Mom scream while Dad hit her. I wanted to see him locked up."

Speaking of it fans the spark of hatred lodged in my heart into the roaring blaze it was that day. The heat of my rage seeps into every cell in my body once again, reminding me of my mission in life. I am *not* my mother, and I vowed to myself that if I survived the assault I would get away—far away—and make a life for myself. I want something to be proud of, the life I could've had if things had been different.

Thomas nods. "Well, you got that."

"Yes, I did." A satisfied smile pulls at the corners of my mouth. It was cathartic in more ways than one. I never wanted to be part of his stupid plots, and now I can rest easy knowing I never will again.

At first, I didn't know I was. Every time we moved, which was every other month or so, I assumed it was to keep my parents from finding me. We colored my hair and pretended to be brother and sister or cousins. Dean encouraged me to make friends, though I never understood why. I trusted him too much.

Right before we left each neighborhood, he'd clean the residents out. When I found out what he was up to and told him to leave me out of it, the manipulation started. *I'm going to do it anyway, Heidi. At least if you help, I have a better chance at getting out without getting caught. You don't want me to get caught, do you? Who will take care of you then? You'll have to go running home to Mommy and Daddy and hope she still loves you and he doesn't kill you.*

I shudder. Dean was a real piece of work.

"What did they call it?" my brother asks.

"What?" I ask, wondering if I missed something while I remembered the not-so-good ol' days. I risk a peek, but his expression is too guarded after years of living with Dad to betray him when he doesn't want it to, and he's giving nothing away now.

"The reason you kept going back?" He watches me closely, like every blink or twitch has something to tell him. *Maybe it does.* A flinch told Chris way too much about me last night.

I take a deep breath and scrub my face with my hands. "Stockholm Syndrome."

My attorney convinced the judge that my involvement was solely due to Dean's manipulation, which started when I was thirteen. He said that Dean took advantage of a neglected child's need for love until I ran away from home with him, and then I was dependent on him because it's not like I could get a job and provide for myself. He argued it was the perfect storm for trauma bonding, also known as Stockholm Syndrome.

I don't know if he was right or wrong, but my sentence wasn't as bad as I feared—a year of probation and court-mandated therapy.

Thomas nods. "So, now what?"

His question makes me smile. An unfamiliar sensation spreads through me, starting in my chest. *Is this what real happiness feels like?* It's . . . warm. And kind of bubbly. I like it. For the first time in years, the future doesn't seem so bad. It can be what I want it to be. *I just have to avoid replacing one abuser with another. Again.* "Well, since you helped me get my GED, my therapist was able to help me find this place and a job. I start at Chambers Freight on Monday." It's a good job. Good pay. Much better than I expected since I have a record now.

He actually smiles. "I've heard that's a great place to work. Have you talked to Mom?"

The little bubble of happiness that came with thinking of my new job bursts. I shake my head. I haven't talked to her in years. "My therapist is encouraging me to reach out to her, but I'm not ready yet."

Thomas nods. "Curt wasn't always a bad guy," he says, correctly guessing my issues with Mom. She put us in a bad situation and kept us there. On some level, I get it. I put myself in a bad situation, and I didn't get out when I should have. But I didn't have kids. My life could be vastly different if she'd left the first time our stepdad raised a hand.

"That doesn't make it better," I whisper. I almost can't believe we're even having this conversation. Thomas lived the same hell I did, longer than I did. But she's our mother, and he will always defend her. She's the only reason he didn't run away on his own.

"No." He absently fingers his nose, crooked now because he stepped between Mom and Dad. "But he was better than Real Dad. At first, anyway. You were too little to remember that, though."

My heart sinks as it always does when he mentions Real Dad. I hate that I can't remember him, but maybe it's better that way. All I know of him is what Thomas has told me—he left a lot, and he left us broke every time. *How did Thomas turn out so good when those were his examples?*

Ultimately, I know I'm responsible for my own decisions, but the decisions she made impacted mine. Maybe someday I can forgive her, but right now, the resentment is buried too deep, right next to my hatred for Dean.

Thomas looks around and his brow wrinkles. "How did you get all of this inside?"

He's changing the subject, but I'm grateful for it. I don't want to argue with Thomas anymore and talking about Mom will only lead us to that point. I tip my head toward Chris's house. "Neighbor had a barbecue last night. His friends are nosey—well-meaning, I think, but nosey—and, well . . ." I wave my hand around at the furniture. "Ten minutes. Twenty if you count the time it took two of them to put my bed together."

His eyebrows lift. "Wow. Not gonna lie, last night, I was pissy and fully ready to tell you to fuck off if you asked me to help you move in, but then Olivia practically held the transcripts in my face until I agreed to read them, and . . ."

Olivia? Why is his girlfriend helping me? We've never met. *That's . . . odd. What does she hope to gain?* Whatever her reasons, I owe her. I'm not even sure I mind in this case. "Yeah, I didn't figure you'd be eager to help, but I was going to ask. I'd rather owe you than some strangers that are exactly the sort of people Dean would've used me to fuck over."

His eyes widen, and he laughs so hard tears roll down his face. "Oh, that's rich."

I smile because he's right. The irony is off the charts. "You have no idea. Obviously, they don't know about any of that, but I kept telling myself if they knew, they'd want nothing to do with me. It was pretty awkward."

His laughter cuts off abruptly. "Heidi, you're as much a victim in all of this as all those people were. He stole a lot more than a watch and some jewelry from you, though."

A sob tears its way out of my throat, refusing to be held back. Thomas bolts out of the chair and sits next to me, hugging me tightly like he used to when Mom and Dad would fight. No, not Dad. Curt. He never did anything to earn the right to be called my father. While I'm breaking up with my abusers, I may as well let go of that old habit too.

Thomas is probably the only guy in the world I don't flinch away from. "I never looked at it that way," I manage to say through tears.

My head moves with his shrug. "It's the truth."

Dean took the last few years of my childhood. My confidence. My innocence. And he almost took my freedom with him, too. *But he didn't break me.* I *will* recover from all of it. Somehow.

"I'm sorry I left without you," I whisper, my voice threatening to break. This whole thing is taking a toll on me, the physical contact, the topic, even apologizing. But I need to embrace this. Get everything off my chest. Heal. Even though it sucks.

Thomas hugs me. "I'm sorry I didn't stop you from going back."

I sit up, but he keeps one arm around me like he knows I need him. Wiping away tears, I ask, "You don't hate me?"

His head shakes a bit. "You're my baby sister. I could never hate you. I wanted to after you went back last time. I really did. When you called to borrow the truck . . . I wanted to hang up on you, but I realized you can't go back this time."

As much as it hurts, I appreciate his honesty. I can't blame Dean for everything. I made the decision to turn my back on my family every time. "I wouldn't even if I could. When he hit me . . . Waking up in the hospital . . . It was eye-opening."

Smirking, Thomas slaps a hand on top of my head and musses my hair. "Good. Because I want my little sister back. I want you to meet Olivia soon. I hope you and Mom can work things out. I hope we can be a family again."

"I want that too." A small grain of happiness settles in my heart, the seed of a pearl wedged in among the resentment, hatred, and bitterness. That is the life I want. Eventually.

It won't be easy for me. Not because I have to forgive Mom, but because I have to unlearn everything Dean ever said to poison me against them. But this is progress. My therapist will be proud. "I don't want to be his victim. I want to be a survivor."

Chapter 5
Heidi

Sunrise finds me in the backyard on Sunday morning, continuing a longstanding family tradition. I don't know if Mom or Thomas still do it, but I kept it up even after I ran away. It was always my favorite part of the week as a child.

It was never anything fancy. Mom would make coffee for herself and something for Thomas and me—sometimes milk if we could afford to buy it that week, occasionally it would be flavored with chocolate, but more often than not, it was lemon water or herbal tea. We'd take our drinks outside wherever we happened to be and watch the sunrise. Mom would read to us, usually from the Bible, but sometimes it would be a book from the library.

As a kid, it felt so magical. It still does, in a way, especially here. There's no traffic noise. No people shouting at each other—no voices to be heard at all, in fact. It's like I have the world to myself, if only for a little while.

Unbidden, my hand reaches for my phone, and I navigate to my contacts to call Thomas. My thumb hovers over the button to end the call, but he answers on the first ring. "Yeah?"

I press my phone to my ear had enough it hurts. "You still do it too?"

"Yeah," he repeats softly. "Have you always?"

"Rarely miss it," I tell him with a smile. "It's my favorite part of the week."

"Mine too. I used to think it was so stupid, but I miss it now."

"Me too." A comfortable silence falls between us. Words aren't necessary. We're miles apart but together in spirit at least as we watch and wait.

I can barely see the sun for all of the trees and two-story houses, but I don't mind. Much. Unbidden, my eyes dart toward Chris's house and the balcony that probably has a perfect view of the sun.

Someday. This situation is temporary. There's nothing wrong with my house. It's a great place to live, and I'm incredibly grateful to my landlord for taking a chance on me and my therapist for the strings he pulled. But someday, I'll have a big house with a little balcony where I can sit and watch the sunrise as often as I want.

The unmistakable sound of a sliding door draws my attention to Chris's house again. Something sails through the air and lands in the yard, then Keaton toddles out, turns, puts both hands on the glass, and starts walking, shoving the door closed behind him. When he's done, he stoops to grab whatever it was that preceded him out the door and looks around. We lock eyes, and he smiles, then starts my way, dragging whatever it is behind him.

Aw, shit. I look behind him, hoping to see some sign of Chris coming to wrangle his brat, but the house is dark. *Does he even know where Keaton is?* "Thomas? Can I call you later?"

"Yeah. Something wrong?" he asks, a defensive edge to his voice.

I frown. "I don't know. The neighbor kid is heading my way."

He laughs softly in my ear. "Alright. Later." And the call ends.

The little boy walks up to me and holds up both arms without dropping the thing in his hand, which turns out to be a Teddy bear. I don't know what makes me do it, but I lean over and grab him under his arms, hefting him into my lap. He's a lot heavier than he looks. *And Chris made this look easy yesterday.*

"Can you talk?" I ask him. I'm almost certain I heard him talking last night, but kids are strange. Just because he *can* doesn't mean he will. He doesn't know me. *Didn't stop him from walking over here and asking me to pick him up.*

"Yes," he says. He lays his head on my chest and yawns.

I freeze. *What is he doing?* What am *I* doing? Why is this happening to me? "Um . . . Where's your dad?" I don't know much about kids, but I do know that parents don't like it when their children go missing.

"Bed," he murmurs.

"Your dad is still asleep?" I ask, needing some clarification here. I wasn't introduced to a girlfriend, but that doesn't mean he doesn't have one. He could be getting laid right now and didn't notice his kid was up.

That thought brings up the memory of the muscled torso his shirt hinted at yesterday. Does he really have abs? I thought those were a myth. If those are real, what about those little 'V' things? And—no. I'm not going to wonder what he looks like naked. Bad idea.

"Yes."

"What are you doing out here then?" I ask him. It's stupid early, and he's obviously still tired. He should be in bed, asleep too.

Keaton's little shoulders twitch in a shrug. I can't imagine that he would've made it this far if he had told Chris first. That means Chris has no idea his child isn't safely tucked in his bed.

Shit.

But what if Chris isn't sleeping? What if Keaton tried to wake him and he didn't respond because he's having a medical emergency or something? I mean, he's *kind* of old . . . he could've had a heart attack or something. Stranger things have happened.

Holding Keaton tight, I stand up and transfer him to a hip like Chris carried him yesterday. It's a lot easier than I imagined it would be. The little boy lays his head on my shoulder and combs his fingers through my hair. *That's . . . kind of nice.*

With him settled and secure, I hurry across the yard. *What do I do?* Do I ring the doorbell and hope it wakes him? Or do I go in the back door and start yelling for him?

Even thinking about entering his house uninvited makes my chest tighten. If he calls the cops that will look so bad. But then again, so will having his child in my possession. I'm still on probation, so I'm screwed either way, but I can't do it. I run to the front door and press the doorbell half a dozen times.

Keaton never stops finger combing my hair. His breath tickles my neck. It's kind of sweet. Maybe he's not all bad, but he did shit in my yard . . .

There's still no sign of life inside. No thundering footsteps—and a guy Chris's size is going to thunder. No lights flicking on. Nothing. *What do I do?* Hands shaking, I ring the bell a few more times and try not to fidget while my heart pounds in my ears.

The panic at the idea of entering the house uninvited is coopted by panic that Chris might be upstairs dying while I wait on his porch. I take a step back and turn, and the door opens.

"Heidi?" His voice has a soft, rumbly, sleepy quality to it. No pain, no agitation because he was about to bust a nut until I rang the bell. "Keaton?" A sharp note of distress cuts through the just-woke-up softness.

I whirl around. His arms snap out, and he snatches his son away. In the space between those two actions, I get a confirmation that abs are definitely not a myth, and those little 'v' thingies definitely exist too. I can't stop staring at where they disappear beneath the loose gym shorts he probably threw on before he came to the door. *Stop it, idiot.*

"What the *hell?*" he shouts, breaking the spell.

Flinching at the volume more than anything else, I hold up my hands so he can see they're empty and take a step back. "I was sitting in my back yard, and he came out your back door."

Chris heaves an audible sigh. "I'm sorry," he says, running his hand over his son's unruly curls. "I didn't mean to shout. I just . . . wasn't expecting to wake up to the doorbell and find my kid on the porch." He steps aside and tips his head toward the door. "Please, come in."

I take another step back, shaking my head. That would be a monumentally stupid thing to do. He's obviously agitated, possibly with me. At least out here, he won't hit me. Probably. All he can do is shout unless he wants witnesses. Someone around here has cameras, I'm sure.

"Heidi," he says, his voice soft and smooth as satin. It works its way through my ears and into my chest, easing the tension knotted around my lungs and heart. "I'm sorry. I'm not upset with *you.*" His arms constrict around Keaton's little body until the boy giggles like it's a game or something. "I was scared. Please, come in and help me figure out what happened? So I can make sure it doesn't happen again."

Is this what a good dad is like? He's not yelling or throwing a fit. He's not angry. He just wants to know what happened. I can understand that, even if the rest is foreign to me. It's still a stupid thing to do, all things considered, but my curiosity gets the best of me, and I step inside. The door closes behind us, and he eases past to lead the way.

Chris

My heart finally settles back into my chest where it belongs and slows to some semblance of a normal beat. Finding Heidi on my porch spiked my adrenaline. The way she rang the bell, I thought something was wrong with her. All signs point to her being abused at some point in her life. What if that person turned up and she ran to me for help?

But seeing Keaton in her arms, on our porch, when he was supposed to be upstairs, in bed, safe and sound asleep, took things to a new level. I've never been so terrified in my life. It never occurred to me that she got inside and took him. She wouldn't be on my porch, ringing the bell if she had.

So many different scenarios flooded my paranoid brain at that point. Did he spend the whole night outside? Get hit by a car? Fall out of a tree? Did she find him wandering down the street? Or did she rescue him from someone else?

She follows me to the kitchen and sits when I offer her a chair. I walk around to the other side, so the table is between us for her peace of mind, and settle Keaton in my lap. He melts into my chest, already half asleep again, but I make him sit up. I need him awake so he can tell me what happened.

"Talk to me, little buddy. What happened?"

He rubs his eyes with his fists and yawns. "I'm sleepy, Daddy."

It takes real effort to keep my voice stern on a good day, but with Heidi across the table, it's next to impossible. I don't want to scare her more, but I have to let Keaton know this is serious. "Then why aren't you in bed right now?"

"I got thirsty," he murmurs, his eyelids drooping.

You got thirsty, so you went to ask Heidi for water instead of me? There's got to be more to this story. "Alright. So why didn't you wake me?"

His nearly invisible eyebrows draw together. "I'm a big boy!"

"Okay. But how did you get downstairs?" Mason installed his old baby gates at the top and bottom of the stairs as soon as he got here on move-in day. Keaton was supposed to be safely contained.

He yawns again. "I opened the gates."

"Who showed you how to do that?" I run through the list of everyone who has been in this house since we moved in. No one would be that irresponsible, though.

"Nobody," he says, confirming my suspicion. He's too smart for my own good.

Fuck. "Okay. So, you opened the gates and then . . . ?"

"I sawd Heidi out the window and wanted to sit with her."

Are you kidding me right now? Some parent I am. First, the baby gates. Then, he decides he's going to go visit a virtual stranger. But how did he get outside?

"But the door was locked." I know it was locked. The last thing I did before bed was check each door and window. Keaton isn't afraid of anything, sure, but he's never done something like this. He's never wandered away. And it's not like it was easy for him . . .

"I unlocked it."

Or maybe it was. Pinching the bridge of my nose with my free hand, I blow out a deep breath and look across the table at Heidi. The fear in her eyes is gone now, which is why I interrogated Keaton first. I wanted to give her time. There's a cute little furrow between her brows now, and her eyes are locked on my son like he's the most fascinating thing in the entire universe.

"You said you saw him go outside?" I ask her. I don't doubt her, and Keaton confessed to it himself, but I'm struggling to grasp that my not-quite-four-year-old opened two baby gates, unlocked a sliding glass door, opened, and—I glance at it—closed it by himself.

Said four-year-old snuggles up against me and rests his head on my chest. It's impossible to be mad at him when he's snuggly like this. *I'm never going to survive parenting.*

She nods. "Yes. He opened the door, threw his bear out, came outside, and closed it behind him."

I heave a sigh. *How is this my life?* "This is insane. I'm so sorry. I'm going to get different gates, and a childproof something for the door, and a door alarm . . . And a fence in the back yard." The fence won't happen overnight, but I can take care of the rest today. *I can't believe he walked out on his own, and I slept right through it.* A shiver of pure terror shakes my body. "Thank you so much for bringing him home."

Her lips stretch into a small smile. "I'm just glad you're okay. I was afraid something was wrong with you."

She was worried about me? That's . . . kind of touching. I didn't consider that angle. I thought she was only trying to do the right thing—return him and alert me to a problem. Now that she's said it, I see it, though. She could've easily opened the back door and put him inside and come by later to tell me what happened. We don't know each other well enough for her to go through the back door first thing, but I suspect that's where she was heading. "I think that knocked a few years off my life, but I'm great. Would you like to stay for breakfast?"

Her eyes widen, and she leans back a bit. "Oh, no! I don't want to intrude!"

"You're not intruding. You were invited." Like inviting her to dinner after Keaton shit in her yard, it's the least I can do.

"You don't have to—"

"I know I don't, but I want to." Keaton obviously likes her. She was quiet at dinner the other night. Not an overwhelmed sort of quiet, but not shy either. She seemed nice enough, though. And she has gorgeous eyes, not that her looks have any impact on the invitation. I didn't place much value on a person's looks before Lydia, but after . . . They matter even less.

It just so happens, I really like looking at Heidi's eyes. And her smile, not that she does that much. But when she does . . .

"Alright," she says softly. "But I can help."

I can work with that. It's been a long time since I shared my kitchen with someone other than Fern, Tara, or now, Trista. I don't date much, and when I do, I'm careful about who I let into Keaton's life and our home. *Not cautious enough, apparently.* I still can't believe my most recent attempt at a relationship ended the way it did. I actually believed Becca and I were going somewhere. I let her in, and she tried to screw me over.

No sleepovers at my place means no waking up in the morning and cooking breakfast together. Or evenings cooking dinner for a night in with a movie. This isn't a date, though. It's breakfast with the neighbor who was nice enough to look out for me and my kid when she could've just ignored it.

Keaton sighs, asleep once more. "Let me put him down."

He doesn't stir when I stand. We're going to have a talk about this later, but for now, he can sleep. I don't even know how to parent this. He's a toddler. What do I do, ground him to his room? Timeout isn't going to cut it this time.

I duck into my room and grab a shirt before I head back downstairs. It doesn't bother me to go without one, but I don't know much about her abuse. She might be more comfortable if I'm fully dressed.

Chapter 6
Chris

Heidi is waiting where I left her when I get back to the kitchen—her hands folded in her lap, on the edge of her seat, with her feet flat on the floor. Other people might not be able to look at her and tell, but her posture tells me she's poised to bolt out of that chair and run for the nearest door.

I want to ask her about it, but she might be embarrassed if it's something she's not comfortable talking about. "Omelets?" I ask instead, giving her something to focus on other than whatever has her so tense.

Keaton and I did a grocery run yesterday, so the fridge is stocked. If omelets aren't her thing, I can come up with something else.

"I'm not picky," she says. She finally stands and creeps closer, joining me in front of the fridge. "Just tell me what I can do to help."

I grab the carton of eggs, some cheese, ham, and a variety of vegetables out of the fridge. I know what I like in an omelet, but she might want something different. We wash our hands, and I get two bowls out of the cabinet, one big and one little, and a whisk from a drawer. "Can you crack eggs?"

She nods and gives me a wistful little smile. "I was a short-order cook at a diner once."

"Really?" Something about that smile, and the way she says it, leads me to believe she's got a colorful work history. I grab a frying pan and put it on the stove, then turn on the burner to heat the pan while we work.

"Yeah, I liked that job." She pops open the carton, grabs an egg, and cracks it one-handed over the little bowl. "How many?"

"However many you want for yours. What else have you done?" I ask, not just to be polite. I really am interested. While she works, I get out a knife and a cutting board to dice some bell peppers, mushrooms, and ham.

She chuckles a bit as she selects the next egg. "Oh, man. I've moved around a lot, so I've had a lot of different jobs. Gas station clerk, waitress, janitor, grocery store cashier . . . So many more. Basically, if it didn't require much schooling and had a high turnover rate, I've done it."

Maybe someone in her family is military. That would explain the moving around. I kind of admire her work ethic. Finding a new job with each move couldn't have been easy, no matter what the turnover rate.

I don't need all of the fingers on one hand to count the jobs I've had. I suppose that makes me lucky, though. I shouldn't suddenly feel like I missed out on a life experience, but this woman probably knows more about life than I do. "And short-order cook was your favorite?"

She opens the cabinet I got the bowl from and takes out another and looks at me expectantly. After her tension when I walked in, I'm glad she's so relaxed and comfortable here now. Maybe a little too much so, because I could get used to this.

"Uh, three," I say, hoping I'm reading her right, and she's asking how many eggs I want in my omelet. "Keaton will eat one, but I'll make his once he's awake."

She cracks the next egg in silence, and I wonder if she'll use the distraction as a reason not to answer. "Yeah," she finally says. "I really didn't have to deal with people. I'm not much of a people person."

After Friday night, I'm really not surprised. I don't comment on that, though. "So, you said you moved around a lot? Is one of your parents in the military? Or both, I suppose?"

She stiffens, her hands stilling in the act of whisking the first bowl of eggs.

I cringe and backpedal. "Sorry, I'm being nosey. I meet a lot of people, but I don't spend a lot of time talking to them outside of walking them through the next exercise."

Heidi gives me a brittle smile. "It's alright. I'm just . . . not used to talking about myself, really. My ex didn't like to stay in one place, so we moved constantly. Can I ask you a question?"

"Shoot." It's only fair, after all. I've pried into her work history, and she knows I own my own business. Maybe she's looking for a job.

"No one mentioned Keaton's mom Friday. What's up with her?"

The unexpected conversational turn surprises me so much, I slip with the knife and nick my thumb. "Crud!" I lay the knife down and quickly back away from the cutting board before I bleed all over the rest of the vegetables.

"Oh, my gosh! I'm sorry!"

"Not your fault," I assure her. I turn on the tap and stick my thumb under the water. It's not a deep cut, but it sure stings.

"Where's your first aid kit?" she asks.

"There's one under the sink." Maybe I went overboard, but I've kept multiples since Keaton was born. There's one in his bag, one in my car, one in every bathroom, and one in the kitchen. I step aside and get a clean rag to dry my hand and apply pressure to the cut while she gets the kit out and finds a bandage.

"Here," she says, holding one out. "Let me help." She grabs my hand and makes quick work of wrapping the bandage around my thumb.

There's nothing heated about her touch at all, but the feel of her skin shoots through me like a lightning bolt. *You're imagining things, man. Get it together.* "Keaton has never met his mother," I tell her, keeping my voice low because I don't want him to overhear if he happens to be awake.

Heidi stops and looks up at me, still holding my hand. "I'm so sorry. That was rude of me. I should've known—"

"It's alright," I cut her off, realizing how that must've sounded to her. "She didn't die. Lydia didn't want to be a mother."

I should stop there, but Heidi watches me with one hand pressed to her mouth, her eyes huge and begging for the rest of the story. I gently extract my hand from hers and move back to the cutting board so I can work while I talk. It's not my favorite topic of discussion. I normally wait until I know someone better before I bring it up, but I feel like I need to explain now. All the same, women usually have strong opinions about this story, one way or the other. I don't want to watch hers form in her eyes.

I listen hard for Keaton at the top of the stairs, or maybe on them since the gates are obviously not an obstacle. Heidi finds another knife and a cutting board, and we work side by side, prepping vegetables and cooking our omelets while I talk. "Lydia and I were together for years. We had our lives all planned out. Get married. Establish our careers. Have kids. I was planning the proposal, even had the ring, and she told me one morning that she missed her birth control shot the month before and was pregnant.

"I was ecstatic. I love kids. Waiting to have them was her idea, not mine. But then she told me she was going to have an abortion because she'd decided she didn't want kids anymore because she didn't want to wreck her body. That wasn't okay with me. It's not like I was some casual fling who wasn't going to take responsibility for the consequences of his actions. I was there, ready to raise this child with her.

"Long story short, she told me I had to choose between her and the baby. Obviously, I chose Keat. She agreed to continue the pregnancy if I agreed to pay for everything, including a bunch of reconstructive surgeries once he was born.

"She carried to term and walked out of the hospital as soon as the doctor discharged her. She wouldn't even look at him in the delivery room," I finish, struggling to keep the disappointment lingering in my heart from bleeding into my voice. I slide the spatula under my omelet and transfer it to the plate, then switch off the burner.

I'll never understand how she could *not* look at our son, the small person she spent nine months making. He was so tiny and helpless and perfect. I thought I was prepared, but I wasn't. My whole world shifted the second I laid eyes on him.

I grab my plate and take it to the table before I get drinks, leaving Heidi to decide how she feels about . . . me. I've lost more than one potential girlfriend because of the choices I made that day. Not that I look at Heidi as a potential girlfriend. She wouldn't be interested in someone like me. But, even if she were, the things she now knows might end that.

I get it. I really do. Under most circumstances, a man has no say in the decisions a woman makes about her body. Our situation wasn't typical, though.

That doesn't ease the guilt.

I grab a couple of glasses and open the fridge. "Juice? Water? Coffee?" I haven't started the coffee maker yet, but I can.

"Um, juice, please," she says.

I fill both glasses with OJ and turn around in time to watch her put her plate on the table next to mine. She pulls out the chair and sits. "So, you paid for all of it?"

I have to fight a smile at her display of trust. Friday night, she was seated between Jam and Noel, and Fern and Tara sat on either side of them, giving Heidi plenty of testosterone-free space. My kitchen table isn't huge, but there's plenty of room for her to put space between us, and she chose not to.

"And I paid her, too," I tell Heidi, placing a glass in front of her before taking my seat. "She said it was only fair because I was treating her like an incubator."

"Chris," Heidi says, the softness of her voice grabbing my attention as sure as if she shouted. "You have to know there was nothing you could've done to stop her from having the abortion. If that's what she really wanted to do, she would've done it."

My heart constricts at the memory of all the times she threatened to do it anyway. "I know," I say, cutting a bite. "She made it clear."

"Then why do you feel so bad about it?"

I pause with my fork halfway to my mouth to look at her. "I don't recall saying that I do."

Her face screws into a scowl. "You don't have to say it. Your body says it for you. Yeah, it's a sh—sucky situation." She changes course mid-curse with a glance upward though Keaton is probably still out. "She's a," she mouths the word *bitch*, "for doing what she did. I could easily argue that you're a . . . *Richard*," her euphemism for dick makes me laugh, but she keeps a straight face, "for encouraging her to go through with a pregnancy she obviously didn't want, but you didn't *force* her to do it! Short of tying her to a bed, there was nothing you could do to prevent her from terminating the pregnancy. Stop beating yourself up for it. Some part of her obviously wanted to see it through."

It's not the first time I've heard that argument, but for some reason, getting it from someone who has absolutely no reason to tell me what I want to hear makes it a little easier to swallow. "Thanks."

She smiles—a true smile that lights up her whole damn face—and we finish our breakfast in comfortable silence.

Heidi

I push my chair back to take my plate to the sink, but Chris grabs it before I can.

"I've got this; you relax. Coffee?" he offers again, already halfway to the sink.

"No. Thank you, though." I don't mind it on occasion, but I don't need it to exist. Dean practically lived on it. In hindsight, I think Dean was too anxious about being caught to relax, so he relied on coffee to keep him sharp.

"I think I've got tea if you'd prefer." Something beeps, and the telltale bubbling and draining burble of a coffee maker fills the room. "Mom usually has some stashed for when she's babysitting here."

I smile, thinking back to the Sunday morning ritual with Mom and Thomas. "Tea would be nice."

"Sure thing."

I don't understand why he's not rushing me out of here. I *really* don't understand why I'm not in a hurry to leave. But I'm not, so I may as well make the most of it. I don't feel unsafe with him, and it's been ages since I could sit and talk to someone new without guarding against forming any sort of connection with them. It's hard to let yourself like someone when you know you're moving in a couple months and your boyfriend is going to wreck their perfect little life before you go. I'll hate myself for it when Chris learns about my past and doesn't want anything to do with me anymore, but for now . . . I'll just keep on deluding myself into thinking I can make friends again. *Dr. Porter would say I'm looking at it wrong.* It's easy for him to say, though. He's not the criminal.

"Are you sure you don't want help?" I glance over my shoulder and am treated to an uninhibited view of his back. *Too bad he put a shirt on.* There are easily thousands of reasons I shouldn't drool over my neighbor, but they're all hard to remember when I can't stop myself from thinking back to that moment at the door. And those "v" thingies.

He looks back, a crooked smile already in place. "Nah, I've got this. Just . . . new house, ya know?"

"I get it." *Boy, do I ever get it.* However, this is the first time in years I've actually bothered to unpack instead of living out of boxes. All that moving around was cool at first—like a never-ending adventure. The cool quickly wore off, though.

And once I figured out what was going on, Dean mostly quit unpacking. Said he only ever did it to keep me from asking questions. Living out of boxes made it quicker to up and leave.

Having all my things unpacked is a surreal feeling, but I love it. The security that comes from seeing my belongings scattered throughout my home makes my heart so light it could float away.

"Is peppermint tea okay?" he asks, holding up a box.

My eyes sting with a sudden onslaught of tears. Peppermint is Mom's favorite. "Sounds wonderful." After talking to Thomas, I feel like the universe is sending me signs that it's time to make peace. But as much as I want to, I can't while she's with Curt.

The tap turns on. Over the noise of running water filling a mug, Chris asks, "So, not to pry, but you mentioned an ex Friday night . . . is the breakup the reason you moved here?"

I hide my cringe, I hope, but it doesn't matter because he turns to put the mug in the microwave. I hate talking about myself, but this time is different. I don't have to lie to avoid divulging information that could lead to someone's arrest. I only have to avoid talking about the more colorful aspects of my past. And Chris isn't pressuring me to answer. "Um, kind of. We split up a little over a year ago, but we were together so long it took me a while to recover, I guess, and get out on my own."

Close enough. As close to the truth as I can get without ruining things. I *was* recovering, just not in the way he'll think, but I also couldn't leave San Antonio until the investigation wrapped up and the trial was over.

He opens the dishwasher to load the dishes he rinsed while I was talking. "How long were you together?"

My cheeks don't get hot; my *whole* face does. It sounds so creepy, and I can practically see people judging me. They never believe that we weren't an actual couple until I was older. I try not to squirm while I speak. "Well, we met when I was thirteen. We didn't date for a few years because he was older, but he waited for me." *That's good.* The truth, just not all of it.

His eyebrows climb his forehead. "Wow. That *is* a long time. You're what . . ." he eyes me from the table up, "twenty?"

"Twenty-two," I correct with a smile. "And you're . . . twenty-eight?" I guess, hoping to steer the conversation away from me.

"Almost right. Just turned twenty-nine last week." He grins, clearly unfazed to be pushing thirty.

I grab my orange juice glass and salute him with it. "Happy late birthday!"

He favors me with another crooked grin that makes my heart beat faster. "Thank you."

The microwave beeps, so he turns and pulls out the mug of boiling water, then drops in a tea bag. He pulls another mug from a cabinet, fills it with coffee, and returns to the table.

"I still can't believe Keat got out," he says, sinking into his seat. He slides my mug in front of me and scrubs his face with his free hand. "And I can't thank you enough for bringing him home. But there's something I'd like to ask you. It's a yes or no question."

"Okay?" I make it a question, and my brain wanders off to consider all of the things he's probably not going to ask me, but I'd like to say yes if he did. *Yes, I absolutely want to watch you do pushups shirtless.*

"I guess it's two questions, but they're both one-word answers. And I don't need explanations."

I tense, and the familiar tightness of apprehension winds around my lungs again.

"Is your ex the reason you flinched Friday night, and is he going to be a problem for you in the future?"

My lungs stall. I knew he suspected something, but I didn't realize I was that easy to read. I suppose it's only logical, though. Not hard to figure out at all.

His eyes narrow and flick left and right, up and down, taking in my reaction. Slowly, he says, "I'm only asking because I want you to know you can always come here if he turns up. I wouldn't even ask, but I want to be prepared if it's a possibility."

"Yes, and no," I rasp out. At least, I think the answer to his second question is no. I don't think Dean is the kind to hunt me down. Even if he does, I'll be long gone by then. There will be no Chris to run to. I look at my hands where they're wrapped around my mug. "He'll be in jail for a long time."

He leans to put his eyes in my line of sight. I'm a goner. There's no resisting that intense gaze. "Even so, you're safe here. Alright?"

For whatever reason, I believe him. Maybe it's because of what I witnessed this morning. A tear breaks free and slips down my cheek. I met this man two days ago, and he's already offering his protection if I need it. *"People like you. They look at you, and they want to know you, to protect you. It's why I convinced you to come with me."*

I swallow that bitter pill and try to smile. At least that inexplicable draw is serving me well this time. And I won't let Chris regret it. *Until he learns the truth, anyway.* "Alright. Thank you."

Smiling softly, he reaches over and grabs my hand, giving me ample time to withdraw if I want. But I let him. His touch doesn't even send me into panic mode. The opposite, in fact. I relax again and wonder how long I can get by with sitting here hand in hand with him. I don't deserve his comfort or his protection, but damn, it's nice to know someone cares. To know there are decent men out there. Well, to assume there are. I still have my doubts.

"You're welcome." He squeezes my hand and releases it. "So, are you all settled in then?"

I sniffle and shut my eyes tightly, locking down my tears. When I'm confident my eyes won't leak, I open them and do my best to pretend he didn't just take a wrecking ball to my defenses. "Yeah. I finished unpacking yesterday."

"Don't need help with anything? Are you looking for a job?"

A smile comes easy this time. "No and no. I actually start at Chambers Freight tomorrow."

Chris grins and huffs out a little laugh. "CFI, huh?"

"Yep. I've heard it's a great place to work." I've heard so much good about it from my therapist I have to work to contain my enthusiasm so I don't regurgitate it all to Chris.

"Well, I've never worked there, but I know the CEO and the CEO in training, I guess. I'm not sure what his official title is." He rubs his stubbly jaw. "You do, too."

"What? Who?" My heart takes off at a gallop. How could I possibly . . . ? *Oh, shit.*

"Mason and Austin Chambers," he says, his grin going lopsided. "Their grandfather, Martin, is the current CEO. Mase will take over for him next year. You working in the warehouse or the office?"

"The office," I whisper. Does this mean they know about my record? If not yet, will they? What then? I mean, I've already got the job despite my past. Surely, they won't fire me when they find out.

"Doing?"

"I'm the new receptionist," I answer on autopilot, my enthusiasm thoroughly doused by this new development.

Chris watches me for a beat like he's waiting for me to laugh. When I don't, his whole body shakes, and he bites his bottom lip in an effort to keep quiet. "But you don't like people?"

I slump forward, but I have to fight the urge to laugh because, as devastated as I am, I can see the humor there. "I know! But I couldn't turn it down." My therapist was so excited about finding me such a great job. Not to mention everything he did to help me get it.

"I get it," he says, still grinning. "If I didn't have the gym, I'd apply there. You'll do fine. It's mostly handing out visitor badges. They'll probably tell you this themselves, but don't be afraid to ask for Mason or Austin if you need them. The Chambers take care of their employees."

Chapter 7
Heidi

The CFI corporate office doesn't open to the public until eight-thirty A.M., but the e-mail I got from HR asked me to arrive an hour early. The heels I bought specifically for this job tap against the concrete sidewalk, as loud as gunshots to my ears despite the typical sounds of early morning commuters in the distance. My skirt feels too tight. It's really not, but it's more restrictive than the jeans I live in. Not like I can take normal steps in these heels anyway. I'm already sweating in my long-sleeved, collared blouse, but the HR e-mail also warned me it's chilly in the lobby year-round.

Clothes like this always make me feel like a fraud—like anyone who looks closely enough will see the scared little girl trying desperately to blend in. Like I am supposed to be here. Like I belong. This outfit is more of a costume than the armor I need to get through life, but it'll have to do.

My hand is steady as I reach to open the door, but my insides are a jittery mess. I pause for a deep, steadying breath and pull. A blast of cold air hits me in the face before I even step inside. The lobby is nothing like I pictured. I had this vision of a giant, dark, empty space, but it's actually bright and inviting. There's plenty of space, but it's not the cavern I imagined.

Despite the lights, it's clear the office isn't open for the day yet. It's deserted except for a silver-haired woman seated at the long desk in the middle of the room, guarding the elevators on the back wall.

This isn't the woman who conducted my interviews. That one was younger and dark-headed. This woman's hair is pulled back in a no-nonsense bun that calls to mind Professor McGonagall from the *Harry Potter* books and movies. Crow's feet bracket her eyes, and the lines around her mouth are deep. Altogether, she doesn't look like anyone I'd want to cross. I swallow hard, trying to force down the feeling that I've been sent to the principal's office.

She looks up and smiles. The lines on her face deepen, but the warmth of her smile melts that stern façade. "Heidi Decker?"

I try to smile as I cross to the desk, but nerves make it more of a twitch. "That's me!" I tell her and immediately cringe. The words come out much higher pitched than I usually speak and way too perky.

Her eyebrows arch upward, and she somehow makes it look graceful.

"Sorry. I'm nervous." *You idiot! Stop talking!*

The lady smiles again. "That's perfectly understandable. There's always so much uncertainty when you start something new." She looks me up and down and nods. "I think you'll do well here, Heidi—do you mind if I call you Heidi?"

The tension tying my muscles into knots fades away quickly under the influence of that smile. Something about it is familiar, but I can't quite place it. At any rate, I'm more at ease with this woman than I've ever been in my life. "No, that's fine."

She claps her hands once in front of her chest. "Wonderful. I'm Lola Chambers, but please, call me Lola." *Chambers!* Chris said the grandfather is the current CEO. Lola must be the grandmother. But what is the CEO's wife doing here with me? "A little bird told me you already know my grandsons. We'll make our way upstairs later and introduce you to Martin, and you can pop in and tell them hello."

"Oh!" I breathe, suddenly nervous all over again. I don't want them curious about me. Especially not since they probably have access to my files, and details of my probation are probably listed. And I definitely don't want any of them to think I was seeking them out to further my position here. I had no idea they were my boss's family. "I wouldn't want to interrupt!"

She waves a hand as if brushing away my objections. "Nonsense. Life is too short to work too hard. That's the first thing to know about CFI. We get things done, but we're pretty laid back—well, except Mason. That poor boy . . . He feels like he has something to prove. Fern is good for him, though. She makes him slow down and enjoy life."

The information overload leaves my head spinning. But I must admit, her forthright attitude only increases her charm. This is a woman who tells it like it is. "I liked Fern," I murmur.

Lola beams at me. "She's such a dear. We're fortunate to have her in our lives."

"Mrs—I mean Lola," she cocks her head at my slip up, and I correct myself with a smile. "I just want to say, I'm really grateful for this opportunity . . ."

She reaches across the desk and pats my arm. "We're thankful to have you here."

"This job is beyond what I—"

Her soft smile stops my own overshare. This woman . . . I feel like I can tell her anything. Like I could lay all my crimes at her feet, and she'd hug me and tell me that everyone makes mistakes. "Heidi, love, Dr. Porter assured me we'd regret it if we *didn't* hire you. I've known Donny his whole life, and I trust his judgment."

"*You* approved my application?" The question comes out barely louder than a whisper because her declaration hit me like a fist to the chest.

Her lips purse. "Well, ultimately, Martin signed off on it, but yes."

Tears blur my vision. I don't know what to say. A hand on my arm turns me, and I'm engulfed in a hug. I never noticed her move. She's quick for a grandma. And this hug, it's the second-best thing that's happened to me in a long time. Physical affection of any sort isn't something I've known a lot of in my life. I had no idea what I was missing. As crazy as it seems, I just want to lay my head on her shoulder and tell her everything because the space between her arms is a no-judgment zone.

My whole body shakes with the sob I'm struggling to hold back, but she passes her hand over my hair slowly and squeezes a little tighter.

"I have faith in you. Sometimes, a little faith is all it takes to alter the course of a person's life."

This woman I've never met before today believes in me more than anyone, except maybe Thomas, ever has. "I won't let you down," I whisper through the knot in my throat. "No one else knows, do they?" I ask when the tears finally give up the fight.

"No, child. Only Martin and me. It's your story to tell. However, I do encourage you to have a little faith in my grandsons and their friends. Those kids . . . They'll surprise you. They surprise me every day."

The very idea of it makes me cringe inwardly. I can't imagine sitting them all down and telling them the things I've been party to, but I smile politely. "I'll keep that in mind, ma'am."

She clicks her tongue at me. "None of this 'ma'am' stuff. But you do that. Obviously, I don't know everything, doctor-patient confidentiality and all that, but I know Donny wouldn't have called me if he didn't have faith in you too. If you ever need someone to talk to, I'm here for you, child. We're going to get you through this, whatever it is."

The air in my lungs freezes. Her willing acceptance eats at me. I have to know. "Dr. Porter did tell you why I was on probation, didn't he?"

She shakes her head. "No, he couldn't."

My stomach drops. She *has* to know already. If she doesn't, she might fire me when she finds out. "But you looked into it?"

"No."

"Then . . . Why did you take a chance on me on nothing more than his word?"

Lola glances at her watch. "Let's go to the break room and get something warm to drink." She wraps her arm around me and leads the way. "Being married to the boss has its perks. It'll be alright if we're a little late getting started."

I let her shepherd me to the break room. Over lemon balm tea, she tells me about her sister, who, like me, found herself the victim of a manipulator. Only Lola couldn't give her the help she needed when she finally broke free, and no one else would. She lost contact with her sister after that, so now that she's in a position to do so, she does what she can to help others out of bad situations. When she's done, I fill her in on my past, starting with the day Mom introduced Thomas and me to Curt.

***

My head still buzzing from everything Lola taught me, I navigate the unfamiliar streets to the address on the card Chris handed me the night we met. I need to talk to him, and he wasn't home when I got off work. I'm not sure if I want to thank him or yell at him for telling Miss Lola that I've already met Mason and Austin. Granted, meeting the Chambers family is part of every new hire's first day if they work at the corporate office. At least, that's what Lola says. I can't imagine why, or that any of them can identify the employees they don't interact with on a daily basis once they walk out of their respective offices.

Mason and Austin both remembered me, though. And they seemed genuinely happy to see me again. Both asked if I got settled in okay and if I needed anything. Both gave me cards with their personal numbers in case I *do* happen to need something.

Finally, my GPS announces that my destination is on my right. I turn into a packed parking lot of a large, warehouse-looking building, set way back from the road, and search for a place to park. Luck is on my side, and I find a spot close to the door.

Inside, I'm greeted by a bored-looking college girl sporting a nametag that reads Leslie. She smiles and welcomes me to The Bar. "What can I help you with?" she asks.

"I'm here to see Chris," I tell her, holding out the card he gave me as proof that I have some sort of right to encroach upon his time.

She smiles brightly. "Right this way! Are you Heidi?"

"Um . . . Yeah?"

"He warned the staff that his new neighbor might drop in sometime. We didn't expect to see you so soon, though. Self-defense class with Ryan starts in about thirty minutes."

My mouth goes dry. Ryan was perfectly nice, but I can't imagine being shut in a room with him. "Oh, no! I—I'm just here to talk to Chris for a minute."

"Sure!" she says. "Between you and me, Ryan's classes can get a little intense. He's great, though. I never knew he could be so patient until I sat in one day."

Leslie chatters on endlessly as she leads me through a large room dominated by different pieces of metal I can only guess at the purpose of, full of men and women performing various movements, accompanied by grunts and groans and swearing. Finally, we enter a hall, and she stops outside the first door. "Here ya go!" she says, knocking on the door before she turns the handle. She pushes the door open and steps back. "Nice to meet you!" She waves and walks away.

The reality of what I'm about to do slaps me in the face. *I've lost my mind. It's the only explanation.* I need to know if Lola told him anything about me when my name came up in their conversation. She may not have known details at the time, but she knew enough to make him suspicious of me. And if they're that close, she could've said more.

I also need to know what *he* said about me. I need to know if the Chambers think I'm a stalker or something. I mean, I do have a record. Lola knows the truth now, but the others don't.

It's too late to back out now. The door is open enough I can see Chris at his desk, looking up at me with a smile on his face that makes my insides all fluttery. Like Saturday morning when he stopped by to drop off those muffins on his way to work, he's wearing a fitted tank top that shows off the muscles of his arms and teases at what's beneath, but I know now, and I can't unsee it. I also can't play this off as a friendly visit—we're not that close—or that I'm really interested in anything this gym has to offer, because I'm not. "Heidi! Come on in."

What kind of an alternate reality have I stepped into? No one in the real world is ever this happy to see me—except maybe Thomas now. "Hi," I mumble, stepping over the threshold. There's a chair in front of his desk, but I'm not sure of the protocol here.

Chris waves the pen in his hand. "You can shut the door if you want. It blocks out some of the noise."

I can't decide if being shut in his office with him is more awkward than listening to the groans from the other room that are occasionally almost obscene without context. Ultimately, I decide closing the door is better than having someone overhear our conversation, and I pull it shut.

"Have a seat," he says, waving his pen again, but at the chair this time. "How was work?"

I clear my throat, uncomfortable with this whole situation. I don't want to be here. If I'm going to see him, I'd rather it be through a window where I can ogle without fear of looking like the creep I apparently am. But here I am. And that smile on his face makes it hard to remember why I'm upset with him. *Focus, Heidi.* "Did you tell Mrs. Chambers about me?" I ask, deciding that it's better to get to the point.

He frowns. "Grandma Lola texted me last night to ask me how I was settling in, and I mentioned that one of their new hires was my neighbor. Why? What did she say?"

I force myself not to react so he doesn't see my relief. I doubt that Chris is a good enough actor to hide it from me if there was more. Everyone has a tell when they're hiding something, and he's perfectly calm. "She only said that a little bird told her I'd met her grandsons."

His chin tips upward. "Yeah, I told her we helped you move in, and you joined us for dinner. I'm sorry . . . is that a problem?"

"No. Maybe." I drop my face into my hands. "I don't know." I don't *think* Lola would tell anyone else everything I told her today, but if she's so close with Chris that they frequently text, who knows what could happen? I mean, it's not like there's anything I could really steal from my desk. Or anywhere else in the building since I have no business being anywhere but my desk, the bathroom, or the break room. But what if she feels the need to warn him that he's living next to a . . . I'm not exactly a thief. I never took anything. I *wouldn't* take anything. But all the same. *Lie down with dogs; you get up with fleas.*

"Heidi?" A creak fills the room, and Chris is suddenly squatting next to my seat, leaning to look up at me between my hands. "What's up? Did Lola say something to upset you?"

I shake my head. Lola was great. Too great. She got me to spill my guts with little more than a hug and a few encouraging words. But there's one thing she said I can't quite get out of my head. *"I encourage you to have a little faith in my grandsons and their friends . . ."*

"Then, what is it? Is it anything I can help with?"

I shake my head again. He *can't* help. It's over and done with. Nothing can change my past. I have to focus on making my future the best it can be. Someday, I may have to tell him the truth, but not yet. "I'm sorry. I was just worried she would think I'm trying to suck up to the bosses or something." It's not exactly a lie; it's just the lesser problem. The one I can talk about.

Chris's nose wrinkles. "Nah. Grandma Lola wouldn't think that. Not unless one of the guys said something to that effect. Mason and Austin have a pretty good eye for people trying to kiss their asses. You've got nothing to worry about. I'm sorry if talking to Lola about you made you uncomfortable, though."

My head shakes again. "No. *I'm* sorry. This job is just important." It's a stepping stone to the future I want. A future where I don't feel like a fraud in the clothes I'm wearing. Where a nice guy like Chris or any of his friends might look twice at me and think I was worth their time. And I have something for people to judge me by other than the life I lived with Dean. Where I can stand on my own two feet with my head held high because I've *earned* it.

Chris slowly reaches out and lays his hand on my shoulder. "You're gonna do great. The Chambers clan won't give up on you. You've got this."

My head involuntarily tips toward his hand to press my cheek to it, but I stop myself. Instead, I manage a smile, and I mean it. "Thanks, Chris. Sorry for barging in here."

"It's no trouble." He squeezes my shoulder and removes his hand to go back to his chair. He leans back with his hands behind his head, elbows splayed. "Barge in anytime. I don't mind. Do you want to hang around for a self-defense class?"

My stomach turns over. "Can I be honest?"

"Absolutely."

"Look, I know Ryan is probably a great guy, but—"

"He scares the shit out of you?" Chris finishes for me.

I nod. That might be putting it mildly.

The corners of his eyes crinkle, and I could swear he's holding back a laugh though he gives no other sign of it. "We get that a lot. But the women who say that usually have the best results with him. He can be intense. But he's great with . . ."

He trails off, and I can practically see his brain working, trying to find a word that describes me without insulting me. "Scared women?" I offer.

One side of his mouth quirks up into a grin. "Yeah. If you want, I can have someone cover my next client and sit with you. You don't have to do anything today, just watch. But if you feel like giving it a try, you're welcome to jump in. Ryan won't push you to participate, but once you do, he'll push you to break through your fear."

"What makes him so much better at this than you?" I think I could work with Chris. I mean, I shut myself in this little room with him without thought for my safety. After yesterday morning, I don't believe Chris *has* a temper or a mean bone in his body. He's unlikely to snap and smack me into a wall for screwing something up.

He grins again. "I'm a pushover. Okay, that's not fair. He really can be. The difference is, he's better at judging someone's limits and stopping within them. I'm better with the women who don't have confidence issues, the ones who already know they can do it. The ones who don't, well, honestly, I just want to wrap y'all in bubble wrap and baby you. It won't help you, though."

He's sweet. It's really nothing to smile about, but that doesn't keep my lips from straining upwards. "I have to admit, I'm impressed that you recognize that about yourself."

Chris's broad shoulders twitch up in a shrug. "I've learned the hard way. Ryan can be the biggest asshole on the planet at times. And man does he ever have anger issues—actually, he's getting better on that front. But when he's working with battered women, he's a different person. So, if you want to sit in, I'll come baby you while you watch. If you want to change in case you decide to participate," he pauses and eyes me, sizing me up, "I can call Jam and see if she has clean clothes in her locker and get her combination. She won't mind letting you borrow something."

Do I want to do this? This could mean I never have to suffer another beating again. Well, avoiding men like that is a big step in the right direction, and I seem to be doing great at that thus far, but knowing I could stop someone if they tried . . . It could be life-changing.

"I think I'd like that. Thank you." I'll probably sit safely on the sidelines, but this way, I know what I'm in for if I ever change my mind.

Chapter 8
Heidi

Between Fern and Jamaica, I'm suitably outfitted. Luckily, they were together when Chris called. Jam's shorts fit me fine, but there was no room for my boobs in her XS bra and shirt. *Damn boobs, anyway.* My feet are bare, but it'll have to do. It doesn't matter if I don't have shoes if I'm watching from the sidelines.

Chris is waiting right outside the door like he promised me he would, just far enough away no one could accuse him of trying to peek in. His lips stretch into a smile the second I step out of the door. Chris doesn't need to smile to be gorgeous, but when he does, I practically need to fan myself or go stand under an AC vent or something. I would do some questionable shit to see that smile.

Whoa.

That thought scares me almost as much as Ryan does. I do *not* have room in my life for notions like that. Objectively admiring Chris from afar is fine, but that's straying into crush territory. *Ain't nobody got time for that.* And someone like me has no place in his life.

"Ready?" he asks, extending a hand to indicate which direction we're heading.

He's so careful not to make me uncomfortable. That level of consideration is almost enough to make a girl swoon. Almost. Some guys try to lead with a touch, a hand on my back or my arm. Not all of them are doing it to be creepy; some people just have no regard for personal space. But I grew up watching Curt use seemingly innocent touches like that to hurt my mother, and even me when I got older, when he decided I was misbehaving in public.

I try to smile back at him, to hide the dark place my mind went, but my heart isn't in it. "As I'll ever be."

"You're gonna be fine."

We walk side by side through the big common area, but he still leads the way, guiding me with a gesture or a word. As contradictory as it may be, I want to hug him for it. But I don't. I walk next to him, following his cues.

"Alright, this is where we do self-defense class, regardless of who is teaching," he says, opening a door and stepping back to allow me space to pass without touching him.

Eight sets of eyes lock on me when I step into the room, five women and three men, one of whom is Ryan. It's obvious what Chris meant when he said Ryan leaves his anger outside this room. The intensity that followed him like a second shadow is gone. *Why can't he do that all the time?*

Not my business. I already know way more about these people than I have any right to.

"Heidi!" he cheers. "Glad you came!"

"Um, hi," I say, caught off guard by his exuberance. The guy I met Friday doesn't seem to be the sort to get that excited about anything.

The door closes behind me, and Chris stops on my right. He's close enough I can feel the heat radiating off him, but not so close as to touch me—letting me know he's here if I need him. *But why? Why does he care? Why do* any *of them care?* "I convinced her to at least watch today," he tells Ryan. "But I told her she could hop in if she thinks she can handle it."

Ryan nods, then locks eyes with me, and I fight the urge to take a step back. The anger might be gone, but my brain knows it's there, waiting under the surface. "At any point," he says. He grabs the shoulder of the guy next to him. "This is Bryce. He's a blackbelt in Jiu-Jitsu and helps with the self-defense classes twice a week. I'll leave the others to introduce themselves when they're ready."

I'm obviously dismissed until I decide to step up because he turns his attention to the students assembled in front of him. "Who's ready to take back their power? Let's warm up!"

The class responds with cheers, clapping and whooping as they spread out.

Chris waves a hand toward the nearest wall, but he doesn't wait for me to follow. He leads the way, talking over his shoulder. "Honestly, you can learn everything you absolutely need to know in a class or two, but we like to teach a wide variety of techniques because sometimes, the basics don't fit the situation."

"What do you mean?" I ask.

He turns around and sinks to the floor, knees bent, back against the wall. Following his lead, I lean against the wall and slide down until my butt hits the ground. "No two attacks are the same, obviously, but there's data that suggests a woman is less likely to defend herself if she feels the techniques she was taught are too harsh for the situation. If someone is verbally harassing you, are you going to feel breaking their nose is justified?"

My mouth goes dry, and a jolt of old fear zaps my heart, sending it into overdrive. It's not hard to imagine myself in that situation. I've lived it. And no, I'm not going to break someone's nose. I'm going to freeze or run and hide. "No," I rasp.

I catch his nod from the corner of my eye. I can't make myself look at him. "Exactly. So, we have basic courses for people who are adept at handling themselves in situations like that but want to know what to do in a physical altercation. Then, we have the more in-depth classes where we help build confidence, teach techniques to de-escalate if possible, and how to make the other person wish they'd stayed in bed if they won't back off."

Silence settles between us while Ryan and Bryce wrap up the warm-up and move into the teaching part of the class. Students pair up and work with each other, practicing hitting pads or these little bag things that they dangle from their hands while the instructors make their way around the room, going from pair to pair to practice hands-on things. It's very interesting until Bryce grabs a woman by the throat and backs her into a wall.

The memory of the night everything went wrong slams into me, and I stop breathing. My throat tightens painfully, and my hands clench so hard my nails dig into my palms.

"You bitch!" Dean's whole body swings with the force behind the backhand I'm too slow to dodge. His hand strikes my cheek hard enough to snap my head back and to the side, slamming it into the wall. "You had one job! One job!"

One of his hands closes around my throat. I grab for it, digging my nails in, anything to get him to let go. My back hits the wall, and he holds me there, laughing at me while I struggle to get free. "You're such an idiot! *How could you miss her leaving?"*

"Heidi?" Chris's voice filters through the memory of Dean screaming like someone yelling at the other end of a tunnel, weak, distorted, and echoey. "Heidi? It's Chris. You're safe here. No one is hurting you. You're not alone. Can you hear me?"

I blink, and the image of Dean is gone. Chris is kneeling in front of me, far enough away he's not touching me in any way but within arm's reach. A jagged, ugly sound tears from my too-tight throat, leaving a trail of fire in its wake. My chest heaves as my lungs work, but no air is getting through.

"You're safe," Chris says calmly, holding his hands up at shoulder height, "what do you need? What can I do?"

Over his shoulder, I see the entire class has come to a halt. Ryan, Bryce, and the lone male student are nowhere to be seen, but the ladies all stand in a group where I can see them. I look left and right, searching for the men. *When did I get so scared of random people?*

"The other guys left the room," Chris tells me. "I didn't want to leave you alone with strangers, but I can go if you need me to."

I shake my head. That's not what I need. I don't know what I need other than to feel safe. Tears gather in my eyes, burning with the need to fall.

"Hey, just slow down and take a deep breath for me. Can you breathe through your nose?"

I shake my head again. I can't breathe at all. *I'm going to pass out right here in front of all these people like the idiot I am.*

Chris smiles, and the grip my fear has on me loosens a bit. "Okay. Hey, it's alright. Breathe through your mouth for now."

"I can't!" I gasp

"Yes, you can. You are, even if it doesn't feel like it. Forget about everything else and focus on the air in your lungs. You take as long as you need to, and I'm right here if you need me."

"The class—" I begin to argue, glancing over his shoulder.

Chris shakes his head and taps two fingers to his cheek at the corner of one eye. "You look right here. Don't worry about them. Some of them understand."

"That's right," a woman says, and others back her up.

"You just look right here and breathe," he says, smiling again. "You're strong enough to get through this, but I'm right here if you need me."

He taps his cheek again, drawing my eyes with the movement. I already know his eyes are chocolate brown, but I didn't notice the flecks of honey in them. *Gorgeous.* I could happily sit here looking at them for the rest of the day.

"There you go," he says, breaking the spell I was falling under. "See, all better now. I knew you could do it."

What? I pull a deep breath through my nose and understand what he means. I'm not on the verge of hyperventilating anymore. The tightness in my chest and throat is gone. It's like it never happened. But the memory is there.

"I'm so proud of you," Chris says. "Do you want to stay or call it a day?"

"C'mon, honey. You stay and fight!" the voice from before calls out. "Don't you let that bastard break you."

The corners of Chris's mouth twitch as he fights a smile. "That's Addi," he whispers.

"My ex-boyfriend gets mean when he drinks tequila. One night, he came home drunk, someone was in his parking spot, he got angry and took it out on me," Addi continues. She edges away from the group and comes to stand behind Chris so she can look me in the eye. A scar bisects her face from just below one eye, under her nose, and across both lips. She points to it. "He did this. Broke my nose and my orbital bone. Dislocated my shoulder and threw me out a second-story window. I let that prick win for about two years before someone talked me into taking self-defense. This is my last week, but I was like you when I walked in here. Ryan scared the piss out of me, but he's a big ol' softy. So are Bryce and Chris. I know it's hard, but so is living in fear. Choose your hard, honey."

A tear drifts down my cheek, but it's not a sad, pathetic tear this time. It's more like solidarity. She gets it, but the woman in front of me isn't afraid of anything. *Could I ever be like her? I never was to begin with.* I don't have visible scars to tell my tale, but there were plenty of broken bones. "My ex broke three ribs," I say barely above a whisper, dropping my eyes to the floor because I can't handle the pity that comes with telling someone what happened or the shame I feel for putting myself in a position for it to happen. "One punctured a lung. He broke my left arm and dislocated that shoulder, shattered my left orbital socket, and fractured my jaw."

Addi nods, just a sharp downward jerk of her chin that I catch in my peripheral vision. "Take back your power, honey. No one deserves to walk through life at the whim of their worst nightmares."

Is there any other way? That's all I've ever known. Even when I thought I was free of the nightmare of living with Curt, I had Dean whispering poison in my ear. I thought I was strong then because I ran away, but I was nothing more than a pawn, manipulated to win a game. I had no power.

But I *want* that power.

"I'll stay," I whisper, though the prospect of another panic attack is overwhelming, and not only because they're exhausting. I don't care if everyone here understands; it's humiliating to be so weak in front of witnesses. But this is where all that bad shit goes to die.

A smile tugs at her scarred lips. "You go, girl. You're one step closer."

Chapter 9
Chris

The patter of running feet wakes me before Keaton makes it to my room. The dimness of the light coming through the window means it's way earlier than I want to be awake. *What does my kid have against sleeping in?* It's Sunday. I don't work until two.

With his running start, he leaps onto the bed. "Daddy!" he says mid-jump. "Miss Heidi is sitting behind her house again!"

"That's great, bud." I grab the covers and raise them for him. "Climb in. Let's go back to sleep."

He ignores the blankets, bouncing in place instead. "Can she come over for breakfast again? Please?"

"How about dinner instead?" It's useless, though. He's awake now. It doesn't matter if dinner sounds better to him; we're up for the day.

"Please?" he repeats. "I want to show her my room."

I want to show her mine too, bud. I should probably be ashamed of myself for thinking that. She's so scared of me she could hardly stand to be shut in my office with me Monday. But, because I'm some sort of twisted fucker, that only makes me want her more. I want to show her how a man should treat his lady.

I'll just have to learn to live with it.

"Alright, Keat. But let's get breakfast ready first." Cooking with her last weekend was great, but very . . . intimate. I should avoid situations like that, or I might start getting ideas.

***

Heidi looks up when the back door opens, so I smile and wave. Keaton takes off like someone fired a starting pistol. He wants to be the one to extend the invitation, so I lag behind and let him do his thing.

"Good morning, Miss Heidi," he begins, and my heart swells with pride for his manners.

"Good morning, Keaton," she replies with a cute little smile that somehow seems uncertain.

"Would you like to come over for breakfast? We're having sausage and eggs and hash browns, and it's all done already, so you can just come and sit and eat."

Wide-eyed, she looks at me over his head and raises her eyebrows. It's a look I'm very familiar with, adults seeking validation for what my child is saying or asking of them. However, it's usually seeking permission to give him the sweets he's asking for. I nod, letting her know I'm in on his plan.

"I don't want to intrude," she says, still addressing me.

Somehow, I expected that reaction. I swear the woman feels like she has to apologize for existing, and I hate it. "It's not intruding when you're invited."

"I cooked the eggs!" Keaton tells her. "Don't worry. Daddy made sure there were no shells in them."

Heidi looks down at Keaton like she can't quite figure him out, but she nods. "If you're sure," she says slowly.

"We're sure!" he says, grabbing her hand. He leads her across the yard, all the way to the kitchen table, with a death grip on her hand like she'll disappear if he lets go.

"Grab a seat," I tell her, waving toward the table. I want to give her as much space as possible, so I go to the stove instead. I usually plate food from here, but this time it's all on serving platters or in bowls I can put on the table.

I'm not surprised when I turn to find Keaton moving his booster seat to occupy the chair next to Heidi. *At least he'll be between us.* That might help her some.

"After breakfast, wanna see my room?" he asks her.

She looks to me, panic in her eyes that doesn't make much sense. Yeah, it's kind of an odd question if you're not used to kids—and I don't think she is—but it's nothing to freak out about.

I shrug. It's her choice. I don't care either way so long as she's not harsh about it if she tells him no.

"Uh, sure," she says.

"I know twice doesn't exactly make a habit, but is sitting outside on Sunday morning your thing?" I ask before Keaton can come up with something else to make her uncomfortable.

That actually gets a smile out of her. I mentally pat myself on the back for earning it. "My mom, brother, and I used to sit together and watch the sunrise on Sunday mornings." She glances out the back door. "Even after I . . . left, I kept doing it. I can't see the horizon here, but I sit and watch for the sun to clear the trees and the houses."

I follow her gaze to the door. I never thought about it before, but I see what she means. "The view probably isn't much better from my balcony, but you're welcome to try sometime."

She freezes and drops her eyes to her plate. I suppose that's as strange an offer as my kid asking her if she wants to see his room, but if it's important to her . . .

"I'd like that," she whispers through that beautiful smile. "Thank you. And thank you for inviting me this morning."

"We're glad you came," I tell her, my voice a little rough from the effect her smile has on me. It hits me like a fist to the heart every damn time.

"Can we do this tomorrow too?" Keaton asks.

I wouldn't mind, but . . . "Heidi and I work in the morning, bud."

His little face screws into a frown. "What day is today?"

"Sunday," Heidi and I answer together.

He nods as if that answers everything. "Okay, then how about next Sunday?"

"We'll see, Keaton." I'm not going to promise him anything. I don't mind at all, but Heidi might have better things to do than hang out with us.

Keat switches on the puppy dog eyes and swings them in Heidi's direction. "Please?"

Her smile gets just a little bigger. "I'd love to if your dad doesn't mind."

"Then it's a—plan." I quickly stop myself from calling it a date. I don't even know why I thought the word. I don't want to freak her out. It's not like that. *Damn it.*

Chapter 10
Chris

A loud crash my brain recognizes as the slamming of a car door jars me awake. Groaning, I roll over and look at the display on my phone. Eight o'clock. *Wow.* Keaton *never* lets me sleep this late. He has no regard for Saturdays, so this is a minor miracle. And Sundays are all about Heidi as far as he's concerned. Sunday morning breakfasts are a thing now, four weeks and counting. Five if I count the day he snuck out.

Shit! Did he wander—

The *thumps* of little feet running down the hall hits the stop button on my panic attack. "Daddy! I think Miss Heidi's car is broked."

"Broken," I correct automatically. "And why do you think that?"

He sucks in a huge breath, my warning that I'm in for a long explanation. "Well, she got in, shut the door, it made a funny noise, she got out, shut the door really hard, kicked the wheel, and sat down on the ground."

Well, I guess he's not wrong. "Think we should call Uncle Ryan and have him come take a look?" I ask him. Keaton loves all my friends, but he practically hero-worships my business partner. And Ryan has no idea. He'd be appalled if he knew—claiming that he's not the kind of guy a kid should look up to. He's wrong, but I keep that to myself. At least until Trista gets him sorted out. She's already worked wonders for his self-esteem.

Keaton launches himself into the air and pumps his tiny fist. "Yeah! Can he bake muffins with us, too?"

Chuckling, I sit up and put my feet on the floor. "We can ask. But let's get check on Miss Heidi first, alright?"

"Okay." He turns on his heel and runs from my room, shouting, "I'll get dressed!"

He insisted he *had* to have the room overlooking the street. I wanted him closer to the master suite, but I caved. He was so excited about being able to sit at his window and wave at the cars going by, not caring that they'd never see him and wave back. Now that we have gates I *know* he can't open, and extra locks and alarms on all the exterior doors, I don't worry so much.

I hurry into clothes and walk down the hall to his room to assess the situation next door, tapping out a text to Ryan as I go. I can see Heidi's backyard from my room, but Keat has a view of her driveway in addition to the road. Sure enough, she's sitting on the ground next to her battered Escort, head down like she might be crying. *She has to be freezing.*

Yeah, it never really gets *cold* here, but the temps have taken a nosedive in the month since we moved in. It's still early enough in the morning the air will have a bite to it. The ground will be downright chilly.

"Ready!" Keaton announces. I turn and give him a once over, checking that his shirt isn't on backward—or his pants—but he managed alright this morning.

"Good job, buddy. Let's go check on Heidi."

He holds my hand down the stairs, but it's more like holding onto the string of a helium balloon—I'm the only thing keeping him on the ground. He's so excited to go help he can hardly stand it. He does the impatient dance while I unlock the front door, then he's off and running.

"Miss Heidi!" he cries, frightening a flock of birds into flight from their perch in the tree in her front yard. Her head whips around about the time he collides with her back, wrapping his arms around her neck to hug her. "Are you alright?"

I cringe and pray for all I'm worth that he didn't send her into a panic attack. She's made a lot of progress in the last few weeks with self-defense class, but a surprise like that might put her over the edge.

She reaches over her shoulder to pat his back with one arm. *Progress indeed.* She's come a long way from looking at him like he's some sort of alien, but he didn't really give her a choice. Every time he sees her, he greets her like she's his all-time favorite rockstar. Between him and the classes, she's not nearly as standoffish as she used to be. "Where's your dad?"

"I'm here," I tell her, knowing she's probably worried he's gone off on his own again. "He says you're having car troubles, so we came to check."

"It won't start," she says on a tired sigh.

"Battery?" I ask, stopping next to her. My knowledge of what makes vehicles go is limited, but I know they need a battery to start and fuel to stay that way.

"I have no idea," she says, her voice tight. Keaton releases her and falls onto his butt on the concrete beside her, resting his head on her shoulder. Heidi carefully moves the arm trapped between them and wraps it around him. Whatever it is holding my heart together disappears, and it collapses into a pile of quivering goo in my chest in the face of so much cuteness.

"Would you—" I stop, surprised by the gravel in my voice, and clear my throat. "Would you like me to check it out?"

Her head whips my direction, and she shakes her head. "Oh no, I don't want to—"

"Heidi..." I softly cut her off. I hate that she feels like she can't ask me for help. I know she's not alone in this city—she's mentioned her mother and a brother—but I'm right here. "It's no trouble."

I can practically see the gears in her head working, turning so hard smoke should be rolling out of her ears. "The keys are in it," she finally whispers, hanging her head.

My phone vibrates in my pocket while I'm opening the door, more than the two short buzzes that indicate a text, so I get it and check the display. "Yeah, Ryan," I answer.

"Battery?" he asks.

"I'm checking now," I say, folding myself into a seat that is much too close to the steering wheel for me. I put my foot on the brake, check that the car is in park, and turn the key. She tries like hell to turn over, but nothing happens. "Sounds like it."

"Alright. My class just started."

"If a jump doesn't help, I'll let you know."

"Sounds good." The call disconnects, which is nothing less than I expected since he made the call mid-class.

I climb out of the car and smile at the worried look Heidi gives me. "Bad news is I'm gonna have to drive on the grass. Good news is I think it's only that your battery needs to be charged. If it's not, Ryan will be by later to take a look."

"What do I need to do?" she asks, eyeing her car skeptically.

"You don't know how to jump a car?" I ask. I'm not surprised. I only know because Ryan taught me one night after work when I forgot to shut my dome light off before work that morning. In the age of AAA and living in the middle of a big city, it's just not something I ever needed to know before.

Heidi's head shakes, sending her ponytail swaying back and forth. *Oh, the things I could do with that ponytail.*

I bite my cheek to keep my brain from wandering down that path. *I won't like how it ends anyway.* "Well, for now, you sit right there. Keaton, you too. When I get the Durango over here, I'll show you what to do."

I jog back to my place and dash upstairs to grab my keys off my nightstand. Back downstairs, I make a side trip to the kitchen and grab a banana for Keat and a second for Heidi. I don't know why I'm treating her like a child who can't fend for herself, but damn it, that girl is just too skinny. It makes me worry she's gone without enough food recently. *At least I know she gets a good breakfast on Sundays.*

The Durango rolls smoothly across the grass patch between her drive and mine, and I ease it as close to her car as I dare, hoping my cables will reach because

I can't line up nose to nose. She's parked too close to the house for that. Before I get out, I kill the engine and pull the lever for the hood.

"Pop the hood," I tell Heidi, stepping out of my vehicle and walking back to the cargo area. She stands and moves towards her car, so I open the back hatch on the Durango and grab the jumper cables.

Heidi beats me to the front of the vehicles and opens the hoods of both. Instead of joining her in the space she needs to work, I walk around and stand next to the driver's side of her vehicle, putting a barrier between us so she doesn't feel trapped, and hand her the cables.

She works while I explain how to connect them, red to positive, black to negative, which end to ground, and how. When she's done, I double-check everything and have her start the Durango. While we wait for the battery to charge, I hand out the bananas then explain how to disconnect everything when it's time.

When we're done, I'll leave my cables in the trunk of her car and go buy a new set. Ryan gave them to me because I didn't have any and needed them. It seems fitting to keep the chain going.

Like Keaton on our way over here, Heidi is practically buzzing with excitement when I give her the go-ahead to start her car. She hustles around to the door and hops in. The motor tries like hell again, but nothing happens. My view through the windshield breaks my heart. That spark in her eyes dies in a blink, drowning in tears that she quickly tries to hide.

Heidi scrambles out of the car, her head hung low. "I'm such an idiot! I must've done it wrong!"

"Hey," I say, reaching for her. Before I can think better of it, my hand is on her shoulder, and I'm pulling her into a hug. I should apologize and give her some space, but holy *shit*, I've wanted to do this since I first saw her. That urge is still a mystery to me, but this . . . This is amazing. *This is what my arms were made for.*

Her arms wrap around my waist before I can bully mine into letting her go. She presses her face into my shoulder, and her body shakes with a sob.

"I'm so sorry. I wasn't thinking. Let go, hon. I'll give you space." She tosses her head side to side, making her ponytail dance again, and clings tighter. I force myself not to respond in kind. I don't want her to feel like she can't get away if she needs to.

She's so close and warm, and she smells like sunshine and fresh air, I have to remind myself that this hug isn't a prelude to something. It's about Heidi needing a shoulder on a bad day. But I'm thankful I wore jeans instead of something I'd work out in. My dick doesn't care about the whys. Its only focus is her body pressed against mine, and it is knocking on my button, begging for freedom. The denim helps keep that situation in check.

Get it together, man. It hasn't been that damn long. There's no reason to react so strongly because it's never gonna happen with Heidi. She needs one thing from me, and it's not my body. At least not in that way.

I rub her back, hoping it's not pushing her boundaries, but I need to do *something* to give her some measure of comfort. And it usually works with Keaton.

Keat! I glance down at where I left him, but he's up and moving now, making right for Heidi. He wraps his chubby toddler arms around her legs and squeezes. She shudders against me with the force of another sob.

"You're not an idiot, Heidi," I tell her over the Durango's motor, still rubbing slow circles on her back. "You did everything right. Sometimes, it just takes a bit. Or your battery could be so far gone it can't hold a charge. You hear me?"

She nods, but her body presses closer until she's plastered against me from shoulder to hip and lower. There's no way in hell she doesn't know I'm harder than Chinese algebra, but she doesn't react. "I don't know what I'm going to do," she sobs. "I need this car. How am I going to get to work? How am I going to get *groceries?*"

"Slow down, hon. It's too early to assume you've gotta throw the whole car out and start over, okay? If we can't get it to start, Ryan will figure it out. If it's not a simple fix, we'll figure that out too. And guess what? I happen to know your boss. I promise you, Mason won't mind swinging by to pick you up for work until you get your car fixed."

More likely than not, he'll even offer to lend her a car, but I can't see Heidi accepting it, and mentioning that will only freak her out more than she already is.

"Uncle Ryan can fix anything!" Keaton proclaims. "And I'll help!"

Her body shakes again, but I think she's laughing this time. Laughter is good, though. The curveballs life throws are harder when you can't find humor in them.

"Where were you off to?" I ask her. The only plan I have today is baking muffins with Keaton like we do every Saturday morning unless I'm working and he's with my mom. If we try again and the motor still won't turn over, I can take her wherever she needs to go.

Heidi finally picks her head up and looks at me. Her eyes are all red, and there's a line on her cheek from the seam in my collar, but she's as beautiful as ever. "To pick up my groceries."

Looking at her now, my reaction to her makes sense. Some, anyway. I don't believe in love at first sight, but I cannot deny my attraction to her. I want this woman in more ways than one. I want to be the one she runs to when the world gets sideways. I want to be the one to light that spark in her eyes and chase her fears away. I want her smiles and her laughter, her hugs, and—God help me—her kisses.

But she's twenty-two. And I'm the twenty-nine-year-old single father who has more baggage than she'll ever want to deal with since it seems she has plenty of her own, assuming she ever even notices me in that way. At her age, I thought people my age were way too old.

All that aside, there's a far more obvious reason we'd never work. She might not be afraid of me right now, but after whatever happened in her past, that recurring fantasy I have about wrapping all that gorgeous blond hair around my fist and everything that goes with it will *terrify* her. I could shove that side of me into a metaphorical box and bury it. I've done it before. She might be worth living that lie again. I'll never know.

I could make excuses all day, tell myself the timing is bad and things will be different later. But they won't. The reality is the things I want right now will never happen. But I can still show her what a man should be.

"Well, then, let's try your car one more time. If it still doesn't start, we'll leave the keys where Ryan can get them in case he turns up before we get back, and Keaton and I will take you to the store. And, afterward, you can bake muffins with us if you'd like." I know what she's going to say, but I'm ready for her this time.

A little of that spark comes back to her eyes, and she smiles, dividing my attention and sending my gaze bouncing from one beautiful sight to the other. It would be so easy . . . Just lean a little, and—I catch myself doing just that and stop. *I am such an asshole. I can't believe I even thought about it.*

"That would be great," she whispers, unaware of the battle in my head. "Thank you so much."

The argument I prepared for the inevitable 'I don't want to be a bother' reply fades away to memory because I'm sure I'll need it later. I force myself to focus on her eyes but find them locked on my mouth like she was maybe thinking along the same lines I was. But that's ridiculous. *Wishful thinking.*

I tip my chin toward the car. "Alright. Give 'er another try."

Her eyelashes flutter a bit, then her arms fall away, and she carefully disentangles her legs from Keaton's grasp. Instead of clinging to her, he wraps both arms around one of my legs and leans into me while Heidi climbs behind the wheel once again. I can't say I'm surprised when the motor cranks but doesn't turn over again. Her battered car has clearly seen better days. It has more dimples than a golf ball, and there's no shortage of rust, but just because it *looks* like it shouldn't be roadworthy doesn't mean it's not sound under the hood. Batteries do go bad.

Shoulders slumped, she climbs out of the car again and closes the door behind her. I supervise the removal of the jumper cables, then get them both situated in the Durango and run her car keys to my place. Ryan knows how to get in to get them when he arrives.

As I maneuver the car back to my drive and into the road, Heidi says, "I don't know how to repay you."

I let her statement hang in the air between us until we reach the stop sign at the end of the block, then look her way. "Easy. You don't. I didn't do this expecting you to return the favor sometime."

What kind of life has she lived to think that every act of kindness has to be tit for tat? Has no one ever done something nice for her because it was the right thing to do? Granted, that wasn't a lesson I learned at home, necessarily. That was a Grandpa Martin and Grandma Lola lesson. My parents had more of a 'not my circus, not my monkeys' outlook on life because life taught them that people are users.

I wait for a longer than strictly necessary break in the Saturday morning traffic before I turn. No point in taking unnecessary risks, especially not with my kid in the car.

"Then why did you do it?" she asks.

The answer to that is surprisingly simple. I don't even have to think about it. "Because I'd want someone to do the same for my family."

Her eyes burn a hole in the side of my head. "So, what, you just treat the whole world like your extended family?"

The memories that question dredges up make me sigh. "Not exactly. It's more that I remember a time when a helping hand was the difference between feeling like I was failing at life and making it through the day without a breakdown."

At the next stop, she pointedly glances back at Keaton, then watches me expectantly. I nod. I spent the first two years of his life terrified that Lydia would change her mind and try to find a loophole in our agreement—or just take him. I wouldn't leave him with anyone I didn't know personally, and they had to be someone I would trust to stand up to her if she showed up and tried to sweet-talk her way in the door.

"So now, I'm paying it forward." I could've done things differently. I could've hired someone to run errands for me, but my sister Callie is a great example of what growing up waited on hand and foot can do to a kid. I'd be the same if not for the Chambers' influence on my life. I want better for Keaton, so I don't buy my way out of hard situations. I do my own shopping. I do my own cooking and cleaning. As a retiree, Mom has more than enough time to spend doting on her grandson and is always happy to babysit while I'm at work. He gets more of her than Callie or I ever did, not that I hold that against him. Parenting is hard. We all just do the best we can and hope like hell we don't fuck up our children too badly.

If taking Heidi to get groceries is the one thing that turns her whole day around, then I'm happy to do it. And hopefully, I'm setting a good example for my son in the process.

Chapter 11
Chris

Thanks to a detour at Starbucks because a banana wasn't nearly enough to keep Keaton full for long, Ryan is already under the hood of Heidi's car when we pull in. I step out and am greeted by him cussing up a storm about something. *That doesn't bode well.*

"Why don't you go unlock your door, and I'll let Keaton out and grab the bags?" It'll take me one trip to get everything, but I'm not sure she can say the same.

"Alright." Her willingness to agree without arguing is surprising, but she lost some of her stubbornness after the conversation in the car on the way to the store. She hops out readily enough, and I move on to the next task on my list. Once I free Keaton, he'll run right to Ryan and attach himself like a burr to his honorary uncle's side.

But as I round the hood of my car to do that, I spot a problem. Heidi has stopped halfway between her drive and mine and is staring at her car. No, at *Ryan.*

He has her keyring. This is the first time she's had to approach him outside the safety of the self-defense classroom.

No matter how badly I want to, I can't step in on this one. I *can't* fix this for her. Not unless she asks. She either needs to face her fear and do it herself or admit she needs help. I hate it, but this isn't about what I want. Like Addi said, Heidi needs to take back her power.

But maybe I can give her a little nudge in the right direction. A buffer, so to speak. The buckles on Keaton's car seat come undone in record time. He's so excited he nearly wiggles out of my hands as I lower him to the ground, and he hits it running. Shouting loudly enough the local HOA will probably beat down my door later—or send me a sternly worded letter—he tears across the yard to hug Ryan's knees.

Even Ryan doesn't come across as threatening with a kid stuck to his leg. Heidi must reach the same conclusion because the tension in her posture eases, and she takes a tentative step forward. Then another.

I've done what I can. The rest is up to her.

But I take my time gathering her bags so she doesn't see me coming and feel rushed.

I have no idea if she needed the extra time, but she's gone when I shut the liftgate and step into the yard. I'll call it a win.

Ryan is scowling at her motor like it insulted his girlfriend when I pass. "That doesn't look like good news," I mutter.

"What?" he asks.

"Your face."

He curls his lip. "It's not, but I only want to say this once, so get her back out here. But you come too so she's not scared shitless. Sending Keaton over was genius, but this will require a lot more than five words from her."

"There's coffee for you in the Durango."

The curl in his upper lip stretches into a grin. "Yay. Coffee." He turns his attention to my son and holds up his grimy hands. "Keat, could you get me one of those wipes, please?" he asks, indicating a fairly clean-looking tub of wet wipes by his feet. They must be new. I've seen what they look like by the time he's hit the bottom of the tub. Just handling the container necessitates the use of the contents.

"Be back." I continue on my way, through the open door and into the kitchen where Heidi is waiting. "Ryan has news," I tell her, "but he's distracted by coffee, for now, so we've got time to put things away before he comes looking for us."

Her answering smile reminds me of the forced one she used the night we met, but I'm not sure if that's due to the news or that she has to talk to Ryan to get it. Either way, she's obviously prepared for the worst. I hate it, but I'll be right here to help her figure it out.

"Alright. You wanna take the cold stuff, and I'll get everything else situated?" she asks.

"Sounds good."

Despite how little she bought, it takes her a long time to get things stored in the cabinets to her liking. I recognize her fussing for what it is, though. She's stalling. I lean against the counter out of her way, giving her space. It would be easy to assume that she doesn't need it after that hug, but I know better. Panic attacks can strike at the damnedest times at the slightest trigger. Still, Ryan is waiting on us . . .

I keep my voice light and as soft as I can manage, but her shoulders still twitch up next to her ears as soon as I speak. "Heidi, you can't avoid this forever."

She sighs and slumps forward, resting her forehead on a cabinet door. "I know. I'm just . . . Not ready."

"For what?" I ask. "The news, or to talk to Ryan?"

"Both, but mostly the news." She sighs again and slowly adds, "I've got some money put away, but . . ."

I nod though she can't see it. It's as much as I expected. "One thing at a time, hon. Let's hear what he has to say before you go putting yourself in debt."

Judging by the way Ryan was glaring at that motor when I walked by, I'd say it's going to take some work. That doesn't mean Heidi will have to cough up her life savings all at once to get it roadworthy again, though. Ryan's never met a car he can't fix, and if he doesn't have the tools he needs on hand to get the job done, it pisses him off, so he goes and buys whatever it is. Bonus, he probably won't mind if she makes payments.

Her back straightens, and she scrubs her face with both hands while sucking in a deep breath. "Let's do this thing," she says with a nod, then she turns around and smiles at me. "In case I forget later, thank you for all this. I know it can't be what you wanted to do with your Saturday morning."

Oh, yeah. Spending the morning with a pretty girl and my son. Total waste of my time . . . So maybe none of this was on my to-do list. I've still had a good time. And I got to hug Heidi. "You're welcome. I've actually enjoyed my morning. We didn't have any plans that can't be done later."

She grins. "You know, the day I moved in here, I thought living next to you was going to be a bad thing. But now, I'm really glad I'm lucky enough to have you for a neighbor."

My brain tries to make more of those words than she likely intends. And maybe my heart does too. "Oh yeah?"

"Yeah. As sappy as it sounds, you're giving me some faith in humanity. I mean, not everyone is an asshole. Who'da thunk?"

Once again, I find myself wondering about her home life as a kid, but I have no business asking. "I think you've spent too much time with the wrong crowd," I say, striving to keep my voice light and teasing so she doesn't take it the wrong way.

She snorts. "You can say that again. C'mon. Let's get this over with."

Outside, Ryan and Keaton are playing tag while they wait. Ryan is "it" and makes a big show of being unable to catch my four-year-old, overshooting the mark, falling to his knees in the cold grass, stumbling, tripping, just hamming it the hell up. Keaton is laughing so hard he falls every few steps. It is the *cutest* damn thing. *And Ryan thinks he'd make a horrible father . . .* I love how my friends love my kid like their own.

Keaton comes to a halt and turns around to face Ryan. "Now push-ups!" he shouts.

Ryan doubles over and braces his hands on his knees, pretending to be out of breath from chasing Keat when he probably didn't break a sweat. "Again?" he pants.

"Yes!"

Ryan tries to hold back a grin, but I know him well enough to recognize the signs. He falls to his hands and knees, then stretches out into plank position and slowly lowers to the ground.

Keaton runs over and climbs onto his back, fisting his hands in Ryan's shirt like it's a handle. "Ready!"

"Alright, here we go. How many are we doing this time?"

"Until I get tired!" Keat cries.

Ryan shakes with restrained laughter, but I don't hold back. That is exactly something Ryan would say in the gym to one of his more advanced clients who isn't putting in enough effort. Even Heidi laughs. Everything about the unbridled joy in the sound makes my heart stutter, then soar. Sure, we haven't spent much time together, but this is the first time I've heard her laugh like she means it, and it's beautiful.

When Ryan doesn't comply quickly enough, Keaton applies his heels to Ryan's ribs like he's wearing spurs, and Ry is a damn horse, which only makes Heidi and me laugh harder. But Ryan gets to work, pushing away from the ground with an extra thirty pounds on his back.

His chest hits the ground again, and Keaton cries out, "One!"

He makes it to ten before Heidi leans my way and whispers, "How long can he do that?"

"Until Keaton gets bored, probably," I say, laughing a little more. "Or until I step in."

Heidi shakes her head. "That's insane."

"Nah. That's good exercise. But we probably should stop them so Ryan can tell us what's up."

"Um . . . Ten!" Keaton proudly proclaims after nineteen.

"Twenty," Ryan and I correct him at the same time.

"Twenty!" he says with the same level of enthusiasm he started with.

Since he's showing no signs of boredom, I run interference. As cute as it is, we need to take care of this car problem. "Hey, bud. You gonna let Uncle Ryan up so he can tell us what's up with Miss Heidi's car?"

He shakes his head and heels Ryan again. "But I'm not tired yet."

Ryan stops at the top of his push-up. "I'll let you check the oil again."

Keaton throws himself off Ryan's back. "Okay!"

He takes off for the car, Ryan hot on his heels. Keaton stops at the front bumper and raises his arms into the air. Ryan scoops him up and settles him on one hip, then leans over for Keaton to grab the dipstick.

"Here's the deal," Ryan says while Keat carefully extracts the dipstick. "Your battery is sh—crap. As old as it is, I'm not sure how it made it this long. Your alternator bit the dust. But what concerns me most . . ." He pauses and waits while Keaton finishes his task.

The tip of the stick finally emerges, liberally coated in black sludge.

"Oh, fu—crud." I do my best not to cuss in front of Keaton, but this time might be an appropriate exception. "This car hasn't had an oil change in . . . ever."

"That's a problem, obviously. Not to mention, there's a lot of questionable uh . . . crud keeping this thing running. Wires taped when they should've been replaced, that sort of thing." He glances at Heidi but looks away just as quickly. "How long have you had this car?"

"I bought it just before I moved here," she says, her eyes fixed on the dipstick while Keaton wipes it off with a towel.

He nods. "You've been lucky so far."

"What are you saying?" Heidi asks.

"Basically, it's a miracle it lasted this long."

"So?" I ask him. I have to remind myself to keep breathing so I don't hold my breath hoping for an answer other than the one I'm expecting after that *glowing* review. Heidi will be devastated if he says what I think he's about to.

Ryan blows out an audible breath. "I mean, I *can* fix it. But it might be cheaper and easier to replace it. I think they topped it off with oil to make the sale, but that's all leaked out now. Coolant is leaking as well. Radiator hoses are *taped* on. Tires are damn near bald. And that's just what I can see from here. More likely than not, it's going to cost more than this thing is worth."

Chapter 12
Heidi

Every word out of Ryan's mouth increases my urge to cry from sheer frustration. My jaw hurts from clenching to hold back the tears, and my eyes burn like I've been awake for two days with someone blowing cigarette smoke in my face nonstop. I gave eight hundred dollars for that car. Yeah, it's ugly, but I'm proud of it because it's not stolen. I tagged it, paid taxes, insured it, the whole nine.

But my knowledge of cars is limited to the value of various makes when delivered to a chop shop. Clearly, my Escort isn't as great as the seller made it out to be, but I was desperate.

And now, all that money is gone.

I wish Thomas was here. He'd know what to do. But, most importantly, I just need a hug. Chris didn't seem to mind earlier, but he'll probably think I'm crazy if I do it again. But damn . . . I don't think I've ever felt so safe. Not even with my brother. Those big arms could do so much damage if he were to hit me, but the only thing he used all that strength for was to hold me tighter when I cried.

"What do you want to do?" Ryan asks me, reminding me that I need to focus on the problem at hand. I can daydream about that hug later.

I can't answer his question the way he's expecting. What I *want* to do is curl up in a ball and pretend this day never happened. I want to delude myself into believing this is all a bad dream, and when I wake up, my car will start and run just fine. "I don't know," I whisper. "I don't know what *to* do."

Yeah, I'm making great money at CFI. It's the best-paying job I've ever had. Lola promised me a Christmas bonus even though Christmas is only a couple months away and I haven't been there all year, and a raise after my first calendar year of employment. I don't *need* all my savings to live comfortably right now. But I don't want to be without it. What if I get sick? What if I get *fired?* How will I pay rent and utilities and buy groceries then?

Ryan says something about a loan, bringing me back to the present once more. "I can't get a loan. I don't have credit."

"Well . . ." he pauses and glances at Chris, who shrugs. "I wasn't talking about a traditional loan."

"What do you mean?" I ask.

"I mean I'll loan you the money. Or Chris will."

I open my mouth, but no words come out. That's insane. They don't know me. I have no way of ensuring them I'll pay them back. I shake my head at the sheer stupidity of it, and Ryan takes that as an answer.

"If you're not comfortable dealing with us, Fern is a viable option."

"Fern is a great option," Chris murmurs.

Ryan nods. "But you'll probably get the same kind of deal from her that you'll get from either of us."

What is wrong with these people? "Do you *hear* yourselves? You don't know me. I've lived here a month! What if I can never pay you back? For all you know, I'll skip town with the car, and you'll never see me again." Not that I *would* do that. That would definitely land me behind bars. What they're offering is incredibly generous, and I'm probably a fool for saying no, but it's just too risky all around. If something goes wrong and they turn me in for theft or something, my record will work against me.

Chris's broad shoulders lift in a shrug, but he addresses Ryan. "You free after work?"

Ryan nods. "Tris and I are gonna work on the Camaro some more, but it's not going anywhere."

"Alright, let Heidi and me talk this out, and then maybe we can go find her something that's not going to fall apart around her ears?" Chris is talking to Ryan, but he's looking at me, asking me with his eyes if it's okay. He can talk all he wants, but he's not going to change my mind, so I nod.

Ryan nods again. "Sounds good. I'm gonna take off then. I left Leslie in charge."

Something about that makes Chris laugh. "I can just see her barking orders at the guys."

"Yep," Ryan says with a grin. "She can probably run the place better than we can."

Keaton, who is now as greasy as Ryan's hands were earlier, reinserts the oil-checker-thing into its spot for approximately the millionth time and wraps his smudged arms around Ryan's neck. "But I don't want you to go, Uncle Ryan. Stay and bake muffins with us!"

"I can't today, little man. I've got to go back to work."

"Bossing people around?"

Ryan nods. "Exactly. Unless you want to wait until this evening to bake. I can bring Aunt Tris over?"

"Yeah!" the little boy cheers.

Ryan leans back a bit to look at Chris, who grins. "That alright?"

"Yeah, sounds great."

"Alright, later you three. Keaton, you're in charge!" he says, handing the little boy back to his father.

Keaton grins. "Can Miss Heidi come too?"

Those twin grins highlight the similarities between them. It's Chris and his mini-me. I've covertly observed the two of them every time the opportunity was presented for the last month. Chris is so careful and attentive, and Keaton tries so hard to be like his dad. They are undeniably adorable together. It's hard to keep myself from wandering outside in hopes of being invited to join them at whatever they're doing that day. But Dean's voice in my head always convinces me I shouldn't get too close.

"You'll have to ask Miss Heidi," Chris says.

Keaton turns his big brown eyes my way, and I swear they get bigger somehow. "Please, Miss Heidi, will you bake muffins with us tonight?"

"Nicely done. Good manners, Keat," Chris murmurs to him while I struggle with my answer.

How do I say no to that? Like, it should be illegal to be that cute. And it's a cuteness overload with him in his father's arms. *Oh, my God. When did I start thinking kids were* cute? Not all kids, though. I'm sure. It's just this one. He's special. It must be how much he looks like his daddy, because that man . . . *Whew, did it get hotter out?*

My resolve to stay in my own lane wavers. I wait for the alien voice in my head to tell me all the reasons accepting this invitation is a bad idea, but nothing happens this time. *My therapist will be so proud at our next monthly check-in.* He'll be even happier if I accept, but I'm not sure I'm ready.

It's not just the prospect of being crammed in Chris's admittedly spacious kitchen with him and Ryan *and* a kid—a kid who I actually kind of like now—but I do have plans today. I need to find a weekend job, especially now that I need a new car. I have goals, and those goals take money. My search can wait another week, but I'd rather not put it off. I'm not sure what to do with all my free time now that Dean doesn't have me out using me as bait. "Maybe . . ."

'Maybe' is easier than 'no' with those puppy dog eyes trained on me. I just won't turn up. I don't even know why he wants me there. He won't notice if I'm a no-show.

Chris tips his chin up, and I could swear he knows what I'm planning. His eyes narrow just a bit, and he almost seems disappointed. He opens his mouth, but whatever he plans to say is interrupted by a silent SUV towing a trailer pulling up along the curb in front of his house.

His mouth snaps shut, and confusion flashes through his eyes before he turns to survey the situation.

"Ronni!" Keaton squeals as he squirms in Chris's arms, trying to get down. "Down, please, Daddy!"

Chris obliges, and the little boy takes off like a shot across the yard to collide with the dark-haired little girl who was here when I moved in. His momentum knocks her on her butt, but she laughs like it's the funniest thing that's ever happened to her.

"Hey!" a deep voice booms. Keaton's head snaps up as Mason steps off the road into the yard and rests his fists on his hips. "Where's my hug?"

"Uncle Mason!" Keat wriggles away from Ronni and shoots toward Mason, who is prepared for the assault and catches the little wrecking ball, swinging him into the air and around in circles until *I'm* dizzy just watching. Fern smiles from the sidelines, and I have to wonder if she finds watching her husband with a child as . . . *interesting* as I find watching Chris and Keaton.

"I forgot!" Chris called across the yard.

"We didn't," Mason calls back to him.

"Obviously. Let me move the Durango, and you can pull around back."

"What are you doing here?" Keaton asks, now resting comfortably on Fern's hip.

Her smile gets a little brighter. "You remember Ronni's old play set?"

Keaton nods.

"Well, it's yours now. We're here to help your daddy put it together."

"What are we doing with the old one?" Mason asks Chris, but his voice carries to me.

"Uhh . . . I have no idea," Chris says. "Know anyone with limited yard space who needs one?"

"Stick it in Ryan's yard for when you're there," Fern suggests.

Both men look at her. "That's a great idea," Mason says.

"Seconded," Chris chuckles.

I don't know why I'm still standing here, watching the five of them. Maybe because it's all so strange to me, even after spending an entire evening with them. There's no struggle for dominance between the adults. It's like they all know and are content with their place in the dynamics of the group. No one is making any sort of play to be dubbed the leader of this get-together, which is different. When Dean's friends got together, there was always some sort of pissing match. Someone had to prove they were the biggest badass in the group.

No one here seems to care who their self-proclaimed leader is. From the outside looking in, they're all badasses in their own right.

But Dean's friends could easily say the same. Yeah, they did bad things, but they were all good at what they did. So what's the difference?

Trust. The answer is surprisingly simple. These people trust each other to the bitter end, whereas no one in Dean's gang trusted anyone other than themselves. For good reason, obviously, because Jack rolled on them as soon as he was cuffed.

But, seeing how much they trust each other kind of makes me think that maybe I can trust them too. And maybe they can trust me. So maybe Ryan's loan proposal *isn't* all that crazy.

"Hey, Heidi!" Fern waves at me from the other yard. "Wanna come sit and supervise? I brought brownies!"

I certainly *want* to be someone they can trust, but that means leaving my lane, and that is hard. It's safe here; no one can use me. No one can hurt me. But it's lonely, too. If I say no, I'll just end up watching out the window, wishing I hadn't while I should be searching online for a job.

So maybe I say yes this time. And maybe I bake muffins tonight, too . . . Maybe. I'll try. Ryan will still be there. Trying is the best I can do.

Now that I've convinced myself, my smile comes easy. This will be fun, I think. I enjoyed myself last time, anyway. There's no reason this time will be any different. And when it's over, I'll be proud of myself for branching out. "I suppose my plans can wait another day. What am I supervising, the construction or the dessert?"

"Yes!"

I just look at her, waiting for her to answer, and I realize that *is* my answer. *One more weekend without a side hustle isn't gonna kill me.* Who knows, maybe one of them knows of something . . . Unless moonlighting is against CFI policy.

Chris backs his Durango out of his drive and pulls into mine. He rolls down his window and sticks his head out. "This alright? My garage is full of boxes of stuff I'm getting rid of."

"I ain't going anywhere," I point out.

He grins. "Yeah, but it's still your driveway. I don't want to be presumptuous."

As presumptuous as that hug? Oh. Em. Gee. Don't *think* about that hug. Save it for later, when it's safe to think about all the things I felt.

"I don't mind." The hug, him parking in my driveway. Any of it. I'm beginning to think there aren't a whole lot of things he could do that I *would* mind. Especially not the things that involve what was pressed against my hip when he hugged me earlier.

"Thanks." He switches the motor off and gets out. We cross our yards together to the others behind his house. He grabs a chair and moves it closer to the construction site for me, near where the kids are playing in a sandbox and Fern is already at work with a wrench, removing rusty bolts from the existing playset. "While you supervise, maybe I can convince you that Ryan's idea isn't as insane as it sounds," he says over his shoulder on his way to help unload the trailer.

"What idea is that?" Mason asks from where he's waiting for Chris on the trailer. "Ryan's ideas *can* be rather crazy sometimes."

"Heidi's car is toast," Chris explains. They grab either end of a long piece of wood and get to work. "He suggested fronting her the money for a replacement, and she kind of . . ."

"Freaked out?" I finish for him. He doesn't have to tiptoe around it. I kind of went off back there, but I still think it was justified.

His back to me, he nods. "Yeah, that. I told Ryan I'd spend the day convincing her we're not crazy and we can maybe go find her something after he gets off work tonight."

Mason purses his lips. "I have a better idea," he says after a moment.

"What's that?" Chris and I ask at the same time.

He looks at me across the yard. "What if CFI were to provide you with a car as part of your wages?"

I start to argue, but he holds up a hand as soon as I open my mouth. I'm not at work, but he *is* my boss after a fashion, so I hold my tongue.

"Hear me out. As long as you have a job with us you have a car. After so long, it will be yours, free and clear. We'll hand you the title. Should you decide to leave before that time, you have the option to buy it."

I take care to keep my tone civil because I don't want him to think I don't appreciate the offer. But I don't want anyone to accuse me of kissing ass. I want to work hard and earn the respect of the people I work with, even if I am just the girl at the door handing out badges. "I don't want special treatment, sir."

He smiles. "Mason, not sir. God, I hate sir."

"Second only to Mister Chambers," Fern says through a giggle.

Mason's eyes close, and I could swear he's counting to ten. When he opens his eyes again and finds me watching him, he grins again and says, "Long story. Anyway, it's not special treatment. It's a perk."

I fight not to roll my eyes, but there's no containing the sarcasm. "Oh, I'm sure you do it for everyone."

Nodding, he follows Chris back to the trailer to grab another piece of wood. "Actually, yes. When we know, at least. We don't make a point of stalking our employees, but if they make their problems known to us, CFI has their back."

I've met Lola. Everything he just said sounds like something she'd do, so it all checks out. I doubt he's making that up on the spot as a favor to me. But still . . . Businesses don't *do* that. I can't count how many times I heard Dean or one of the others preach about CEOs only caring about lining their pockets. "Why would you do that?"

They drop the next beam, and he rests his hands on his hips. "Happy employees stay. They take pride in the company and their work. CFI wouldn't be what it is today without our employees. They take care of the company; the company takes care of them. So go pick out your car—any car you want. Chris or Ryan will pay a deposit so the dealership will hold it," he looks over at Chris for confirmation and receives it, "and CFI will pay them back. Monday morning, my assistant will take you to finalize the purchase."

I have no idea what he's talking about, but it mostly sounds logical to me. Except . . . "But if you have the title, how do I tag it and insure it?"

He smiles again. "You don't. We do."

"But—"

He flashes that blinding smile and cuts me off. "Perks. Trust me."

Trust. That word is coming up a lot today.

He hops on the trailer again, still talking. "I benefit in no way from screwing you over on this. Neither does CFI. We, the company and I, only want to help."

My throat constricts around the emotions threatening to choke me. My old crowd was wrong about a lot of things. Maybe this is another one, or maybe CFI is just an anomaly.

"And you're already living in a company house," he says over his shoulder on his way back to the trailer.

"*What?*" There's no way I heard him right. I mean, I've never met my landlord, but I don't send my rent check to CFI.

Mason turns to look at me and cocks his head to the side. "Didn't Grandma tell you? She bought that house in the company's name after they made the decision to hire you. That's why rent is so low."

Lola. I suppose that's all the explanation I need. Still... That lump of emotions in my throat gets a little larger, robbing me of my ability to speak. I mentally add her to the list of reasons I have to achieve my goal—I will not let her down. Someday, maybe I can help her help others too.

"But it wasn't for sale," Chris says. "I looked at it before I looked at this place and decided I was tired of renting."

Mason shrugs and squats down to grab another board. "You ever heard *anyone* tell Grandma Lola no?"

"Point taken," Chris mutters.

"Grandma wasn't going to charge rent at all, but Granddad thought it was important. Standing on your own two feet and all that. So they worked out a deal." He stops to look at me again when that board joins the pile on the ground. "At this point, I have to swear you to secrecy because I'm not supposed to tell you this and Grandma will be devastated if she finds out I've ruined the surprise."

I almost don't want to know. I'm not sure how much of this brand of crazy I can handle today. Curiosity will kill me, though. I make a show of zipping my lips, locking them, and throwing away the key like I'm a little kid again. "My lips are sealed," I promise him. I'm good with secrets.

One side of his mouth kicks up into a crooked smile that *should* make me dizzy, but it pales in comparison to another. "You're going to be given an option on Monday. The money you pay in rent every month will either go towards renovating the house and the yard, or it will be applied as payments toward the house."

Payments? Is Lola insane? "Your grandmother thinks I can buy a house on *that?*"

"Oh, there's more," he says, the other side of his mouth joining the smile. "If you go that route, she's decided to personally match your payments."

I'd think I heard him wrong—again—but after all the insanity spewed at me today, it's really not hard to make that leap. "Why? Why would anyone do that?" Hiring me was one thing, but buying a whole *house* just so I have a place? That takes extra to a new extreme.

He shrugs. "Grandma likes you. She says that sometimes, all a person needs to succeed in life is for someone else to lend them the tools necessary to lay the foundation for their future."

"If she weren't doing it for you, she'd be doing it for someone else," Fern says over the clicking noise her tool is making. "Actually, I guarantee you she *is* doing it for someone else too. That's just Lola."

"She says CFI changes the world on a large scale, but she prefers to work one-on-one," Mason adds with a confident nod.

Is this how Alice felt when she landed in Wonderland? The words they're saying make sense, but the actions they indicate do not. Life has taught me that people just don't do things like this for other people. No one cares that much. It's eat or be eaten out here.

"I just . . . Look, in my world, people like y'all don't exist." Horrified, I clamp my mouth shut. I didn't mean to say that. It reveals too much. They're going to ask questions that I'm not ready to answer. Then things will get complicated.

The three of them share a look, but it's Chris who speaks. "Well, we do now."

As much as I try, I can't doubt him. In the short time I've known these people, they've provided me with a load of evidence to back up his claim. They *are* good people, but I thought Dean was a good person until—wait. No. That's the Stockholm Syndrome talking. Dean convinced me to run away from home so he could use me to rob people. He was never a good person. And that's why I don't know what to do with people who are.

Even if they *are* good, it doesn't change that they won't like me anymore if they ever find out about my past. They can't *all* be like Lola, even if some of them are related to her.

Chapter 13
Chris

Ryan's Barracuda announces their arrival long before they park in front of the house. The rumble of the big motor gives me goosebumps. Before I found out about Keaton, Ryan and I were spending the spare time we really didn't have searching for a resto car for me. We were going to work on it together someday, and it was going to be my baby. But then I had an actual baby, and there was even less time. *Someday.*

When Keaton is older, we'll find a car, and he will help us with it too. That'll make it even better.

The new-to-us playset is long finished, and the old one is trailered, but that's as far as we made it. Mason and Fern packed up their tools and pulled up chairs while I threw burgers on the grill for lunch for everyone. We barely got the kids to sit still long enough to eat, and we turned them loose immediately after. Not much has changed since. The four of us whiled away the hours bullshitting and watching the kids play.

"Knock knock," Ryan says as he and Trista pass the edge of the house. "Heard the kids and figured we wouldn't bother with the door."

"Good call," I tell him. He would've had to let himself in again if he had. There's no way I'd hear the bell over the kids.

"What the heck? Looks like we missed a party!" he says, eyeing the half-empty brownie pan in the middle of the table.

"You missed playset construction," I correct him.

A frown tugs at his lips for a moment but smooths out. He loves putting things together. And taking them apart. Mostly taking them apart.

I lean back in my seat and stretch. From the corner of my eye, I catch Heidi hunkering down in her seat, trying her hardest not to catch his attention. I hate that, but there's nothing I can really do about it. It'll just take time. "I suppose you're here to go car shopping."

"Yep."

"Hmmm," Fern hums. She gives the kids the side-eye and then sweeps her gaze around the table. "I propose Mason and I stay here to watch Keaton while you do your thing. I'll call Austin and have him pick up steaks. The others can bring sides. You call when you're on your way back, and dinner will be ready when you get here."

"I like this plan," Mason says, settling deeper into his chair and lacing his fingers over his stomach.

Before Ryan or I can weigh in on the matter, the shrieking cuts off. Every adult but Heidi looks toward the children. Keaton is running across the yard as fast as his little legs can carry him, holding one hand out in front of him.

Breathless from excitement more than the running, he stops next to Heidi, who still hasn't noticed him, and holds out his hand. "Miss Heidi!"

She jumps, startled, but quickly turns to look at him. "What's up?"

"This is for you!" he says, proudly holding his hand just a little higher.

From where I sit on the other side of Keaton, I'm privy to the full range of emotions that flash through her eyes, but the wonder that brings up the rear of the parade is my favorite.

"It's a heart!" he says as she reaches out.

When she withdraws her hand, she holds a deep red leaf shaped like a heart. She swallows hard and favors him with one of her rare real smiles. "It's beautiful, Keaton. Thank you."

Grinning from ear to ear, he turns and runs back to the playset. He stops about halfway and turns to shout, "You're welcome!" garnering laughs from everyone at the table.

"That's so sweet," Heidi whispers, her eyes fixed on the leaf. From the awe on her face, you'd think she was holding a raw diamond or a gold nugget, not an ordinary leaf. There are probably a million more littering the yard. But that one is special because Keaton gave it to her. And I understand completely. It's not just a leaf anymore; it's a bit of magic. That's what children do. They take the ordinary and make it magical.

I don't think I'm meant to hear it, so I don't comment, but I don't think I'm the only one with a little bit of a crush on our neighbor.

"That sounds like a good plan to me too," Ryan says, dragging everyone back to the topic at hand. His eyes zero in on Heidi, and he asks, "Are you going to be okay in a car with me, or should we drive separately?"

She looks up from her leaf, and her eyes go round. I've lost track of the number of times today her mouth has opened, but no words have found their way out.

Ryan smiles at her. There's nothing he can physically do to *not* look threatening, but that smile usually helps. "Heidi," he says softly, "you're not going to hurt my feelings. I know it's nothing personal."

She looks at me, takes a deep breath, and lets it out before she tries to answer again. "I want to try, at least."

He and I both smile at that. We don't *know* what it's costing her, but we know there's a price for trying. But I'm so proud of her for being willing to pay it.

"You can do it," I murmur to her. I look up at Trista and ask, "Are you going too?"

"You bet," she says with a smile for Heidi. "You're not alone. I used to be scared of him too. I promise, he's a big marshmallow."

Ryan sighs and shakes his head, but he doesn't bother trying to deny it. Everyone at this table knows better except for Heidi, and I think even she suspects it after watching him play with Keaton this morning.

I stand up and stretch again. I've sat far too long today, and I never got my workout in unless constructing the playset counts. "Shall we, then?" I ask.

Heidi just nods and stands up.

"Keaton, come here, please," I call over his laughter.

"Awww!" He hops off the swing and comes running, but not as quickly as he did to bring Heidi her leaf.

I crouch down to get on his level and give him a hug, but he doesn't hug me back. "I'm going out for a bit, alright?"

"Just you?" he asks.

"No, I'm going with Ryan and Trista and Heidi. Mason, Fern, and Ronni are going to stay here with you, alright? And when I get back, we'll all have dinner."

He squints at me and thinks on it a bit before asking, "Like before?"

'Before' could mean anything from yesterday to some random Sunday two years ago, so I specify. "Like our first weekend in this house, yes."

Bouncing on the balls of his feet—something he picked up from Fern—he smiles really big. "Okay, bye!"

So eager to get rid of me . . . Though, he's never been one to cling. I admire his independence—when he's not sneaking out of the house at sunrise. "Okay. I love you."

"Love you too, Daddy." He throws his arms around my neck and squeezes until I can scarcely breathe.

"You be good, okay?" I ask on what little breath I have left.

"Okay. You too."

I chuckle at that. "I will."

He turns to run away but stops when Ryan calls, "Hey! What about me?"

Keaton's cherubic smile lights up his little face. I swear someday my heart is going to explode from how much I love this little human. "You be good too, Uncle Ryan."

"That's not what I mean, you little punk!" Ryan shouts while the rest of us laugh. "Get over here and give me a hug!"

"Nuh-uh!" Still grinning, Keaton whirls around and takes off running, and the chase is on. Unlike their game of tag this morning, this is over quickly.

Ryan catches up within five steps and lifts the giggling, wriggling little punk over his head. "Gotcha! Now! Where's. My. Hug?"

"I lost it!" he screams through his laughter.

"Well, you'd best find it, little man."

"Or what?"

"Or I'm gonna tickle it out of you!"

A soft laugh causes me to glance over at Heidi. She's watching the two of them, rapt as if it were her favorite movie. Austin swears that watching men interacting with children does something to a woman, and I have to say, there's something to that, but I didn't expect it from Heidi. Especially not watching Ryan.

And doesn't that just suck? There's something ugly going on in my chest—like something with tentacles is wrapping all of them around parts of me best left untouched. *Jealousy.* It's ridiculous. For one, Ryan is happily off-limits. For another, I've already established that there is not now, nor will there ever be, anything between Heidi and me. *Between me and anyone, at least not until Keaton is grown.*

Mason lucked out and found someone who loves his kid as much as he does. Fern must be a fucking unicorn because I haven't been lucky enough to find another woman like her.

"Alright. We can go now," Ryan says, pulling me out of my pity party. He puts Keaton down, and the little shit runs around the table to hug Trista. The two of them are thick as thieves now that she's with Ryan.

When she puts him down, he turns, his face bright with excitement, until his eyes land on the space Heidi occupied just moments ago. The brightness dims, and his bottom lip pokes out in a pout. He looks at me and that lower lip quivers. *What the hell?* Wordlessly, I point toward the street and Heidi's retreating back. She's already halfway to the car.

Keaton whirls around and takes off running. "Wait!" She turns, and he barrels into her legs with enough force, she stumbles backward, but she recovers before she falls. "You didn't say goodbye!" he wails.

"Oh, Chris," Fern murmurs, a small smile curving up the corners of her mouth. "I think he might be a little attached already."

"I was noticing he seems to have a crush," I confess. It's cute now, but what happens if she moves? He'll be heartbroken. *I won't be too happy myself.*

She shakes her head. "I'm not sure that's the case, but he's definitely fond of her."

Whatever it is, I'm not sure Heidi is prepared for what it entails. She hasn't said as much, but I don't think she's a fan of children. She isn't mean to Keaton or anything, but her initial reaction to things he does gives her away, like her confusion when he gifted her the leaf. Of course, it could be that they got off to a bad start.

Heidi

"Wait!" The raw emotion in that little voice is enough to stop my heart. I turn just in time for him to crash into my legs, sending me stumbling and fighting to maintain my balance so I don't take us both down. "You didn't say goodbye!"

What do I do with this? He barely knows me. I'm not one of his fake aunts. I didn't think he'd notice if I walked away when the love-fest got to be too much. This kid has known more love in his short life than I ever have. *Or will.* I don't blame him for it, but watching his father's friends shower him with adoration is a little more than I can handle. They don't owe it to him, but they love him anyway. Unlike my stepfather, who promised Mom he'd love us like his own but made our lives hell.

Maybe that's how he would've loved his own kids? If that's the case, I'm glad Mom never got pregnant by him. A newborn wouldn't have survived life with Curt. The yelling. The smoke. The hunger. He probably would've shaken the baby in a fit of rage if it cried while he was trying to sleep after an all-nighter at the casino.

"I'm sorry, Keaton. I didn't think—" What do I say, that he'd care? That he'd *want* to tell me goodbye? I'm no one to him. A virtual stranger. It just so happens I live next door.

Keaton smiles at me, and I'm clearly forgiven. A little knot of worry in my chest eases, but I didn't even know it was there until it was gone. *What's going on here?* "It's okay now. I'll miss you, Miss Heidi. Have fun with Daddy. I'll save you a seat at dinner!"

Could he get *any sweeter!* I can't even with this kid. The more time I spend with him, the more confused I get. "Uh . . . Okay. I'll miss you too, Keaton."

And I mean it! I've come to look forward to spending time with him. He's a bright spot in my life. I may not understand him, but I don't doubt his sincerity. He's too little to be fake. He means everything that comes out of his mouth. That's something that used to annoy me about kids. Their honesty could cause so much trouble. But when this one says he's gonna miss me, it makes my heart go *squish*. I don't want to leave now.

I didn't want to assume I was included in the dinner plans. I mean, yeah, they included me last time, but that doesn't mean it's an open invitation. Heck, I don't even know if I *want* to be included except to see Keaton again. Yeah, food I don't have to cook sounds pretty good, but I'm about peopled out today. I'm not about to promise him that I'll be here until I'm invited and decide if I can handle a whole crowd of people who make no sense to me. He'll have forgotten all about it by the time we get back anyway.

I crouch down in front of him like Chris did earlier and let him wind his chubby arms around my neck. Hugging his little body is awkward. He's so tiny. What if I squeeze too hard and hurt him? It must be enough for him, though, because he lets me go and takes off running for the playset again.

When I look up, the others are all smiling at me like they know something I don't. What I do know is that I don't like it.

"What?" I ask, scowling at them.

Fern's smile somehow gets even bigger. "Nothing. We were just talking about how Keaton has latched onto you."

Coming from any of the others, I might not believe it. But her . . . One look at that woman's eyes and you know she doesn't have an ounce of guile in her body. Maybe I'm setting myself up for another kick, but I trust her to tell me the truth. "Oh. So, are we going, then?"

Smirking, Ryan steps forward, leading the way while the other two call their goodbyes. I wait for Chris and fall in step beside him so that Ryan isn't behind me, not that it bothered me as much as I thought it would before, and because being near Chris makes me happy.

Trista reaches for the passenger door handle, but Ryan stops her with a hand on her arm. He looks over his shoulder at me and asks, "Would riding up front make this easier?"

Memories of Curt twisting Mom's arm as he drove down the road or backhanding her without ever even swerving flood my brain. My jaw locks and my mouth goes dry. I always thought Thomas put me behind Curt in the car because I was shorter and didn't need as much legroom. I believed that at first, but the real reason was it was the one place Curt couldn't reach in a fit of anger.

"Hey," Ryan says, "it's okay. You can sit wherever you want."

On the one hand, I could say getting in the car at all is a huge step. On the other, it doesn't because I know Chris isn't going to let anyone hurt me. So how is cowering in the seat behind Ryan taking back my power?

"I'll do it." I force the words between clenched teeth, but they're out.

A hand brushes my shoulder, light as a feather, and is gone. *Chris.* I know it's him without looking. There's a certain gentleness to his touch and a sense of peace. I wish he wouldn't pull away so quickly, but I don't know how to tell him that without making things weird.

"Are you sure?" Chris asks. "You don't have to. He wasn't implying—"

"I know," I cut him off. I let my breath huff out and make a decision. These people have done so much for me already, and they just keep going. I want them to know that I appreciate it and why I am the way I am. Maybe it's time to extend a little bit of trust in return. "If my mother did anything to irritate my stepdad while we were out, he'd hurt her on the way home. Or he'd threaten to cause an accident and kill us all. He'd also lash out at my brother and me if we got on his nerves in the car. My brother always insisted he was too tall to sit behind Curt. I didn't understand until later that he was doing it to keep me out Curt's reach."

I hold my breath and wait for their reactions. I don't know what to expect. The only people I've ever talked to about this have similar backgrounds, other than my therapist. All of my old friends had a rough childhood. It's what banded us together; at least, that's what Dean said. They'd shake their heads and mutter some version of 'that's fucked up.'

There's a heartbeat of nothing, then everything happens all at once. A storm rolls across Ryan's face, and his hands ball into fists at his sides. Chris steps forward, surging into the space between his friend and me, shielding me from that anger, while Trista grabs both of my hands and squeezes, then pulls me into a hug. Neither reaction from the guys surprises me. It's Trista's who catches me off guard.

"Don't mind him," she says, her voice soft and low. "That anger isn't at you. He's angry *for* you. We're both so sorry you had to live like that."

Every muscle in my body clenches with the effort of holding back tears. This isn't a time to cry. I put a piece of myself out there—a fragile piece—and I can't protect it. I don't want to advertise how easily they could hurt me right now. The others would've taken advantage of that in a heartbeat. So I fight for all I'm worth, refusing to blink and grinding my teeth until the wave of emotion passes and the tears subside.

"Thank you," I whisper because I don't know what else to say. I don't know why any of them care, but it's clear to me they do. Why else would Ryan be angry on my behalf—if Trista is right. Why else would she hug me? Why would Chris step in to shield me? *Because they're good people.*

"You don't have to—never mind. You're welcome." Tris pats my back and steps back but rests her hands on my shoulders. "You're gonna be alright."

Ryan sidesteps Chris to stand next to his girlfriend and opens his arms to me. "I know I scare you, but I'll swear on anything you'd like that I don't hurt people who don't try to hurt me first. And sometimes, facing a fear conquers it."

That makes sense. I got over my fear of the dark by forcing myself to walk into dark rooms. And I *had* to get over that fear because I spent a lot of time in dark spaces once I ran away. If I'm going to spend any sort of time around Ryan, and obviously I am because I've lived here a month now and this is technically my fourth encounter with him outside of the gym, I need to get over it. Sooner rather than later. *Take back your power.*

I nod. Smiling, Tris squeezes my shoulder and lets her hands fall away. I didn't think about how she might feel about her boyfriend hugging another woman, but she doesn't seem to mind. At least, if she does, there's no outward sign of it.

"It's alright," she whispers as if sensing my trepidation.

So I grit my teeth again and take a step toward Ryan. Then another. And another. And then his arms close around me and, just like when Chris hugged me this morning, he's nothing but gentle. Still, my heart pounds in my ears, and my lungs work like the bellows I once saw at a Renaissance Festival where Dean was pickpocketing.

"Deep breaths," he murmurs. "You're fine. I would never intentionally hurt you."

There's a note of command in his voice that's impossible to ignore, but I suppose that's what makes him so good at working with women like me. He demands you to listen without shouting and without the threat of violence.

A hand rests on my shoulder, and I know that it's Chris's without looking—again. "Thank *you* for trusting us with the truth. It's easier when we know what your triggers are," he says.

I nod, acknowledging his words the only way I know how because I don't know what to say to that. No one has ever thanked me for anything like that before. But between his hand on my shoulder and his soft, soothing voice, it's easier to relax.

"Are we good now?" Ryan asks me.

A deep, shuddering sigh works its way up from somewhere in the soles of my feet, and I breathe all the tension I was holding out with it. "Better anyway," I reply.

"Progress is progress. Don't discount it." He releases me and pulls Tris to his side.

I don't have to hide a sigh of relief to be away from him because there isn't one. As hard as it was to do, it really did help. I faced my fear, and that pride settles in my chest—in my heart—along with the happiness that took up residence there after my talk with Thomas. It glows as bright as an ember and warms me clear to my toes.

"My turn?" Chris asks, holding out his arms.

Have I ever had this many hugs in one day? Maybe when I was little. Before Curt. But I like it. Especially once Chris has his arms around me again. I want to lay my head on his shoulder and let it all out while he rubs my back and murmurs sweet things. Every tear, fear, and nightmare. All the things Curt and Dean ever did or said. It's stupid. Doing so would give them way too much power over me. My heart doesn't think that's such a bad thing right now, but my mind says to wait.

Fern helps me make that decision, reminding me that standing next to the road when we're supposed to be getting in the car and leaving isn't the best time or place for a tell-all. "Alright, I dunno what's going on over here, but there are a lot of hugs, and I need in on this."

"We're just over here bonding," Trista says lightly, making a joke of it, which is nice because I had no idea how to explain what's going on without saying it all again. "Heidi gave us some insight as to why Ryan scares her."

"Ah," Fern intones, her voice heavy with understanding. "And hugs are magic."

What an odd thing to say... But I can't argue. I do feel a lot better about life right now. I would happily stand here in Chris's arms all day long, which is terrifying on multiple levels, but I let him go and turn to the others. "Don't take this the wrong way because it's not a bad thing, but y'all are the strangest people I've ever met in my life."

"We try," Fern says with a shrug.

Trista giggles. "You don't know the half of it."

Maybe I don't, but I think I'd like to learn. I hold my arms out to Fern, offering her a hug too. Because why not? I'm on a roll here. When in Rome and all that.

Over her shoulder, I watch the kids run across the yard with Mason trailing behind them.

"Hugs!" Ronni shouts.

Fern lets me go and steps aside, making way for her stepdaughter. I lean forward and accept Ronni's offering with tears in my eyes. "Hugs are magic!" the little girl whispers in my ear. "They let hearts talk and heal."

Is that what this is? She might be onto something there.

Ronni releases me so Keaton can hug me again. Then Mason shrugs and hugs me too. And I climb into the front seat of Ryan's car, smiling and laughing, my heart light as a feather for the first time in . . . ever.

Maybe it's not the hugs that are magic. Maybe it's these people. Whatever it is, I'm glad I'm here and that they decided to share that magic with me.

Chapter 14
Chris

I'm still shaking my head, as I've done intermittently since walking off the car lot, when we finally join the others for dinner in my backyard. The scent of cooking meat hits my nose, making my stomach rumble, and I forget for a moment why I was even shaking my head to begin with. Mason's trailer with the old playset is gone, and his and Fern's patio heaters are spaced strategically around the yard to ward off the evening chill. The cars out front mean everyone's here, but the only other people in the backyard are Mason, Fern, and Gabe. And the kids, of course.

Next to me, Heidi gasps. I turn to look, afraid something has happened to upset her. She's been a *lot* better since the hug-fest before we left, but . . . You never know.

"You saved my leaf!" she cries, so excited she's bouncing—again—and pointing at where it rests on the table, secured with a rock.

"I did," Fern says with a smile. "And he found a pretty rock for you, too."

Heidi gasps again and bounces forward to grab both of the treasures while Fern catches my eye and grins.

Heidi straightens, the leaf clutched in one hand, the rock in the other, and both held to her chest. "I'll be right ba—" Some of the light in her eyes dies. She catches her bottom lip between her teeth and glances around at the table, the people, and the yard.

She thinks she's not invited . . . When did I get so good at understanding the things she doesn't say? But, since she says more that way than she does with words at times, I guess it makes sense. How do I fix this without embarrassing her? Of course, she's invited. She was here when we made the plans. We want her here. *I* want her here.

"Alright," I tell her, ignoring the way she left that sentence unfinished. "We'll be here."

"We'll wait for you," Fern chimes in. "And get the littles cleaned up and situated." She turns and calls for the kids, ready to herd them into the house to wash.

Heidi's eyes lock on mine. For a while today, they lost that dullness. They were a stunning navy blue that threatened to knock me on my ass anytime she looked at me. That spark is gone now, though, and the loss of it leaves me a little off balance. "Are you sure?" she whispers.

"Count the chairs," I whisper back.

Her eyes circle around the table, her lips moving as she counts without a sound. Noel must've convinced Colton to come because I noticed his car is out front, so we have two extra chairs tonight. I'm glad he's here. Noel won't admit it, but I think it hurts her feelings when he refuses to join us for things. Introducing Heidi to him will be interesting. He makes Ryan look small, but he lacks the angry vibes. Hopefully, he won't scare her too.

When Heidi finishes counting chairs, she counts people, then looks at me with something a lot like hope burning those pretty eyes.

"I'll be right back," she whispers.

"We'll be right here."

Beaming again, she whirls around so fast her hair fans out behind her and takes off at a sprint for her front door. My eyes follow her until she disappears from sight.

"So," Mason begins, reminding me that I have company and it's weird to stand and stare at the place Heidi disappeared until she comes back. "What did she pick?"

Ryan and I share a look. He closes his eyes and sighs. I shake my head for about the millionth time.

"A '71 VW Beetle," Trista says, laughter coloring her voice. "The guys tried like hell to talk her into something newer, but she just . . ."

"Lit up like a sparkler on the fucking Fourth of July when she saw it," I finish for her, turning around to give my full attention to my friends. The memory replays itself in my head again, bringing with it the same fierce sense of satisfaction as a result of her excitement. I can't take credit, but seeing her so happy just does something for me. I shove that aside to analyze later.

"Yeah, that," Trista agrees with a smirk.

Mason is silent for a moment, then asks, "How much?"

"Twenty," Ryan grunts.

Mason's eyebrows raise, but his eyes narrow. "That's it? Does it need work?"

I had the same thought. Those are collector cars now. But as it turns out, they're not all that expensive unless they've had a lot of work done to them. This one wasn't bad; it was clearly garage kept and a one-owner, but it wasn't something the original owner sank a lot of money into."

"Eh," Ryan intones. "A little bodywork, and the interior is a little banged up. It's clean under the hood . . . trunk, whatever you want to call it. Runs alright. Not an unreasonable amount of miles."

Mason waits a beat for Ryan to continue, but when nothing else is said, he asks, "So, what's the problem?"

Ryan rolls his eyes. "It's fifty years old."

Mason clears his throat and leans to the side, looking around the house to where Ryan's Barracuda is parked on the street. His '71 Barracuda.

Growling, Ryan scratches at the scruff on his jaw. "I can fix it if it breaks!"

"You just said the VW runs clean," Mason argues.

"Yeah, but—"

Mason isn't having it. "I'll have Darren leave the Vee-Dub at your place on Monday. You can go over it with a fine-toothed comb, fix anything that isn't up to your standards. Send me the bill. Len will get Heidi to and from work and wherever else she needs to go until you're done." He raises his eyebrows and watches Ryan expectantly. "Happy?"

Heidi *won't* be happy about this. She won't like relying on someone else to drive her, but I don't think Len, Mason's driver-slash-security chief, will scare her. On the contrary, I think she'll feel safe with him. The green monster in my chest tightens its tentacles around my heart at the thought. But I ignore it. I want Heidi to feel safe. And Len is a great guy.

"Yes," Ryan agrees. "But wouldn't it be easier to insist she picks something—"

Mase shakes his head. "If it makes her that damn happy, let her have it. That girl needs *something* to light up about."

Just like that, any and all arguments die. He's right. Deep down, Ryan and I both knew it. That's why we didn't fight harder. It was impossible to look at the excitement written all over every inch of her body the moment she saw it and tell her no. It wasn't just excitement, either. It was her inner child coming to life, probably for the first time since her stepdad came into the picture. That's a big assumption, but one I'm comfortable making based on the evidence she's provided so far. It was like telling Keaton no when the ice cream truck drives by the park. I folded like a cheap paper napkin as soon as she looked at me. Ryan didn't last much longer.

Tipping my head toward the house, I change the subject. "Do they need help in there?"

Mason smirks. "Does my wife ever confess to needing help with anything?"

"Point taken. But—" the back door opens, cutting me off, and Fern steps out carrying a platter that's nearly as big as she is, piled with steaks. The others file out behind her, each loaded down with a bowl or a plate of something. The kids follow after, Ronni closing the door behind Keaton, and they both run to grab chairs.

"I'm back!" Heidi shouts, breathless, as she sprints over. "Sorry, I wanted to brush my hair out, then my brother called."

Her enthusiasm makes me smile. "That's alright. The food just got here. We were just telling Mason about your car."

She stops in her tracks and cringes. "I can—"

Mason doesn't let her finish, which is unlike him. "My assistant will take it to Ryan's after the paperwork is signed Monday. Ryan will go over it and make any repairs he deems necessary."

"But—"

"While he's working on it, my driver, Len, will get you to and from work. I'll make sure you have his number in case you need to go anywhere else, and I do mean anywhere. Don't hesitate to call him. I promise he doesn't mind at all, and I compensate him well for his time."

"But . . ." She stops like she's expecting Mason to cut her off again and looks at her feet.

"Yes?" he asks while he pulls out a chair for Fern.

Heidi looks up. Her face flushed. "I don't—do you really pay him just to drive you around?"

Mason's face lights up with a smile. "He's also my security chief. But yes, he drives my family and me places if there are other things we need to be doing with the time on the road."

Austin grins at Heidi. "What he's trying to say is he's a workaholic, and he uses this commute to get more work done, but he can't do that if he has to drive himself."

"Eff off," Mason says, scowling at him. But we all know Austin is right—even Mason.

"Um," Heidi begins. We all look at her, but she's dragging the toe of her shoe back and forth in the grass, studiously *not* looking at any of us. "Speaking of work . . . is it like, against company policy for me to have a weekend job?"

Mason's mouth falls open, but no words come out. A lot of looks are exchanged, but no one says anything. If she's not making enough at CFI . . .

"No, it's not," Mason says slowly. "But if you *need*—"

"I just don't know how to *not* be busy," Heidi tells him in a rush. For whatever reason, relief surges through me. I hate to think of her struggling to make ends meet. I already worry that she doesn't eat enough.

Tara looks up at Heidi from her seat next to Gabe. "Can you use a sewing machine?"

Heidi shakes her head. "No, but I'm a fast learner."

"Got plans tomorrow?" Tara asks her.

"No?"

Tara's eyes light up. "We're going to need someone to help pick up my slack once the baby comes. I don't mind training someone."

Before anything else can be said, Keaton thumps the seat next to him. "Miss Heidi! I saved you a place!"

I was too distracted by Heidi's distress to notice before, but everyone else is seated and the only places left are the one Keaton indicated as hers and the seat next to it. To say I'm disappointed would be a lie, but I planned to put her between two of the girls or one of the girls and one of the kids. Somewhere safely away from me and my green monster that just needs to take a hint already. But it's too late now.

"The boss has spoken," I tell her, stepping forward to pull out her chair.

Her eyes bounce between the chair and me, and she doesn't move. *Ah, I should've known.* While probably not for the same reason, she's like Jamaica, who doesn't need someone to help her with a door or a chair. That's fine. I hold up my hands and back away.

"What are you doing?" Heidi asks quietly.

"Moving?" I mean, isn't it obvious?

"No, before?"

Before? What the hell is she talking about? "I was . . . going to help you with your chair?"

Her eyes light up again. "Like in the movies?"

"Uh, yeah?" I'm missing something here. That's the only explanation.

She cocks her head to the side. "People still do that?"

Is she insinuating I'm old? Or just old-fashioned? I guess that just proves what I thought earlier; I'm too old for her. "Sometimes?"

Her face falls. "Darn."

"What?" Did I say something wrong? I mean, it was a one-word answer. What did she expect?

"No one's ever done that for me before."

So, she really didn't know why I was standing there? It's no big thing at all. If she wants me to help her, I will. "I thought you didn't want me to."

"I didn't know . . ." she stops and scowls. "Why *wouldn't* someone want you to?"

I have no idea how to answer that. I don't quite understand it myself. It's not like I've ever assumed a woman is incapable. I'm just doing it to be nice. Polite. Helpful. Whatever. Maybe her question is a good one. Why *do* we do it?

"Feminism," Jamaica says when I don't reply. "We are strong, independent women. We don't need their help."

"But manners are kind of sexy," Fern adds, making Mason grin.

Jamaica sighs. "Unfortunately, she's right. Austin broke me."

Austin chokes on his drink, coughs a couple times, and gives her a smile that is *not* fit for the public.

"I'm so confused," Heidi whispers, her eyes now roving between Jam, Fern, and myself.

You and me both.

"Just do the thing," Jamaica tells me. "Someone needs to show the woman some manners once in her life."

The back of my neck burns now that everyone is focused on us, but Jam has a point. It would seem that most of the men in Heidi's life to this point are prime examples of what a man shouldn't be. But I'll fix that. *We'll* fix that. Not me. Us. Collectively.

"Come here," I tell her, hoping like hell no one can tell how freaked out I am about my mental slip.

She steps forward and stops next to me. "What do I do?"

"Just sit. You'll understand."

She does, and when she's all scooted up to the table, she grins at me and says, "I feel like a princess. Thank you."

My face puts off as much heat as the patio heaters around the table, but, as embarrassed as I am, I'm also a little proud of myself. Even if it makes no sense. "You're welcome."

"And that is why I'm broken," Jam murmurs.

"It's good to be queen," Tara adds.

While the other women murmur their assent, I glance over at Heidi in time to see a single tear fall and land on her plate. I reach for her but stop myself before I get anywhere close to touching her. Not because I think she'll mind anymore, but because I *shouldn't*. I have no right to. And I like it too much.

"Are you alright?" I whisper.

She smiles at me, twisting the tangle of confusing emotions in my chest just a little more, giving the green monster something else to grab onto. "Yeah. I've just . . . never been so happy."

Things make more sense now that I know about her stepfather, but I still feel like there are pieces of the story missing. There had to be *some* point in time when she was free from either of them before now. "I'm glad you're happy, but I'm sorry it's a new thing for you."

"I thought I was happy before," she says, wiping at her eyes with the back of one hand. "Six months ago, if you'd told me that any of this would happen, I would've laughed at you. I don't know how I ended up here, but I'm so thankful I did."

I don't know why Grandma Lola decided on the house next to mine, but I'm certain she knew that little fact when she bought it. It's not uncommon for CFI to provide their employees with houses if they have to move for the job. But maybe she knew the person she was buying it for needed friends, and this was the best way to put her in our path. Whatever it was that brought Heidi here, I'm pretty thankful for it, too.

I only wish things were different and I could consider indulging the urges to ask her out. But it's pretty clear that's not anything she wants. At least not from me.

Chapter 15
Heidi

My head is buzzing when I finally fall into bed, and I didn't touch the wine Fern supplied. This day was one surprise after another, but most of them were good. I might go so far as to call it the best day of my life. I *love* my car. Dinner was great, and I wasn't even tired of being around people. And Tara offered me a job! I'll get to learn a new skill! Dr. Porter will be so pleased with my progress at our next monthly check-in call.

But I know in my heart that the buzz is mostly from sitting next to Chris all night. And Keaton. It's only been a month and that little doll has me wondering what I ever found to hate about kids. I don't know what it is about him, but I've reached the conclusion I'll do just about anything to make him smile. I've never felt that way about anyone before him.

And his father.

That's another problem I can't quite figure out. I shouldn't want anything to do with either of them, but I do.

There were so many moments tonight when I thought Chris was going to reach for me. Not just *thought*, I know he was going to. But he always stopped himself. I suppose I shouldn't be surprised since I tend to freak out. He's just trying to be nice and give me space. But I don't want it from him. That's as scary as it is exciting. Not so long ago, I thought I'd never want to look at a man again. I've come so far. That ember of pride burns a little brighter.

My mind drifts back to that hug this morning. It was obvious he did it without thinking, like he would for one of his friends if they were having a bad day—

something I didn't know people did before. I could tell the exact second he realized what he'd done. He froze; stopped breathing even. And maybe I should've panicked like he thought I would. I've known him for a month. A *month*. But since the moment I ducked behind him to put myself out of the line of sight when Ryan and Fern were messing around, I've had a sense that Chris will never give me a reason to fear him. Even if I did forget when Keaton wandered into my yard. That was a special circumstance.

But this morning, in his arms, it was like . . . home. A feeling I haven't had in so long, I barely remember it. And at one point, I really thought he was going to kiss me. I *wanted* him to. I've never wanted anything as much as I wanted him to keep going when he leaned closer. My lips burn again just thinking about it, sparking a fire in my blood that gathers between my legs.

Get a grip. Dean's voice in my head douses that fire, but he has a point. It's probably just hero worship on my part or something. He keeps popping in to save me, after all.

And I'm the last thing a guy like Chris would want. I'm too young. He has a business. A kid. He doesn't need my drama. He probably looks at me as another kid to take care of.

That bulge in his pants this morning disagrees.

I have no answer for that one. At least not one that sticks. Maybe an automatic response to hugging a woman? But I hugged Ryan and Mason today, and neither of them got . . . *excited* about it.

Chris didn't the second time, either. But I did just kind of drop a bomb on him. *And maybe that was the moment he decided I wasn't worth the hassle?* He's had enough female-initiated drama in his life after what his ex did. I'm happy she left if she didn't want to be a mother. She would've made life hell for all of them. But I hate that she put Chris through that, and I really hope she doesn't wake up one day and realize she's missed out on something wonderful.

Really, it doesn't matter. I can't have any sort of close relationship with someone without them eventually learning the truth about my time with Dean. Whatever his reasons for keeping his distance, it's probably better this way. Even if he doesn't shut me out completely when he finds out the truth, he'd never consider me as anything other than a friend to be wary of. I may not know a lot about love or life, but I know that a person can only handle so much rejection, and I've met my quota.

The memory of Chris's hard cock pressed against me rekindles that fire, which roars to life and melts that newfound resolve. I know what I felt, and I know what I saw. There's no point in bullshitting myself. Maybe I've only ever been with one guy, but I'm not stupid. He wanted me.

And I wanted him.

I *still* want him. So much that my center throbs. The last man to put his hands on me hurt me, but maybe this one can heal me. Or help me heal myself.

Maybe it's a chance I have to take, like trusting him and his friends today.

I toss and turn, willing away the incessant pulsing I don't want to act on. I don't want to think of him that way yet. How am I supposed to look him in the eye after imagining all the things I want him to do to me? But my mind conjures such things anyway, what those calloused hands would feel like on my skin, and the beard he's wearing now that the days are cooler. His lips, teeth, and tongue.

Frustrated, I roll over and open the drawer on my new nightstand. I grab my vibrator, wiggle out of my panties, and let my imagination take over. His arms around me, holding his body suspended over mine while our hips work together. His heat inside me as he plunges in and out, pushing us both closer and closer to—I come so hard I cry out. The throbbing doesn't stop, though. I still want more, but not from BOB, my battery-operated boyfriend.

I want him. But I want more than just a bit of fun. I want everything. I want to know what it's like to hold his hand and be able to hug him on a whim. Kiss him. To someday tuck Keaton into bed at night with him, and wake up to both of them in the morning. But how do I convince him that whatever made him pull back today isn't an issue?

And how do I tell him about my past without losing him?

Chapter 16
Chris

Heidi moans beneath me and thrusts her hips faster, urging me to keep up. I gladly comply, sliding myself in and out of her wet heat, earning another moan. *I can't believe I got her in bed.*

Wait. How did we get here?

She moans again and grabs my ass, pulling me closer. "Harder," she pants. My questions slip away. They're not important right now. I'm going to give this woman the best—

"Daddy!"

I lunge upright and pull the covers over . . . an empty bed.

A dream. It was just a dream. Bitter disappointment washes through me. I'd rather it be real, even if we were interrupted, because at least it happened then. *Aren't I too old for wet dreams?* Better question, why couldn't he let me finish that one? I'd feel so much better. But this is our new Sunday ritual. He wakes up and runs in here to check if Heidi is on her back porch. The dream is a new addition, though.

"Daddy?" Keaton says again, his face pressed to the windowpane. "Miss Heidi is up! She's in her backyard already!"

I swear he's trying to beat her out of bed.

"Are you okay, Daddy?" he asks without looking away. "You were making funny noises."

I scrub my face with both hands and try to come to terms with reality. "Yeah, buddy. I'm fine. It was just a dream." *Damn it.* It was a good dream.

He finally peels his attention away from the woman next door to look at me. "Can we start breakfast now?"

"Yeah, buddy. Let me shower, and we'll head downstairs, then you can go invite her over." I don't *need* a shower yet, but I need some alone time after that dream, and a shower is the only way I'm going to get it. And only if I let him play a game on my phone. "You can even play that game you like while I clean up."

Keaton's eyes light up more and more with every word. "This is the bestest Sunday ever!"

"Best," I correct out of habit.

He climbs into my bed while I unlock my phone for him. The colorful steam engines on the screen command every iota of his attention. Even so, I have to hurry. His attention span is unpredictable when it comes to Heidi. *I can say the same about my dick . . .*

I close the door behind me and wedge a towel in front of it. Keaton can still get in if he needs me, but it'll slow him down, and I'll have a warning. While the shower heats up, I let my mind wander back to that dream. Her moans. The way she pulled me in closer. Begged me for more. Real-life Heidi probably prefers careful and gentle and sweet, not that I'll ever know. But fantasy-Heidi . . . she's okay with playing a little rough, which is good for me.

My dick is already weeping pre-cum when I step into the shower and brace against the wall. My imagination isn't nearly as vivid as that dream, but I picture flipping her onto her stomach to take her from behind. Wrapping that ponytail around my hand to remind her that I'm in control and she's going to love every second of it. The way she'll tighten around me, and the fluttering pulses of her orgasm as mine overtakes me, sending ropes of cum spurting all over the shower wall. My body sags with the relief of sweet release, but it's short lived.

I shouldn't have done that. The intensity of my desire for her is rivaled by the guilt burning in my heart for giving in. She doesn't want me thirsting after her. She probably hates men after everything she's been through. And here's me, being some sort of pervert . . .

But there was a moment yesterday morning when I could swear she was thinking about kissing me. The memory eases my guilt. What if she was? The idea of her thinking about me the way I just imagined her ignites a firestorm of desire, redirecting my blood flow to my dick again. Maybe I have time—

"Daddy?" Keaton asks from the door. "What's taking so long?"

Fuck. His timing today is horrible. I should thank him, though. It doesn't matter what I want; or what Heidi may or may not want. I have to put Keaton first.

I look over my shoulder, keeping my back to him because the last thing I want right now are questions about why my penis is big, or, God forbid, for him to mention it to Heidi later. "I'll be right out, bud. Why don't you go get dressed?"

"Okay!" He turns and runs off.

Sighing, I grab my shampoo. He already cares too much about Heidi for me to risk ruining our friendship. And I can't date another woman who views Keaton as an obstacle.

The look on Heidi's face yesterday when she took the leaf flashes through my mind. The memory of her excitement when she found her leaf on the table under that rock follows it. And the way she clutched them both to her chest.

That wasn't her humoring him—not that I can fault anyone for that. Even I do it sometimes. But those reactions were genuine.

Maybe . . .

As unlikely as it is, what if she *is* interested and she *doesn't* view my son as a problem? Maybe she's my unicorn. If so, I'm depriving myself and my son of something special by refusing to explore the possibility.

Heidi

"Miss Heidi!" The sliding glass door was a split-second warning before Keaton came flying across the yard, yelling for me. "It's time for breakfast!"

Chris waves from the warmth of his kitchen, but I ask anyway. It's the first time Keaton has come out without him since the day he let himself out. "Does your daddy know you're out here?"

I fight a smile. It's funny how fast things have changed. I can't think of anything better than breakfast with these two handsome guys. It's my favorite part of the week.

A smile brightens Keaton's already excited eyes. "Yeah." He grabs my hand and pulls. "Let's go!"

"Alright, alright. I'm coming." After last night, the word 'coming' makes me blush. But it's chilly enough out this morning I can blame it on that if Chris mentions it. Standing, I put my mug down next to my chair and fold the blanket I brought out to drape it over the chair. "By the way, thank you for the pretty rock. I forgot to tell you that last night."

"Did you like it?" he asks without pausing or looking back.

You have no idea. I don't know why, but that leaf and rock are the sweetest gifts I've ever gotten. "I *love* it. I put it on a shelf in my front room so I can look at it every day. And I'm pressing the heart leaf you gave me."

"What's pressing?" he asks.

"It's a thing people do to make flowers and leaves stay pretty longer." I have vague memories of my grandmother, or maybe my mother, pressing flowers in the summer. I thought it was some sort of magic back then, and now I get to do it.

"Cool." We reach his back door, and he struggles to open it. "I got it," he insists when I reach to help. "Uncle Mason says we always open doors for ladies."

He is so sweet! This little boy is going to steal my heart one pretty rock and opened door at a time.

"For anyone behind us," Chris corrects through the inch-wide gap Keaton has managed. Grinning, he winks at me through the glass. "But pretty ladies especially."

That wink makes my whole face hot. *I don't think I'm going to be able to blame the cold now.* The heat from my cheeks seeps into my bloodstream, spreading further with each beat of my heart until my whole body is burning for him. Again. Was that—Is he . . . Did he just flirt, or was that wishful thinking?

His eyes scan my face, which is probably stoplight red, and the corners of his mouth curve up into a cocky little smile that more or less confirms it. He was flirting. And he's pleased with my reaction. *Maybe convincing him to take a chance on me will be easier than I thought?*

"Yeah, that," Keaton agrees, huffing and puffing while he works on the door. Chris reaches out and grabs the top, helping Keaton out without letting him know. Once it's open, Keaton looks up at me with the sweetest smile. "After you!"

"Thank you!" I step inside, breathing in the wonderful aroma of sausage, onions, and peppers, and move out of the way so Chris can help Keaton with the door again.

"You're welcome!" Keaton says.

I turn in time to catch Chris smiling down at Keaton, glowing with pride. He glances at me, and that pride gives way to something intense that makes my heart flutter like a bird trapped in a cage.

"Breakfast!" Keaton cries.

"Breakfast," Chris agrees, his eyes on me still.

"Thank you for inviting me." I cringe inwardly, kicking myself because the breathy way those words came out sounds more like a starstruck teenager than a grown woman. The exact opposite of what I need to do if I'm going to convince him I'm not just a kid.

That cocky smile makes a comeback, and my heart loops the loop. I'm snared in some sort of trap, scarcely able to breathe.

So much has changed in the last month, but I give Keaton credit for this one. He eroded my defenses a little at a time. I didn't even notice it happening until it was too late. Yesterday, when my car wouldn't start, he burst right through what was left with a hug, and once he was inside, he blew the walls to pieces with a leaf, letting the others find their way in as well.

Keaton tugs at the leg of Chris's jeans. "Daddy, I'm hungry," he says, shattering the tension between his father and me.

Chris reaches to mess up his red curls. "You're *always* hungry."

"I'm growing!"

"I know! Stop it!"

"But I can't!"

"You can if I put a brick on your head."

"No!" Keaton scoffs, devolving into a giggle fit that knocks him off balance. Chris and I lunge to catch him at the same time.

I'm too far away to get to him in time, but Chris isn't. "Careful, buddy," he murmurs, but his eyes are on me, and that intense look is back.

My mouth goes dry. *What if I—*

"I'm okay," Keaton says, breaking the building tension once more.

I clear my throat. "You're a little wrecking ball; that's what you are!" It's not the first time I've thought of him that way, but it's the first time I've realized how apt the description is.

"You've got that right," Chris mutters. He catches my eye and grins, then mouths, 'watch this.' "Alright, breakfast. Who wants mudpies?"

"Daddy!" Keaton giggles. "We already cooked burritos!"

"Roadkill?"

"Daddy, no!"

"Dog food?"

Keaton is laughing so hard he can't talk, but he grabs Chris's leg to keep himself from falling over again. That laugh is infectious, and I end up giggling with him at the outrageous suggestions Chris lists off rapid-fire.

"Sardines? Kitty litter? Knuckle sandwiches?"

Keaton finally slides down Chris's leg and falls on his butt, laughing so hard tears stream down his face. Grinning still, Chris says, "Gets him every time."

It's not the words, but the hollow ache in my chest they evoke, that sobers me. *I want to be here every time. I don't want to miss a minute of this.*

What is this feeling?

Keaton's laughter subsides, and he climbs to his feet again. "Burritos!"

Chris slaps his forehead. "Burritos! Oh, man. Why didn't I think of that? Good call, buddy."

Keaton grabs my hand and pulls me toward the table and what has unofficially become my seat. "It's all cooked. We just have to build them."

Chris is right there to help me with my chair again like he did last night. "That'll get easier when you get taller, buddy," he tells his son, who is scowling at him for helping.

He scowls harder when Chris tells him he can't help carry the food or the drinks. "Why don't you sit down and keep Heidi company while I get the food? Tell her about your Halloween costume."

The little boy perks up at that and climbs into the booster seat in the chair on my right. "I'm gonna be Ryder!"

"What?" I ask. That was apparently the wrong question to ask because it earns me a scowl, too.

"Dude on *Paw Patrol*," Chris explains. He puts a package of tortillas and cheese on the table. "It was a close call between Ryder and Gekko from *PJ Masks*, but I guess he still has a soft spot for *Paw Patrol*." Sour cream and salsa join the growing pile of ingredients.

"I see," I say, but I really don't. It's all gibberish to me. "Are you excited?" I ask Keaton, hoping to shift the topic to one I can keep up with.

"Yes! We're going to trick-or-treat with Ronni and Mallie and Lottie and Marnie!"

"Who?" Ronni I know, but the other three are a mystery. None of the others have mentioned children, aside from the one Tara's carrying, of course.

"Mason's nieces, Mallory, Charlotte, and Marnie," Chris says, placing a pan of steaming sausage, peppers, and onions on a trivet in the middle of the table. "Don't touch, Keat. That's hot."

"You should come with us, Miss Heidi!" Keaton cries, bouncing in his little booster seat thing, making it squeak and squeal.

My first instinct is to say no, but that's not me talking. *I* want to go; it's the fear telling me not to. This is another thing I don't want to miss. But unless Chris consents . . .

He comes back to the table with plates and utensils. "Help yourself," he says, passing me a plate. "And you should come along. It's always fun. The Chambers family makes a big thing of it. There's a hayrack ride—I have no idea where they get the hay. Len dresses up like Lerch from Addams Family and hauls everyone around. It always ends with a bonfire, s'mores, and hot drinks out at Grandma and Grandpa Chambers' place."

"Are you sure?" I want to go so badly, but I don't want to make things weird. I don't have a kid to take, after all. And I don't want him to feel like he has to say yes to be polite.

He pauses in the act of spooning sausage and veggies onto the burrito he's making for Keaton to look at me. "Absolutely. We'd love to have you."

"Yeah!" Keaton says around a mouthful of his burrito.

"Don't talk with your mouth full, Keat," Chris scolds.

"Alright, that sounds like a lot of fun." I can't remember the last time I went trick-or-treating. It was before Curt, or maybe the year Mom married him. But after that, Thomas and I weren't allowed to go begging for stuff to rot our teeth out because he wouldn't pay to fix them. It'll be like reclaiming a bit of my childhood.

Chapter 17
Heidi

I can't stand another second of sitting inside, staring out the window, waiting for Tara, so I grab my keys and my bag and head outside. At least the scenery is different. And I have more room to pace.

There's no chance of seeing Chris or Keaton, though. They've left for the afternoon. Chris had to work, and Keaton was going to spend the rest of the day with his grandmother. I've given up trying to figure out Chris's schedule. We normally leave around the same time in the morning on workdays, but he gets home much later somedays. Others, he doesn't. And weekends are unpredictable. It's all chaotic. I asked him one Sunday over breakfast, and he said he's working on it.

A silver car turns my way, and I freeze, my heart pounding in my ears. This is it. This is . . . not Tara. The car passes without even slowing down. I sit down on my front step and prop my elbows on my knees, resting my chin in my palm. I'm going to wear myself out waiting at this rate.

Another car turns. A bright green Dodge Charger that would sell for a pretty penny to the right people. *Stop thinking like that. You're not a criminal anymore.* I watch the car, expecting it to speed past, but it slows, and the turn signal flashes to life. I blink a few times, certain I'm seeing things when it turns into my drive. But the head of blond curls behind the wheel is easily identifiable.

I cross my yard in a daze and open the passenger door to slide inside.

"Hey there!" Tara greets me. "Sorry, Gabe took my SUV to Ryan to get new brakes and who knows what else. Nesting is my job, but I swear he's trying to take over. He's suddenly concerned my vehicle isn't safe enough for the baby. I'm like, it's been driving us around for eight months now!"

The funny thing is, I can see it. He fussed over her and the baby so much last night there's no doubt in my mind what she's saying is probably a watered-down version of the truth. While she drives, she recounts all the silly things he's done, from the sympathy cravings to over babyproofing their house. "We have tamper-proof outlets, but he bought outlet covers!" she rants as she unlocks the door to a suite at a busy open-air mall.

I don't know the first thing about babies or being pregnant, but that's kind of cute to me. "At least you know he cares."

Her face softens, and a smile drifts across her lips. "Yeah. He really does." She gives herself a little shake and opens the door. "Anyway, enough about baby drama. Welcome to The Boutique! It used to have a real name, but no one ever used it, so we jokingly changed it to The Boutique when we moved here a few months ago. We used to be closed on Sundays, but we're trying something new. One of the salesgirls will be in any minute now to run the floor, but you and I will be in the back today."

She works her way through the racks and displays on the sales floor. Everywhere I turn, there is something beautiful to look at, but the mannequins in the windows on either side of the door keep pulling me back. They are dressed for Halloween, but not in the cheaply made costumes prominently featured at Superstores and pop-up holiday shops. These are handmade works of art.

Since I was *just* invited to a Halloween party of sorts this morning, it almost feels like a sign. Maybe I need a costume. Not one of these, of course. Not on my budget. But something.

A fairy costume catches my eye first—dainty wings and a floaty skirt sprinkled with flowers. There's an angel too, but it's not just a big white sack with wings. It's like something out of a movie where angels go to war, complete with a sword. A bodysuit that looks like mummy wrappings. And—

"Are you Halloween crazy, too?" Tara asks from a door at the back of the room, interrupting my inspection. "Madi is. She plans costumes all year long."

Crap. I'm here to work, not to gawk, but she doesn't seem upset that I fell behind. I hustle to catch up with her. "Sorry, no. Just got to thinking. Keaton invited me to go trick-or-treating with him, and I don't know if he's expecting me to dress up."

She looks back at me, her eyes glowing so bright they rival the sun. "Oh, definitely. They go with the Chambers crew, and that family doesn't half-ass anything. *Everyone* will be in costume. Want to try one on?"

I suck in a breath. "Oh, n-no, thank you. They're beautiful but—"

"You can rent one," she says, cutting off my objections. "And we can consider it today's pay."

I try to fight it, but my eyes are pulled back to the displays. I shouldn't do it, especially now that I have a car to pay for. I can go buy a cheap costume and not be out an entire afternoon's pay. But . . . Maybe just this once I can splurge for no reason other than I want to.

As if sensing my moment of weakness, Tara smiles. "Wait right there." She disappears into a backroom but keeps talking, raising her voice to make herself heard. "We have just the one in the back. Someone commissioned it but backed out. Madi will be *thrilled* to have someone wear it. She's so proud of it. And she should be. It's gorgeous."

The bells over the front door tinkle, announcing a new arrival. I turn to find two women—one with purple hair and the other blond—watching me. The blond narrows her eyes, causing me to freeze like a kid caught with their hand caught in a cookie jar. "You must be Heidi," she says.

I swallow hard, not trusting myself to speak without squeaking under that scrutiny. "I am."

The crinkles at the corners of her eyes shift from suspicion to a smile that matches the one on her lips. "I'm Madi." She jerks a thumb toward her companion. "This is Teagan. Tara told me she was bringing you in, but she said you'd be in the back."

"I'm here," Tara says, puffing and panting. "Sorry, belly got in the way, and this thing is heavier than it looks," she says, giving the garment bag in her hand a little shake."

Madi narrows her eyes again. Now that she's not glaring at me, I note they're tinged pink like she's been crying. It's none of my business, though, so I keep my mouth shut about it. "What are you doing with Reni?"

"Heidi is going to try her on," she replies. I must look confused because she grins and explains, "Madi names her dresses. This one is Reni, short for Renaissance since it's based on a ballgown from the period."

"Oh," Madi breathes, rushing forward to take the dress from Tara. She grabs me by the arm and hauls me along in her wake. "You're a genius, T. Reni will look *fantastic* on her."

I hold my breath and wait for the panic, but it doesn't come. Madi pulls me into a dressing room and slams the door behind us, then freezes. Our eyes meet in the mirror, and she bursts out laughing. "I'm sorry. We just met and—" she's laughing too hard to continue.

So I'm not the only one who noticed this is awkward . . .

"This dress," she finally manages, "is a two-person job. I probably should've led with that, but I got a little excited."

"A little?" Tara yells through the door.

"Hey!" Madi shouts. "I worked my butt off on this dress, and poor Reni was just discarded because that hoity-toity ol' bag changed her mind!"

"Heidi, are you alright?" Tara asks, ignoring Madi's rant.

"Yeah, I'm good." There's nothing threatening about Madi now that she's not squinting at me like I'm a fly to be swatted.

Madi holds up a flat hand as if swearing an oath. "I promise, I'm not checking you out. I do this all day. So I'm just gonna turn around while you get undressed, then I'll help you into it."

I have questions, but I do as she says and pull my shirt over my head. "Um . . . If it takes two people to get into it, how am I supposed to . . ."

Madi's reflection in the mirror waves a hand dismissively. "Once you know how it goes on, you can get into it again. You'll need someone to tie the laces, though. The lady who commissioned it didn't want a zipper."

"I'll come help," Tara says. "Or you can get ready with Fern. She's going to need help too, and not the kind Mason is going to want to give her."

"The only help she's gonna need is keeping him off her," Madi mutters to me. "She's going as Black Widow."

It's not hard to imagine Fern in a black leather jumpsuit. I almost feel bad for Mason. *Maybe I should find something Chris can't keep his eyes off . . .* That fairy costume was kind of revealing. It won't keep me very warm, though.

"Alright, I'm ready," I tell Madi.

She unzips the garment bag and starts pulling out pieces. "Alright, here's how this baby works . . ."

It takes ten minutes to get me into the dress, but most of it is her teaching me what goes where. It's not completely true to period, but the woman who commissioned it wanted it as close as possible. With the amount of time and money that went into this dress, I should be paying by the minute to wear it.

Tears collect in Madi's lower lashes, and she fans her face with both hands. "I'm gonna bawl."

I'm not sure if that's good or bad. She's kept herself between me and the mirror, so I haven't seen myself yet. I don't need the mirror to know a lot of my assets are on display, which isn't necessarily a bad thing. But if she's that worked up about it, maybe I should go with something else. "Are you sure it's okay if I—"

"Yes!" she and Tara say at the same time.

Madi squints at me again. "If you don't wear it, I'll . . . I don't know, but you won't like it!"

"But what if I—"

"You won't!" they say, speaking in sync again.

"Are you two twins?" I ask. I swear, they're reading each other's minds. It's kind of creepy. I went to school with twin sisters who finished each other's sentences and talked in sync like these two. I always thought they practiced it, but now . . .

"Nope, but we spend a lot of time together," Madi tells me, fussing with the skirt. "Seriously, the deposit on this dress covered the materials. I'm not out any money, only time. And you can't do anything to this dress I can't fix."

"Don't jinx yourself!" Tara cries.

Madi looks up and rolls her eyes. "Okay, so there might be some things, but as long as you don't come to bodily harm, we should be okay. Are you ready to see it?"

"Yes, please." I'm *beyond* ready to see it, even if I'm nervous about wearing it. I feel like a movie star in this costume, like I'm about to walk out on set and say my lines.

She grabs me by the shoulders and turns me around. "Let's go to the big mirror."

I reach for the handle on the door, but it opens before I grasp it. Tara and Teagan are just outside, pressed close together so they can both see into the little dressing room.

"Holy shit," Teagan says, then slaps a hand over her mouth. "Sorry," she says, though it's muffled.

Tara shakes her head. "Nope. You're right. That's about the best way to put it." She pats Teagan on the shoulder but continues speaking to me. "Chris is gonna lose his shit when he sees you in that."

"*What?*" I ask, but Madi asks the same thing at the same time, distracting me for a moment. *Maybe it's just a Madi thing?*

"I don't know what you're—"

Tara rolls her eyes and cuts off my denial. "Oh, please. What is it with all y'all? First Tris and Ryan, now you and Chris. Do you think we're all blind? Or stupid?"

"I'm . . . sorry?" I try, unsure of what she's talking about or how to respond.

She looks at me again, and her jaw goes slack, parting her lips. "You really have no idea, do you?"

It's clear she expects me to answer, but I don't want another scolding. *I'll probably get one either way.* "No?"

Her eyes flutter closed. She takes a deep breath and cants her head toward the ceiling before she opens her eyes again. "Honey, that man about turned himself inside out last night trying to keep his hands off you. And *you*. *You* just look at him like he hung the moon and every star in the sky. *I* thought you two were fooling around and trying to keep it a secret, at least from Keaton."

Cheeks burning, I shake my head. *Was I really that obvious?* If I was, does *he* know?

Tara searches my face for something, and a small smile turns up the corners of her mouth. "But you want to be?"

She's got me dead to rights. There's no point in lying now, so I nod. It's probably ridiculous, but I do.

"And Keaton?" she asks. Before I can say a word, she's smiling again, so my face must say it all. "I kinda thought so. Have you two at least *talked* about it?"

I shake my head. We haven't really been alone together since the day Keaton snuck out, and it doesn't seem like the sort of thing we should talk about in front of him. But, even if we did have a chance, what would I say? *Look, I know you probably think I'm just a kid, but I'd really like to jump your bones. I'm as shocked as you are.*

I never thought I'd go for a dad, but here we are . . . But it's so much more than that. *That part seems sane compared to the rest.*

She looks over my shoulder at Madi and shakes her head. "I already know everything he's going to say . . . But he's wrong. The logistics are for the two of you to figure out, but I reckon it doesn't hurt to help you help him pull his head out of his ass, and this costume will do it. Come on, girls. Let's catch a man."

She makes that sound so easy. Those logistics she's talking about are terrifying because that means telling him about my past. The excitement inspired by this costume and Tara's insistence that this thing I have for Chris isn't one-sided is no match for that dose of reality.

One step at a time, Heidi girl. If this doesn't work, I never have to tell him. But if it does, he has to know. There's no other way. If I don't tell him, everything will be a lie, and it will be that much worse when he somehow *does* find out.

Tara holds up a finger. "First off, don't you *dare* tell him about your costume. Let it be a surprise. Otherwise, it might lose the wow factor."

I can keep secrets. That's not a problem, at least I don't think it is. I've never had a secret I was excited to share. I don't understand why it matters, but I'll try anything.

She leads me to a three-way mirror and helps me up onto a little stage in front of it. I don't even recognize myself. The deep blue, ivory, and bronze material make my eyes the color of a stormy sea, and my skin glows. I've always felt kind of plain, but the woman in the mirror is gorgeous. But . . . "What am I supposed to be?"

Grinning, Tara gathers my hair and twists it back in a clip. Teagan hands her something, and in the mirror, I watch her place a tiara on my head. "A queen."

Chapter 18
Chris

It's hard to focus on the schedule I'm supposed to be making when my eyes keep drifting to the clock on my desktop. Heidi has been by every Monday for class since the first one, when she had her breakdown, and she should be here any minute. She doesn't always stop by my office, but I make an excuse to go talk to her when she doesn't. I don't know what kind of day today will be, but after yesterday, I need to see her without Keaton around to interrupt. There's a question I never found the right moment to ask.

But I also need to get this done.

Ryan practically lived here before he and Trista got together. Now, he wants a little more free time—not that I blame him. Figuring out how to juggle it all is the problem. *We need a manager. Someone we trust to handle shit when neither of us can be here.*

A tap on my door moves the problem in front of me to the back of my mind. It's not going anywhere, and it's not going to change anything this week. "It's open," I call, mentally crossing my fingers and toes that a certain blue-eyed blonde is waiting on the other side.

The door opens, and Heidi breezes in, already talking. "Okay, so you were right. Len is awesome."

I ignore the green monster in my chest and smile at that. And at the change in her since the day we met. Instead of creeping in and hesitating to close the door, she walks in like she has every right to be here and shuts the door behind her without a second thought. As cliché as it may be, her newfound confidence is breathtaking.

It's amusing that Len doesn't terrify her. He may well be the most dangerous person Heidi has ever met, but he hides it well under a veneer of patience and gentleness. I don't know what he did before Mason hired him, but Fern told me once that he has connections that scare gang members. And Heidi will never know.

"Good. I'm glad you're comfortable with him." I sit back in my chair, content to let her chatter until she's said everything she needs to say. There will be time to pose my question after.

"Darren is pretty cool too," she continues, pulling the chair across from me closer to my desk and sitting down. That one doesn't surprise me either. Mason's assistant is unflappably calm. *And married.* "But I'm pretty sure Mason is a few cards short of a full deck because he thinks I'll have the car paid off in less than five years."

I don't doubt him. I haven't seen the numbers to run them myself, but Mason is good with them, too. If he thinks she can do it, she can do it. "I'm sure he's right. He's not going to do anything to hurt you, the company, or himself, I assure you."

She slumps forward and rests her head on the edge of my desk. My hand twitches, longing to reach for her and brush back her hair, offer her some sort of comfort, but I can't. "I just . . . I want to be able to say I paid for it."

Since I can't touch her, maybe I can comfort her with words. It doesn't soothe my urge for contact, but all that matters is that she feels better. "And you will. Or, at the very least, you will work to earn it. They're not giving you a handout, hon. They're giving you a leg up. Do you plan on quitting once the car is paid off?"

Fuck I hope not. The future isn't something either of us has discussed. I mean, mine is pretty well mapped out at this point, but hers isn't. She has so many possibilities ahead of her . . .

She sits up to look at me, her lips pursed. "No, I like my job. And they're great to work for."

I swallow a sigh of relief. She'll understand someday. A loyal employee is priceless. "Exactly. How did things go with Tara?"

A smile teases her lips, but it's there and gone in a blink. "Good, I think . . ."

"You think?" I ask, as curious about that smile as I am about why she only thinks it was good. *Is she hiding something?*

She looks behind me, checking the time on the clock I keep saying I'm going to move because I always feel like someone is standing behind me when people do that, and pushes her chair back. "Well," she begins, rising. It must be time for her to change, "I didn't break anything. And I didn't mess anything up. But it was all just kind of . . . easy."

I wish I could stop time just to have a little more with her right now. "Well, did you expect them to start you off with something too hard to manage?" I ask, hoping to get her off on a tangent so she'll stay longer. I don't want to blurt out an invitation to dinner. I hoped we'd kind of segue into it somehow. I'd bring up yesterday and go from there.

She shrugs. "I really don't know what I expected. I liked it, though. And I liked Madi and Teagan. But it's time for class. See ya!"

"Alright. See ya." She walks out, leaving me to stew in my disappointment at the missed opportunity. She never leaves that fast. She must be running behind today. Once the door is closed behind her, I turn to glare at the clock. *What the . . . ?* She's still got twenty minutes. Did I say something to upset her? She didn't act like it. That little smile that almost wasn't pops into my head. Did she not want to talk about her new job? Or was I right, and she's hiding something?

Damn it! I should've just come right out and asked her.

Chapter 19
Chris

Me: Don't forget 4:30 tonight. Did you get the address?

I know she did. I sent it to her twice, but Heidi has been strange since her brief visit to my office Monday. Every time I see her, she's in a hurry. Like she can't wait to get away from me. *God, I hope she doesn't bail on us tonight.* Keaton will be crushed. He's told everything with a pulse that "his" Miss Heidi is trick-or-treating with him this year, even the other neighbor's dog.

I don't know what the hell I've done to make her avoid me, but I'll never forgive either of us if she doesn't at least make an appearance tonight—her for not talking to me about it and myself for whatever the fuck I did.

My phone screen lights up.

Heidi: Yep. I'm riding with Fern and Mason. See you there!

Oh, thank fuck. I let out a sigh and drop my phone on my bed. I wish I had texted her sooner instead of agonizing about it all day, but I was afraid of her answer. I was scared of having to break the news to Keaton.

"Daddy?" he yells from the direction of his bedroom. "Can I put my costume on yet?"

"Not yet, buddy." I leave my room and head for his to make sure he's not already in it. He's tried to live in the damn thing since I brought it home.

"How much longer?" he asks, his impatience bringing out a whine.

"Two hours," I say, leaning against his doorframe. Happily, his costume is still on the hanger where it belongs. That hanger is now on his bed instead of in his closet, though. *How am I going to distract him for two hours?* "Hey, let's take a nap, so we're not too tired to party later!"

That's one way to distract him. And *damn*, I need a nap. I haven't slept well all week, alternately agonizing over whatever I did to upset Heidi and staring at my phone, wondering if asking her out via text is some sort of faux pas since it would be our first date. *When did I get so bad at dating?* It hasn't been *that* long! I met Becca a year ago!

A long silence follows my suggestion. Keaton *hates* naps. I haven't got him to take one regularly in two years. But occasionally, if I give a good enough reason, he'll try. But he has to decide it's acceptable. "Alright," he finally says. "But only because I want to eat a hundred million s'mores tonight."

"A hundred million, huh?" I ask, chuckling to myself. "That's a lot of s'mores. You better save some for everyone else. My bed or the couch?"

"Your bed!"

I try not to let my relief show. He kicks way too much for the couch, but it's his preferred spot if he's going to nap. "Lead the way."

Keaton is out almost as soon as his head hits the pillow. *For someone who hates to sleep, he's sure good at it.* I stare at the ceiling, ignoring my phone and the burning desire to text Heidi again.

***

"Where's Miss Heidi?" Keaton demands as soon as I shut the car off.

I scan the row of cars lining the parking area in front of the Chambers's mansion and spot Fern's Camaro. "She's here somewhere, bud. She said she was riding with Fern."

"Is Fern here?" He strains to sit up taller and looks out the window, but all he can see is the truck next to us.

"I see her car. That's all I can say until we get inside."

I climb out and open his door to unfasten the harness holding his wiggly little body in place. The second his feet hit the ground, he's off and running, as at home here as I am. I grab his candy bucket and follow, in no hurry now that he's here. Heidi will probably avoid him if I'm around him anyway. I have no idea what I'm going to do about it, but I need to fix it before Sunday breakfast.

The front door opens, and Grandma Lola appears dressed in a baggy blue jumpsuit with a red bandana tied around her white hair. "Hello, m'boy!" she greets Keaton. "Come give Grandma Lola a hug! You've grown so much!"

He gives her a quick hug and hurries on by. "Well," she says, standing to give me room to pass. "What's got his tail in a knot?"

I shake my head and accept my hug. "He's anxious to see Heidi. I don't know why, but he's very attached to her."

"I think a lot of young men are going to be very attached to her tonight," Lola says, mischief lighting her eyes. "And where is *your* costume?"

"Ryan brought it," I tell her, shrugging. I don't really care about dressing up, but Keaton insisted this year. He even picked.

"I'll wager you know where to find it then," she says, pulling me into a hug.

Indeed, I do—in the corner suite that is unofficially Mason's. He never lived here, but they always kept a room ready for all three of their grandchildren. And it was a pretty sweet spot to hang out when we were younger. It still is, actually.

"Head on up," she tells me, waving toward the stairs. "Everyone else is already in the backyard. The kids are harassing Mason to light the fire. They want hotdogs before you all leave."

"Before?" I ask, surprised. That's a bit of a break from tradition. It's not a bad thing, though. They're usually so full of candy by the time we get back that we can't get them to eat anything.

Lola nods. "Nicole declared there will be no candy consumed prior to dinner."

I cringe. "Oof. And she used the mom voice, didn't she?" I can't recall a time that Nicole *didn't* use the mom voice. Those kids are in for it because the five of us gave her a lot of practice when we were all kids.

"Of course!" Lola laughs. The doorbell rings, so she waves me toward the stairs again. "I'll see you outside, Christopher."

***

Sighing, I grab the red, white, and blue plastic shield and give myself another once-over. *I didn't think this through.* When Keaton said I should be Captain America because I'm the strongest man in the world, I thought it was a cool idea. Now that I'm in the costume . . . not so much. But it's only for a few hours. When we get back from trick-or-treating, I can change again.

And the sooner I get downstairs, the sooner we can leave.

The house is deserted, but that's a good thing. I don't want to get caught up in idle chatter right now. *I want to see Heidi.* No, I don't. I *think* I want to see Heidi. When she makes an excuse to get away from me, I'll regret that I wanted to see her *and* doing or saying whatever it was that has her treating me like I'm 'it' in a game of tag.

Just get it over with.

There's a bite in the late afternoon air that has me grateful for the warmth of my costume if nothing else about it. I manage to slip outside without being noticed, or at least called out, and scan the crowd, looking for those blue eyes that make my stomach think it's a trapeze artist or dirty blond hair that begs me to wrap it around my fist.

It would help if I knew what her costume was. Keaton begged until I texted her to ask, but she said it was a surprise.

I don't recognize Austin at first. The shoulder-length blond wig he's wearing throws me off since I'm accustomed to seeing him with short, dark hair. The huge hammer he's brandishing makes the wig make sense, though. He's Thor, from the first movie if I remember the outfit right. Jam is next to him. It takes me a moment to puzzle out who she's supposed to be, but when I do, I laugh. She makes a great Shuri.

Picking out familiar faces becomes easier after those two. I finally understand why Mason hasn't shaved his face in a while—so he can pull of Tony Stark's goatee without makeup. He's not great about keeping his hands off his wife on a normal day, but it's hard to blame him tonight with Fern in a black jumpsuit à la Black Widow.

The silver sleeve of Ryan's Winter Soldier costume glints in the sunlight. I'm not even going to analyze how fitting that costume choice is. Trista is *stunning* in a tight red dress and a black and white wig to give her Cruella's signature look.

Tara is also rocking red, but her dress is a replica of Buttercup's from *The Princess Bride*—her favorite movie. Gabe broke the Marvel streak the guys continued by dressing up as Westley to match her. I know who he's supposed to be, but I just *have* to give him a hard time and ask him if he's supposed to be Zorro.

Even Colton and Noel came dressed as Khal Drogo and Daenerys Targaryen, though she has the hair to pull it off, and he doesn't. *I'm* not about to call him on that, though. I like my nose the way it is. She must have convinced him to pretend Gabe doesn't exist for an evening. It would be nice if he'd let go of his grudge, but as long as he's clung to it I doubt it's over yet.

But where is . . . ? A woman in a blue dress with a whole lot of skirt turns to talk to Tara, revealing a profile I could sketch in my sleep. *Oh, fuck me.* She was right there with her back to me all along, tucked between Fern and Tara. And she is . . . I'm sure there's a fitting word, but my brain refuses to supply one other than *wow.*

I should do something, but my feet don't want to move. If I stay right here, I can look at Heidi without her knowing, without her leaving to avoid me for whatever reason. I can memorize every detail. All that silky hair is curled and arranged in an updo that only leaves a few loose tendrils on each side to frame her face. A tiara sparkles and shines from where it's perched in the nest of curls. Her eyes glow brighter than the jewels in her earrings and the ones dangling from a wide ribbon tied around her throat.

And her smile . . . I want that smile. It's rare and more precious than diamonds and rubies—worth more to me than all the money in the world. As precious to me as my son.

I'm in motion before I realize my brain sent a command to my feet for them to move. Last weekend in my kitchen, I could've sworn we had a moment, as corny as that sounds. More than one, actually. But this week, she vanishes faster than any magician's assistant every time I see her. And we're not leaving here tonight until I know why.

I can't handle the hot and cold treatment. I'm good either way, but I need consistency.

"Look who finally decided to join us!" Austin shouts, spotting me over Heidi's shoulder as I approach. "We thought you bailed on us, Cap!"

For some reason, Tara growls and steps forward to punch him in the arm.

"Ow!" he cries, clutching at his bicep. He glares at Colton. "Did you teach her that?"

Colton smirks at him and holds out a fist to his sister, who obliges him with a fist bump. "You bet your ass I did."

Tara moves closer to Gabe, making room for me next to Heidi. Watching Heidi from the corner of my eye to see how she reacts, I step forward, mentally crossing my fingers that she doesn't cut and run. I'd love nothing more than to look at her again, to ask her what the hell is going on, but that moment has passed. I'll have to wait. Again.

"I didn't know this was a Marvel party," I say before Austin's mouth can dig him into a hole. I love the guy, but sometimes he doesn't have the sense God gave a goose.

Austin scoffs and brandishes his hammer again. "This is a princess party." He points the replica Mjölnir at Jamaica. "She's a princess." The hammer swings to Tara. "Princess." On to Heidi. "Princess."

"I am a *queen*, thank you very much," she corrects him. *Yes, you fucking are!*

"Yeah!" Tara cries. I hold my tongue, though I'm inclined to agree. And I'm proud of her for speaking up.

Austin rolls his eyes. "Whatever. Close enough." He aims at Noel, "Yet another princess, queen, whatever. Belle is running around here somewhere. I swear I saw a fairy princess. And, of course, there's you and me," he says, pointing the hammer my way and grinning from ear to ear.

Mason clears his throat, breaking the awkward silence that follows that proclamation. "You just called yourself a princess."

Austin puffs out his chest. "Thor is the ultimate Disney Princess."

I *think* I know what he's talking about—some dumb meme—which is good enough for Austin logic. But that has nothing to do with Captain America. "Okay, I'll give you that, but why Cap? He's not even royalty."

He waves the hammer again. "Just accept it. You can lift the hammer. You're a princess too."

Jam's eyebrows rocket toward her hairline. "He better not touch your hammer."

"It's all yours," I promise her over the roar of laughter. And, because I *never* have the opportunity to get Ryan back for all of his jokes, I add, "He's not my type, but Bucky, over here . . ."

"Damn it! You finally got me!" Ryan cries, but I barely hear it. The confusion on Heidi's face when I glance her way commands every iota of my attention.

"It's a joke," I tell her, hoping she doesn't already have the wrong idea firmly fixed in her brain. *At least she's still standing here and didn't run off the second I joined them.*

Fern, oblivious to my crisis, leans back like she's looking at something behind me and scoffs. She stands upright again and smirks at me. "Mr. Whitmore, I hate to tell you this, but that suit does nothing for your ass."

She's the only one who manages to keep a straight face. Even Heidi laughs at that, which eases some of my worries—about her avoiding me *and* her taking that joke the wrong way.

"What the hell is this, a roast?" I look at Mason. "Dude, are you going to just stand there and let your wife look at my ass?"

He shrugs and holds up his left hand, showing off his wedding band. "She can look at your ass all she wants, so long as mine is the only hammer she wields."

"Don't listen to her, Chris," Trista says over a fresh wave of laughter. "That's America's ass."

Shaking my head, I turn to Ryan. "Dude!"

He spreads his hands. "Well, she's not wrong. You do have a nice ass."

"Oh, man." I scrub a hand over my face. "Why is this my life?"

"Because we love you," Tara tells me.

A small herd of children—mine included—comes sprinting across the patio, darting around and through other groups of guests, screaming, "Daddy!" and "Uncle Mason!" as appropriate. Their excitement becomes more of a frenzy as they reach him, like sharks when there's blood in the water. "We picked up all the trash. Can you start the fire now, please? Please? Please, please, please?"

"A fire? There's a fire? Where? We better call 9-1-1!" He shields his eyes with his hand and makes a show of checking the sky for smoke while the kids moan and groan about there not being a fire.

While he's hamming it up, Fern and Austin slip away from the group. Fern snags a propane torch off a table as they pass. As she does, Heidi gasps and grabs my arm. I tense; the lingering frustration with her for avoiding me gives way to a fear that she has some aversion to fire. Her eyes are locked on Fern and brimming with excitement.

This might be my best opportunity to talk to her, to clear the air, for hours. I lean closer to whisper, "You've been avoiding me."

She bites her bottom lip and nods without taking her eyes off Fern.

"Why?" Do I need to apologize for something? Did she decide that whatever passed between us last Sunday was too much? She seemed alright when she walked into my office Monday. But something happened in that brief window that changed things. Whatever her reason, I just need to know.

Her throat works as she swallows. "Because my costume was supposed to be a surprise, and I was afraid I wouldn't be able to resist telling you."

Seriously? That's all it was? I don't even know how to process that. It's . . . Irritating. I've spent the last five days agonizing over what I did to upset her when she was only trying to keep a secret? But at least that's all it was. "You could've just said so. I wouldn't have pushed you . . ." I don't even understand why it was that big of a deal. I mean, yeah, it's a beautiful costume, and she looks fantastic, but—

She turns her head to look at me. Her pupils dilate, and I'm thrown back to that first moment in my kitchen Sunday. It's not my imagination. There's *something* going on here. Something I really want to explore, unless she doesn't feel the same. But that look in her eyes . . .

"I *wanted* to tell you," she says, her voice taking on a rasp I've never heard from her before.

Against my will, my eyes drop to the neckline of her dress—the one place I've avoided at all costs since I first saw her standing here. If that dress were cut any lower, there'd be no keeping her in it.

My lips move before my brain re-engages. "Heidi, I was wondering if—"

"I don't see a fire," Mason says, his voice much louder than it needs to be. Loud enough to ruin the moment.

I swallow my irritation at yet another interruption. Before the night is over, I'll have a chance to ask her properly. I just have to be patient. She deserves more than just a question whispered in a stolen moment when my kid is otherwise occupied. *She deserves better than me because that's all I'll ever be able to give her.*

But damn it, there's *something* here, and I can't ignore it anymore. I want to say that it's too fast and too strong to be anything more than physical, but that argument doesn't hold up well surrounded by my friends.

"That's 'cause there's not one!" Keaton yells, tugging on Mason's pant leg.

"*Oh!* Should there be?" he asks, frowning and looking around like he's searching for something.

"Yes!" All the kids shout together.

"Okay, Well, maybe you should ask someone to light one. Fern likes fire. You should ask her."

"Daddy!" Ronni pouts.

"Yes?" he asks, drawing the one syllable out.

She clasps her hands under her chin and bats her eyes at him. "Please?"

"Okay, okay." Grinning, he points toward the firepit. The wood was already laid out and, thanks to Fern and that blow torch, is well on its way to being ready for the hotdogs Austin is busy skewering. "Let there be fire!"

"Daddy!" Ronni huffs. She grabs his arm and takes off walking like she's going to drag him to the firepit, only to drop it and take off running. "It *worked!*" she cries. "Come on, guys!"

Heidi

"Yes," I murmur to Chris while we watch the kids mob Fern and Austin. The rest of his friends—or are they our friends now?—drift that way as well, but I'm rooted in place. At least until Chris goes.

I could've sworn he was about to ask me on a date before Mason got loud. Even if a date isn't where he was going with that, if it involves him and Keaton, I'm in. But the heat in his eyes before that indicates he had something other than Sunday morning breakfast in mind.

He blinks at me. "Yes, what?"

"To whatever you were about to ask."

That heat flares again but is doused just as quickly. "Heidi, I—Later, okay? When we have more than ten seconds to talk without someone—"

"Daddy!" Keaton shouts, underscoring his point. "I'm cooking my own hotdog!"

Chris squeezes his eyes shut and sighs. "Tonight, once Keaton's asleep, alright? I'll call you—or you can come over?"

My heart sinks, but I shove aside the disappointment and smile. "Alright."

I don't care if we have to talk around the interruptions, I can keep up with multiple conversations, but Chris clearly minds.

His smile is pained, but he slowly reaches out to cup my cheek in his hand. The searing heat of his skin lights my body up. It's amazing I'm not shining brighter than the bonfire. "You have the most hypnotic eyes," he whispers. "I'm sorry."

The compliment makes my heart race. "For what?" I lean into his hand and will him to close the gap between us and kiss me, to do anything to clarify these mixed signals. But he doesn't. He only looks at me.

"For . . . everything." He opens his mouth to say something else, but Keaton calls for him to come see how great he's doing. His hand falls away, exposing my cheek to the cold air that is even chillier for the absence of his warmth. "Later, alright?"

"Alright," I murmur, but he's already gone.

I really hope this isn't the beginning of the end of whatever this thing between us is, but that's what it feels like. If this conversation goes the way I hope it does and he expresses interest in something more than friendship, I have to tell him the truth. Then, he won't want anything to do with me anymore. But I can't start something more with him with that hanging over my head. My heart won't allow it. That outcome is exactly what I want, but I didn't think it would happen so fast. I'm not ready.

"So, you and Chris, huh?" Noel saunters over to stand next to me. I didn't know she was watching. I didn't know *anyone* was watching, but I should've. We're at a party.

"No . . ." She tilts her head and looks at me, clearly not buying it, so I try again. "Maybe. I don't know," I sigh.

She lifts her chin with a small smile that speaks of understanding. "For a simple guy, Chris is pretty complicated."

"You two . . . ?" I shouldn't be surprised. Noel is gorgeous. What guy wouldn't be interested in her? But there's none of the tension between them that usually comes with that sort of thing.

She shakes her head. "I've never dated Chris. But I've known him for years. Has he told you about Lydia?" she asks, turning to look at the man we're speaking of, who is now crouched down behind his son, covertly helping him keep his hotdog out of the ashes. I know Fern was only joking, but she's wrong. He has a great ass.

"Yeah."

"Well, that's where the complicated started. Keaton isn't the only person Lydia abandoned. As has every woman he's dated since. Obviously, he's not going to blame Keaton for that, and instead of putting the blame where it rightfully belongs—on grown-ass women who are as selfish as Lydia—he blames himself."

"I guess I can see how he might do that." Don't I do the same? It's a hard habit to break, blaming yourself for what others did to wrong you. But what does that have to do with me? Or us? Is she saying he already thinks I'll abandon him too?

"If *they're* what you really want, don't let him give you the runaround. But you're not just getting Chris; you're getting both of them. If you can't handle that, then stop this before it goes any further. You're not doing anyone any favors by pretending."

Noel is surprisingly insightful, but she's not telling me anything I don't already know. Still, I appreciate that she's looking out for her friend. It doesn't matter if Chris tries to give me the runaround or not. "Later" might not end well. If I had more time, maybe I could convince him that I didn't want that life, but I didn't know how to get out of it. That I'm not that person. That I can be better. But if things go the way I hope, I'm out of time to do that. I can only pray he won't judge me for the choices I made in my past.

"I understand." She has no idea how much I understand that. Curt didn't want Thomas and me; he only wanted Mom. But Noel's wrong about one thing, sort of. It wasn't selfish of those women to leave. They may have had self-serving reasons, but staying and making Keaton's life hell because they didn't want him too would've been selfish. *How could anyone watch them together and not want them both?*

Noel's little lecture had nothing to do with my mother. All the same, her pointing out that Chris blames himself for the failed relationships raises questions for me. Did Mom stay with Curt because he was the only guy who didn't leave her? For years, I've blamed her and wondered why she stayed with him, but I never questioned what drove her to date him in the first place. Maybe Curt is an opportunistic asshole like Dean and found someone he could easily take advantage of. *"No one loves you anymore—no one but me—and no one ever will, because to them, you're nothing more than a lowlife thief."*

But it doesn't matter. I've come to realize that as long as Curt is still in her life, there is no place for her in mine. It doesn't matter if I'm ready to make peace, I can't do that to myself.

"Miss Heidi! Come see!"

It's impossible not to smile at his excitement, even with Dean's voice haunting me for the first time in weeks. I pick up my skirts and join the crowd around the bonfire, taking care to stay far enough back no stray sparks land on my rented dress.

"I'm cooking this one for you!" Keaton tells me.

Chris looks at me and flashes that pained smile again.

Chapter 20
Heidi

The candy is all collected and inspected. Marshmallows have been toasted. Apples have been bobbed for. And little eyes are drooping. Keaton is awake on willpower alone, his head resting on Chris's shoulder. Keaton toys with his father's curls while Chris pats his back, trying to lull the little boy into giving up the fight.

Fern claimed her youngest niece, Marnie, and is singing softly to the overtired baby. Lottie is asleep on Mason, Mallie is curled into Austin's side, and Ronni is leaning hard on Ryan. I wasn't too sure about the girls at first—convinced that my affection for Keaton was a fluke—but they quickly wrapped me around their little fingers along with all the others. Maybe kids aren't so bad after all. Especially when they're sweet and cuddly like this.

Keat picks his head up and looks around until he finds me. "I want my Miss Heidi," he says, attempting to wriggle out of Chris's arms.

My Miss Heidi. He grabs another little piece of my heart and claims it for his own with three words.

"Keat, buddy, you need to go to sleep," Chris murmurs. "You can see Heidi again tomorrow if she's not busy. It's Sunday, after all. We've got to get up early and cook her breakfast."

Every other head turns to look between Chris and me, but he doesn't seem to notice. Things between us have been off since he promised we'd talk later. It's all my fault, but I can't seem to stop myself from trying to guard my heart against what's coming. Still, having him acknowledge our Sunday morning . . . Whatever it is gives me all kinds of flutters that should be a good thing, but they're hollow. An echo.

"I'll go to sleep for Miss Heidi," the tired little boy whines, a tinge of hysteria creeping into his tone.

Chris looks up and meets my eyes. *"You have the most hypnotic eyes."* Just remembering that should make me giggly as a teenager with her first crush, but it doesn't. I'm still waiting for the but. "Do you mind?" he asks.

I shake my head. I don't mind at all. I should, because losing whatever I have with Chris means losing Keaton too, but it's not his fault. It's not fair to keep my distance from him.

I've already changed out of my dress and stashed it in Tara's car, so it's not my problem anymore. I don't care about chocolate smudges and sticky fingers. Chris sets Keaton on his feet, and the little boy staggers to me and climbs into my lap, straddling my hips and laying his sweet little cheek on my shoulder. His fingers go to my hair, and he toys with the curls that are no longer pinned on top of my head.

"You're going to put me to sleep," I tell him.

He yawns. "Grandma Lola will get us a blanket. We can just sleep here tonight."

A low laugh ripples through the group. The guests are all gone now except for the people the Chambers's have adopted as family, and since I came here with Fern and Mason, that includes me tonight. It's bittersweet. I've loved every second of my time here with these people. They make me feel included. Valued. Maybe even loved. But I can't count on it lasting.

"It might be a little cold for that, sweet one," Martin says.

"What do you think, Rainbow?" Fern asks her stepdaughter. "Is it time to head for the hut?"

"Yeah," Ronni says, slowly sitting up. Ryan gives her a push in the right direction, then steadies her when she wobbles on her way up.

Damn. Tears sting my eyes, but I blink them away. I'm not ready to give him up, but if Fern and Mason are leaving, I have no choice. "Sorry, sugar bear, but that's my ride. You're gonna have to go back to your daddy."

"We can give you a ride," Chris says. His eyes light up with laughter, and he grins. "It's not that far out of the way."

"I'd hate to be an imposition," I tease back. My smile feels as hollow as those flutters, but I try.

His grin disappears. "You're never an imposition." His voice is so sharp I flinch. "Sorry," he says, ducking his head. "Didn't mean to snap."

"It's okay," I whisper. And it is, really. But I'm not. He's never anything other than careful and kind, even tonight with me keeping him at arm's length. But that will change soon. *"You're just as worthless as the rest of us as far as the world is concerned."*

There's no place for me in this circle of friends—*family.* Because that's what they are. They may not share blood, but the bonds that bind them are every bit as strong. Somehow, I allowed myself to forget that I don't fit in with their perfect, shiny lives. I got sucked into this fantasy that this fresh start meant I could belong, that I could really matter to Chris and Keaton and all the others. Now I'm going to pay for it. Just as I knew I would. Because I'm losing him tonight.

Even if he doesn't try to give me the runaround like Noel thinks he will, he'll want nothing to do with me once he learns about the things I've done.

Chris sighs and stands up. "No, it's not. Do you want me to carry him, or do you have him?"

"I've got him," I say, ignoring his first comment. It's not worth arguing over. I wobble a bit when standing, but hands reach out to steady me. Keaton is heavy, but I can get him to the car, I think. I'm gonna try like hell at any rate. I'm getting all the cuddles I can while I can. I don't know what the coming talk with Chris will do to my growing relationship with Keaton, and the possibility that this might be the last time I get to hug him opens a fissure in my heart. I never thought I'd care about a kid, but this one gave me no choice.

As if Chris standing were some sort of sign, everyone else rises as well. Those who aren't holding sleeping children begin gathering wayward cups and dropped candy wrappers, stacking chairs, and putting things in order while Martin and Lola tell them not to fuss and are generally ignored.

Tara grabs Chris by the arm and pushes him my way. "Go. We've got this. Get that boy home before he melts."

I know what she's doing, and it has nothing to do with getting Keaton home. While I appreciate the attempt, I can't help but feel it's wasted effort on her part.

Chapter 21
Chris

Keaton is asleep before we make it out of Martin and Lola's driveway. Heidi sits next to me, stiff as a board and just as silent, staring out the windshield. She hasn't been this distant since the day we met, and I don't like it. It's worse even than her disappearing act this week because she's right fucking here, but she's not.

I expected things to change when I told her we needed to talk, but not like this. *Maybe I should've kissed her.* I swear, she was begging me to with a look. But nothing about that situation was right. There were too many people around. It wasn't romantic at all. She deserves an effort on my part. I can absolutely do that. I haven't forgotten how all that works.

I bet Heidi likes flowers. I can buy her some. Or, better yet, have some delivered to her at work. And dinner. Movies. Maybe some dancing. Time with *me*. Not just *us*. Not just spare moments. *But that's all I have* . . .

I brush that thought away. I will *find* more time. Somehow. I can work different hours or something. Stay up later. Get up earlier. *Something.* Whatever it takes.

I turn into my driveway and switch off the motor. I need to get out, get Keaton, take him inside, get him out of his costume, and clean up his sticky hands and face, all without waking him. But I just sit because after I do all that, I have to convince Heidi that I'm worth the risk. That I can make her happy and that there is room for her in my life, even though it might not always look like it.

"Chris?" Heidi whispers, barely louder than the wind outside.

"Will you come in?" I ask, hoping and praying that she says yes, or at least tells me to call her once I have him down.

In answer, she unbuckles her seatbelt and opens her door. She gets out and opens Keaton's door while I'm scrambling to catch up with her. She's still fighting with his harness when I make it around the Durango.

"Here, let me," I murmur, keeping my voice low so I don't disturb him.

She shakes her head. "I can get it," but her frustration rings through in her voice.

I'm sure she can, but I'm also sure it took me a *long* time to get good at it. I step up behind her and reach around to guide her hands to where they need to be. "Like this. Push here."

What I've done hits us both at the same time. I freeze, but Heidi melts. The tension leaves her in a rush, but her hands never stop. And neither of us says a word.

The buckle gives. "Hey, sugar bear," she murmurs. "Miss Heidi's got you."

She lifts him out of his seat and hugs him to her chest. He sighs in his sleep and turns his head, nuzzling into her neck.

There's not much that competes with the moment my son was laid in my arms, but what's happening now is a close second. Heidi isn't doing this for show as one of the women I dated did—she's not trying to win my affection by sucking up to my kid. I haven't known her long, but I don't think that's Heidi's style. She's not fake. She's not going to pretend to care about Keaton.

This right here is real. Maybe she doesn't care for him as much as I do, but maybe she can learn to. And if she can, maybe this can work.

I lead the way to the house and let us in. Heidi heads straight for the stairs and carries Keaton to his bed. He doesn't fuss when she lays him down or when she takes his shoes off. Getting his costume off takes both of us, though.

Heidi disappears while I'm wrestling him into his pajamas and returns with a warm, damp washcloth. She picks up one of his hands and carefully, if clumsily, cleans each sticky finger and his palm, then moves to the other. Then, she gently wipes the sticky residue off his mouth, chin, cheeks, and his nose.

Her eyes remain fixed on him, but she straightens up and backs away. "How do you just . . . leave him?" she whispers.

I sigh because I know exactly what she means, but it's not an easy answer. He's so vibrant and full of life when he's awake, but asleep he's so small and defenseless. I always want to stay right here and watch over him all night. "The first night he slept in his own room, I jumped up and ran at every little noise. I had to convince myself not to sleep on the floor outside his door. It's hard, even now. Everything about parenting is hard. But you have to do it."

I move closer to the head of the bed and lean over to kiss his head. "Good night, little buddy. I love you so much."

She's watching me when I step back. Her eyes dart to Keaton's sleeping form, then back to me. "May I?"

"Of course." I back away, giving her space.

She smooths his hair back and presses her lips to his forehead. "Good night, sugar bear. Your Miss Heidi loves you," she whispers. It takes all the strength I have to hold my ground because I want to kiss her so badly now. Her voice gets soft enough I have to strain to hear it, "I'll see you around, alright?"

My heartbeat quickens at her words. *Why does it feel like she's telling him goodbye? Did I say or do something to lead her to believe the talk we need to have is a bad thing? Is that why she's so distant now?*

She kisses his forehead once again, then straightens up. Now that I'm looking for it, there's a goodbye in her eyes. It's plain to see even in the dim light of Keaton's nightlight. I've seen it before. I don't even have her yet, and I'm losing her. But why? What did I do this time?

Am I just supposed to let her drift away like I have others in the past? Or am I supposed to fight for what might be?

I can't stop her if it's what she wants, but I don't have to sit by and watch. I can try to change her mind. Give her a reason to at least try.

"Where do you want this?" she asks, holding up the washcloth as she steps past me into the hallway.

The washcloth is the furthest thing from my mind. My self-control snaps. I follow her out and close the door behind us, then grab her, one arm around her waist, the other hand cupping the back of her neck, and pull her against me. She gasps just before my lips claim hers.

That little sound gets to me, making it hard to remember all the reasons I should stop because every cell in my body is urging me to go. It's wrong of me. I know better. She's been abused. She's afraid. She's . . . kissing me back, pressing her lips to mine hard enough to bruise. *Oh, shit.* I need to stop this before things get any more out of control. Before *I* get any more out of control and scare her.

I pull away and hold my hands up in the air, shoulder height, to let her know I'm sorry and that I'm thinking again. I back up to put some space against us, but she matches me step for step, staying close.

"I'm sorry," I whisper.

"I'm not," she replies.

She reaches for me, but that's not going to work. I don't trust myself with her hands on me. I catch her wrists in one hand and turn to push her against the wall, pinning her hands over her head. She gasps again. We need to talk, and if she gets her hands on me, there won't be a lot of words exchanged.

"I'm sorry," I pant again, searching her face for any trace of fear, but there's none to be found. Its absence gives me a glimmer of hope that things may actually *work* between us. If she'll just hear me out. "I will let you go, but I kind of need you to keep your hands to yourself, or my brain isn't going to stay in the driver's seat here, alright?"

She sucks in a deep breath and lets it out slowly, then nods.

"Do you have plans this weekend?"

"Chris, I—"

There's a sadness in her eyes that scares me. What just happened is proof there is something here. We both know it, but we need to talk this out. "Please, Heidi. Don't. I don't know what I did but talk to me. Give me a chance."

Her eyes flare wide, and she shakes her head. "Oh, Chris," she says softly, squeezing her eyes shut. "You didn't—It's not—I need to tell you something."

"Don't tell me you're married."

"No! It's . . . worse."

"How is it worse?" What could *possibly* be worse than finding out the woman you think is the unicorn you've been looking for is already married to someone else? *Oh, fuck.* Is she sick? Is that why she was so skinny? I don't care, though! I still want her.

She sighs and hangs her head. "I have a criminal record."

Her words cut through my mental tailspin, putting an end to my theories. "I'm sorry, what?"

She's not married. She's not sick. She . . . did something stupid? It's obviously a big thing to her, but I don't understand why she seems to think it's going to have any impact on us.

Heidi hangs her head, and her muscles coil tightly, like they were that first Sunday in my kitchen so many weeks ago. "Can we . . . I don't know, sit down or something?" she murmurs.

"Sure." I release her hands and lead her back downstairs. My room is closer, but that's not conducive to talking.

I sit on my couch, making sure there's enough room for both of us, but she lowers herself into a chair nearby and looks everywhere but at me. "You already know that I didn't have a happy home life." Her words are slow and halting, like she'd rather be *anywhere,* talking about *anything* other than this.

I nod to let her know I'm following, but I'm scared of what she's going to say next. I can't imagine her doing anything that would change the way I feel unless she's a very good actress, and I seem to have a thing for that type. But I don't think that's the case this time.

"Well, my stepdad has a gambling problem, so we didn't have a lot of money growing up. Life was just . . . not happy. I told you I met my ex when I was thirteen. That was a really rough year for me. It was when Curt started abusing me, too. And Dean convinced me to run away from him."

That raises goosebumps on my arms. Trista almost ran away with a boy when she was a teenager too, but I have a feeling it was for a different reason than Heidi. I listen patiently while Heidi relives some of the worst moments of her life, my arms aching to hold her and comfort her through it all.

Yes, it's horrible. I hate that she had to endure it. But I'm not sure why she seems to think it changes anything. It's not like she killed someone. We all make stupid decisions when we're young. And she was a victim—manipulated into jumping from one bad situation to another.

If anything, it makes me more determined to make her life better.

She runs out of words and sits staring at her hands.

Heidi

I sit and wait, bracing myself for Chris to tell me to get the fuck out of his house. To stay away from him and not even look at his son ever again.

The silence hangs between us way too long. I finally sneak a peek at him. He's watching me like he's waiting for me to continue, but that's all I've got. Maybe he didn't understand something I said? I thought I was clear enough. It's hard to misunderstand words like theft and accomplice. Or maybe he thinks I'm being dramatic, like it's not nearly as bad as I'm making it out to be.

Before I can anxiously ramble on, repeating the same thing in different words until he gets it, he leans forward to grab my hand. I tense, waiting for the hammer to fall. "I appreciate you making me aware of this before we . . . figure things out. I know that wasn't easy for you, and that you didn't have to tell me."

I shake my head. "No, I did have to. I couldn't do this . . ." I clamp down on thoughts of that kiss and the way my heart raced in a good way when he pushed me up against the wall to gesture between us, "without telling you. You deserve to know that I'm not a good person."

He tugs on my hand, inviting me to move to the space next to him. I hold my ground, though, afraid to get my hopes up until I'm sure we're on the same page.

He doesn't push for me to move. "Again, I appreciate the honesty, but I don't understand how being abused, manipulated, and used your whole life makes you a bad person."

How can he not understand? "Chris, I have a criminal record! I helped other bad people fuck over people like you for *years*. It doesn't matter that I didn't want to, that I hated it, that I felt like I had to and I had no way out. I still did it."

Chris shrugs like it's nothing. "Heidi, you said yourself you were diagnosed with Stockholm Syndrome. I'm guessing there's some PTSD as well?" He raises his eyebrows, making it a question.

I nod. I don't understand the PTSD part. That's what soldiers get. Cops. Firefighters. Good people who survive truly fucked-up, life-altering shit while trying to make the world a better place. Not . . . me.

Chris's mouth twitches into another frown. "That's what I thought. I don't care that you have a record. So does Ryan, technically. He lost his temper at a frat party and knocked some guy out for saying he was going to get a girl drunk and take advantage of her. The guy pressed charges."

That's kind of awesome. I'm glad Ryan was there to stand up for that girl because far too often, no one does. That's not the point right now, though.

"But, I . . ." I stop. I don't know what to say. I told him *everything*. I didn't try to downplay it. And he just doesn't care?

Chris squeezes my hand. "I didn't know you then. I know who you are based on the choices that led you where you are now. You were *manipulated* into making bad choices, and when you broke out of that cycle, you made good ones. But the bottom line is, you're no less worthy of love because of what you've been through."

That breaks me. The last remnants of my defenses crumble to dust. I fall apart a little piece at a time, tear by tear, until I can hardly see because everything is so blurry. He knows it all, and he doesn't hate me? Dean was actually wrong?

Objectively, I know he was. He manipulated me, twisting my brain into a dark, miserable place where he was the only good. Some of the things he said linger in my brain, like splinters that are in too deep to easily remove. They have to fester their way out, or someone has to go in after them. By telling me I'm worthy of love, Chris worked one free.

Strong arms circle me and my head lands on Chris's shoulder. "Shhhhh," he soothes. "It's okay, Heidi. It's okay. I'm here. I'm not letting you go." He presses a kiss to the top of my head. One of his arms shifts, moving under my knees, and he lifts me up. We turn, and he sits, settling me in his lap. "I'm right here. Lean on me, honey. I've got you."

I've got you. I know what he means, but he says it like he's never letting me go. *I hope he means that too.*

Chris holds me, petting my hair and talking to me the whole time. He doesn't care. He's not pushing me away. He still wants me in his life—in his son's life. I'm not losing him or Keaton. Oh, my god. Keaton. I get to see his smiling face tomorrow. I get to hug him and snuggle him and laugh at the silly things he does. And I can have both of them.

I get to keep them both.

"Heidi, honey, how can I help?"

I shake my head. I don't know. He's already done so much. I just need this. Him. Someone to help me believe that Dean was wrong.

"I'm here for you. Whatever you need."

I nod, but the tears keep coming. I was so sure he would hate me. It's such a relief to know that he doesn't.

My tears eventually run their course, leaving me a sniffling, hiccupping mess. Chris pushes me upright and grabs my chin, turning my head until our eyes are locked. There's a softness in his gaze that causes a lump to form in my throat. *It's almost the same look he gives Keaton.* He slowly leans in and presses his lips to mine again, not caring that I'm a mess. It's a quick kiss, but it's more than everything.

Chris brings a hand up to cup my cheek. "Are you alright?"

I swipe at my nose with the back of my hand and nod. "I was so scared you'd hate me," I whisper.

"I don't." He leans in until we're forehead to forehead, nose to nose, and looks into my eyes. "I admire you for breaking away from a hard situation when so many people would have stayed."

He admires me? Getting out was hard each time, until Dean made it easy, but I never considered that people who didn't know me before would recognize that. *Because he's special*... Some people won't see it that way—people who will say I brought it upon myself or that I asked for it. But maybe they don't matter.

"Fern and Mason are celebrating the one-year anniversary of their contract this weekend." He pauses to clear his throat and sits back, offering me a shy smile. "Will you come with me? As my date?"

A date? Something in my chest swells, like a balloon inflating. I've never been on a date before. I didn't need to date Dean. Our relationship was a given, though he only pursued it to keep me around. The prospect is kind of exciting, even if I don't know what to expect. "Are you sure?"

"Absolutely." He presses another kiss to my lips. "Nothing would make me happier."

"I'd love to. If you're sure," I repeat, giving him another out in case he has even a sliver of a doubt.

He smiles at me. "I'm sure."

Holding my breath, I lean in, searching for another kiss. Chris obliges eagerly. I take a chance and tease his lower lip with my tongue, pushing things a bit further. I want to continue what he started upstairs, but he leans back.

He swallows hard and shakes his head, but his eyes are fixed on my lips, softening the rejection. "Heidi, I want to take you upstairs so much it hurts me. But I want to date you even more."

"What?" There's a difference anymore? Dating is stuff you see in movies or read about in books. Or maybe I've got it all wrong. I'm beginning to understand that absolutely nothing about my life up to this point was typical. That my old life was the stuff of movie plots and all the things I used to think never really happened *do*.

A furrow forms between his brows. "Have you ever been on a date?"

I roll my eyes. "Only if all of us dining and dashing counts." It wasn't that we didn't have the money for the meal. They just enjoyed the thrill. They'd drag me out so I couldn't pay and ruin their fun.

The corners of his mouth turn down. "It doesn't."

I shrug. That's the best I can do. Dean's idea of romance was boosting a car and joyriding until it was out of gas. Lifting something from a store for me. I hated it. I still do. There was nothing romantic about any of it. None of it meant anything to him. He only did it to show off.

"Heidi, I can't promise to be perfect, but if you give me a chance, I can show you what a real relationship is supposed to be like."

"I'd like that." I'd like anything that involves him and Keaton. Especially now that I'm sure he's not going to turn his back on me for something I've left behind me. I don't have to worry anymore.

"Good. But I need a favor, alright?"

"What's that?" I ask, biting my lip. I can't imagine him asking me anything I won't agree to, but I'm not jumping in blindly. I've learned that lesson the hard way.

He toys with one of my curls. "It's nothing bad. I need this to stay between us for now, for Keaton's sake." His fingers don't cease while he tells me about Becca and her scheming, and the women who left because dating a dad wasn't what they thought it would be.

As much as I hate lying to Keaton about anything, I agree because I understand where he's coming from. He wants to be sure of us and to find a way to reassure Keaton I won't leave like others have.

I lay my head on his shoulder again, and we sit like that until keeping my eyes open becomes a struggle.

Chris walks me home, insisting that Keaton will be alright for five minutes. A good night kiss later, and I'm leaning against my door, wondering if I should pinch myself because this has to be a dream.

Chapter 22
Chris

"Daddy?" The confusion in Keaton's voice brings a smile to my lips. I haven't beat him awake on a Sunday morning in a while, but I was too excited to sleep in this morning. I even set an alarm.

"I'm down here," I call to him. He can navigate the stairs just fine. I just don't like him doing it in the middle of the night when he's half asleep.

I flip the last pancake as he walks into the kitchen. He looks around at the plates sitting out and the pans of steaming food on the stove. "You cooked without me?"

I brace myself for his reaction because he's not going to be happy. The question is, how bad is it going to be? He got to bed late last night, and he's up earlier than normal. That combination normally results in an overly emotional little boy. "Yeah, I did," I say, removing the pancake from the pan and adding it to the others on the plate next to the stove.

Everything is ready now. Heidi's tea and my coffee are waiting in insulated cups, as well as glasses of juice. We only have to plate food and go.

His lower lip pokes out and begins to tremble. "But I wanted to help."

I've got one chance to save this before he melts into a puddle, so I play my trump card. "I know, bud, but we're doing something different today, alright? Heidi is going to love it." I'm already smiling just thinking about how excited she'll be, and I love that I can do this for her. It's a little thing, but sometimes those are the most important.

That does away with the pout. Anything Heidi will love is alright with him. "She will?"

"Mmhmm." I check the time and glance out the window. He finally beat her. Her kitchen light is on, but she's not outside yet. "Why don't you go knock on her back door?"

He takes a step toward the door and stops. "You'll watch?"

"I'll watch." He's so careful since I lectured him on the dangers of wandering off on his own. I was afraid I'd scare him, but, so far, as long as he knows I'm watching, he's alright. I'm glad I managed to toe the line between terrifying him and helping him understand.

We open the door together, and he's off and running through the pre-dawn gloom. I lean out to watch. He makes it about halfway before her door opens and she shuffles out onto her little porch.

"Miss Heidi!" Keaton shouts loudly enough to wake the neighbors. *They'll get over it.*

She stops and looks our way, then runs to meet him. She picks him up and hugs him close, and I *melt*. Her whispered good-bye to him echoes in my mind, and it hits me. Last night, when she said that, she truly believed it was goodbye forever. That there would be no more Sunday morning breakfasts or spur-of-the-moment barbecues with the others. She was preparing herself to never see him again, not for some distance and maybe less time together.

Everything about her behavior last night makes sense now. It wasn't that she thought what I had to say was bad; it was that she thought I'd discard her like some broken object the moment I learned she had a shit childhood. She was shutting me out to protect herself. *Never again.*

It takes everything I have not to run across the yard and join them. But I can't do that yet. We need to figure things out before we clue Keaton in. I'll have to be content with feeding her breakfast and watching the sunrise together.

There's not enough light to tell for sure, but I think she's smiling. "Good morning, sugar bear! What are you doing here so early?"

"Breakfast is ready! Daddy says we're doing something different today and you're gonna love it!"

I glance to the east. "We've gotta hurry, though." I leave the door open and move to the stove to make Keaton's plate and mine. They're right behind me, and we make it upstairs with time to spare.

My balcony isn't big by any means. There's just enough space for a chair or two and maybe a small side table when I get around to it, but that doesn't matter today. Keaton settles himself between us on the blankets I've layered to soften the cold concrete and is oblivious to the smiles and glances exchanged over his head.

He babbles on about how much fun trick-or-treating was while we eat and watch the sun inch over the horizon. There are still houses and trees blocking her view, but it's better than on the ground.

It's perfect for me because I watch the sun's progress in her eyes. Maybe I'm jumping the gun, but I'd happily do this every Sunday for the rest of my life.

"It's beautiful," she whispers. "Thank you."
"So beautiful," I agree, never taking my eyes off her.

Chapter 23
Heidi

A warm front moves through Wednesday. Even after sundown, it's beautiful out. Just chilly enough to curl up with a blanket and a good book for a while before bed, so that's what I do. It would be a shame to waste weather like this.

It's hard to focus on the words on the page, though. My mind keeps drifting to Chris and Keaton.

"Damn it, Annalise!"

The angry shout from the house next door shatters the peace. My hands tighten around the book. I'm damaging the pages, but I can't force myself to relax my grip. My lungs stop, refusing to contract or expand again. My pulse thunders in my ears, and my fight or flight instinct triggers, urging me to flee.

What do I do? Where do I go?

Chris! I lunge to my feet, dumping my blanket and the plate that was perched on my knee onto the ground. The plate lands with a crash, sending shards of glass everywhere. Heedless of my bare feet, I run. The pain of my feet being sliced open registers, but it's more of a distant annoyance. Getting away is the only thing that matters. Getting to safety.

I fly across his yard to the back door. The kitchen is dark. The whole house is dark, but I pound on the glass anyway.

"Please, please, please," I chant like a prayer. A light comes on deeper in the house, and Chris comes running into view.

He unlocks the door and opens it with a quick yank. "Heidi? Honey, what's wrong?"

I can't make my mouth work. It opens, but the sound is stuck somewhere.

His eyes travel down my body, looking for the problem. "Honey, you're bleeding. What the hell happened?"

I shake my head. I can't talk right now. I just need to be safe. Chris carefully pries the book from my hands and tosses it on the table. Then, he leans and hooks an arm behind my knees, the other behind my shoulders, and picks me up. "You can talk to me while we get your feet cleaned up, alright?"

I nod. I might be able to do that. Once the door is closed. And as long as he stays with me. The warmth of his arms around me eases the panic, loosening the iron bands around my lungs, making it easier to breathe. That makes room for my brain to register the pain in my feet, though. It's nothing I can't handle, but *damn*, that stings. There's also room to worry about Annalise—whoever she may be. I've never heard anyone yelling from that house before. Maybe I should've checked on her?

Chris carries me up the stairs and turns right, toward a part of the house I've never visited. Keaton showed me his room and everything he loves about it, but we didn't venture this way. He steps into a dark room, and it must be his because he continues on through to an ensuite bathroom.

"Alright," he says, placing me on the vanity counter, "wait right here. Let's get you cleaned up and patched up." He opens a cabinet and produces a huge first aid kit, then pulls a washcloth from a drawer. Reaching across me, he turns on the tap, then grabs one of my now-throbbing feet. "Let's see here." He whistles long and low. "What did you step on, honey?"

"Plate," I say, closing my eyes and gritting my teeth against the sting.

"Does blood bother you? Is that why you came over?"

I shake my head hard enough to make myself dizzy. "Neighbor was yelling."

Chris stills, his fingers flexing around my ankle. "At you?"

I shake my head again. "Someone named Annalise."

He tips his chin up and wets the washcloth. "Do you think someone needs to check on this Annalise?"

I shrug. If this is a common thing, which I don't think it is, Annalise will deny everything. She'll take the blame. So many people tried to help Mom over the years, but she always brushed it off as no big deal. If it's not common . . . "Maybe."

The concern in his eyes hardens into an angry resolve I've never seen from him. "Alright. Once you're patched up, I'll go check on her. Unless you think I should call the cops?"

"I don't know." I don't want to send him into the middle of a domestic dispute and put him at risk, but calling the cops might make things worse. Curt always got even angrier if officers showed up at the door. If neighbors rang the bell because they heard shouting, he'd only cuss about them being nosey once they were gone.

"So, the neighbor started shouting, and . . . ?" he asks, gently dabbing at the blood on the bottom of one foot. I grit my teeth again, holding back the yelp of pain so I don't wake Keaton.

"I don't know," I mumble. He must think I'm insane. Someone I don't know yelled at someone else I don't know, and I panicked. I swallow hard, wishing I could force down the heat in my cheeks as easily as the lump in my throat. "I just freaked out. I didn't feel safe."

"And you came to me." There's no anger in his statement. No irritation. No judgment. In fact, I'd almost say he's pleased, but that makes no sense. Sure, he told me I could come here to be safe, but I wasn't actually in danger. I probably woke him up. And if I didn't, I could've woken Keaton. I didn't even consider that at the time.

The knot in my throat is back. "I'm sorry."

He pauses, looking me in the eyes. "I'm not."

I suck in a shaky breath and do everything I can to hold back the tears threatening to fall. It's all so much to handle, the panic and fear, his acceptance. But I refuse to cry. I've had enough tears in the past year to last me a lifetime.

"I told you," he whispers, switching to the other foot, "you're safe here. You can always come to me, alright?"

Sniffling, I nod. I do feel safe here—anywhere he is, actually. *I don't want to leave.* I'm okay now, but the thought of returning home triggers the return of those iron bands around my lungs. *Maybe I don't have to.* He has a guest room—and a couch. "Can I—I mean, do you think—Would it be alright if . . ." *What am I thinking?* I can't believe I even considered asking. There's no reason for me to stay here. There's no reason for him to let me. I live right next door. He's a call away if something happens. And what would he tell Keaton in the morning? "Never mind."

He stops again to look at me but doesn't acknowledge my flubbed attempt to ask to stay here. "You're not going to like this next part."

Fear makes my muscles tighten again. "What?"

"You have some slivers of glass in your foot." I relax again. I can deal with that. I'm already adjusting to the pain. "I *think* I can get them out without hauling you to Urgent Care or maybe calling Fern to see if it's something she can do."

"Just do it," I tell him. "I'll be fine. I've had worse."

Shaking his head, he closes his eyes and tilts his head toward the ceiling. "Do I even want to know?"

"Probably not. I was a runaway, Chris," I remind him. "My boyfriend and all of the people I called friends were career criminals. I couldn't exactly pop in to see a doctor anytime I got hurt or sick."

He takes a deep breath and mutters to himself, then shakes his head again. "Alright. I'll try. But if you cry, I'm probably calling Fern."

"Whatever." I'm not sure why he thinks Fern would be any better at this than him. It's just like removing a splinter, only you have to dig a bit. I've done it before.

Never to myself, but I know I can do it. "I'll try before you do that, though. No need to bother her."

"I hate this," he sighs, digging through the first aid kit to find tweezers.

"Here," I say, reaching to take the tiny silver torture device from him. "I can do it. It's okay."

He shakes his head. "No. I can do it. I hate that it happened and that you're hurting and that I'm going to hurt you more. And you're sitting here acting like you're in absolutely no pain when I know that has to be excruciating."

"It stings a bit," I admit. A lot, actually, but I wasn't lying. I've had worse. I can deal with the pain.

"Heidi," he sighs. He lays the tweezers down and cups my face in his hands. "You don't have to be tough all the time." He leans forward and presses his warm lips to my forehead.

He thinks I'm tough? I haven't thought of myself that way in years, not since I realized running away wasn't an act of strength. My lower lip does that annoying trembling thing it sometimes does when the tears are too strong to fight, so I bite it. I don't want him to see me weak. I want him to continue seeing me as a strong person—the person he likes enough to want to date.

"Alright, let's get this over with," he whispers.

***

My eyes burn from unshed tears, and my lip is probably on the verge of bleeding from me biting it, but my feet are finally bandaged. Chris scoops me off the vanity and carries me out of the bathroom.

"I can walk," I whisper. Yeah, it's going to hurt, but putting it off isn't going to help.

He ignores me and carries me to his bed and puts me down on the edge of it. "Wait here. It's late, but I'm going to go check on your neighbors. They're probably already in bed, but I want to make sure he's not still over there yelling at her."

A fresh wave of anxiety swamps my brain. What if it's the wrong thing to do? What if it only makes things worse? What if Chris gets hurt? *Trust. I have to trust him.* He teaches self-defense classes, after all. He's not going to do something to escalate the situation. "Alright."

"I'll be right back," he promises.

"Be careful . . ." Even knowing he can handle it, I'm still worried.

He kisses my forehead again. "I can take care of myself."

Once he's gone, I settle back against the pillows and try not to dwell on it. Nothing bad is going to happen. It was just a commonplace marital spat. Everyone loses their cool from time to time. They're already in bed, and he'll be back before I know it.

The stress of it all weighs on me, pulling me down until I can't keep my eyes open any longer.

***

"Heidi?" Chris's soft voice coaxes me awake.

Everything comes rushing back. Fear ties my insides in knots while my cheeks get hot enough to fry eggs on because I fell asleep in his bed. "What happened?" I ask.

"Lights were out at the neighbors," he says, holding out a grocery sack for me to take, so I do, "but I cleaned up your back porch and grabbed a few things I thought you might want."

My sleep-drugged brain struggles to make sense of the bag or the last thing he said. "What?" I ask, looking in the bag like its contents might clear things up. But they don't.

"I didn't want to worry about you getting cut cleaning up the glass, so I got it all. And while I was there, I grabbed your pajamas and your toothbrush."

Squish. There goes my heart again. "Thank you so much, but you didn't have to do that."

A red stain spreads across his cheeks. "Do you want me to carry you to the bathroom, or do you want to try walking? Walking might make your feet start bleeding again."

"If you don't mind then . . . But why am I going to the bathroom? Just get me to the door so I don't get blood all over your house, and I'll walk from there."

"You're not going home tonight."

"Huh?"

"You heard me. That's what you were trying to ask earlier, isn't it? If you can stay here tonight?"

My face flushes. *I never should've opened my mouth.* I don't want to make things awkward. Things between us are tenuous enough right now. "Yes, but—"

Ignoring me, he scoops me up off of the bed and carries me to his bathroom again. "Just get ready for bed," he says, putting me on my feet in front of the sink. "Let me know if you need anything."

He backs out of the room and closes the door behind him. *Okay then . . .*

On some level, his insistence is a relief. I probably won't sleep if I go home; I'll be too anxious. If the yelling starts again, I'll be running right back here. And Chris offered, so it's not *as* weird as me asking. He wouldn't offer if he wasn't okay with it.

I quickly change and hop up on the vanity to give my feet a break. He was right; walking is going to hurt. I can deal with it, but I'll feel bad if I get even more blood all over his floor. I sit there and brush my teeth, then call for him to come get me.

He picks me up again as easily as if I were a rag doll.

"Thank you for letting me stay here," I whisper.

"You're welcome," he says. Instead of carrying me out the door, he walks around to the far side of his bed and sits me on the edge. Then, he grabs the covers and pulls them back. "Climb in."

I don't move. "I didn't mean *here*, here. I meant your guest room or the couch. I don't . . . I'm not—" *How do you tell a guy you desperately want to get naked with that you're not particularly interested right this moment?*

Chris seems to read my mind. "Heidi, you're hurt. I'm not after sex. We can share a bed without sharing our bodies. If you'd be more comfortable down the hall, that's fine. Otherwise, climb in."

I don't have an argument for that. The guest room or the couch would be fine, but to pass the night so close to him, safe within his reach . . . I'm not strong enough to say no. I climb up the bed and lie down, letting him pull the covers up over me and tuck me in like he does Keaton. Only, he doesn't kiss my forehead or my cheek like he does for his son. He places a soft kiss on my lips instead before walking around the bed to join me.

Chris

I slide into bed, shut off the lamp on my nightstand, and scoot to the middle. Once I'm settled, I reach for Heidi and pull her across the bed to me. "Okay?" I ask, worried it might be too much for her and trigger another panic attack. I need her close to me, though. I need to know she's not curled up in a ball somewhere, crying or afraid while I sleep.

"Okay," she replies in a voice so small it breaks my heart into more pieces than that plate she dropped. "I'm sorry."

"I'm not," I tell her, recycling her reply from last night. I hope I never have to dig glass out of her feet again, but being the one she runs to is a role I'm alright filling. I'm a single dad. I'm used to wearing a multitude of hats. I'm happy to add another to my collection.

With the lamp off and the shades down, my room is pitch black—just the way I like it, usually. I could go for a little more light just now, though, so I can see her face and watch her fall asleep.

I wasn't lying when I told her I wasn't bringing her to my bed for sex. Someday, but not like this. I just want to hold her. Still, I find her chin in the darkness and tip her head back until I can put my lips on hers again. It's difficult to sneak kisses with Keaton around, so it's hard to waste this opportunity to do so.

She sighs, and her body softens against me. My head and my heart know nothing more will happen, but my body hasn't given up hope. There's a beautiful woman in my arms, in my bed, melting into my kiss. I'd be worried if I *wasn't* hard.

I want to pull her leg up over my hip. Grab her ass and press her closer while I grind myself against the cleft between her legs. Roll her over and pin her wrists over her head to see if she reacts the same here as she did against the wall Saturday night.

If she doesn't, we may have a problem. But we'll figure that out later.

"Good night," I whisper, brushing one last kiss against her lips and another on her forehead.

She squirms in my arms until her head is tucked under my chin. "Good night," she whispers. "And thank you."

She doesn't need to thank me. This right here is thanks enough. But telling her so will spark another thirty-minute debate, and we both have to work in the morning, so I let it go. "You're welcome."

Chapter 24
Heidi

An unfamiliar noise rips me from a perfectly good dream. I was asleep in Chris's bed. In his arms. He held me all night, and despite his obvious desire, he never pushed me for sex.

I gasp and open my eyes, trying to sit up at the same time, but a weight across my waist stops me. So does the view. Instead of staring at my boring beige wall, I'm looking into a pair of brown eyes that never cease to make my heart do stupid, fluttery things. "It wasn't a dream," I whisper. The panic attack, the glass in my feet, it was all real. As if awakened by the thought, the cuts on my feet twinge in confirmation.

"Just my alarm." Chris grins and raises his arms over his head, stretching, and the weight holding me down is gone. "Do you dream of me, sweet Heidi?"

My blush starts in my cheeks, but the heat quickly spreads throughout my whole body. "Maybe," I concede purely out of curiosity. I want to see his reaction.

His eyes drop to my cheeks, then down to my neck, and lower to the neckline of my shirt, and his grin stretches into the sexiest smile in the history of ever. "I've had some good dreams about you," he continues.

That heat intensifies at the implication, but I don't comment. If I speak again, I'll do something stupid, like beg him to have his way with me right now, before we go to work. I want to carry that secret with me all day, the scent of his skin on mine.

"Maybe I'll get to tell you about them someday."

He hasn't said anything blatantly suggestive, but my pussy throbs in time with my heartbeat, and my breath comes in quick bursts. *Maybe you can show me instead.*

His eyes snag mine again and pull me under their spell. I can't blink. I can't look away. He is everything. "Or maybe I'll get to show you. Would you like that?"

His eyes demand an answer whether I want to give it or not. I can't stop myself from nodding. I would like that very much. Right now. Tonight. Again in the morning. Every available opportunity in between. "Chris," I whisper, lightheaded with need for him.

He shakes his head. "I've wanted you since the moment I laid eyes on you. I can wait a little longer for the sake of doing this right."

"If we both want it, how is it wrong?" Yeah, getting caught would be bad, but his door locks, I'm sure. Nothing about my life has been "right" so far. At other times, I like that he cares about things like that. Just not now when I want him inside me.

"Because I need to know you understand what you're getting yourself into."

"Oh, I do. I'm not a virgin, Chris."

"That's not what I mean." Quick as a thought, he rolls me onto my back with his body, pinning me beneath him with his hips while one of his big hands gathers my wrists and pins them over my head. My heart pounds. Excitement heats my blood, increasing my longing for him.

"This is what I mean," he says, his eyes boring into mine like they're sharing secrets. "I like control, and I don't want that to scare you."

"It doesn't," I promise, tossing my head back and forth. Nothing about this situation is frightening to me. The opposite, in fact. It's . . . hot. Who would've guessed that sweet, laid-back Chris likes to play a little rough? But is it that, or is he a dom? Either way, I'm not worried. "You know I ran away from home as a teen. Most of my sex-ed came from a couple we worked with—a dom and his sub who weren't shy about telling it like it is. Or about anything, really. I know a *lot* about sex, even if my experience is limited to one guy." *And that one guy wasn't exactly boring.* I'm not telling Chris that, though. It's not a competition.

His eyes flare wide and his dick throbs where it's trapped between us. When he speaks, his voice is more of a growl, "I don't care. Your ex pinned you to a wall and beat you."

It's not like I've forgotten. I slam the door on the memories that want to take his words as an invitation to invade my head. I will not let my past drag me down right now. This is Chris. I'm not afraid of him. I've known from the day we met that he would never hurt me, even if I didn't trust that knowledge right away. "Just don't grab my throat." That probably *would* send me into a panic attack, even with him.

Chris shakes his head. "That's not my thing. I don't need to hurt you or myself. I just like being in charge."

"I'm okay with that," I whimper, digging my heels into the mattress to push my hips against his. His hard shaft presses against me, so close to where I want it but so far away, sending another surge of longing through me. I'm okay with whatever gets us naked. Like, now.

He shakes his head again. "No, you *think* you are because we're here like this. Once you leave, you may feel differently. I'm a patient man. I can wait until you're ready. Delayed gratification is always worth it."

"Please." My gratification is already delayed. I'm so close all it would take is him *looking* at my clit to make me come. He might be patient, but I'm not. I don't know how to wait. I've never had to. Dean was always happy to indulge me, even if he was a one-and-done kind of guy. And if he was busy, or I wasn't content, BOB was always around.

His smile is slow and sharp. He lowers his mouth to my ear, and I hold my breath, certain he's giving in. His beard tickles my neck as his breath warms my skin, raising goosebumps that make no sense while lightning bolts of need shoot straight to my pussy. "No," he whispers.

I smother a frustrated groan and thrust my hips against his again. "Please!"

"Do you touch yourself and think of me?" he asks, purring the question directly into my ear. Somehow, I feel his words between my legs where I long for his touch.

"Yes," I gasp, hoping that's the proof he needs that I'm ready for this. I'm not afraid of him. Dates and dick can coexist. There's no need to wait.

"Don't." That sexy purr is gone, replaced by a commanding growl that brooks no argument. "Your next orgasm comes from me, got it?"

"For how long?" I ask louder than I mean to, but damn it! I had every intention of doing just that when I got home, whether he does it for me now or not. Orgasms are too good to stop at one. It must suck to be a guy.

The corners of his mouth twitch like he's fighting a grin. "As long as it takes."

That really sounds like an 'or else.' Like if I don't listen, there will be no sexy fun time. *I don't like this.* "And if I do?"

He shrugs, and his lips pull to one side. "Then you're not ready."

"How does that mean I'm not ready?" That makes no sense! I'm so fucking ready I'm getting myself off to thoughts of him. How can I not be ready?

"Because you're not listening."

Control. Oh, shit. This is a test. My first order. It's not about how much I want him; it's about how willing I am to play his game. *Very.* The alternative is no Chris-induced orgasm, and I have a feeling he's much better than BOB ever thought about being. "Are you going to do this every time?"

"What do you mean?"

"Insist I never get myself off if I want to sleep with you?" If he is, we might have a problem unless he's ready to play as often as I am.

He smiles again. "No. I want to know you're giving this serious thought. If you're horny, you'll think about it a lot."

You have no idea . . . "Saturday."

Little crinkles form in the corners of his eyes as he narrows them at me. "What about it?"

"You will—" he raises his eyebrows, and I stop, considering his reaction. If control in the bedroom is his thing, he probably doesn't like being told what he will or won't do. That's not giving him control. "I will do what you want, but Saturday gives me time to think on it."

"We'll see," he says, fighting another grin.

"You're evil." That's three whole days without an orgasm. As badly as I want him right now, I'm not sure I can make it that long. *I'm going to lose my marbles.*

His eyes scan my face, and I could swear he knows exactly what he's doing to me. It's not fair. He seems so . . . unaffected, except for the rock-hard dick pressed maddeningly close to where I want it to be. "No, I know that it's worth waiting to make sure this is something we'll both enjoy."

I buck my hips again, hoping the third time is a charm, but he only smiles and shakes his head. *Control indeed.* But what if I don't make it? Or what if I don't enjoy his particular brand of control? The taste he's given me so far is fun, but it's just that—a sample. "So, what if I decide your kink doesn't work for me?"

Something shifts in his eyes until I don't recognize them anymore. The bright, playful, challenging spark that was just there is nowhere to be found. "I don't know. I guess we'll figure that out when the time comes." He rolls off me and out of bed and keeps his back to me to adjust his pants. Then, he turns and reaches out a hand for mine. "C'mon. We're going to be late. I'll walk you home before I wake Keaton."

Chris

The walk to Heidi's is quiet, but not uncomfortably so. Walking down the stairs didn't re-open her cuts, and it didn't bother her too much, so she didn't want me to carry her. I gave her a lot to think about this morning. I didn't mean to. That conversation could've waited a few weeks, but the way she blushed when I asked her if she dreams of me . . . I couldn't leave it alone.

Mutual desire is a powerful thing. I've witnessed what it does four times now—five if you count Gabe and Tara's second go at it. No matter how hard any of them fought it, it pulled them together in the end.

The longing between Heidi and me is stretched to the breaking point now. When it snaps, nothing will ever be the same, good or bad. But this time, I think I got it right.

I can't speak for her, but I think my soul has been screaming at me since the day we met that this one is special. Some people find love at first sight, but the rest of us have to take a second glance to know for sure.

Heidi stops at her front door and rummages around in the bag I packed last night to find her keys. She unlocks the door, then turns to look at me. Her frustration is impossible to miss.

"Have a good day," I tell her. I want to hug her again, but I'm not sure if she's open to that after my repeated refusal to give in and fuck her senseless this morning.

She opens her arms and pulls me into a hug. "You too. Thank you for taking care of me last night," she whispers against my neck, sending a thrill straight to my dick. It can't get any harder, though. And I may as well get used to it. I told her she couldn't touch herself, so I won't either. It's only fair.

I've never warned a woman about my proclivities in the bedroom. Despite what Heidi labeled it, I don't consider it a kink. I don't have to have control to enjoy sex, but I've always felt like I was hiding part of myself when past partners didn't respond well.

I'm not hiding this time. She will either accept it, or she won't, but she'll know either way.

"Anytime, but please don't make a habit of hurting yourself." I keep my voice light so she knows I'm teasing about her hurting herself.

She bites her bottom lip. "Can . . . Can I see you tonight?"

I turn my head and press a kiss to her neck. There are other things we can do that don't result in orgasms. Is that what made her hesitate to ask, because that's what she wants? "With or without Keaton?"

She swallows hard, and her breathing gets shallow. "Either. Both."

Straightening up, I look her in the eye and ask, "You really don't mind spending time with him?" She shakes her head, confirming what I already knew. But it's nice to be reassured. "I have a late class tonight, but I'll let you know when we get home. I'll pick up dinner somewhere."

She flashes that smile that makes my heart do flips. "Okay!"

"And after dinner, if it's not too late, maybe we can watch a movie." I'm rushing things, but this woman already spends time in my home with my son. It's too late to impose limits on such things now. But maybe keep the touchy-feely stuff to ourselves until he's asleep. And then we can make out on my couch until we can't take it anymore.

"I'd like that."

A smile breaks free. *If she only knew what I was thinking just then . . .* "Me too." Maybe I had it all wrong before. Maybe I don't have to rearrange my life to make room for her. Maybe she's already found her spot and was just waiting for me to let her in.

Chapter 25
Chris

"Go get her, bud. I'll have the back door open." I lower Keaton to the ground and turn him loose. He sprints to Heidi's door as fast as his little legs will carry him while I grab the takeout bags and his backpack. I'd love to stand out here and watch the interaction between them, but as soon as her door opens, I head inside to unlock the back door and set the table for dinner.

I barely beat them to the door. Keaton's excited about having dinner with "his" Miss Heidi in the middle of the week for no apparent reason.

"Miss Heidi! I have something for you!" he says, leaving the door wide open in favor of running for the backpack I left draped over a chair.

Giggling, Heidi closes the door and follows him, shooting me a smile as she passes. I want to kiss that smile so fucking bad, but not in front of Keaton. Not yet.

"I found it at school!" he says, holding up a bright blue feather. "My teacher tried to make me leave it outside, but I was afraid it would get lost, so she let me put it in my backpack if I *promised* not to get it out again until I got home."

She takes it and clutches it to her chest, just like she did with the rock and the leaf. "I love it, sugar bear. I'll put it on the shelf with my rock, alright?"

She kept *that*? Not that I don't have a collection of various odds and ends he's presented me with over the years, but I'm his dad. She's just... not "just" anything. She's his Miss Heidi, and, somehow, she might love him as much as I do.

I drop what I'm doing and join them at the table. "Hey, Keat," I say, so much gravel in my voice I could rock the driveway, "do you think Miss Heidi needs hugs?"

"Cuddle puddle!" he cries, immediately latching onto the idea and taking it where I hoped he would. He wraps his arms around her legs and squeezes for all he's worth.

"What's a cuddle puddle?" she asks through her laughter.

"This," I say, wrapping my arms around her from behind. "It's something a client at the gym does. Keaton latched onto it."

"I like this," she whispers.

I look down at Keaton, but he's not paying us any attention, so I press a kiss to Heidi's neck. "I do too."

"Daddy, can we eat while we watch a movie tonight? Please?"

Food belongs on the table, especially for the almost-four-year-old. But I think I can make an exception this once. "Sure, bud. We can do that tonight. Why don't you go pick a movie? Heidi will help me with dinner, and we'll be right in."

"Okay!" he says, already running for the remote.

Once he's out of sight, I turn Heidi and greet her properly, kissing that smile I've spent the whole day shaking out of my head. "Is it weird to say I missed you?" I whisper.

"Only if it's weird for me to say I missed you too." She throws her arms around my neck and pushes up on her toes, bringing her mouth to mine for another kiss.

I could get used to this. But maybe not having to hide it. "Careful," I whisper, looking to the other room to make sure Keaton isn't watching. "I don't want him to know yet."

"I understand," she says, dropping back onto her heels to step back, letting me go.

Damn it. I scrub my face with one hand and pull her close again with the other while I try to explain before I hurt her feelings—if the damage isn't already done. "I don't *want* to keep it from him," I tell her. "I just want us to both be sure about this before we tell him. I don't want to confuse him."

"Chris," she says, a small smile turning up the corners of her mouth. "I get it. But he'll catch on pretty quick. No kid is stupid, and he's quicker than most."

"I guess you would know, wouldn't you?" I murmur. "Sorry. I just . . . whatever happens, I don't want to ruin your relationship with him. I never want you to feel like you don't have a place in his life, alright? I know you're important to him, but I feel like it goes both ways."

Tears gather in her eyes. Nodding, she throws her arms around me again. "Thank you. I never intended for it to happen, but I love that little boy, Chris."

"He loves you too." *And so do I.* I shove that thought and the flicker of alarm it causes aside. It's much too soon to know that for sure. It might be true, but it might be lust.

"Daddy? Miss Heidi?"

Like a couple of teens caught with their hands in inappropriate places, both of our heads whip around to the door where Keaton waits, watching us like we're bugs under a microscope.

Fuck. "Heidi was just . . . giving me a hug to thank me for dinner," I tell him, grasping at straws.

"Yep!" she says too quickly, backing me up. "These cheeseburgers sure smell good. Do you have a movie ready?"

"Uh-huh," he says slowly, his eyes darting between Heidi's face and mine. But neither of us breaks. "We're watching *Alvin and the Chipmunks*."

"Oh yay! I love that one!" Heidi grabs the stack of Styrofoam boxes off the counter, shoots me a wide-eyed look, and follows Keaton to the couch.

"I'll get drinks," I tell them. I need a minute anyway. That was close. *What the hell am I doing?* Maybe I should just tell him now? But what do I say? Every woman I've ever introduced him to as anything more than a friend has moonwalked out of his life. I don't want him to assume Heidi will do the same just because we're more than friends.

His sweet little voice drifts back to me from the living room. "Miss Heidi, I love you."

"Aw, little sugar bear. I love you too. You know that, right?"

"Uh-huh. I'm going to draw you a picture tomorrow at pre-school."

"I can't wait, sugar bear. I'll put it on my shelf with my rock and my feather."

I glance at the counter where she placed the feather for safekeeping before picking up the food. Maybe I'm worrying over nothing.

***

A bath, three stories read by Heidi, five kisses from each of us, and about a dozen 'I love you's' each, and Keaton is finally down for the count. I exhale a sigh of relief and follow Heidi out of his room. I've never been so excited for him to fall asleep.

I close his door and grab Heidi's hand, leading her down the stairs. It's time for us, now. Whatever that looks like. All I know for sure is our clothes are staying on, and hands are staying above the belt because I'm so hot for her I'll come on the spot if her skin comes in contact with my dick.

Once seated, I grab her hips and pull her into my lap, straddling me. She comes willingly and leans in to kiss me. My hands go to her hair. It's not tied back in its usual ponytail tonight, so I gather it all in one hand and wrap it tightly around my fist, giving her just a taste of what it means to come to my bed. I use her hair to tilt her head back, exposing her neck to my lips, and press my lips to the fluttering pulse point on one side of her neck, then the other. The pent-up frustration comes roaring back to life—but it's fun.

She rocks her hips against mine, grinding against my dick for relief. "Heidi," I whisper, warning her. She can chase that relief all she wants, but if she finds it, we start over.

"Damn it," she whines. "Please! I want you."

"I want you too, but we're waiting." She has no idea how much her begging is wearing on my control, though. I want this mouthy woman so much. I want to turn her begging and bargaining into whimpers and moans. I want to hear her chanting yes and begging for more.

"But why?"

"Because I said so." And because my son is upstairs, and I don't want to hold back to keep from waking him. But I can't tell her that; she'll promise to be quiet. I'm sure she can do it, but I don't want her to. I want her to scream for me.

"Control freak." She spits the words like they're a bad thing, but the excitement in her eyes reveals the truth. She may be frustrated, but she's enjoying this too. I didn't know I needed the reassurance, but part of me was worried about pushing her too far by not giving her what she wants.

I smile and kiss her neck again. "Yes, I am. You're going to love it."

One corner of her mouth twitches like she's holding back a smile. "Prove it."

"I will," I say, tugging her hair again to watch the fire in her eyes burn hotter. I love that's she's not afraid to show me how much she wants me. It makes me want her even more.

"Now," she gasps.

Fuck, that's hot. Maybe I can just—No. No 'justs.' I won't lose control.

"Nope." *Maybe* Saturday. Depending on our date.

I don't know who I think I'm kidding. At this point, I'm only holding back on principle. I said we'd wait. I'm not going back on my word. This woman is bad for my self-control, but I kind of like it.

Chapter 26
Heidi

Len is waiting for me right in front of the door at five o'clock on Friday, and he's grinning like someone just told him his favorite sunglasses are BOGO right now. "Miss Decker," he greets me just as he always does, even though I've told him to call me by first name. Every. Single. Day. He opens my door and says, "There's been a slight change of plans today."

"Good evening, Len. What do you mean?" I ask, climbing into the back seat.

Len glances at his watch and smiles at me. "Three . . . Two . . . One."

My phone rings on one. *What the hell?* I check the caller ID to find Tara's smiling face on my screen. I tap the green icon and raise the phone to my ear. "What's going on?"

Len closes the door and walks around to get behind the wheel.

"Oh, good. You're already in the car," Tara says, having obviously heard the doors closing. "Fern just called to tell me that Chris invited you tomorrow, but he couldn't remember if he told you about the dress code. Guys have it so easy. Just throw on a suit, and *voila!*"

"There's a dress code?" I ask as I put pieces into place. Chris called Fern. Fern called Len, then Tara. Or maybe Tara, then Len.

"Yes. Nineteen-twenties themed. Fern said she was having Len bring you to The Boutique. I'm pulling some dresses now that might work for you. We're kind of the unofficial dressmakers for the place now. Fern sends a lot of business our way."

"Fern does?" I ask, confused. Last I knew, Fern didn't have a job. That's not to say she's not busy as a one-legged man in an ass-kicking contest, but she wasn't gainfully employed anywhere.

"Oh, damn it, Chris. He didn't tell you anything, did he? We'll get you lined out when you get here."

"Okay, see you soon." I hang up the phone and look up, meeting Len's eyes in the rearview mirror. "What did I get myself into this time?"

It's a rhetorical question, but he smiles and answers anyway. "Fun. That's what."

I sit back and try not to fret about how I'm going to pay for what is sure to be an expensive dress *and* make my car payments. Mason won't let me pay until the car is in my possession, but I'm still putting money aside for it.

I'm so deep in thought I don't notice we've stopped until Len opens my door, startling me to the here and now. "Here we are, Miss Decker." I climb out, and he closes the door behind me. "I'll be going home now. Mrs. Martin said you can ride home with her."

"Alright, thank you, Len." I take a deep breath and will my feet to carry me onward.

The bells over the door chime my arrival. Tara looks up and smiles. "Oh, good. You're here." She beckons me toward a dressing room. "I've got some selections in here. I still think Zelda for her, Madi." She holds up a turquoise dress with what I can now identify as a drop waist and beaded fringe.

Madi, busy undressing a mannequin, pauses and looks me over from head to toe. "But the neckline on Olive would do great things for the girls."

"Maybe we have time to make a few alterations . . ."

"What are you thinking?"

"Either alter the neckline on Zelda or combine the two. The top of Olive and the bottom of Zelda."

While they debate the pros and cons of both options, I grab the hanger from Tara's hand and shut myself in a fitting room to try it on. The black would probably make my eyes stand out more, but the turquoise looks great with my skin tone.

The option to show more cleavage *is* attractive since Chris doesn't seem to be struggling with the ban on orgasms as much as I am. However, I'm excited for tomorrow for more than just the promise of finally getting dicked. I'm going on a *date*. One I have to dress up for. I don't want him to spend the entire evening staring at my boobs. Not this time. We can play that game later.

I step out, cutting off their chatter about alterations, and turn around for Tara to zip me in.

"Alright, Zelda it is," Madi says. "That color is just . . . damn."

"I don't think we need to change the neckline, either," Tara murmurs, walking circles around me to check the fit. "I mean, we *can*. But we'll lose some of the swish from the fringe."

"She still needs an LBD," Madi says.

"Yes, but a dedicated LBD. Something timeless that will work for any occasion. The Olive isn't really that."

"Are you two going to keep talking about me like I'm not here?" I ask, fighting back a laugh. It's kind of cute when they get like this.

They both shake their heads. "Sorry," they say together.

Madi offers me an apologetic smile. "We kind of get—"

"In a zone," I finish for her, grinning. "I've noticed."

"Why don't you get changed, and you can browse some catalogs while I alter Zelda here real quick," Tara says. "It won't take long. And I'll work on sketching an LBD for you this weekend."

"Uh, question . . ."

"What's up?" Tara asks.

"What exactly is an LBD, and why do I need one?"

"Little Black Dress," they say together.

"And for your next date," Madi adds.

"*Next* date?" They're awfully confident. Not that I'm not, but they don't know the things I do.

"We're playing it safe!" Tara says. "That way, you're not rushing in here last minute all the time because Chris is a guy and forgets that we women need time to prepare for such things."

"But I can't—"

"Fern says Chris is paying for this one," Tara says, indicating the turquoise dress I'm still wearing. "And you'll make your LBD yourself, so just materials."

"You think I'm ready for that?" I ask. I've done a lot of simple work for them since I started, but I've never made a whole dress. I'm just beginning to grasp the patterns they use to cut the fabric.

"Definitely. We'll be there to guide you. You can have it done in a couple of Sundays. You could also come in after work during the week if you wanted."

My excitement shows itself in a silly, wiggly little dance. If they think I'm ready for this, it won't be much longer before I'm sewing dresses for Tara instead of practicing on scraps of fabric and the occasional alteration they say I can't mess up. "Sweet!"

I change back into my work clothes and hand Tara the dress . . . Zelda. I'm trying to adjust to calling a garment by a human name, but it's a work in progress. *Like my life.*

But honestly, my life is pretty damn great right now. I have a job—two, even. I have friends because, as hard as it was for me to accept at first, Chris's friends are my friends too. I'll have a car soon. Things with Chris are . . . well, unfolding in their own time. And I have Keaton. What more could I possibly want?

Chapter 27
Heidi

Noel steps back to survey her handiwork, then comes at me with a fluffy brush to assault my eyes one more time. Madi grabs another section of my hair and wraps it around her odd, cone-shaped curling iron. She's already spent a ridiculous amount of time doing something with the back of it, and now she's adding curls. Jam is on my other side, carefully applying polish to my fingernails, and Fern is kneeling off to the side, out of Noel's way, painting my toes while Tara looks on from a chair Mason carried up for her.

Fern's bathroom is some kind of warzone. There are discarded plates, chocolate wrappers, cups in various stages of fullness, and enough beauty products to supply a salon scattered on every available surface. It's overwhelming, but so much fun. I've never done anything like this, much less had friends to do it with. The women in my life before weren't interested in female bonding, as Mason referred to our time today.

I'm not sure where the music is coming from, but the song changes, and Fern hums along. Among her other talents, that woman can *sing*. She says the others can as well, but they all deny it.

"I'm done here," Jam says, screwing the cap back on the nail polish.

Fern's humming cuts off. "Almost there," she murmurs.

"Will it be dry in time?" I ask, eyeing my dress where it's hanging from a towel rack with all the others. I don't want to ruin my new dress. Chris is going to love it.

I'm so excited to put it on, even if I still feel a bit like an imposter in it. If it were just Chris and me tonight, I'd be fine. He knows the truth now. The others don't, though. Chris's acceptance gives me hope for the others, but until I work up the guts to tell them, I'll continue to feel as if I'm pretending I belong.

"Oh yeah," Jam says. "This stuff dries fast. It's the best. I still can't believe you've never had your nails painted before."

I force back the urge to cringe. That slip-up earned me some strange looks. It was easy enough to cite strict parents, which isn't far from the truth. Curt wouldn't have allowed me to spend money he could lose gambling on nail polish or make-up.

Fern glances up at me. I've only had my hair or makeup done by someone else once, and she knows it. She taught me how to use a curling iron and makeup besides eyeliner while we were preparing for the Halloween party. *How much longer are you going to lie to them? Yeah, Chris seems okay with your past, but he also wants to fuck you. These women won't be so easy to convince.*

I can't shake my head to drive Dean's voice out, or Madi might burn one of us, so I bite my cheek instead.

"You guys?" No one stops what they're doing—we're on a timeline after all, but I know they're all listening. "Thanks for this. I've had a great day."

They all murmur various forms of 'you're welcome,' but the ones still working stay focused on what they're doing.

Fern caps the polish she was using, a glittery silver that matches the sequins dotting my dress, and stands up. I can't see, but from the sounds of things, she and Jam are attempting to tame the mess on the counter. "I'm glad you're here. I'm glad you're all here. I wish Tris could've made it. This was fun."

"Oh, Tris was having fun," Noel murmurs. "The horizontal kind."

"Okay, I would've stayed home too," Madi says. "There is a severe lack of horizontal fun in my life."

"Some broken things can't be mended," Tara murmurs softly.

"I know," Madi says on a sigh. "But we've been together so long."

That doesn't justify wasting more of your life on someone who doesn't make you happy. She hasn't come right out and said it in my presence, but I can read between the lines. Her relationship is strained.

Tara clears her throat pointedly. Madi is preaching to the choir there. I haven't got the whole story yet, but I know Tara and Gabe were high school sweethearts and have been married twice now.

"I know, I know," Madi grumbles. "I'm just . . . waiting for a sign, I guess."

Tara cracks the door open and yells, "Mason! I need a piece of paper and a marker!"

Madi snorts. "There's no way he heard that."

"Hide and watch," Fern says dryly. *Where are we supposed to hide?* No one moves to do so though, and I follow their lead. It must be one of Fern's funny sayings that make no sense to me until after the fact.

Silence falls, and it's quickly broken by soft footsteps on the stairs. "Everyone decent?" Mason asks from right outside the bathroom door.

Tara opens the door to let him in and takes the paper and marker. She turns around and braces the paper against the wall to write, *here's your fucking sign* in all caps.

"Bionic. Fucking. Hearing," Fern says, making us all giggle.

"Does that mean you've heard *every* word we've said?" I ask him. Not that anything said here today was some great secret, I'm merely curious.

"Eh," he says, tilting his head from side to side. "If I wanted to, but I have a sister, and she taught me to respect the sanctity of female bonding time."

I try to put myself and Thomas in that sort of situation and come up blank. We were all each other had. But, if things had been different . . . I think Thomas would've done the same as Mason, but more out of annoyance than respect. It makes me smile. "How'd she do that?"

He wrinkles his nose. "I did not need to know that much about my sister's menstrual cycle. That said, unless anyone else needs something, I'm out."

"Thank you, Mase," Tara says, smiling as she passes back the marker. "I think we're good."

"You're running out of time, ladies." He snags a belt loop on Fern's jeans and tugs until she turns to kiss him.

"We'll be ready," she promises. "We're mostly down to changing."

Mason leaves and closes the door behind him, sealing us back into our bubble.

"I'm done here," Noel says, laying down her brushes and dusting off her hands. "Hurry up, Madi. We need to get this girl in a dress so she can see this perfection."

"I'm done except for the feather," Madi replies. "You ready?" she asks, patting my shoulder.

A fresh wave of nerves churns my stomach. I try to muster my earlier enthusiasm to hide my anxiety, but my assent comes out much too bright. "Yeah!"

The other women smile, and there's no malice in any of them. They're actually . . . encouraging. Like they understand, and they're here for me.

"This is my first date," I explain, blurting out the words before I lose my nerve.

Fern cocks her head to the side. "Because of your parents?"

I shake my head. "I met my ex when I was thirteen. We were just . . . always together after that. When I turned seventeen, we . . . our relationship changed. He was older, you see . . ."

"So, if you were together so long, why is he an ex?" Madi asks.

Maybe if I give them a piece of the truth at a time, it'll be easier. Revealing any of it makes me anxious, though. Even this piece, because I'm afraid of their reactions. I don't want their pity. It's over and done with. I survived, and he's in prison. I don't need them to feel sorry for me. But they don't pity each other for the things they've been through. That's reassuring enough to help me get the words out.

"He got mad because I messed something up, and he put me in the hospital." After all their lighthearted girl talk, Madi's relationship woes aside, my confession slides into the room like a storm cloud on a sunny day. But damn it, it feels good to say it. They've opened their arms and welcomed me into their lives. I want to do the same as much as I can without driving them away.

"Damn it!" Tara says, her voice strained with the effort of holding back tears. "I'm gonna ruin my makeup!" She fans her face and takes some deep breaths, trying to control the pregnancy hormones. "I'd say I need a hug, but I really will bawl then. So someone hug her for me."

"Cuddle puddle!" Madi says.

The others laugh, and I'm quickly pulled into a group hug, minus Tara.

"On the bright side, now you have Chris," Jam says. "And all of us. And the other guys. And none of us will ever let anything bad happen to you again."

She has *no* idea how much I want to believe that, but they still don't know the whole truth. Until they do, their support is something I desperately want, hovering just beyond my reach, that could be snatched away at any moment.

"That's right," Fern says. "The guys consider themselves brothers. That makes us sisters. Sisters have each other's backs. Always."

Sisters. As nice as it sounds, I'm on the outside looking in. And that's where I'll remain as long as I keep this secret. I don't want that. I'm tired of living life half in the shadows. I want to be all in. Or all out. I want to grab onto all those things just beyond my reach and hold on for dear life. *". . . have a little faith in my grandsons and their friends."*

So why am I waiting? Why put myself through one more minute of uncertainty? Losing the possibility of their support will hurt, but it will be better to know one way or another. "Can I tell y'all something?"

"You can tell us anything so long as you can talk and get dressed at the same time," Noel says, stepping out of the group to grab her dress. She opens the frosted glass shower stall and steps inside to change. "Spill it."

"I'm just . . ." I suck in a deep, shuddering breath and let it out, but I do not cry. After crying at the slightest provocation for so long, that's a huge win. "I'm afraid you won't like me very much anymore."

"I mean, unless you club seals when no one is looking, I think we'll be alright," Jam says, unbuttoning her shirt because, in her words, she's not body shy.

I don't give them nearly as many details as I gave Chris because I don't want to be a sobbing mess again, but the abridged version is bad enough.

To my relief, they all continue getting themselves dressed instead of stopping to stare at me like I'm some sideshow oddity. Even when I'm done, they act as if I didn't just confess to being an accessory to countless crimes.

"I knew your name was familiar," Fern says slowly. She pauses to touch up her lipstick. "I used to live in your neighborhood. There were flyers all over the place."

My heart sinks. I can just imagine my mother and Thomas out stapling flyers to every lamp post and taping them in every window they could after I disappeared. At least, I hope they were missing person flyers and not wanted posters.

Noel purses her lips, and I brace for her to prove Dean right and tell me I'm a trash human being. "Heidi, what you did takes balls—all of it. Running away, getting out of that situation, even telling us now. I'm sorry that shit happened to you, but everyone deserves a second chance." Her words give me goosebumps, and it takes all the determination I have to keep myself from sagging forward, bowled over by relief. The others murmur their agreement while she takes my dress off the hanger. "Now, get dressed and straighten your crown. You've been given a fresh start, and in this one, you're a fucking queen."

"I don't *feel* like a queen," I murmur. Are they really not going to make a thing of this? I had myself all worked up over nothing? All those times I spent dreading the day I let something slip, and they pried the whole story out of me ... And they're just rolling with it?

"Too bad," Tara sobs.

"Oh, T," Madi groans, smacking herself in the forehead.

Fern pulls several tissues from a box on the vanity and passes them to Tara.

"It's the hormones," Tara says, dabbing at her eyes in a futile attempt to dry them without ruining her makeup. "They make me a crybaby."

"Hormones are evil little bitches," Fern says with a knowing smile. Nothing about her face says she's trying to be funny, but everyone laughs.

Tara sniffles some more, then gives me a watery smile. "No one feels like a queen on the hard days. It's how you handle those days and the days after that makes you a queen. Everyone makes mistakes sometimes. A queen owns up to them, learns from them, and resolves to do better."

I swallow hard to clear the knot from my throat. *Haven't I done just that?* At least, I have now. I have no illusions about them keeping this a secret from their partners, and I wouldn't want them to. So I have now fully owned my mistakes. I definitely learned from them. And I *will* do better.

Noel holds up a hand before anyone can say another word. "Okay. This has to stop now, or I'm going to cry too. And then I'm gonna have to hurt someone because I don't cry. We're all queens here. Let's get Tara fixed and go knock 'em dead."

In the commotion that follows, I pinch myself, sure I must be dreaming. I can't try to say that they didn't understand like I did with Chris. I was brutally honest about it all. But here I am, and for the first time in my life, I'm not hiding in the shadows, praying that no one looks too close and discerns the truth.

It's fucking wonderful.

Chapter 28
Chris

I walk out my front door and cast one last look toward Heidi's house. She's not home, but I can't help but wish she'd come walking out.

I didn't want this to be a big thing. I wanted to show up to dinner with Heidi once the others were there and get the questions and the comments out of the way all at once; just rip that Band-Aid off and get it over with. The girls had other plans, though, since Fern let the cat out of the bag.

My friends have never been anything other than supportive when I've introduced them to women in the past, but it's different this time. This thing with Heidi is fragile. *Heidi* is fragile, which is sometimes hard to remember because she hides it so well. But the slightest indication of disapproval from any of our friends could ruin this thing we're building. I can only hope the girls aren't making her uncomfortable.

Just because they all *like* Heidi doesn't mean they'll approve of me *dating* her. *One way or another, everything changes tonight.*

The limo Mason hired to recreate his first—impromptu—date with Fern is waiting on the curb. It's hard to believe a whole year has passed since four of us set out to discover the secrets of Easy Speak's Killer Queen and dragged those two along for the ride. *Little did we know* . . . And so much has changed since then. Not just for me, for all of us. It had its ups and downs, but the results were great.

Ryan and Trista are already on board. I climb in and settle into the seat across from them. "So, why didn't you get ready with the others?" I ask Trista. The girls gathering to prep and primp at Fern's house seems to be a tradition in the making.

Her cheeks flush. "I needed a shower," she says.

There are showers in the Chambers's home, but the self-satisfied smirk on Ryan's face tells me more than I need to know. *Lucky bastard.*

It's my own doing, though. The opportunity was there, but I refused to take it. Tonight, Heidi and I fall or fly. If things don't go well, we can at least still be friends. That might not be true if anything had happened, and nothing is worth that risk.

I try to relax, to tell myself that everything is going to be fine, but I'm too anxious. Are the others giving Heidi a hard time? They're all very protective of Keaton, especially after what happened with Becca. What if they say something that makes her change her mind?

"What the hell, Chris?" Ryan asks.

I look around, trying to figure out what his problem is. *Did I spill something on my shirt?* I look down, but it's snow-white. "What?" I finally ask.

He waves a hand at me. "Your leg is bouncing hard enough to shake the whole damn car. What's up with you?" His pierced eyebrow quirks upward, then he flashes a big smile. "You're bringing a date, aren't you?"

"Figured I shouldn't be the odd man out," I say, hoping to deflect his scrutiny. The longer I can put off the inquisition, the better.

He nods. "It's about time. I know it hasn't been all that long, but I was afraid you were going to give up after that bitch pulled her shit." He's not far off the mark. I had no intention of dating again. But Heidi happened. "Please tell me it's your neighbor," he continues.

Words fail me, so I nod. Was I that obvious, or is that just a general observation? He sees a lot. And he seems so . . . pleased about it. It's the outcome I hoped for, but I wasn't prepared for it. The knot of tension in my chest loosens a little, giving me room to breathe.

Ryan smiles. "Fucking finally. I thought we were going to have to draw you two a map."

I glare at him. He's got *no* room to talk. "Really, coming from you?"

"That was different," he grumbles, crossing his arms over his chest. Next to him, Trista smothers a smile.

I can't pass up the chance to pick on him. He'd do the same for me. "So you ignoring your feelings for five years is different than me missing signs for a few weeks?"

"Fuck off," he says, playfully kicking my shoe. "Seriously though, glad you opened your fucking eyes. That woman looks at you like the sun shines out of your ass. Quite the accomplishment considering your head was wedged so far up there."

"Dude, go fuck yourself." I can't say it with a straight face. He's right. I was willfully obtuse, but I had good reasons. At least, I thought I did. "I didn't think she'd be interested in my old ass."

Trista scowls at me. "You're not old."

The car stops for Gabe, so I slide over to make room. "You have to say that. Your boyfriend is older than I am."

"And she's younger than me, too," Ryan points out, tipping his head Trista's direction.

I roll my eyes. "Two years, big whoop."

"What's going on?" Gabe asks.

"Chris invited Heidi tonight," Ryan says.

Gabe nods. "Oh, that? Yeah, Tara and Fern were on the phone for half the morning." While I don't doubt that they talked, half the morning is probably an exaggeration.

Ryan looks at Trista. "Why didn't you tell me?"

Tris gives him a *look*. One that plainly reads *'really?'* "Because you two," she swivels a finger between Ryan and me, "tell each other *everything*. If *he* didn't tell you, I wasn't about to!"

I make a fist and hold it out to Tris, who bumps it with her own. "Thank you," I tell her. "Glad to know someone has my back. Fern wasn't supposed to tell anyone, and we can see how well that worked."

Trista winces. "Well, she didn't *mean* to tell *everyone*. But she realized that you maybe forgot to tell Heidi about the dress code, so she called Tara to see what could be done about that. So, Madi found out, of course. And Jam was with Fern . . ."

Gabe snorts. "Then Tara had a pregnancy moment today and broke down on the phone with Noel and Trista about how pretty Heidi looks in her dress and how that color was just *made* for her."

"But she swore us to secrecy when she realized she slipped," Trista says, picking up the threads of the story again. "So Colton probably doesn't know. But Mason definitely knows since she's there getting dressed. And Austin is there too. So . . . everyone but Colton."

I drag in a slow, deep breath and let it out slowly while I try to talk myself down from an anxiety attack. I'm only anxious because this is important to me, and I don't want anything to mess it up. But I need to stop obsessing over silly little things that are unlikely to happen and enjoy myself. "So I may as well have taken out a billboard on the freeway?" I ask with a grin, relaxing for the first time since I dropped Keaton off at Nicole's.

"Two people can keep a secret if one of them's dead," Ryan deadpans. "Really, man, what's the big deal? She's not a child. No one batted an eye when Austin and Jam hooked up."

I throw my hands into the air and accidentally smack the headliner of the limo. "Austin's not seven years older than Jam. He doesn't have a child that Jam is barely old enough to be the mother of without straying into statutory rape territory."

"Big fucking deal," Ryan says. "Age don't mean shit. That woman is an old soul trapped in a young body."

He's not wrong there. That's part of the reason I love seeing her get so excited about the little things, like the rocks Keaton gives her or when we invite her over for *anything*. "I just hoped that seeing us together and happy would kill any concerns before they were voiced."

Gabe shrugs. "Everyone deserves to be happy. If the two of you make each other happy, that's all that matters."

"And Keaton loves her already," Ryan adds, throwing out the real kicker.

"You know, I didn't expect you all to argue this for me," I tell them, chuckling at the irony of it. "Honestly, I was afraid you'd try to talk me out of it. You all saw how she was with Keaton the day she moved in."

"We saw her with Keaton the last time we were over too," Gabe points out with a shrug. "People grow. We saw it before you did."

"How?" I ask. I guess I really *was* that obvious. It's not just that Ryan is overly observant—which he is.

"Well, let's see here," he begins. "You couldn't stop staring at her the day she moved in. Last time we all had dinner together, you had this strange twitch where you kept reaching her direction then yanking your hand back like you were going to get burnt. Don't get me started on the Halloween party . . ."

"Oh, my gosh," Trista says. "It's a good thing looks can't get her pregnant, or you'd have another one on the way after Halloween."

Oh, fuck. Halloween . . . I can't think about that right now, or I'm going to have an awkward situation in my pants. "And to think I spent all afternoon stressing," I mutter.

Ryan scoffs. "You worry too much about the wrong things, my friend."

"I'd drink to that," Gabe says, "but, you know . . . Seriously though, as long as you're not harboring doubts and hoping we'll give you an out, I'm happy for you."

The car turns and begins the trek up Mason's long drive. "I'm really not," I assure him.

"Are we going in or are they coming out?" Gabe asks.

Ryan shrugs and hooks a finger in the collar of his shirt, trying to stretch it out. "Dunno, but I hope they hurry either way. I'm ready to be done with dinner so I can unbutton this damn thing before I pass out."

Gabe shoves my shoulder. "Go."

"Huh?"

He shoves me again. "Get your ass out of the car, Chris. She spent all afternoon here getting mobbed by the others. Go let her see you appreciate it. As much time as you've probably spent imagining getting her out of whatever she's wearing, she's spent picturing your face when you get your first look at her tonight. Don't let that moment be when she climbs in this fucking car."

Ryan spreads his hands. "The man has a point."

It seems like solid advice to me, so I edge between the seats and make my way out of the car. My hands shake when I reach for the door, but more from excitement than nerves now. I can't wait to see her.

"To be fair," Trista says as I reach for the door to shut it behind me, "we spend just as much time imagining getting our guys out of whatever they're wearing."

Chuckling to myself, I shut the door. I tried to write off the way Heidi looked at me the few times she saw me shirtless, to discount it as something other than attraction, but I know better now. But thinking about her thinking about getting me naked is not something I should do right now. I want to grant that wish.

I try the handle, and it gives, so I open the door and walk on in. Austin, Mason, and, surprisingly enough, Colton, are seated in the living room, drinks in hand. *Maybe Colt did decide to let bygones be bygones after all.* Their eyes leave the television and swing my way, and they couldn't have synchronized it better if they had planned it. "I was going to ask how it's going, but I think you just answered."

Laughter drifts down the stairs. Austin sighs. Colton shakes his head. Mason just smiles. "Go say something," he tells the other two. "I *dare* you."

"Fuck off," Austin mutters. "I'm fucking done with dares."

"Chickenshit," his big brother taunts.

"I like my balls where they are, thank you very much."

"In Jam's purse?" Colton asks him.

Austin finishes his drink and smacks his lips. "Yep. At least there, she takes them out and plays with them."

Mason looks at me and waves over his shoulder toward his office. "Grab a drink. I'll text the others to come in. This could take a while."

"It's already *taken* a while," Austin complains.

"Just let them do their thing," Mason says. "The end results are always worth it."

Colton raises his glass. "Amen to that."

I let their banter wash away the residual stress and chuckle to myself. "Where are they?" I ask.

"My bathroom," Mason says. "Enter at your own risk. These two pestered them until Jam threatened bodily harm to the next person who interrupts."

Colton chuckles. "Which is hilarious because she couldn't hurt a fly."

Austin glares at him. "Lead the way, big guy."

"Fuck no," Colton cries, shaking his head. "I want to get laid tonight. Noel will tell me to give her some fucking space, or I'll be back to dating my hand. I *just* got out of that relationship, man. I ain't going back."

"Send Ryan," Austin says. "He's good at crisis management."

I look up at the ceiling when the girls laugh again. "I didn't know it was a crisis." It doesn't sound like one.

Austin grabs a water bottle off the table and opens it. "It's probably not. But Ryan can get answers about how much longer it will take without setting off that bomb," he says over the crinkle of protesting plastic.

Shaking my head, I decide to take one for the team. Or maybe I'm just hoping for a glimpse of Heidi. I move toward the stairs. "Allow me."

"Been nice knowing you," Austin calls after me.

"He's the safest of all of us," Colton says, pitching his voice loudly enough for me to hear. "None of them officially own his balls. They won't do anything to him until that changes."

I wouldn't bet on that. But I should be able to get answers without making any of them feel like I'm rushing them.

I let myself into Mason and Fern's bedroom and tap lightly on the bathroom door. The chatter within cuts off.

"Colton, go away," Noel snaps.

Maybe they were right to warn me ... I'm not giving up that easily, though. I'm not Colton, so her bark is worse than her bite. "I'm just checking to see if you ladies need anything in there. Water? Wine? Margaritas?"

"Chris!" six distinct voices say at once, making me laugh.

"Oh shit, we're late!" Fern says. The door opens a crack, and she beams up at me. "We'll be right out! Just had a little makeup emergency."

"And to think, Colton and Austin said y'all would have my balls for interrupting," I tell her, grinning.

"It was the offer of margaritas that saved you," Noel says.

"Chocolate would've worked too," Tara adds.

"Duly noted. But really, do you need anything?"

"Just for you to go away," one of them mutters, just loud enough for me to hear but too soft to determine who, but my money is on Noel.

I hold up both hands and take a step back. I'm dying to know how Heidi's holding up, but I know when it's time to bow out gracefully, and it's time. "I'll be downstairs."

Austin jumps up off the couch and throws his hands up in the air. "He *lives!*"

"They'll be right down," I say, rolling my eyes. "The official excuse is a makeup emergency, but I think they lost track of time."

"They lost track of their minds," Colton mutters.

"Remember that when Noel comes down the stairs," Mason tells him.

Colton laughs. "Have you *seen* my wife? She knows she doesn't have to dress up for me."

Heels on hardwood announce the impending arrival of one of the ladies we're waiting for. My heart beats a little harder with every step closer. *Breathe, Chris.*

Mason's eyebrows inch upwards. "Women don't dress up for us. They dress up for themselves; it's just a bonus if we like it. If they were doing it for us, they'd stay home and put on lingerie. Or just get naked. Naked is always good."

Noel's voice precedes her down the stairs. "Give the man a cookie!"

She steps into view, but I'm watching Colton. His eyes lock on her, and I'm not sure he's aware anyone else is in the room. He clenches his jaw and swallows hard.

Mason laughs. He smiles and somehow manages to look innocent when his words are anything but, "Fern has my favorite cookie."

"Guess you'll just have to eat dessert later," Noel says with a shrug and a perfectly straight face while the rest of us laugh.

"What's so funny?" Fern says from the top of the stairs. She practically runs down them in her ridiculously high heels, but Tara follows at a sedate pace, clutching the railing for balance in a way that makes me want to help her, but I know better. She'll ask if she needs a hand. She clears the stairs and heads straight for the door, patting my arm as she passes.

"Cookies," Mason says.

Fern scowls at him. "We're going to dinner! You can eat cookies when we get home."

He eyes her up and down. "I intend to."

Fern's cheeks turn pink, but she waves toward the door. "The others are right behind us. Let's head out."

"Good," I say, glancing toward the stairs again in hopes of some sign of Heidi. "I wasn't going to say it earlier, but Ryan thinks his shirt is going to kill him."

"He'll live," Noel says. She grabs Colton's arm and tugs. "Come on."

"What's the rush?" he asks, resisting her attempts to move him with no effort on his part. "We've waited on you. I'm not done with my drink."

Mason and I wince. This is *not* going to end well.

Austin smirks. "You enjoy flirting with death, don't you?" he asks Colton.

Colton grins at him. "What can I say? She's fun when she's mad."

"See how fun you think I am when you're sleeping on the couch. Outside. Now."

Her threat has him shooting to his feet. "Yes, ma'am."

"We know who wears the pants in that relationship," Austin mutters.

"I think lack of pants is the point," his brother says.

"It is!" Colton calls from the front door.

"Touché," Austin says, trying and failing horribly, to mimic Ryan's French accent.

Fern grabs Mason by the arm and tugs. "After you, m'love," he says as he rises. "I'll follow you anywhere. Especially if you're wearing that dress."

The staccato taps of multiple pairs of heels pull my attention to the stairs again. I hold my breath, but it's only Madi and Jam. "What's so funny down here?" Madi asks over the fresh wave of laughter. She and Jam descend side by side, and they both grin at me.

"These guys think they're comedians," Fern calls back to her.

Jam marches straight to Austin and drags him out too, but Madi comes to me. She waits until the door is closed behind them to speak. "Heidi is nervous," she whispers.

"What's wrong?" I ask, ready to charge up the stairs and offer her whatever reassurance she needs. My mind runs away with me, conjuring different scenarios. I'm sure it's nothing to do with her dress or any of that, or the girls would have it resolved already. Is it something to do with me?

Madi turns and looks toward the stairs, pitching her voice low in case Heidi should make an appearance. "It's her first date, Chris. And . . . She told us about her ex and everything. I think she expected us to kick her out after, and we didn't. I'm not sure she knows how to handle that."

She told them? I'm so proud of her, but worried too. Madi is right. She's probably overwhelmed. I take a step toward the stairs without making a conscious decision to do so, and Madi grabs my arm, holding me back. "Give her a minute to come down on her own before you go charging up there. Sometimes, a queen needs to be her own hero if she's going to hold her head high."

I want to argue, but I can't refute the wisdom there. There's a difference between Heidi *needing* my help and wanting it. This isn't like the night she showed up at my door in a panic. She needs to face this one herself.

Still, it sucks. I don't *want* her to face it alone. "Thanks, Madi."

She pats my arms and turns for the door. I track her movement with my ears, but my eyes stay on the stairs. The door opens and closes, then the house falls silent. I listen hard, straining to detect the slightest hint of distress from upstairs. Any sign that it's time for me to step in.

Heels strike the floor upstairs—slow, cautious steps as opposed to the confident strides of the others.

"It's just you and me, honey," I call up to her, letting her know it's safe if she's worried about facing anyone else right now.

A foot comes into view, then the other. Glittery toes peek out of the end of black heels. Another step reveals tanned, toned calves. Turquoise fringe flutters around her thighs, swinging to and fro with each step she takes. My eyes devour her as she descends one slow step at a time until she's standing before me, her eyes a storm of emotions—excitement, uncertainty, maybe a little bit of lust. I need to say something, but the words are lost somewhere between my brain and my throat.

She turns in a slow circle, giving me a good look at the low-cut back of her dress and that cute little ass.

Facing me again, she smiles. "When Noel said we were gonna knock y'all dead, I didn't think she meant it literally."

"I'm sorry. I'm just . . ."

"Speechless?"

"Yes."

"I'll take it."

Now that my mouth has remembered how words work, more of them are coming back to me. "Madi said you're nervous?"

"I'm alright now," she says with a small shrug of her shoulders. "Today was just . . . a lot."

"Do you need to talk about it?"

"The others are waiting," she says, leaning to look toward the door.

"They'll wait."

She shakes her head, making the feather in her hair bob and sway. "I'm alright. Maybe later, once I've had more time to think about it all."

I'm so proud of her. She's come so far since she moved in. But, as Ryan and Gabe just proved to me, sometimes the best way to get over anxiety about something is to face it. "I can understand that. Are you ready then?"

"Not quite yet." She steps forward, closing the distance I was careful to keep between us, and throws her arms around my neck. "I haven't seen you in two whole days."

My hands span her waist, trying to maintain some distance between us. I'm already hard as steel after watching her walk down the stairs. Having her pressed against me will make it worse.

"Did you miss me?" I ask. I wish I could kiss her, but I don't want to mess up her makeup. Those two days were hard for me too.

"So much," she whispers, inching her mouth closer to mine.

"I don't want to ruin your lipstick."

"I have more in my bag."

"Yeah? You planning on needing it?"

"Mmmhmm. If my—I mean you—"

I cut her off, stealing her words with a kiss. *Boyfriend.* She was about to say boyfriend. I haven't been that to anyone since Lydia, really. Becca was the closest I came, but she couldn't commit to me *and* my son. That's the defining factor for me, and Heidi already met that requirement.

"Were you about to call me your boyfriend, sweet Heidi?"

Her cheeks flush as red as her lipstick. "Sorry," she whispers.

"I'm not." This thing is progressing fast. Faster than any relationship I've ever pursued. It's just . . . right. Natural. Easy as breathing. "Not if that's what you want."

Her eyes shine so brightly it almost hurts to look at them. "It is."

"Well then, I guess that's what I am. Are you ready?" It's a loaded question. Ready for tonight. Ready to be mine. Ready for whatever that means for our future. Ready *for* that future.

Heidi steals another sweet kiss. "Ready when you are."

Chapter 29
Heidi

The limo turns down a side street in a questionable area of town. The sort of place Dean and I lived for the first couple of years after we ran away—dark streets, ramshackle abandoned buildings, and a populace who didn't see anything. The perfect place for a couple of kids to get lost because none of the other inhabitants want to draw the attention of the law by reporting them.

Those areas aren't safe, though. Reflexively, I scoot a little closer to Chris and try my best to look at everything at once. We *must* have taken a wrong turn . . . who would put a nightclub in a place like this? And why would these well-to-do people frequent it? It's one big fuckup waiting to happen.

I open my mouth to ask if we're lost, but the limo stops and everyone else prepares to get out. *What the hell is going on?* The driver opens the door and Ryan, the closest to it, climbs out first. The others join him one by one until it's my turn. He's still there, waiting with his hand out to help me. *I never thought I'd feel safer because Ryan was with me.* He smiles when I take his hand like he's having the same thoughts.

"Where *are* we?" I ask, whipping my head back and forth the check the shadows for other shadows. The group is large enough to deter most petty thieves, but numbers are not a deterrent if there's enough of them, and they're armed. I've witnessed it.

People line the block in front of us. It's hard to tell in the gloom, but they all appear to be dressed up—just like us. *They can't be serious.*

"It's safer than it looks," Fern tells me. "The owners put a lot of money back into the community and, surprisingly, no one has screwed that up for everyone else yet."

The limo dropped us off at the back of the line, but she saunters past the queue like it doesn't exist. Chris grabs my hand and pulls me along after her.

"What about the line?" I whisper, but he doesn't hear me.

The bouncer on door duty nods and reaches for the velvet rope. "Your majesty," he says with a grin, bowing deeply. "Good to have you back."

"Thank you, Teddy," she says, leaving Mason's side to hug the man like he's an old friend. "Are we gonna do our song later?"

"You know it," Teddy says, patting her back. "Have a good evening, y'all."

"Man, that is such bullshit!" a guy near the front of the line complains. "I've been waiting here for two hours, and you just let them in? It's my birthday, damn it!"

"Keep runnin' your mouth, and you can find your way to the back of the line," Teddy tells him. "The owners don't wait in line."

Owners? . . . Fern. That would explain why she knows what the owners do for the community. And why she's comfortable walking past the line like she, well . . . owns the place. The guy keeps grumbling, but he lowers his voice. Chris pushes me ahead of him, and I fall in line between him and Trista, who reaches back to grab my hand.

"Hang on," she calls over the noise coming from the open door. She pulls me through the door, and it's like stepping into another world. Fog curls through the air like cigarette smoke without the vile scent. Lights dance and strobe. Music vibrates my bones. And there are so many people. *This would be a pickpocket's dream.*

Tris tugs my hand, reminding me to keep moving when I want to stop and gawk. Ryan cuts a path through the crowd to a metal stairway and steps aside, waving Tris and me onward. I follow her up, expecting her to drop my hand, but she doesn't. When we reach the top, she leads me to the edge of the balcony.

"This is the best view," she says over the fading notes of the song. There's a stage against one wall and a little area next to it that's separated from the chaos by an L-shaped counter. A huge bar takes up most of another wall, and there are some tables scattered around the edges of the room. But the middle of the floor is packed with dancers.

The song's last note dies, and the swirling, colorful lights go out with it. The old warehouse seems to hold its breath, waiting for whatever comes next. The lights come back up, but they're all yellow this time, bathing everything in a golden glow. The crowd cheers loudly enough to vibrate the floor under my feet.

"Ladies and gentlemen," a voice comes across the loudspeaker. "You know what that means. And if you don't, well, you're in for a treat. The one and only Killer Queen has blessed us with her presence tonight."

The guy behind the counter next to the stage holds his hand in front of a microphone and begins snapping his fingers. The rhythm is quickly picked up by the people on the dancefloor and carries on when the next song starts.

"Who is the Killer Queen?" I ask Trista.

"Fern," she says. "It was her stage name when she sang here for tips—before she bought the place, obviously."

"This is so wild," I murmur. My life has turned on its head. I have friends. They work. They *buy* things. Not just things, whole fucking businesses. I can go places with them without worrying about them getting caught breaking the law. *This is amazing.*

A pretty woman who looks like a living statue approaches us to take our drink orders. She's different shades of bronze from head to toe—even her dress. She asks for my ID, and for the first time in my life, I don't have to pray because it's not a fake.

The waitress leaves, and so does Trista. She goes to Ryan and leads him downstairs by his tie, which is now hanging loose around his neck, and the collar he covertly fussed with all through dinner is unbuttoned.

An arm slips around my waist, and the body it's attached presses close behind me. "Dance with me, gorgeous," Chris purrs in my ear.

That one sentence, somewhere between a question and an order, sends a thrill down my spine. His hand finds mine, and he leads me to the stairs. We find a space on the dancefloor that's not in the way of five different couples and their fancy moves, and Chris turns me to face him.

"I don't know how to do all that," I tell him, tipping my head toward a couple in the middle of some complicated spin.

He smiles and leans in to rest his forehead against mine. "We'll teach you."

"You *can* do that?" I ask, trying to hold back the excitement bubbling in my chest. That looks like a lot of fun. I'd love to learn how.

"Yep. It's just a two-step."

I watch from the corner of my eye. "They're taking a lot more than two steps . . ."

Chris laughs and hugs me. "Martin and Lola taught all of us when we were kids," he says, a hint of hero-worship for the couple warming his voice. "It's easier than it looks. But for now, we'll just stay right here." He sways us side to side.

Fern's lovely voice settles over the room like a magic spell. She croons an old slow song I vaguely remember listening to in the car with my mom once while Chris and I dance. "She's amazing," I say on a sigh.

Chris nods. "She is. But so are you. I'm proud of you for telling the girls. I know how hard it was to make that decision."

I squeeze him tightly and lay my head on his shoulder. "It was harder to live with the fear. I finally realized that."

He turns his head and his warm breath fans across my cheek before he kisses it. "And now, you have nothing left to be afraid of."

He's right. I don't. I'm finally free.

For the second time today, I have the urge to pinch myself. This has to be a dream. Tonight, I'm not hiding anything from anyone. Keaton isn't going to come running in and catch us. The girls all know my story, and if their guys don't already,

I'm sure they will soon enough. I can stay right here, in Chris's arms, all night without a care in the world.

Chapter 30
Heidi

E asy Speak is great. So are dates—if the one is anything to judge the rest by. And dancing... The simple joy of being able to do so quickly morphed into something primal thanks to his breath on my skin and his body held so close to mine. The warmth of his arm around me. Our clasped hands. The gleam of excitement in his eyes slowly burning brighter and hotter with each new song.

No words are spoken. We don't need them. We can say it all with looks and smiles.

But I'm not sad when Mason taps Chris on the shoulder to say it's time to go. I'm ready to go home—my house, his, I don't care as long as there is privacy. A place where we can communicate with touches and kisses.

I did as he asked. It was hell, but I made it. Now, I want my reward.

No one is interested in talking much on the ride home. From the secret looks and shared smiles, it's pretty obvious everyone in the car has one thing on their minds. Chris passes the time by taking my hair down, his patient fingers searching out every single pin. As innocent as it may be, that touch is fuel for a fire that's already burning too hot after weeks of wanting and days of teasing. I press my thighs together, willing myself to hold on just a little longer.

To my delight, the driver drops us off in reverse order, starting at Fern and Mason's, so we're the third stop. The driver opens the door and helps me out. I step aside but linger on the sidewalk, waiting for Chris to lead the way.

Unlike before, he guides me with a hand on my back. After hours spent in his arms, so close to what I wanted but couldn't have, my panties are drenched. The heat of his hand sends a rush of heat spreading down my thighs.

His front door closes behind us, hiding us away from the rest of the world. I reach for him, but he grabs my hands. "No. Wait until we're upstairs."

Groaning, I turn and follow him to his room, my hands shaking with the effort of keeping them to myself. He closes the bedroom door behind us and flips on the lights. I reach for him again, but he stops me. "Wait."

"Why?" I asked, forcing the word between clenched teeth. *I didn't know control meant torture by withholding to him.*

"Why not? What's the rush?" He looks at me with eyes full of promises, and whatever he sees on my face makes him smile. "Patience, sweet Heidi. And keep your hands to yourself until I say otherwise. Did you wait for me?"

"Yes." I hated every minute of it, but I did it. I wrap my arms around my middle to control the urge to touch him.

"Good. Turn around."

I growl to vent my frustration with everything about this situation, that I've waited *days* to get off. That he won't let me touch him. That he won't touch *me*. "Why?"

"Because I told you to."

Rolling my eyes, I do as ordered. The heat of his body washes over my back, but he keeps some small space between us. His hands gather my hair and sweep it over my shoulder, then his warm lips brush across the base of my neck, sending a shiver of need down my spine.

"Oh," I sigh, giving myself over to his touch.

He blows softly on that same spot, the cool air causing my skin to erupt in goosebumps after the heat of his mouth. "Please," I whisper. There's time later for foreplay. I don't need it tonight, and I doubt he does either.

If he hears my plea, he ignores it. His head dips lower and lower, kissing his way down the exposed skin of my spine until he reaches my dress. He pauses there and traces the line of my dress with a calloused finger.

"Please!" I try again, begging him to put his mouth on me again.

"I love it when you beg," he murmurs as he grasps the tab on my zipper. He tugs it down a bit and presses a kiss to the newly exposed skin. Again and again, until he's kneeling behind me. My skin is so sensitive that I feel every brush of his lips between my legs by the time he runs out of zipper.

I reach to push the straps off my shoulders, but he stops me with a word. "Why?" I ask.

"Because I want to do it." His calloused hands skim up my back, sending bolts of pleasure straight to my throbbing core. He nudges the straps off my shoulders, and his hands follow them down my arms.

"Damn it, Chris. You're driving me crazy!"

"But it feels good, doesn't it?" he asks, easing my dress over my hips.

I hate to admit it, but he's right. "Yes," I answer before he can decide he needs to make me.

His lips chase my dress down my legs until it's a turquoise puddle around my feet and I'm standing before him in nothing but my bra and panties. I don't feel exposed or vulnerable, though. He already knows my darkest secrets. Revealing my body is nothing in comparison.

Each new kiss sends a rush of sensation *everywhere* until I'm certain the slightest touch anywhere on my body will send me headfirst into the best orgasm of my life. "Step out," he says, smoothing his hand up the back of my thigh to my butt.

I lift each foot, stepping clear of my dress. He grabs it and rises, taking it to his closet. "No sense in leaving it on the floor to get wrinkled," he says, flinging a crooked smile over his shoulder at me.

I bite my tongue to keep quiet. I don't know if I want to groan, sigh, or beg him to come back, or maybe a combination of the three. The touches and kisses were nothing compared to the torture of him stopping. *He's just hanging up my dress. He'll be right back. I can do this.*

But he's still smiling that same, crooked smile when he turns around, and I question my assumption. *He's going to make me wait.* Those wicked hands go to his tie. He loosens it and lifts it over his head, then hangs it on a hook inside his closet. He shrugs out of his suit jacket and hangs it up as well. Starting at his cuffs, he unbuttons his shirt with meticulous care, watching me all the while. His eyes roam my body, leaving a trail of heat in their wake that sustains my need for him.

"You're beautiful," he whispers while he works. "I should tell you that more, but I don't care much about a person's looks, and I was afraid you'd misunderstand. So let me explain."

His white button-down comes off, and he tosses it in a basket, followed by his undershirt, leaving him naked from the waist up. And this time, I don't have to pretend I don't want to look. My eyes bounce between his abs and his hands while he takes off his belt. I wrap my arms around my middle again and force myself to stand my ground. I'll be able to explore him later.

"What's outside is just a shell; it's what's inside that matters to me." His pants slide down his legs, but it's the crown of his dick peeking out of the waistband of his boxer briefs that holds my attention as his words wash over me. "But you're just as beautiful inside as you are out."

A tear rolls down my cheek, but I ignore it. Who I am as a person has never mattered to anyone else. I don't know that he's right, but I try to be a good person. Me standing here, transfixed by his body, probably indicates otherwise, but what he's saying about me is true for him as well. I've known he was a beautiful soul since the day we met, when he gave me space to handle my panic on my own. *And that's when I started to fall.*

The random thought startles me, but it's the truth. I fall for him a little more every day, but I can't tell him that. Not until I'm sure he's ready to catch me.

His pants and socks land in the clothes basket. "I wanted you to know that before we go any further." Clad in nothing but his underwear, he comes to stand before me and pulls me into a hug. Every inch of me he's touching flares to life again, burning for more of his brand of sweet torture. "And, as corny as it probably sounds, your soul talks to mine. I don't know how else to put it, but I feel it every time I see you. Especially when I hold you," he whispers the last words as if saying them too loudly will frighten me. His eyes betray his concern, but he has nothing to fear.

"I feel it too," I whisper. It's something different than falling for him. Something bigger. I didn't recognize it before, but it was there all along—the little voice in the back of my mind urging me to trust him.

It wasn't just my subconscious. It was something more. *Home. This is home.* Try as I might, I can't write it off, and I can't deny it. It doesn't matter that we hardly know each other, or that I'm younger, or that he has a kid. This is where I'm meant to be, always and forever.

Chris cups my face in his hands. He leans in until his lips brush mine and whispers, "Good," before laying claim to my mouth. His tongue slides against mine, urging it into a dance as one of his hands skims down my side to the waistband of my panties. I moan, anticipating the moment his fingers find their way under that elastic to explore my most intimate place. I *need* his touch more than oxygen or food or water. Nothing else will do now.

He breaks our kiss to ask, "Is this what you want? We can stop." There's a smile in his eyes that says he's joking, but I know he'll follow through if I say yes.

But *hell no*, that's not what I want. At this point, I don't care if he slides my panties to the side and fucks me with them on. "Don't you *dare* stop," I say, my voice breathy with need.

Still smiling, he walks his fingers lower over the thin cotton barrier that is no protection from his heat. He grazes my clit, making me moan again. "Sweet Heidi, you're soaked. Do you want me?"

"Fuck yes." My hips rock against his fingers, seeking relief, but he withdraws his hand. "Please!"

"Soon enough."

"You are evil!" How can he build me up until I'm about to burst and then stop? Is he trying to push me until I break? Maybe I'll appreciate it more in the future, when I'm not starving for him, but this teasing is so *frustrating*. I don't want to wait anymore!

"No, I'm patient," he says, just like last time I called him evil. "Enjoy the ride."

I grab his hand and pull, trying to place it where I want it, but he resists. "I'm fucking trying to!"

"No," he says through laughter, "you want to enjoy the destination. Enjoy it all, and I'll get you to that destination more times than you think you can handle."

I scoff. "I've heard that before." Dean always talked big but couldn't back it up. He had no control. *Maybe Chris* can *keep that promise.*

He thrusts his hips against mine, teasing me with his proximity. "Honey, I may be a little out of practice, but I'm not some boy fumbling around in the dark. Trust me."

I can't contain the sass. I was willing to play nice, but nice went out the window when I crossed the line between needy and desperate. "Fine. But I have a vibrator, and I'm not afraid to use it."

Chris laughs again. "Well, that could be fun. But if you *need* it tonight, I'm doing this wrong."

"Just tonight?" I ask, just to make him laugh again. And it works.

"Eh, Keaton isn't gone every night," he says with a shrug. "Sometimes, quick and easy wins. Are you ready to trust me?"

I already do. More than you'll ever comprehend. We wouldn't be here now if I didn't. "For the sake of orgasms," I say, keeping my voice light and teasing.

"Good." He reaches around me to unclasp my bra, letting it fall to the floor, then hooks his thumbs under the elastic of my panties and tugs them down. *Yes! Finally!*

"So fucking wet," he whispers. "Damn, I love it. Get on your knees."

"Why?" I ask, but I hit my knees, my mouth already watering for that dick.

Smiling, he shakes his head. "What happened to trust?"

I look up at him and tease my bottom lip with my tongue, knowing it'll get to that control of his. "What happened to orgasms?"

His eyes zero in on my lips. In my peripheral vision, his dick twitches, straining to break free. "Heidi . . . stop being contrary for the sake of it and suck my dick."

That demand sends a jolt of excitement zinging through my center. The wait is finally over, and I'm so excited I can scarcely breathe. He told me to keep my hands to myself, so I snag the waistband of his underwear with my teeth and tug.

"Oh, fuck," he breathes.

I work them down his body, taking my time, letting my hair tease him as I go. It's only fair, after all. They land on the floor, and I sit upright again. I look up at him and swirl my tongue around his crown. *Enjoy the ride indeed.* His jaw clenches, but he fails to hold back a groan.

"Is this one of your dreams?" I ask him. I don't wait for an answer before drawing the tip of him into my mouth and sucking gently, teasing him a little more.

"No," he grits out. "But it should've been."

Why is that so hot? Another rush of liquid heat surges down my thighs. Why it's hot doesn't matter. Having a dick in my mouth shouldn't be sexy either, but it's always gotten to me. Mr. Control Freak put the power in my hands when he told me to suck him off. Little by little, I take more of him in and suck a little harder with each inch. He breathes my name, and it becomes a chant, becoming louder with each repetition.

He never rescinded his order to keep my hands to myself, but I figure it's better to ask forgiveness than permission. Cupping his balls, I squeeze, increasing the pressure until he threads his fingers through my hair and his hips begin to rock. I want him frayed around the edges, not completely undone, or he'll try to fuck my mouth. I know from experience that doesn't work for me.

His dick thickens and pulses, and my mouth fills with the salty sweetness of his precum. His balls begin to tighten in my hand, and his hands fist in my hair. *Soon.* I bring my other hand to his shaft, stroking and squeezing, urging him closer.

"I'm there," he gasps out a warning.

That warning surprises me. I expected him to take his pleasure however he wanted, not give me the option to stop. I suck once more and lean back, squeezing his shaft and his balls a little tighter. Hot ropes of cum spurt forth, painting my chest with his release. Marking me as his, if only for us.

Wild-eyed and panting, he falls on his ass on the bed, staring at his seed dripping down my breasts. "I'm sorry. I—"

"I'm not," I say, cutting him off. "You gave me a warning. This was my choice."

He blinks, then one corner of his mouth hooks up into a grin. "And you called me kinky."

I shrug. I learned more than the mechanics of stealing shit in my time with Dean and the others. "I didn't say it was a bad thing or that I wasn't. Besides, you're the one staring." I don't mind. I want him to look. It excites me in a different way, not physically but soul deep.

"I can't help it," he says, his eyes still fixed on my tits. His obvious appreciation fills me with a heady sense of power. "That's . . . fucking hot. Jesus, I think I could go again already."

Good. There's a lot more riding left to enjoy. "Well, unless you want to wear it too, I need to clean up."

He stands up and brushes a strand of hair out of my face. "Wait there."

I sit back on my heels to give my knees a break and wait while he gets a warm washcloth from the bathroom.

"May I?" he asks when he returns, his gaze glued to my tits again.

I bite back a laugh at the question. As silly as it seems, I do appreciate his consideration. "You just shot your load all over my boobs, Chris . . . yes, you can wipe it off."

He kneels in front of me and carefully wipes me clean, supporting me with one arm while he works. There's a whole book's worth of words in his eyes, but he doesn't say a thing.

"On the bed," he murmurs when he's done, then he rises and returns the washcloth to the bathroom.

He didn't specify, so I perch on the edge of the bed and wait, equal parts preoccupied with the look in his eyes before he left and excited for what happens next. He comes back and kneels on the floor in front of me again, reaching up to thread his fingers through my hair and pull me to him for a kiss.

"I'm sorry," he whispers when we break apart.

"For what?" Aside from making me wait, he's done nothing to apologize for. And really, if he follows through on his promise of multiple orgasms, I'll gladly forgive him for teasing me.

His eyes drift closed, and he lays another soft kiss on my lips. "I didn't consider that you may have been sexually abused."

Oh. That. I suppose, in a way, I was lucky there. I should've made it clear to him from the start.

"I wasn't," I assure him. "Not once. I just . . . didn't have a parent or society telling me that something was right or wrong. It's sex. Sex is fun and orgasms are good. As long as we both consent, who cares? Now. You promised me orgasms. Lots of them."

His eyes bore into mine like he's attempting to unravel the secrets of my soul. It's really not that complicated. *Peace, love, and orgasms.* "You're sure?" he murmurs.

I smile and nip at his bottom lip, hoping to inspire him into action. "I'm sure if you don't make me come soon, I'm going home to get my vibrator. And you don't get to watch."

He lunges for me, pushing me over backward. "Stay there." His hands slide up my calves to the backs of my knees, and he pushes my legs apart. *Yes!* The promise of what comes next steals my breath again and leaves me panting and pulsing with desire. "*Still* so fucking wet. Did you like sucking my dick?"

"So much," I moan, already giving myself over to anticipation. *Please don't let him be all talk.* "Next time, I'll swallow every drop you give me."

"Fuck," he whispers. "It's your turn here. You don't have to talk dirty to me."

I prop myself up on my elbows and smile. "I like it." Everything about it is perfect. He knows how I feel, what I think, what I want. And it keeps him primed and ready.

His breathing gets ragged. Eyes on mine, he inches forward and drags his velvet-soft tongue slowly up my slit. The pent-up tension from his teasing comes rushing back. My hips surge forward, begging for more while I moan his name. "Please don't stop. I'm so close."

"I knew there was a reason I call you honey," he rumbles. My clit disappears between his lips, stealing my breath. His teeth graze the sensitive little nub, and lighting bolts of sensation zip through my veins. It's pleasure and pain. It's too much and not enough. It's perfect. I need more.

"Yes, yes, yes," I whisper. "Do that. Make me come. Please."

The soft caress of his tongue is maddening after the rush of pleasure from the threat of his teeth, but he laps at me repeatedly, gentle sparks of pleasure that build and build. My muscles clench, ready for release, but he holds me on the edge of sweet bliss. My hips move faster, trying to direct him, but he throws an arm across them, holding me down.

"Please!" I whine. I've never needed to come so badly in my life, but if I don't soon, the tension in my muscles is going to break me in two.

He sucks my clit into his mouth again, and I shatter into a million pieces of pure bliss.

"Don't move," he orders.

I wasn't planning to, but I'm too content to care to talk back. He gets up, and a drawer opens and closes. Foil crinkles, then he steps back into my line of sight, rolling a condom on his thick length.

My inner muscles clench. For once, I'm not sure if I'm ready for another orgasm. But I'm going to find out.

Chapter 31
Chris

Heidi's gorgeous tits heave with her breath. Watching my cum spurt all over them was one of the most satisfyingly erotic things that has ever happened to me. Knowing she did it on purpose . . . That tops the list.

I roll the condom on with shaking hands and step between her thighs, which are still spread from my feast. Maybe she was too tired to move, but I don't think so. She's not ashamed of her body or her sexuality, which is a surprise. I expected her to be shy, or at least play coy when I told her to suck my dick. But she was eager . . .

I lift her hips off the bed and seat myself deep within her in one hard, claiming thrust. Her mouth was fantastic, but this . . . this is heaven. Tension builds in my groin, but I force myself to relax. I'm not going that easily.

"Oh, shit!" she cries, her upper body coming up off the bed. I freeze, afraid I pushed her too far. But she rests back on her elbows and rolls her hips, urging me to move. "Do it again." The walls holding me are already constricting again. She'll go easy this time if I do as she says, but that's not what I want.

I want this to last.

I want her to feel me tomorrow and remember that she's mine. She gave herself to me in more ways than one tonight.

I withdraw as quickly as I went in, smiling at her breathy cries of "yes." Her hips roll to meet me on my next thrust, but I give her the tip and hold there, enjoying the heat and the fluttering pull of her walls trying to draw me deeper and milk me for all I'm worth. *Not yet.*

As I teased her with my kisses before, I tease her with my dick this time. Forcing aside my enjoyment, I focus on her, driving just deep enough to hit that sensitive spot within but not giving her what she wants. Not yet.

"Oh, my God! What are you doing to me?" she cries. She throws herself back against the mattress and tries to take control, to fuck me harder, but she's not strong enough to break my hold.

"Enjoy the ride," I say, bracing for her sassy comeback. She only tosses her head side to side and begs me.

"I can't take it! What *is* that!" No matter what she says, I know she can. Her walls squeeze tighter still, contracting to the point I almost don't fit. It's nearly impossible to ignore how good she feels—like she was made to hold my dick—but I refuse to give in to that siren's call yet.

Sweat drips down my body from the exertion of holding myself back, but I have a promise to keep. She's going to throw out that vibrator when I'm done with her. "Come for me. Now. I know you can."

Her body goes rigid once more, and she comes screaming my name so loudly it's a damn good thing Keaton isn't home. *We're going to have to work on that.* I grit my teeth and endure the sweet agony of her orgasm trying to coax me to my own, but I'm not ready yet.

"I'm not done with you." I direct her to move up the bed and settle myself between her knees, doing my best to recreate my first dream about her.

"Oh, fuck yes. I already like this," she murmurs when I guide one of her legs to my shoulder.

"I won't last long," I warn her. I take my time sliding home this time, enjoying her heat and the way her inner walls hug me. "You were testing my limits with that last one."

She slides one hand between her legs to toy with her clit. "I'll take care of myself. Just give me that dick until you can't anymore."

Oh, fuck. My eyes follow her hand, wishing for a better angle. I could watch her touch herself all night, but the need to fuck her is all-consuming. I slide out and slam home again, eliciting a cry from her.

"Harder!" she urges. "Stop holding back, Chris. Fuck me like you dream about."

The threads of my control slip through my fingers, and I give myself over to her urgings, driving myself in hard and fast until release tears through me again. Heidi pulses around me again, and I collapse on top of her, nuzzling my face into her neck.

That was unbelievable. Hands down the best sex I've ever had in my life. I don't know if it's because I didn't hide anything or because she was such a willing participant. Her eagerness definitely didn't hurt. I just hope it was as good for her as it was for me.

I get up to deal with the condom, hating every second I'm away from her.

When I climb back in bed, I pull her body to mine like I did last time she slept here. Like last time, there's a sense of rightness to having her in my bed. Not just for sex, but for the quiet moments before sleep where touches and kisses carry a different sort of intimacy. *I want this every night.* It's the perfect end to a day.

Silence settles over us like a blanket. Her fingers comb through my hair, playing with my curls. I feel like I should say *something,* but I'll be damned if I know what.

"I thought abs were a myth," she whispers, breaking the silence. "And that sexy little V thingy you've got going on there." She leaves off playing with my hair to ghost her fingers over the muscles in question.

"Obliques," I correct her. "And no, they're not a myth. They just take a lot of work to achieve and maintain."

She hums appreciatively. "I don't care what you call them. I like them. Keep up the good work."

"Yes, ma'am," I tell her, laughing. "So, did I fulfill my promise to your satisfaction?" I finally ask.

She breathes out a little laugh. "I never thought I'd say this, but I think I had enough orgasms for one night."

"I'll take that as a yes."

"Definitely," she says on a sleepy sigh.

"Good. Good night, sweet Heidi," I whisper, hugging her closer.

"Good night."

Chapter 32
Chris

Sunshine on my face wakes me up. *I forgot to close the shades.* Heidi sighs and mumbles in her sleep. Only one word is distinguishable—"mom." I know she mentioned wanting to reach out to her mother again when she told me about her trauma. I wonder if she ever did. Is it wrong of me to hope she didn't? At least, not if her stepdad is still in the picture. Heidi's turnaround might be the impetus her mother needs to break her own cycle and get away from her abuser, but what would it cost Heidi to welcome that drama back into her life?

Heidi! The sleep fog clouding my brain clears under the assault of memories from last night. Her mouth—my *cum* on her tits. The lack of judgment. Her utter delight in the things we did with our bodies. It was all so unexpected. And so unbelievably sexy. I didn't know I needed it. Others have merely humored me, but not Heidi.

She sighs, her breath tickling a bit as it fans across my chest, and her breathing changes. Instead of the slow, even tides that come with sleep, each breath comes quicker. She's awake but maybe not ready to be.

Should I let her go back to sleep if that's what she wants, or should I give her a couple more orgasms? There's time before I have to go collect Keaton . . .

Her hand slips off my waist and goes to my abs. What she said last night rings in my ears, *"I thought abs were a myth. And that sexy little 'V' thingy you've got going on there."* I do my best not to react and let her explore as she will, but each stroke of those soft fingers increases the likelihood of orgasms. I was already hard, but it's no longer merely morning wood.

Still, I control my body and pray she lets her hand stray lower. There's something there she can explore for a while too.

Try as I might, it's impossible to stay relaxed. She has to know I'm awake, but she gives no sign of it if she does. I grit my teeth to keep myself from begging her as she did me last night.

Little by little, her hand inches closer. My dick twitches, trying desperately to catch her attention, but she doesn't seem to notice. Her concentration is fixed on exploring the dips and ridges of my abs and obliques.

It twitches again, and her body shakes with a silent giggle. She reaches lower and wraps those curious fingers around my shaft, squeezing me like she did last night with my dick in her mouth. It's all I can take not to jack my hips and fuck her hand.

"Fucking finally," I breathe.

She giggles again, out loud this time. "I wasn't sure if you were awake or not. You were so still!"

"I was giving you time to confirm that abs are real."

She hums a hungry note and squeezes me again. "Yes, they are."

I shift my upper body to the side so I can see her. She looks up at me, but the tilt of her head and her guarded eyes come across as timid. "What's wrong?" I ask. If she doesn't want sex this morning, she only has to say so. I can take care of myself—she can even watch if she wants to. I don't care if that's what does it for her.

"Nothing," she says quickly.

"Heidi, after everything we did last night, how can you look shy with my dick in your hand?"

Her cheeks flush a beautiful shade of pink. It might be my new favorite color. *I'll have to compare it to the shade between her legs.* "A good night of sleep and morning light . . . change things."

Fear grips my spine, redirecting my blood flow to my brain to support the adrenaline rush. I was too much for her last night. It was all great at the time, when she was frustrated and horny. But now . . . *Then why is she still holding my dick?*

"I'm . . . sorry?" I ask, not bothering to mask my confusion.

She shakes her head. "I'm not. Last night was great. But . . ."

"But?"

"I just . . . am sorry if I was too . . . everything."

I have no idea what that means, but she wasn't 'too' anything. "What you were is fucking sexy," I tell her. "Last night was the best sex of my life, no holds barred. The only reason I didn't roll you over and fuck you again when I first realized you were awake is that you didn't move, so I thought you needed more sleep. But if you'd like me to prove that I was lying here, thinking about last night and going crazy to have you again, just say the word."

"Oh, thank fuck." She sits up and grabs the blankets, ripping them off our bodies to throw her leg over me.

Her relief is but an echo of mine. After that heart-stopping panic, my desire for her is more of a need—one she seems happy to meet.

"Condom!" I say, stopping her from immediately seating herself on my dick.

She groans and huffs out a sigh but lunges for my nightstand. I reach to take the foil packet from her, but she tears it open and sits back on my thighs to roll it on. She sits up on her knees again and notches the tip of my dick in her glistening pussy.

"You're not going to stop me?" she asks, watching me. There's a hint of defiance looking back at me, like she might make me work for it if I decide to try. But we played by my rules last night. She can run things today.

"Why the fuck would I stop you?" If I wanted to be in control, she wouldn't have gotten that far. Watching her take charge is fucking sexy, and there's no way in hell I want her to stop.

She shrugs. "Well, you like to be bossy."

"Sometimes. I don't need it every time. Unless you *want* me to." I always enjoy it, but I only crave it when something in life feels like it's spiraling out of control.

"Don't care." She lowers herself onto me slowly. Agonizingly slow, but I enjoy every second it takes for her tight little pussy to take me in. My eyes dart from the sight of my dick disappearing within her and the sheer bliss on her face that becomes more pronounced with every inch of me she takes. "Oh," she breathes. "It's even better than I remember."

"Yes, it is," I agree through gritted teeth, pushing down the need to move within her. "You were made for my dick."

She opens her mouth, no doubt to smart off judging by the fire in her eyes. My phone rings before she utters a syllable.

"Seriously?" she asks when I reach for it, wiggling her hips to prove a point.

"Could be Keaton."

"Oh . . . good point."

Nicole's name glares up at me from the screen, over a picture of her smiling at me behind an extended middle finger. The picture usually makes me laugh, but something's wrong if she's calling now. Heart pounding as my brain jumps to a variety of worst-case scenarios, I swipe to answer the call and mash the phone to my ear.

"What's wrong?" I ask.

"Nothing is . . . *wrong*. But I learned the hard way what a morning after a first date at Easy Speak looks like. So I'm calling to warn you that Fern and Mason picked Ronni up early because she wasn't feeling well, and Keaton begged them to take him home."

Relief sweeps through me. "And they caved." Of course, they caved. Since I'm balls deep in my beautiful new girlfriend, this is really nothing to smile about, but I can't help it.

She makes a noise in the affirmative. "Like a wet paper sack. So this is your twenty-minute warning to have your ass decent when your kid gets home unless you want to field some really awkward questions about pee-pees and hoo-has."

"Noted. Thanks for the heads up."

"You assholes owe me."

"Yeah, we do." I clear my throat. "I always love to pick on you, Nikki, but uh—"

"Go. Get laid. Have glorious loud sex without fear of disturbing Keaton. But it's my turn soon." She hangs up before I can tell her to pick a date.

"What's wrong?" Heidi asks, forcing my focus where it belongs now that I know everything is alright with a rock of her hips.

"Mase and Fern are bringing Keaton home. We've got fifteen minutes if you want to get home before he does so he can come invite you to breakfast."

"We better hurry then."

She grabs my hands and moves them to her tits. *I fucking love this.* I tease my thumbs over her nipples. Her answering moan is sweet music. She braces her hands on my chest and rolls her hips, moving faster and faster, squeezing tighter with every thrust. "Don't you dare come yet," she orders breathlessly.

Fuck, I like it when she's bossy. I knew I liked issuing orders, but the reverse is new for me and just as good. My jaw is clenched too tightly to speak, so I shake my head. I won't until she does.

She shifts, adjusting her angle so that her clit slides against my dick, then drops her head to watch. *Fuck, that's hot.*

"Heidi!" I manage to bite out as she pushes me dangerously close to my bliss.

"No," she says without looking away from the place we're joined. "Don't. Hold on for me."

"Hurry." I pinch her nipples and tug, hoping the shock of it will send her over the edge.

The muscles around me clench one more time, then pulse and flutter. "Not yet!" she cries. "Wait."

She's so tight and so hot, and each quiver of her inner walls beckons me closer to my release.

Her movements slow. She sits upright and switches from rolling her hips to working herself up and down, her tits bouncing in my hands. She slips one hand between us and works her clit. "Almost," she whispers.

This isn't a woman. This is a magnificent sex goddess. I push her hand away and replace it with mine, soaking my fingers in her juices and lavishing her greedy little clit with the attention it deserves. Her head falls back, allowing her long hair to tease my thighs with every bounce. It's almost too much. My balls tighten, anticipating release from this beautiful agony.

"So close!" She grabs her tits, pinching her nipples and rolling them between her thumbs and index fingers. *She needs to hurry.* I can only hold back so long, and with her doing sexy little things like that, my limit is close. "Tell me."

"Come for me," I say, knowing exactly what she needs from me. Her body goes rigid, and that delicious bouncing slows. She bows forward, her pussy spasming around me again. My orgasm bulldozes through my control, refusing to wait another second. I come so hard my vision blurs, and my body shakes with the force of it, leaving me utterly spent.

"Oh my God..." she moans, her words slurred from her sex drunkenness. "You did it. I didn't think you could do it."

"Huh?" I grunt, incapable of forming words.

"You waited for me."

I force my arm to cooperate and grab my phone to check the time. *Ten minutes. She came twice in ten minutes...* "Don't ask me how. You were killing me. Do you have any idea how fucking sexy you are?"

Her post-orgasm glow deepens to a blush, and she ducks her head, letting her hair fall forward to hide her face.

"I'll take that as a no. We'll work on that because you are a fucking goddess, and I am not worthy. But, you'd best let me up to deal with this damn condom. And you need to clean up and get your cute little ass home. What do you want for breakfast?"

Biting her bottom lip, she peers at me through the curtain of her hair. "You," she says, a smile slowly spreading across her face.

"Two wasn't enough?"

She clears her throat. "Ordinarily, I'd say one can never have enough orgasms. But last night, you introduced me to quality over quantity. However, I'm greedy, and now I need both."

I check the time again, but after what she just did to me there's no way in *hell* I can be ready to go again before my son gets home. "Well, if you can wait until this evening, I'd be happy to oblige. But we're going to have to work on keeping it down."

"Oh, I can be quiet," she says, climbing off me. "I just don't want to if I don't have to." She moves to crawl out of bed but stops. An angelic smile lights her face in the morning sunlight as she leans in for a kiss. "Good morning."

"Yes, it is," I murmur against her lips.

"I'm borrowing one of your shirts to wear home. You clean up. I'll let myself out, and I'll see you again in a little bit."

She steals one more kiss and bounces out of bed. How is this my life? Because I am one lucky sonofabitch.

Heidi

I clean up as best I can without jumping in the shower and scramble into clothes. Bits and pieces of memories from last night and this morning pop into my head like bubbles in a champagne glass, making it hard to concentrate on anything other than Chris. Last night was phenomenal. That's the only word for it. Absolutely worth the wait. Ten out of ten, would ride that ride again.

Either I took longer cleaning up than I thought or Chris's fifteen-minute guesstimate was off, because Keaton knocks on my back door while I'm buttoning my jeans.

I rush to the back door, eager to see his bright smile again, but find him in his father's arms. One look at that little face and my heart breaks. His eyes are all red and swollen, and his face is wet with tears shining in the morning light. I yank the door open and reach out to him. "What's wrong?"

He balls up both fists and rubs his eyes. "I—I—I—" he can't get the words out through his sobs.

"Mase said he cried all the way here," Chris tells me. "I haven't been able to get more than 'Heidi' and 'breakfast' out of him, so I thought I'd bring him over to see if you can cheer him up while I start breakfast."

"Oh, sugar bear. Come here." I reach for him, and he practically throws himself into my arms. "We'll be alright," I mouth to Chris once Keaton is settled on my hip.

He nods and waves and grabs the door to close it behind me. "Come on over when you're ready."

Keaton's sobs continue full force until I get to the living room to sit down. He catches sight of my shelf full of the treasures he's given me, and his sobs quiet into hiccups and sniffles. "Wo-ow! I-it's beautif-f-ful."

I kiss his cheek and cross to the shelf so he can see better. "They're my favorite decorations ever. I'll keep them always."

"Really?"

"Really." While he looks his fill, I rub his back. "You wanna tell us why you were so upset?" Hopefully, my question won't cause a new wave of tears.

His face puckers again, but he holds back the sobs long enough to wail, "The sun is up. I missed breakfast."

"You didn't miss anything! We waited for you." It's not *quite* the truth, but it also isn't a lie. I don't think food was high on the priority list for either of us.

"But we missed the sun!"

"Oh, sugar bear." I hug him as tight as I dare and try not to melt into a big puddle of goo. "Do you know why my favorite part of Sunday morning breakfast is?"

"The sun?" he asks, his words muffled by my shoulder.

"Nope. It's spending time with you."

"And Daddy?"

"... Yes." I hesitate to answer, worried I might cross a line by doing so, but I don't want to lie to him and make him think I don't care for his father. That will only confuse him when Chris *does* tell him about us. "And your daddy. It's okay if we miss the sunrise sometimes, as long as I get to see you. Should we go see what your dad is cooking?"

He sniffles and nods. "Yeah."

I slide my feet into my slip-on house shoes because I don't want to put Keaton down in case doing so causes more tears, and shuffle across the yard.

Chris looks over his shoulder and his obvious relief to see his child tear-free changes to a knowing, impish smile that sets off a cascade of flutters in my middle when his eyes slide to me. "Good morning," he says, throwing in a wink that has me trying to smile and bite my lip all at once. "I'm being lazy today. We're having egg sandwiches."

It takes some effort, but I manage to tamp down my giddiness while I help Keaton close the door. It would be easy enough to explain away my excitement—I'm just so happy to see him—but I don't want to invite his curiosity. It's best if I can just act normal. "Sounds good to me." I crouch down and set Keaton on his feet. "He was upset because he missed sunrise, but we've got it all lined out, don't we sugar bear?"

Keaton nods and wraps his arms around my leg. "Daddy, can we eat outside upstairs again?"

Chris looks over his shoulder again and mouths, "outside upstairs . . . Oh! On the balcony? No problem, bud. Why don't you show Heidi where the blankets are, and the two of you can lay them out?"

"Okay. Come on." He releases my leg to grab my hand and lead me out of the room. I glance at Chris, and he winks again, causing another wave of flutters. *Breakfast is going to be . . . interesting.*

Chapter 33
Chris

With a yawn, I plug my phone in for the night. It's late—for me—but since Keaton's birthday is tomorrow, I wanted to put his present together before turning in. It went much smoother than anticipated with Heidi's help, though.

I can't believe she's been mine for a whole month now. That night in early November when she claimed me as her boyfriend seems like forever ago now. On Thanksgiving, even my mother mentioned that Heidi just seemed to belong, though Heidi herself said she felt awkward and out of place all day.

My phone buzzes, alerting me to a text. Concerned something might be wrong next door, I unlock my phone to check it.

Lydia: We need to talk

I don't need all the fingers on one hand to count the number of times Lydia has attempted to contact me in the last four years. Rolling my eyes, I tap out a reply.

Me: Becca won't be bothering you again.

The rolling ellipses pops up before I can put my phone down again, so I wait.

Lydia: I want to see him.

My phone falls to my nightstand with a clatter. *Is she fucking serious?* There's no way in hell I'm allowing that to happen. Maybe I'm a heartless bastard, but he's not an animal in a zoo she can visit on a whim and then never see again. I will *not* put my son through that.

Me: You should've thought about that four years ago. The answer is no.

I switch my phone to Do Not Disturb and lay it face-down on my nightstand. *I wish I'd never checked that message.*

I brush my teeth and climb into bed, but sleep eludes me.

***

December seventh dawns bright and clear. I sit on the edge of my bed, watching the sun creep over the trees, absorbing the quiet and attempting to clear my head. This day is always special for me, but Lydia's text tainted it this year.

The sleepless night was good for me, though. It gave me time to think.

So much has changed in the last month. They're good changes, but they weigh on me today—the cost of keeping a secret.

I love the routine Heidi and I have settled into, but hiding the truth from Keaton is getting tired. It's so hard to remember I can't kiss her in front of him, or hold her hand, put my arm around her, *anything*. I live for the moment I tuck him in bed, and she can sneak over, and that's not right. It needs to end.

Like clockwork, she comes scurrying across the yard for our few minutes alone before I have to wake Keaton, get him ready for school, and get myself ready for work. I get up and hurry down the stairs. "Morning, gorgeous," I greet her, pulling her inside for a kiss. "I was thinking, since it's Keaton's birthday, would you like to stick around and help me wake him? We can give him his present."

She gasps and does a cute little happy dance. "Yes!"

I sigh. It's best to get this out of the way now. Then we can put it behind us and have a great day. "I need to talk to you first, though."

She stops dancing and bites her lip. "Alright."

I gesture toward the table, but she shakes her head and wraps her arms around my waist. I hug her back and sigh again. "So, Lydia texted me last night." Heidi's body goes rigid at the mention of my ex. "She said she wants to see Keaton, but I told her it's not happening."

Her arms tighten around me like she knows I need the extra comfort. "Okay?" she asks, concern dampening the excitement in her eyes.

I shrug. "I just wanted you to know. I mean, I'd want to know if your ex reached out to you—mostly so I could kick his ass, but still."

That makes her smile as I hoped it would. "I appreciate that—and that you told me about Lydia."

That makes *me* smile. "Alright, should we go wake the birthday boy?"

The excitement sets her eyes ablaze again. "Absolutely. I need my sugar bear snuggles before work."

Hand in hand, we climb the stairs. He doesn't stir when we open the door. I drop Heidi's hand and give her a little push in his direction. He sees me every damn morning. I can let her have today. And, hopefully soon, we can do this together every day without fear of him figuring us out.

She climbs into his twin-sized bed and puts herself between him and the wall, then pointedly looks over him at the scant empty space on the outside edge.

Smiling to myself, I lay down behind him, keeping one foot braced on the ground so I don't fall on my ass.

"Keaton," Heidi croons softly. "Wake up, sugar bear."

He turns his head into his pillow, hiding his eyes behind his favorite puppy snuggly. Heidi grins at me and sings, "Happy birthday to you."

I join her for the rest of it, and Keaton smiles. He keeps his eyes hidden, though, pretending to be asleep.

"I guess he's going to sleep through his birthday," I say, knowing it'll get some sort of reaction out of him.

Sure enough, he giggles a bit and wiggles around, but he keeps his eyes hidden.

"Hmm, does that mean we get his presents?"

"Presents?" Keaton shouts, all pretense of sleep abandoned. "I get presents?"

"You get presents," I confirm. "Miss Heidi and I have one downstairs you can open now, but the rest have to wait until after dinner."

He stands up and climbs over me to get out of bed. "Let's go!"

"Oh, we're in a hurry now?" I tease him.

"Yes! Carry me, please, Daddy! Let's run!"

"You heard the birthday boy," Heidi says, reaching across the tiny bed to shove me out. "Let's go!"

Rolling to my feet, I scoop Keaton up and dash out the door, through the baby gate we left open on our way up, and down the stairs, right past his present.

Keaton is laughing so hard he can barely breathe, let alone speak, but he gets words out somehow. "Daddy, wait! Go back!"

To give Heidi more time to get downstairs and into position to record him, I circle the island in the kitchen before I take him back to the living room. "Oh! There it is! I forgot where I put it!" I tell him.

Heidi gives me a thumbs up, so I put Keaton down and hustle around to the other side to watch his face. It was too big to wrap, so we draped a sheet over it. He grabs one corner and takes off, walking backward to uncover the train table he's wanted for more than a year. He stops, transfixed as his bright eyes dart over every bit of the track, taking it all in.

"I promised I'd get you one for your birthday when we had a house big enough for it," I remind him.

"I love it," he says in an awed whisper. His eyes finally leave the table to look at me. "This is the best birthday ever."

"You said that last year too," I chuckle.

Squealing, he runs the few steps to the table and grabs a train. "Thank you, Daddy. Thank you, Miss Heidi!"

Pride settles in my throat and blurs my vision. The words come out thick, but I don't care. "You're welcome, bud. And good manners." I don't know how I get to be his dad, but I'm so thankful I do. Each birthday is bittersweet, the ending and beginning of another year with this amazing little human being, but I cherish each one.

Heidi gives my hand a quick squeeze and steps away, supporting me, but giving me space to deal. She crouches next to him and asks him questions about the different trains until her phone chimes a warning. "Alright, sugar bear. I need to go. Can I have a hug?"

Keat barely stops playing long enough to throw one arm around her neck and kiss her cheek. "I love you, Miss Heidi."

She gives him a big squeeze. "I love you too. You have a great day."

"Okay," he murmurs, already absorbed in his trains again.

I walk her to the back door and sneak a quick kiss. "I'll see you after work?"

"Yep. You have a great day too." Looking over my shoulder, she steals another kiss and hurries out the door.

That's the last time we hide from Keaton.

Heidi

I manage to pretend that everything is fine until Chris closes the door behind me. As soon as he can't see my face anymore, the dread I've held at bay since he mentioned the text from his ex comes flooding in. I know he still has feelings for her. He never said the words, but some things don't need to be said. It was plain as day in his voice when he was telling me about her.

It never occurred to me to worry about those lingering feelings before now. It was pretty clear to me that both of them were done with their relationship. Once again, he never said the words, but his body language and the words he didn't say spoke loud and clear. But I never thought she'd contact him.

Maybe he told her no this time, but what about next time? I don't believe she'll give up that easily. She's too selfish to. She'll reach out again and again until he caves. What happens then?

They have a kid together. How can I compete with that if she decides she wants him back?

I climb into my car and rest my forehead on the steering wheel. The last month has been the best month of my life. Chris and Keaton seem happy too. Things will only get better once Keaton knows. For now, I need to focus on that. I'll deal with Lydia when I have to.

Chapter 34
Chris

Heidi's front door flies open as soon as I turn into my drive like she was watching the street, waiting for us to get home. She runs across the yard and flings herself into my arms.

"Well, hello to you too," I greet her, lifting her bare feet off the ground for a moment. "What's this about?"

She shakes her head and buries her face in my neck. "I just . . . really needed a hug."

"You came to the right place," I murmur, squeezing her a little tighter. "Is there something wrong?"

"No, I just needed a hug."

I love this. Smiling, I give her one last big squeeze. "Let's get Keaton out, shall we?"

She winces and wiggles out of my grasp. "I'm sorry," she says, glancing toward the Durango.

"I'm not." I lace her fingers through mine and lead her around the car. "I grabbed dinner."

"Really?" she asks, her skepticism clear in her voice.

I know why she's skeptical. She's already had dinner with us twice this week. We try to keep it to a minimum so Keaton doesn't get curious. But no more. "Yep. I thought we might . . . stop pretending." There's no reason to anymore. Any uncertainty about us and her feelings toward him are resolved.

Her eyes go wide. "Really?" she repeats.

Because I can, I reach out and lay my hand on her cheek, reveling in the freedom. "Yeah. It's time. I hate hiding this."

She leans into my palm. "Me too."

Heidi gathers the takeout bags while I release the Keaton. He scampers on ahead, chattering to her about his morning at pre-school and his afternoon with Nana.

He pauses to draw a breath, so I ask, "Do you think Heidi should help us put the Christmas tree up this weekend?"

I didn't own a tree before Keaton, but I always wait until after his birthday to put it up to keep some separation between the two events. I'm excited to include her in our tradition this year. Not hiding means we can spend more time together and I'm looking forward to it.

He jumps, punching the air. "Yes! Please, Miss Heidi?"

"I'd love to," she says, laughing at his enthusiasm.

Keaton and Heidi set the table while I unpack dinner. It's a comfortable routine now, whether I pick up something on the way home or cook.

"Can we watch a movie after dinner?" Keaton asks, placing napkins next to each plate.

"Sure, bud," I say, adding a scoop of rice to his plate.

"Miss Heidi too?"

I pause in the middle of scooping orange chicken onto his rice to look at her. Her bottom lip is trapped between her teeth like she's trying to hold back her answer. She's watching me and waiting to follow my lead as she always does where he's concerned. "I don't care. You have to ask her."

"Please stay, Miss Heidi?"

"I'd love to, sugar bear."

***

After dinner, Keaton snuggles in next to Heidi on the couch. I sit next to him and pick him up, putting him on my lap instead.

He squirms and tries to move but doesn't get very far because I don't let him. "Daddy, no! I want to sit by Miss Heidi."

"Hold on," I tell him, wrapping one arm around his middle. Standing, I step to the side and sit down again, as close to Heidi as can be. "There. You're next to Miss Heidi."

Smiling, Heidi leans over and lays her head on my shoulder.

Keaton looks at her, then up at me, and scowls. "My Miss Heidi!"

With him watching, I slip my arm around her and squeeze. "What if she's *our* Heidi? I kind of like her too, you know."

He crosses his arms over his chest. "No. My Miss Heidi."

I stifle a laugh, but I can't stop my smile. "Alright. She's your Heidi, but she's my girlfriend."

The scowl doesn't budge, but he tilts his head like he's considering it. "Like Aunt Trista is Uncle Ryan's girlfriend?"

Next to me, Heidi giggles.

"Exactly like that, bud," I confirm.

His scowl melts. He must decide that's an acceptable variation because he sits back, getting comfortable like I'm his own personal La-Z-Boy. "Okay."

Grabbing the remote, I start the movie and sigh. *Life is good.*

Chapter 35
Heidi

Saturday morning, I wake to a text.
    Chris: The back door is open.
    I pop out of bed and jump into the first clothes I grab. I'm so excited about decorating Chris's house for Christmas. And eager to see my guys.
    I rush across the yard and let myself in, locking the door behind me and taking care to engage the child locks to be safe. "Knock knock!"
    "Miss Heidi!" Keaton comes galloping into the kitchen, still clad in his footie pajamas, clutching a sprig of some sort of plant in one hand. He stops in front of me and holds it out. "Come here!"
    Am I missing something? "I am here."
    "Bend down," Chris calls from the living room.
    Bracing my hands on my knees, I bend down until I'm eye level with Keat. He holds the plant over my head and giggles, then smacks a big kiss on my cheek. "Mwah!"
    It clicks. "Mistletoe!" Once again, I didn't know people actually did that.
    Chris laughs. "He *had* to have it when I told him what it was for."
    Keaton pushes the sprig into my hand. "My turn!"
    Grinning, I hold it over his head and kiss his cheek. "Now Daddy," he whispers.
    "Alright." *He's handling our relationship so well.* Giggling along with him, I pick Keaton up and settle him on my hip, holding him in place with one arm and the mistletoe in the other. "Let's get him."

The living room is complete chaos. There are boxes *everywhere*. One for the Christmas tree. Another for ornaments. Lights. Garland. Wreathes. Chris is seated on the couch, his coffee in one hand, his phone in the other, frowning at the device.

The mess brings me to a stop. "Didn't you live in an apartment before?"

Chris looks up and smiles, but it doesn't quite reach his eyes. "Yeah. I started shopping for decorations last month. I guess I went a little overboard."

My eyes search his face, trying to puzzle out what could possibly be wrong today. Armed with the mistletoe, I wade through the boxes and hold it over his head. His smile is genuine this time, and it chases away the shadows in his eyes. Bending down, I kiss him on one cheek, and Keaton kisses the other.

"Thanks, you two. Hey Keat, can you go get dressed for me?"

"Okay, Daddy."

"Be careful on the stairs."

"I will. I'm four now. I'm a big boy."

"I know you are, buddy."

We watch Keaton climb the stairs and disappear around the corner. "What's wrong?" I ask.

"Logan isn't feeling well. I have to go in to cover the rest of his shift."

My heart sinks, but I try my best to hide that from him. "Okay, so we decorate when you get home. Or tomorrow. Or a little of both. Where's Keaton going?"

Chris scrubs his face with both hands and scratches at his jaw. "I haven't figured that out yet. Mom is out of town. My sister doesn't watch her own kids. Maybe Mase . . ."

"Or . . ." It's crazy. I've never been alone with a child for more than a few minutes. But . . . "I could stay here with him."

Chris's eyebrows dart halfway up his forehead. "Are you sure? Not that you're not great with him, I just know you don't have a lot of experience with kids."

"Sure! It'll be great. We'll play with his train table and his other presents. I make a mean peanut butter and jelly sandwich. I've got this!" So maybe I'm a little optimistic, but how bad could it be?

"That would be great, honey." He leans forward to put his coffee on the table and rises. "You have no idea how much I appreciate this."

"I'm glad to do it. We'll have a great time."

***

I work my phone out of the back pocket of my jeans without disturbing Keaton to snap a picture of us. Chris jokes that the little boy is allergic to naps, but here he is, sound asleep with his head on my chest. I need proof.

But he *should* be tired. We've played with trains, built a pillow fort, organized all of the Christmas decoration chaos in preparation for the actual decorating, baked cookies with a recipe Fern was kind enough to text to me, and played tag in the back yard until we couldn't giggle and run anymore. It was great, though. All the things I never got as a kid, but now I get to do them with him.

Still, it was a relief when he asked to watch a movie. To sit and snuggle.

I send the picture to Chris and stash my phone again, then wiggle out from under Keaton to use the restroom. My phone buzzes with a message, a smiley emoji with heart eyes from Chris. Another one follows it.

Chris: Shift just ended. Be home soon.

The doorbell rings. The house is so quiet, and I was so focused on texting, that the sudden noise makes me jump. I fumble my phone but catch it before it hits the floor. Scowling at the door and whoever is on the other side of it for daring to be so loud, I hurry across the room and check the peephole.

The woman waiting on the front porch could've just walked right off the pages of a magazine to come here. Perfectly curled, golden blond hair cascades over her shoulders, falling to her hips. High waisted jeans and a cropped top show off her perfectly curved figure and her perfectly flat stomach. Even through the displeased scowl, her face is perfect. Full, pouty lips, big brown eyes, high cheekbones, and a small, straight nose.

I'm positively shabby by comparison. Not that it *matters*.

She reaches for the bell again, so I grab the handle and open the door, blocking her view into the house with my body.

"Can I help you?" I ask, letting some of my irritation with her ring through—both for her perfection and for ringing the bell while Keaton is napping.

She rolls her eyes, somehow managing to look bored out of her mind as she does so, clearly communicating that she believes dealing with me is beneath her. "Where's Chris? Oh, I'm sorry. That's Mr. Whitmore to you."

Excuse me? I bite my tongue to keep myself from saying the first thing that comes to mind. Chris has a sister. They look nothing alike, but this could be her. He won't appreciate her attitude, but I don't need to make it worse. "*Chris* had to go in to work for a few hours this morning. He should get home soon. If you'd like to leave contact information, I'll make sure he knows you're stopped by."

I'm *not* letting Bitchy Barbie into his home with him gone. She can leave a message and take her attitude somewhere else.

She rolls her eyes again. "He *would* be friendly with the help. Whatever. I'll wait." She steps forward like she expects me to move aside and let her pass. When I don't, her upper lip curls into an impressive snarl. "Move!"

"If you'd like to wait, you may do so in your vehicle. I'm not letting you in. I don't know you. Chris isn't home, and his son is asleep."

"*My* son!" she snaps.

My heart doesn't just sink. It freefalls to the other side of the planet. *This* is Lydia. *Of course, it is.* She's gorgeous, the kind of woman people would expect to see on the arm of a handsome man like Chris. I hoped to have a bit more time before she slithered back into his life and tried to ruin things. I'm not fool enough to give up what I've got without a fight. She already had her chance and blew it. Too bad, so sad. They're mine.

But why is she here? He hasn't mentioned her again since she texted him.

Lydia tries to take advantage of my surprise and crowd me, but Ryan trained me for something like this. I shove one bare foot behind the door, blocking it from opening farther. It hurts, but I will *not* let this witch get to Keaton. Not without Chris's permission. On reflex, my right hand snaps upward, and I thrust the heel of my hand into her nose.

Oh, shit.

I didn't really mean to do that . . . Can't say I regret it, though.

Lydia screams and clutches her nose. Blood seeps between her fingers, dripping down her arm and staining her perfect white shirt. "You *bitch!* You broke my fucking nose!"

"I told you, you're not coming in. If you'd like to return when Chris is home, by all means. Until then, hop on your broom and go West. Your flying monkeys probably miss you."

"I'm calling the cops."

Oh, shit. This is going to be bad. I *can't* get in trouble again. But I'd rather deal with whatever happens, even if it means going to prison, than let her break her son's heart. Because, inevitably, that's what it'll come to. She didn't have time for him for four whole years. She won't have time for him again; it's only a matter of time.

Mustering every last ounce of willpower and confidence I possess, I smile at her. "By all means, do." And I slam the door in her face.

"Miss Heidi?" The fear in Keaton's little voice rips my heart into tiny slivers of confetti. "Who was that?"

I twist the knobs to lock and bolt the door. "No one, sugar bear."

A shriek stops me in the act of turning to comfort him. "You can't keep me from my son! I have rights!"

A chill zaps down my spine. Unfortunately, that's true. But that's between her and Chris. My job today is to take care of Keaton, and that's what I'm doing.

I turn around, dismissing the psycho because Keaton needs me right now. He's still on the couch, knees pulled up to his chest like he's trying to protect himself. *I wish I could break her nose again for scaring him.*

"What kind of woman are you anyway? I'm his *mother!* He needs me!"

I banish my fear over what might happen if she follows through on her threat to call the law and smile at Keaton. "Come on, sugar bear. Let's have a dance party." I can turn the music up and drown her out.

"Don't you have a heart?"

Don't you? "In the office." It's as far away from the door as it's possible to get. Keaton points at the door. "Why is that lady yelling?"

That's no lady. Fern is a lady. Tara. Jam. Trista. Madi. Noel. They're ladies. That's a bitch. "She's throwing a tantrum because she didn't get her way."

He purses his lips. "She needs to go to timeout."

I bite my lip to hold back a smile. "She really does. Come on. Chris will be home soon, and he'll—" the words *make her leave* die on my tongue. I can't say that because I don't know that he will, and I shouldn't make promises I can't keep. "Your dad will take care of it."

On the way up the stairs, I get my phone and send a message to Chris. He should have a heads up.

Chapter 36
Chris

Heidi: Heads up, Lydia the psycho bitch is on your front porch screaming. And I might've broken her nose.

Fuck. My. Life. I push the button on the steering wheel to call Heidi. This is too much to text.

"Hello," she answers on the first ring.

"Is Keaton alright?"

"Mostly. Kinda confused. And scared."

My baby. I need to get home now. My foot gets a little heavier on the accelerator, edging my speed closer to ten miles per hour over the legal limit. "You broke her nose?" I ask.

There's an awkward pause. "Well, she tried to kind of force her way in after I told her it wasn't happening. And one of the self-defense lessons was—"

"Heidi," I cut her off because I know what the lesson is, "I'm so fucking proud of you. But she's still there?"

"Yes. Standing there screaming." The doorbell rings in the background. "And now ringing apparently."

"Where are you two?" I navigate a turn that puts me three blocks away. *Fuck.* I *can't* speed on this road. My son needs me, but it's not worth the risk of hitting someone else's. "I'm almost there."

"Guest room. We're going to have a dance party to drown out the noise."

I'd love to see that. "Good idea. I'll see you in a bit." *I love you.*

Oh. Oh shit. I love her.

The house comes into view, pushing that revelation to the side. I can analyze, celebrate, whatever later. Right now, I have to deal with Lydia.

She parked in the middle of the drive because of course, she did. It's big enough for two cars—hell, I have a two-car garage, I just never use it—but I park on the curb because Lydia doesn't care about anyone other than Lydia. And blocking her in would be counterproductive.

Arms crossed under her tits, pressing them up to show off her cleavage, she waits for me at the top of the stairs, tapping her foot. It's impossible to miss the bloodstains on her otherwise pristine white shirt, as well as on her face and likely her hands.

The show starts as soon as I open my door. "Your fucking *babysitter* broke my fucking nose!" she yells loud enough for the whole neighborhood to hear.

Taking a deep breath to fortify myself, I step out of the vehicle and close the door. I will not engage in a shouting match. I will not stoop to her level.

I climb the stairs and walk past her, putting myself between her and the door. Between her and my son.

She turns with me as I pass and invades my space. "Did you *hear* me?"

Crossing my arms, I lean against the door. "I did. So did everyone else on the block. My *girlfriend* already told me she denied you entry into my home and you refused to accept that. You can't blame her for reacting on instinct when you tried to force your way inside."

Lydia takes a step back. "She should have let me in. And . . . girlfriend? Seriously? Where did you find her? Her high school graduation?"

I'm not taking the bait. "What do you want, Lydia?"

A smile splits her blood-stained face, showing off her too-white teeth. She looks up at me through half-closed eyes and drops her chin just a little, trying to be sexy and seductive. Once upon a time, it worked on me. Now, I see it for the act it is. And, with all that blood, it's rather comical. She'd have a fit if she could see herself.

Her hands come to rest on my chest and slide upwards. I know this, too. She'll put her arms around my neck and rub her boobs on me. I'm not interested.

I grab her wrists and remove her hands from my body. "I *just* told you I have a girlfriend."

She rolls her eyes and takes another step closer, pressing her body to mine as I predicted. "That's not a girlfriend. That's a distraction. An easy lay while you wait."

Grabbing her by the shoulders. I force her to take a step back. Moving is not an option for me, both because I can't step back and I'm not stepping away from the door. "And what do you suppose I'm waiting for?"

She flutters her lashes at me. "Me. I'm ready, Chris. We can be a family, just like you wanted. We were great together, weren't we? We can be again."

The absurdity penetrates my brain, and I laugh before I can stop myself. "*Wanted*, Lydia. Past tense. That ended the day you made it clear our child was nothing more than a parasitic inconvenience to you. Get off my property."

Her sexy façade is swept away on a wave of shock. Rejection isn't something she had a lot of experience with when I knew her, and it seems as if things haven't changed much. "I get that you're still upset—"

"No. I'm not upset. I got over it. I got over you. There is no place for you in my life or his. Goodbye, Lydia. Stay gone this time."

She draws herself up to her full height, glaring at me with righteous indignation that is entirely fake burning in her eyes. "I'm his *mother!*"

The ridiculous claim shatters my resolve to stay calm. "You're an egg donor!" She takes a step back and opens her mouth, but I'm not done. I latch onto my patience so I don't snap again, but I don't allow her time to speak. "A mother would've stayed. Would've at least tried."

"I'm ready to try! It's his birthday, Chris. Come on."

Is she serious? She doesn't even remember his birthdate? That little factoid cuts through my anger and I settle into a resolved calm. "His birthday? That's why you came today?"

She smiles and bats her eyes again. "Of course! How could I forget?"

"His birthday was four days ago." I thought that's why she texted me when she did.

Her smile slips and her eyes widen for a fraction of a second. She recovers and flicks her wrist dismissively. "I—that's what I meant!"

"Don't lie to me. You're fucking clueless. You don't know the first thing about him."

"And who's fault is that? You could've e-mailed me or something!"

"I did. You told me to stop."

"Oh . . ." Her mouth works like she's got something to say, but it takes a while for words to come. "Well, I was really mad back then!"

"And that justifies it? What do you really want, Lydia? Because I know it's not Keaton or me."

Her eyes drop to her feet. *Bullseye.* "I—nothing. Just to be family again."

"Don't lie to me. You need money, don't you?" It's not even a question, really. What else could she really want from me? Still, it's devastating to know she'd try to use our son for money.

Her shoulders droop.

"So you thought you'd come suck up to me so I'd fix all your problems. Then you'd leave again. Go. I won't say it again. I'll call the cops on you for trespassing."

"Good!" she shouts, looking up at me again with fire in her eyes. "Call them! I want to press charges. Your *girlfriend* assaulted me. I'm taking her to court!"

"You do that." I sidestep out from between her and the door and head for the porch stairs. "I'll go talk to the neighbor across the street—the paranoid one who has cameras watching every inch of his property. He told me once to let him know if I have any problems with porch pirates because—"

She cuts me off with a scream. "You asshole!" She pushes past me and runs down the stairs, all the way to her car.

"'Bye, Lydia!" I wave.

She lowers her window to flip me off.

I need to go inside, but I drop to my ass on the top step. I wasn't lying, I have no feelings for Lydia anymore, but her act got to me in a different way. How many times is she going to try to weasel her way into my life for money? And how could she consider doing that to Keaton?

More importantly, what am I going to say to him? I don't have time to figure it out, though. Keaton is waiting on me.

Heidi

"I'm tired of dancing. Where's my daddy?"

It's been a while since Chris called. He should be home by now. "I don't know, sugar bear. Shut off the music, and I'll go check on him. But stay upstairs, okay?"

"Okay," he mumbles, already muttering the numbers to unlock my phone to pause the music. I set the code to his birthday weeks ago so I'd never forget it, but it's a blessing in disguise today. I don't have to unlock the phone for him every time he wants to hear a different song.

I creep down the stairs to check on him. He might say he doesn't feel bad about everything that happened, but I know he carries some guilt, even if it's just a little. She might try to use that against him.

I don't know what I think I'll do about it if she *does,* but I can at least be there to support him through it like he does for me when I freak out.

I press my ear to the door and can just make out what Lydia is saying. "We can be a family, just like you wanted. We were great together, weren't we? We can be again."

My blood turns to ice in my veins. I never should've come downstairs. Turning, I run for the stairs, back to Keaton's room to play Candy Land and forget what I heard. She abandoned them. There's no way he'll take her back.

But she's Keaton's mom. That's . . . something. Something that will always bind them. I don't remember it, but Thomas says that Mom took my real dad back several times before she met Curt.

I know deep down that he still has some feelings for his ex, but Chris is a different person than my mom. He won't fall into that trap. *I hope.*

Keaton has the game set up when I walk in. We choose our game pieces, and I try to put my fears aside and be upbeat and positive for him.

It doesn't work. My stomach is in knots by the time the front door closes, and the fear is plain to see in Keaton's eyes.

"Daddy!" he shouts. He lunges to his feet and runs. I follow him out the door and grab him at the top of the stairs. Chris is already on his way up.

He meets my eyes, but there's no smile to be found, just a bleakness that drives my worries deeper into my brain. "I'm sorry."

I don't know what to say to that. I don't know *why* he's sorry, and I don't want to ask in front of Keaton. So I change the subject. "Is she gone?"

He sighs and stops a step or two down, putting himself at eye level with me. "Yeah."

Keaton leans forward, reaching for his father. He was so brave through the whole thing. Instead of taking him, Chris joins us on the landing and wraps his arms around both of us to hug us tightly.

"Who was that lady?" Keaton asks.

Chris sighs again and leans back to look at me. "I think we're going to have to reschedule the decorating. I need to talk to Keat."

That's a dismissal if I've ever heard one. I get it, though. He needs some space. *They* need some father-son time. That was hard on both of them. I paste on a smile and try to pretend like everything is fine, even though I'm pretty sure the world is on fire. "Alright. No problem. I'll head home. Just . . . let me know."

Chris turns toward Keaton's room. "I will," he says without looking back. "I just need to figure out what to do."

And that's a goodbye if I've ever heard one.

I open my mouth to call out to him, but the words won't come. If he's decided to give Lydia another chance, begging and pleading won't change anything. It'll just make it harder for all of us.

"No one feels like a queen on the hard days, Heidi. It's how you handle those days and the days after that makes you a queen."

I'm no expert, but I don't think a queen would make a spectacle of herself. At least not a good one. I let myself out and walk across the yard like I would any other day.

Somewhere, a car fires up and accelerates too fast. It's odd. There are a lot of kids in this neighborhood and the residents are usually mindful of that. I turn to look, but they're already gone. I'm sure I'm not the only one who noticed though, so someone will speak with the driver in question.

I manage to hold back my tears until I'm safely hidden from the rest of the world, but then I break.

Chapter 37
Chris

I grab my phone as soon as I open my eyes and check my messages, but Heidi still hasn't responded to the text I sent her before bed last night. *Maybe she went to sleep early.*

She'll be up soon, so I fire off another text to let her know Sunday breakfast will have to be dinner instead. Logan is still sick. I hate that I didn't get to talk to her about what happened last night, but I was wiped out. And she didn't text me back.

Me: Good morning, gorgeous. I have to cover Logan's shift again this morning and I'm down to work this afternoon. Sorry we have to miss breakfast. Dinner tonight instead? I miss you.

I get dressed and check for messages before tucking my phone in my pocket to go wake Keaton. Since I haven't heard from Heidi, he'll spend the day with Ronni.

Heidi

The sun has cleared the tops of the tallest trees, but here I sit like the fool I am, waiting for Keaton to run across the yard and invite me to breakfast like he does every Sunday morning. I knew when I got out of bed that he wouldn't come today, but I had to try. I hope Chris hasn't been trying to call or text me, because I have no idea where my phone ended up when I got home yesterday. I was too upset to care. *He'd come over if he wanted to talk to me badly enough.*

Sighing, I stand up and take my tea to the sink to dump it. It's too cold to drink now, and I never wanted it anyway. I've got time to kill before I have to be to The Boutique. Maybe Tara would let me pick up a key and go in early? It would be better than sitting around moping all morning.

Someone knocks on my door, sending my heart leaping into my throat. *Chris!* I run and throw it open without looking because who else could it be?

Lydia is standing there, tape on her nose and two black eyes. I don't bother to hide my smile. She had it coming.

To my surprise, she smiles back. "Good morning. I think we got off on the wrong foot."

"I really don't think we did. How did you find me?"

"Oh! Chris told me." She flicks her wrist like it's no big deal.

The implication makes my stomach clench, but I'm not letting her get under my skin. I force myself to relax. "I don't have anything else to say to you." I move to close the door, but her hand shoots out to stop it. *She's a slow learner.*

"Did Chris talk to you?" I hesitate, and her smile grows. "He's so soft-hearted. He doesn't want to hurt your feelings. Can I come in?"

"No." I have absolutely nothing to say to her, and I doubt I want to hear what she came to say. I start to close the door again, and she sticks out a boot-clad foot to stop me again.

Undeterred, she tosses her hair over her shoulder and says, "Chris and I decided to give it another go, for Keaton's sake."

The words echo in my ears like a bad sound effect. Each repetition is another slice across my heart, but I refuse to give her the satisfaction of a reaction.

She offers me a smile that I suppose is meant to be sympathetic, but the sparkle in her eyes tells me she's enjoying this. *How can Keaton be any part of her?* "Kids who grow up with both parents do better in life, you know."

Did she just . . . ? No. I'm imagining things. She can't know my dad wasn't in the picture.

"I'm sure you understand. Obviously, that means Chris won't be seeing you anymore. And it's probably best that you stay away from Keaton too. We don't want to confuse him."

Is this really happening? It would be harder to believe if Chris had talked to me last night. Or if breakfast had happened this morning. Or if he'd even texted me—of course, since I can't prove that he hasn't since I can't find my phone. But we haven't communicated since he walked away without so much as a backward glance last night.

I grit my teeth to hold back my tears. I will not give her the satisfaction of seeing me cry. "Are you done?"

A slow, malicious smile spreads across her face. *I hope that hurts like hell.* She points to her nose. "If you come near my family, I'll file charges against you for assault. It'll be your word against mine, and you have a motive."

Pain arcs through my chest like she just shoved her hand in and ripped out my heart. My lower lip trembles, betraying me. I don't have the luxury of doubting her. I'm still on parole. Her eyes latch onto the movement, and she laughs. She's still laughing when I slam the door in her face. My feet carry me to my room. I throw myself across my bed and let the tears come.

I don't want to believe that he would let things end this way, that what we had meant so little to him, but what did I expect? It hasn't been that long. Just because I fell so fast doesn't mean he feels the same. If Lydia had waited a few more months, maybe the time would've changed things. Or maybe I was doomed to lose him from the start.

Maybe I wasn't meant to be happy. Guys like him don't really look twice at girls like me.

***

"Heidi?"

I jump, startled out of a deep, ugly cry-induced sleep by Tara's voice.

"Heidi? Are you home? Your back door was unlocked."

"Yeah," I call to her, my voice broken from tears and sleep. I sit up and scrub at my face with my hands like I can wipe away the evidence of what happened, but it's useless.

Tara stops in my bedroom doorway and gasps. "Oh, sweetie. What happened? I hated to come barging in, but you didn't come today, and you didn't answer your phone, so I got worried."

Oh shit. It's Sunday. I don't even know what time it is. Or where my phone is at. I've been too scared to look for it. What if I have a text from Chris confirming everything Lydia said? "I'm sorry."

She sits down beside me on the edge of the bed. "Don't be. What's wrong?"

"It's—"

She cuts me off with a look. "If you say nothing, so help me, God, I will assume the worst, and I will call every last one of the girls over."

I laugh. It's rusty and broken, like the first time I met her, but it's a laugh. It's actually sweet that she cares enough to make that threat. "What's the worst?"

She hesitates. "I'm not sure. But it must be bad if you're brushing it off. I'm not a guy, remember. I speak 'nothing' and 'fine' fluently." She slings her arm around me and pulls my head down onto her shoulder. "Tell me about it."

"I was babysitting Keaton yesterday, and Lydia turned up." Remembering all the fun we had before that bitch showed up makes me tear up again.

"Oh shit." Tara grabs a box of tissues off my nightstand and hands me one. "You didn't let her in, did you?"

I dab at my eyes, trying to control the tears. "No. I broke her nose."

"I—you . . ." She kisses the top of my head and throws her other arm around me to hug me. "I love you. You're my hero. I want to be you when I grow up. Continue."

That's hilarious, considering you're the better role model here. "Chris came home, and they talked. I overheard her telling him that she was ready to be a mom and they could be the family he always wanted. When he came inside, he was just . . . different. He apologized and told me we'd have to decorate for Christmas another day. He promised to let me know when he figured things out. And he just walked away with Keaton. I haven't heard from him since."

She strokes my hair, and I can't help but think she'll be a great mom. Her little one is lucky to have her. "Oh, sweetie. You didn't hear the rest of the conversation? How do you know he fell for that?"

I clear my throat and grab a fresh tissue for the next tear outbreak. "Lydia came by this morning. She said they've decided to try again for Keaton. They think it will be best for him if I stay away. And she threatened to press charges against me for breaking her nose if I come near them."

Tara gasps. "Okay, first of all, can she *do* that?"

I twist the tissue in my hand, turning it into a rope while I talk. "Well, she'd be lying, but my record will work against me. I wasn't violent, but I was a criminal, and I'm still on parole. She just has to cry and say I attacked her because my boyfriend broke up with me for her. It's her word against mine. There were no witnesses to back me."

Tara makes an unhappy noise. "I don't like this."

"I don't either."

She shakes her head. "No, I mean it's not right. Chris wouldn't do that. He wouldn't take her back."

I want to agree with her, but it's better if I don't get my hopes up. Men have been failing me since birth. "I don't want to believe it, either. But he hasn't reached out at all."

She turns and grabs my shoulders, holding me at arm's length to look into my eyes. "Heidi, don't believe it until you hear it from Chris. Don't listen to Lydia. Even if it is the truth, Chris owes it to you to tell you himself. He wouldn't let her do his dirty work for him. He's not a coward like that."

Tara is right, but I can see the truth in what Lydia said too. He *is* softhearted. "She said he didn't want to hurt my feelings."

Tara squeezes her eyes shut, unable to refute that claim. "I don't care. Don't buy it."

"I'll try." It's the best I can do. Under the circumstances, I think it's best if he's the one to initiate any sort of conversation. If it *is* true, I don't want to provoke Lydia into making good on her threat.

"What *is* it with the men in my life being complete idiots?" she mutters to herself. She shakes her head and turns her attention to me again. "Do you need anything?"

"Tara, you're due in less than a week. Go home. Don't stress. I'll be alright." And I will. I've survived worse than this. Yeah, it hurts. I don't want it to end. There's a gaping hole in my chest because my heart is next door, cleaved perfectly in two so they each have a piece. But I'm a survivor.

The words I said to my brother the day after I moved in here spring to mind. *"I don't want to be his victim. I want to be a survivor."*

I did it, Thomas. I had a lot of help, but I did it.

"I think I might go sleep on my brother's couch for a few days. I haven't seen him in a while, and it might be good to get some distance." Though they don't happen every week, our Sunday chats are something I look forward to. My showing up on his doorstep with a bag probably isn't something he's bargained for, but I don't think he'll turn me away.

Tara frowns. "Just don't ignore Chris if he calls, Heidi."

That's assuming I find my phone. "I won't."

Chapter 38
Chris

Heidi's house is dark, and her little VW is gone when I finally pull into my drive. *That's odd.* Maybe she's working late with Tara or decided to go out for dinner. I hope that's all it is, anyway. She still hasn't replied to my texts. I hope she's not upset about yesterday . . . She handled Lydia like a champ. There's nothing to be upset about.

I really wish she were home, though. After the weekend I've had, I could use a hug. And I want to talk about what to do if Lydia shows up again. *I should've gone over last night once Keaton was down.*

Coulda, shoulda, woulda, though. Keaton was so upset about the lady throwing a temper tantrum on the porch it took the rest of the day to calm him down and dodge the hard questions he asked because I never did figure out how to explain it to him. I was wrung out by bedtime.

Three vehicles pull up the curb while I'm unfastening Keaton's harness. The rumble of Ryan's Barracuda is a dead giveaway. *Did I forget something?* It's late on a Sunday. We never do anything at this time.

What the hell is going on?

From those three vehicles come my four best friends in the world, plus their partners, Ronni, Colton, and Noel. "What's going on?" I ask as they approach. "Where's Madi?" The others are here; it's odd for her to be left out now unless she's holed up in the back room sewing.

"That's what I'd like to know," Colton mutters, obviously addressing the first question. The other guys mutter their agreement. Ryan just shrugs when I look at him. We were *just* at The Bar together not thirty minutes ago.

"I was told to get my ass outside and get in Colton's car," Austin offers. "So, ladies, would one of you care to enlighten us?"

"Madi is sick. This is an intervention," Tara says. "Ronni, would you take Keaton inside, please?"

"Yes, Aunt T." Ronni grabs Keaton's hand, and they make for the door.

"Now, wait a minute!" I put a hand on Ronni's shoulder to stop her. She can't get in without the key, but there's some sort of misunderstanding here. I don't need an intervention. "Why do I need an intervention?"

"Here, Ronni." Ryan holds out his key ring, on which is a key to my house. "It's the one painted blue."

I glare at him. "You're in on this?"

He glares right back. "I didn't *plan* it, but I provided insider information."

The click of the door closing seems to be a signal. Noel grabs my arm and drags me toward the patio table. "Sit."

There's no way for her to force me, short of racking me, but I comply. The sooner we get this over with, the better. I'm hungry, and it's been a long fucking day after picking up Logan's shift and working my own. I've been gone since five-thirty, I missed breakfast with Heidi, and she's not answering my texts. I'm *not* in the mood for this. "Someone start talking."

The girls arrange themselves in front of me, wearing matching *I will eat you alive* expressions. It's actually enough to make my heart skip a beat or two. This many angry women is *never* a good thing. The guys stand behind their respective partners, but they exchange glances and shrug, except for Ryan.

"Where is Lydia?" Tara asks.

Lydia? What does she have to do with anything? I shrug. "Fuck if I know. Probably looking for someone else to manipulate into being her sugar daddy."

The girls exchange glances, the anger on their faces giving away to confusion.

Ryan clears his throat. "I think you'd better explain what happened yesterday before they murder you. Because, as things stand, I'm not sure I'll stop them."

What the hell did I do to get *him* on their side? He's my fucking business partner! But he did hate Lydia . . . "With Lydia? Nothing happened for me. She showed up. Heidi broke her nose. I sent her ass packing."

Ryan holds up both hands, forming a T. "Timeout! Heidi *broke her nose?*"

Grinning, I nod. I was dying to tell him, but we were so busy all day, I never had a chance. "Lydia tried to get in the house. Heidi broke her nose with a palm heel strike."

Ryan's laughter echoes through the neighborhood. "That's my girl! Sorry, Pixie Stix, but I'm sending another woman flowers."

Trista inclines her head. "I'll allow it."

"So Lydia didn't tell you she wants to try again?" Tara, the apparent spokeswoman, asks, pulling us back on task. She cringes and glances at Trista, who shrugs. *What the hell?*

I squint at her. There's no way she can know about that. "She did . . . How do you know that? I haven't told anyone." There was no need to, except maybe to make them all laugh.

They're not laughing, though.

Tara sighs and looks around at the other women. "Do I just come right out and say it, or try to lead him to the correct conclusion?"

My patience is dangerously close to its limits. I'm not in the mood for games tonight unless they involve Heidi and orgasms. "Tara, just spit it out. I have no idea why you seem to be upset with me. I've had a shitty weekend. I want to go inside and cook dinner and call my girlfriend."

I don't know if that was the right or wrong thing to say, but it must help Tara decide because she nods. "And your girlfriend is . . . ?"

I wave a hand toward Heidi's. "I don't know where she is. I've texted her half a dozen times, and she's not replying. I thought she was maybe working late with you, but you're here so . . . you tell me."

Tara squeezes her eyes shut, then looks to the sky and sighs. "But Heidi is your girlfriend?"

Why do I feel like I'm on fucking trial? And why can't she just tell me what the hell is going on? "Is this a trick question?"

Tara sighs again. A weird look crosses her face, and she reaches behind her to brace a hand against her back. Fern glances at her and frowns a little. *Is she thinking what I'm thinking?* "Look, I'm trying to lead you to a problem you're obviously not aware of without breaking a sister's trust. So work with me here, damn it! Because I think I'm in labor."

Behind her, Gabe freezes. His eyes get huge, and the color drains from his face. He sways a little, and Mason puts a hand on his shoulder to steady him.

I point to a chair. "Sit the fuck down, Gabe."

He ignores me and grabs onto Tara, which is a horrible idea. If he falls, he'll take her and the baby down with him. Mason and Ryan *might* be able to stop him. They're pretty quick, but dead weight is a bitch. "Are you sure, Princess? Do we need to—oh my God, we don't have your bag. I need to—"

"You need to sit your ass in that chair," I say, nudging it away from the table with the toe of my shoe. Ryan grabs him by the shoulder and strong-arms him into it, instructing him to put his head between his knees before he passes the fuck out. With him somewhat under control, I turn back to Tara. "What do you need, T?"

"How long?" Fern asks, her past medical training kicking in.

Tara waves her off like labor is nothing. "Oh, I'm fine. They started about an hour ago. Nothing to worry about yet. The doctor told me not to go in until they've been five minutes apart and one minute long for an hour. I just can't figure out how to make this bonehead understand that his relationship is broken!" She cringes again and throws her hands up in frustration. "Damn it! I shouldn't have said that!"

My relationship is broken? How? Things were great yesterday before Lydia showed up. In fact, we took a huge step forward with Heidi volunteering to watch Keaton. It hasn't been very long, but that woman is everything I never knew I wanted in a partner. "Well, I heard that. But I'm not sure why you think that."

Tara sighs and begins pacing. This is good, though. Walking can help. "Heidi didn't come to work today. I came by to check on her."

I count to ten before I speak so I don't snap at the pregnant lady. I don't need Ryan and Fern going mama bear on me and mauling my ass. "So you know something I don't know, something that impacts my relationship, but you can't tell me what it is?"

Tara claps. "That is correct."

I'm reaching here, but I take a stab at connecting another dot. "And it has something to do with Lydia coming by yesterday?"

She claps again. "Also correct. Just call her. Please."

Why didn't you just lead with that? I blame pregnancy brain. It is real, and I need *something* to blame to save my sanity right now. I pull my phone from my pocket and hit the icon to dial her number. I didn't try to call her today because I was busy and I assumed she was too since she wasn't replying, but now . . . I put it on speaker so Tara can be satisfied that she actually answers, and we all listen while it rings through to voicemail.

"Damn it!" Tara scowls at my phone. "She promised she wouldn't ignore you if you called."

Sonofabitch. Maybe I really do have a relationship problem. It's unlike Heidi to ignore calls. But she could be busy—driving or . . . "Where *is* she?"

Tara looks at Fern, and they both bite their lips. Fern shrugs. "I don't know, T . . . That's not exactly divulging confidential information."

Jam shakes her head. "But it kind of is."

Fern pulls out her phone. "Let me call her.

"That's kind of cheating if she's ignoring his calls," Noel says.

Trista wrinkles her nose. "She doesn't have to tell her she's with him."

Tara snaps her fingers. "Oh! Tell her I'm in labor."

"Good, this works," Jam says with a nod.

What the fuck is this shit? I look at the guys, hoping for clarification, and am met with identical looks of confusion. Even Mason doesn't quite seem to understand.

Fern dials Heidi's number. It rings and rings, and just as voicemail picks up, the back door flies open. Ronni and Keaton come boiling out, Ronni holding a phone I immediately recognize. "Mama! We found this phone upstairs. It was ringing a lot, and it says you're calling."

Sonofabitch. I can't decide if I'm relieved because Heidi isn't intentionally ignoring me or upset that I can't get ahold of her. Where could she be? Maybe she's out retracing her steps looking for her phone? But where did she go if she wasn't working with Tara?

She takes the phone. "Thank you, Rainbow." Once the kids are back inside, she looks at the phone in her hand and mutters, "Well, shit."

Tara bites her lip and drops her head. "She mentioned she might go to her brother's . . . Do you know how to get ahold of him?"

I take a deep breath and scrub my face with my hands. "No. We haven't done the meet the family thing on her side yet."

"I don't suppose you know the code?" Jam asks.

I shake my head. It's not something I felt the need to know. Calling her is a dead end, and I have no idea where she went aside from knowing she's probably with family, but there's a more immediate problem. I can take care of things with Heidi *after* Tara leaves. "Okay, T. I have a problem. I'm going to fix it. What—"

She pins me with the most perfect Mom glare I've ever been on the receiving end of in my life. "Do you promise?"

"I—what?" My self-preservation instincts kick in, and I'm almost scared to speak for fear of incurring her wrath.

"Do you promise me you're going to fix it?"

"Of course. Why would you even have to ask that?" It's not like I *want* to have relationship problems. I don't even know for sure why I have them!

She glances toward the house where the kids disappeared after handing over the phone, then at Mason and rubs her belly. "Childbirth is never guaranteed to go as planned."

"Oh, T." Fern pulls the taller woman into her arms, and Mason rests a hand on her shoulder, the tears in his eyes glittering in the glow of the porch light. But they don't promise our friend that everything will be fine. No one does.

Tara sniffles, succumbing to the hormones and fear. "Will you all come? I know it's just to sit in the waiting room, but I'll feel so much better if I know you're all close by."

We all talk over each other, swearing to be there, even if it takes all night.

She looks at me and sniffles again. "Heidi, too."

No matter what. "I'll find her, Tara. We'll be there. Is that why you brought everyone here?"

She nods. "Two birds with one stone." She gasps and presses a hand to her back again.

Gabe makes a strangled sound and tries to stand.

Ryan pushes him back down. "Gabe, she'll know when it's time to go. If you want to help her, stop freaking out and let her do her thing."

Trista lets out a whoop and punches the air with the hand not holding a glowing phone screen. "I got it! The code was Keaton's birthday."

She holds it out to me, and I begin navigating the unfamiliar icons. Her brother's name is easy for me to remember. Keaton might be enamored with *Paw Patrol* and *PJ Masks* right now, But *Thomas & Friends* will always be king. At least for a few more years. I find his name in her contacts and call him, hoping he might know where to find her.

"Alright, T. I'm fixing it. Go."

She nods and leans over to hug me. Gabe pulls her off of me, and there is general confusion as people decide who is going and who is waiting with me.

"Hello?" a soft, albeit angry voice says in my ear. "Who is this?"

"This is Chris—don't hang up!" I don't know what he knows. I don't know if he's angry with me. All I know is something about yesterday's encounter with my ex has my girlfriend upset, and I need to talk to her.

"Why shouldn't I?" he asks. "You're just another asshole who doesn't respect my sister."

I squeeze the arm of my chair so hard my fingers ache to alleviate my anger. Nothing could be further from the truth. "That's not true . . . I have the utmost respect for Heidi."

"Yeah, dumping her for your psychotic ex is respecting the hell out of her. Way to go."

"What the hell did you say?" Tara might've had a problem with divulging information, but Thomas clearly does not. *At least I know what the hell is going on.*

"I said what I said."

Why the hell would Heidi think that? I've told her how my relationship with Lydia ended. Why would she think anything could fix that? "Look, I'm going to lay it all out for you—cards on the table. I have no idea what's going on here. I didn't know there was a problem until I got home from work and all my friends mobbed me, calling it an intervention. The girls seemed to know something, but I've got more information out of you than I could get out of them because they're on some sisters before misters kick, which I would usually applaud, but apparently, my love life is involved, and that's just not cool.

"My ex can go play in fucking traffic on the freeway for all I care. I love your sister, but if you tell her that before I do, I will make you regret that you were ever born. If you know where she is, will you please tell me? I would like to speak to her face to face so we can figure this out. We have a mutual friend in labor, and that friend wants us both there, so I'm on a timeline, and I don't even know how I fucked up."

The other end of the line is silent so long I start to squirm. The phone buzzes in my hand with an incoming text. "I texted an address to her number. If you hurt her no one will ever find your body," he whispers. And the line goes dead.

I look up to find everyone staring at me. "Alright, Tara, I'm going. Go home. Rest if you can."

She nods, and Gabe leaps into action. "Are you sure we should go home? We can get your bag and go—"

Tara glares him into silence. "They're not five minutes apart yet. Chill. Just get me home."

Hiding a smile, Fern heads for the door. "I'll go have Keaton pack a bag. He's coming home with us tonight. Go."

I lunge to my feet and pull her into a hug. "You're the best." I kiss her on the cheek and let her go, running for my Durango.

Chapter 39
Heidi

"Are you expecting someone?" I call. Thomas and Olivia are making so much noise cleaning up after dinner they probably didn't hear the knock on the door. No one buzzed to get inside, but one of his friends might know the code to get in the door of the apartment building. Or maybe it's a neighbor.

"Yeah," Thomas calls back. "Can you get it for me?"

I look out, because I've learned my lesson about answering doors without knowing who is on the other side. And I gasp. I quell the urge to rip the door off its hinges in my excitement. *But why am I excited? How did he find me?*

"Heidi?" I look over my shoulder at my brother. "Are you going to open it?"

"Maybe. I'm—"

"I told him where to find you."

I while around to glare at him. "*You* told him? How?"

Thomas shrugs. "He has your phone."

How does he—the dance party! I remember now. I left it in his office.

"Heidi, at least hear the man out."

I turn again to stare at the door. Thomas told him how to find me. He convinced Thomas to give him that information. My brother walks up behind me and reaches around me to open the door.

"No one." With that cryptic message, which must mean something to Chris because he nods, Thomas shoves me out the door and closes it behind me.

"Um, hi?" *Oh, way to go. That was so sophisticated.*

Chris smiles and backs across the hall, putting his back to the wall. *Giving me space.* I hate every millimeter of it. He stares at me as if committing every last detail to memory but doesn't say a word.

"What do you want, Chris?" Thomas is inclined to agree with Tara. He says no man would end a relationship that way. Olivia blew a raspberry at him and said he was so cute. So maybe Tara was right, and he's here to "do the right thing."

"I'm sorry," he murmurs. "Can we talk outside?"

"I'm good here." At least here I don't have far to go if this ends the way I think it will. I mean, he was willing to give *me* a second chance, and I never did anything to him. Why wouldn't he give her one too? And if that's the case, of course, he's going to choose *her* over *me*. She's . . . well, she's a bitch, but a gorgeous one. And the mother of his child. I've got nothing to top that.

Chris sighs. ""Talk to me, Heidi. Please."

I shake my head and shove my hands in my pockets. "I think you should go first."

"Honey, I don't even know where to start. I didn't even know we had a problem until—you know what? That's a long story. I can tell you later. Why do you suddenly think I'm breaking up with you for my ex?"

I hug my middle against the renewed surge of pain. "She told me so. And I heard her tell you that she was ready to settle down and be the family you always wanted."

He holds up a hand. "You heard that?"

I blush, embarrassed to confess to eavesdropping, even if I had good reason. "Yeah. I went downstairs to check on you. Keaton and I were worried because you hadn't come inside yet. I know you don't feel the greatest about the whole deal with her, so I was afraid she was making you feel horrible."

Chris's eyes drift shut. "But why would you think I'd go for that?"

"You were just . . . distant when you came inside. You just kind of dismissed me and told me you needed to figure things out. I didn't know what to think. And why *wouldn't* you give her a second chance? You gave me one." Saying it feels like I'm accusing him of something horrible when it's the best thing anyone has ever done for me, but it is, in my mind, a valid point.

He frowns at me. "You're comparing apples to oranges. I've already told you how I feel about her. Nothing will change that. But why didn't you *say* something?"

I look away, unable to meet his eyes. When he puts it like that, it all seems so silly. And now *he's* probably mad at *me* for making a thing out of nothing. "Because you had enough on your plate with Keaton! What was I supposed to do, beg you not to leave me? Throw a tantrum like she did and keep you from giving Keaton the reassurance he needed? I was waiting for you to call or something today and she showed up—"

"She *what?*" He pushes off the wall and crosses the hallway in one step to stand in front of me and grab my arms. My brain screams *panic and run*, but my body trusts him completely and doesn't move to obey. A deep breath dispels the need to flee.

I look down and wiggle my toes, watching them glitter against the drab carpet. "She said you told her where I live and that the two of you decided to give it another go for Keaton's sake, but you were too softhearted to tell me. Between that and what I heard yesterday, and the way you were when you came inside, well... it wasn't too hard to believe. And then she threatened to press charges if I came near any of you again. Since she could say I did it in a fit of jealous rage and I'm on parole, so I thought it was best to visit Thomas for a day or two, even if I couldn't find my phone."

He pulls me into a hug and heaves a shuddering sigh. Being in his arms again slams through my hastily erected defenses and relief comes flooding in. The tears that have plagued me off and on all day—ready to fall at the slightest provocation—come rushing back, but I hold them off.

"Oh, honey. I'm so sorry. No." He sighs again, and his fingers comb through my hair. "Lydia was only after money. She didn't really want Keaton or me. I should've talked to you last night, but I was just so upset at the whole situation—her showing up and scaring Keaton and the fact that she was using him as a tool to get to me. I wasn't dismissing you. You could've stayed. I wish you *would* have stayed. I was just lost in my own head trying to figure out how to explain it to him."

I hope that bitch's nose heals crooked. If she's trying to con her way into Chris's life for his money, she can't afford to pay to have it fixed. But, as mad as I am at her, I'm angrier with myself for falling for it. "So we're okay?" I'm almost too afraid of the answer to ask, but I need to hear him say it. What if he says we're not? How do I make it up to him?

He squeezes a little tighter. "You tell me." His phone rings before I can answer. "Always fucking interrupted," he mutters, fishing it out of his pocket.

The person on the other end doesn't give him a chance to speak. "It's time."

The call ends. That short message must mean something to Chris too, but he smiles this time. "If we *are* okay, how do you feel about going to meet our new niece or nephew?"

The words take a moment to make sense, but when they do, I fly into action, pushing away from Chris to get my things. "Tara's in labor? Oh my God! Let me get my purse! And I need to tell Thomas—oh my God!" The door is locked, so I pound on it. "Thomas! Let me in! I've got to—"

Chris grabs my hips and turns me around. "There's something I want to say before we go."

"But—"

"We have time for this, Heidi. We'll *make* time for this." He leans in and places the softest of kisses on my lips. "I love you."

Behind me, the lock clicks. But I don't care. I throw my arms around Chris's neck and pull him back for a real kiss. "I love you too," I gasp, out of breath, when we finally break apart. "And I'll never leave again."

"Good," Thomas says behind me. "But my previous statement stands. No one."

I look over my shoulder at him, then back at Chris to find him grinning. "You have nothing to worry about."

Thomas reaches around me to extend at hand to Chris. The two of them shake like they're making some sort of pact. I can figure it out later, though. I have the rest of my life to pester the details out of one of them. I have places to be tonight.

Chris

Hand in hand, Heidi and I run through the halls of the maternity wing. We burst through the door, and a sea of familiar faces turns our way. Someone claps like we just made a big announcement or something, but after the drama, I suppose coming in together is exactly that.

Keaton is asleep, sprawled across Ryan's chest, so I don't need to worry about him. I scan the faces until I find Tara's father and brothers. Her *real* brothers, not the ones who adopted her. "How is she?"

Colton answers for them, the only one of the four who isn't a little pale. "Mom texted a few minutes ago. She's giving Gabe hell but doing great. It shouldn't be long now."

Fern paces past, one hand pressed to her stomach. I reach out and snag her arm, redirecting her so I can hug her with one arm because the other isn't letting go of Heidi. "She's going to be fine. They both are."

She nods, but her eyes are a million miles away.

A sob shatters the silence, drawing everyone's attention to the woman on my other side. "What's wrong?" I ask Heidi, pulling her a little closer.

"I'm just . . . I'm so happy to call y'all my friends."

Fern steps around me and takes Heidi into her arms for a hug. "We're happy we have you. You were one of our missing pieces."

"Missing pieces?" It makes a certain sort of sense, but I want to hear her take on it.

Jam walks over and joins Fern and Heidi, wrapping her arms around both women. "You were missing your other half, and Madi still is."

Heidi sniffs and hiccups. "I thought Madi had a boyfriend?"

"Madi has a bedwarmer," Noel mutters, joining the group hug.

Ryan somehow stands without disturbing my child. "Alright, break it up. It's my turn." He wades through the women crowded around Heidi to sling his free arm around her shoulders. "I'm so proud of you I might cry." He squeezes as hard as he can. "I just wish I was there when it happened."

"When what happened?" Heidi asks, leaning around him to ask me for clarification with a look.

"When you broke that bitch's nose!"

Someone claps again, a polite golf clap, and several others pick it up.

"Oh," Heidi says, hiding her face against Ryan's side. "I really shouldn't have done that."

"Yeah, you really should have," he says on a laugh.

Colton leaps to his feet, smiling broadly at his phone. "I hate to break up the lovefest, but—"

Gabe bursts into the room. "It's a girl!"

Ronni clasps her hands under her chin. "Yes!"

Gabe is gone again before anyone can congratulate him, not that I blame him. There's time for that later, and he needs to be with that little miracle. We shake hands with the proud grandparents—even Gabe's father is teary-eyed—and hug each other.

It reminds me of the day a little over four years ago when I walked into this same waiting room to announce the birth of my son. There was so much love and support here that day, and it has grown exponentially since. One little room can scarcely contain it. Eyes blurry with tears, I look around and marvel at what we've become. Five inseparable boys grew up to create this kaleidoscope of love, all the more unique and beautiful for each different piece in the frame.

Epilogue
Chris

My backyard buzzes with conversation, laughter, and love. It's been a whole year since we gathered here for the first time. There are more of us now, but there's always room. The new additions blend in seamlessly. We're one big happy family.

Tara's daughter Haven wails, pulling up to stand with the help of her mother's chair, and tugs at Tara's arm. Tara sighs but laughs off her daughter's jealousy and shifts Fern and Mason's son Jackson to one arm to make room for both babies in her lap.

Everyone is content. Keaton is playing with Ronni. They won't miss Heidi or me for a few minutes, and a few minutes is all I need. I lean over and ask, "Would you help me with something, please?"

"Sure!"

I catch Thomas's eye, then take my time leading Heidi inside, giving her brother time to take his place. We stop in the kitchen, my heart pounding in my ears. I spent months trying to plan the perfect way to do this and kept coming up empty. It wasn't until I realized that any way is perfect that it came to me. And it is only right that *everyone* is here. And that anyone could interrupt at any moment because that's what our life is. And it's perfect.

"What are we doing?" she asks, looking around for something that needs doing.

I walk to the refrigerator, glancing down the hall to ensure Thomas and Olivia are ready. He peers around the corner and grins, giving me a thumbs up. He still likes to remind me that no one will find my body if I upset his sister, but it's more of a joke now than anything. *I think.*

Hands shaking, I pull a little blue box from the top of the fridge and turn, dropping to one knee. Heidi gasps and slaps a hand over her mouth. "Heidi—"

The back door slides open, and Trista walks in. "Hey, Chris, Keaton fell—" She stops talking and backs out of the kitchen. "Never mind. I've got this." She closes the door behind her.

"Yes!" Heidi says, flinging her arms around my neck.

My heart swells to the bursting point at her answer. But I shake my head and sigh. "I didn't even get to ask!"

She giggles and kisses my neck. "Like you were going to get a chance."

"Well, if it matters, I asked your brother for your hand in marriage."

She gasps again. "You did?"

"He did," Thomas confirms. He and Olivia join us in the kitchen. Heidi shoots to her feet and throws herself into his arms.

Rising, I turn in time to watch his face turns red. "Wow. When he asked, I didn't think you'd care that much what I thought."

"Of course I care!" Heidi cries.

Thomas smirks at me. "Just as long as he remembers no one will ever find his body if he hurts you."

Heidi steps back and punches him in the shoulder, making him wince. "Stop threatening to off my fiancé!"

"Do you want to see your ring?" I ask before he can say anything else to get himself hurt. He might be stronger than her, but Heidi trains with a single-minded determination since her run-in with Lydia. She can take him.

"Yes!" She shoves him back and turns to me, holding out her left hand for me to slide the ring into place. I open the box and carefully remove the ring from its nest of silk to slide it on her finger. The pearl gleams in the streams of late afternoon light pouring through the window. It's not perfectly round like cultured pearls, nor is it perfectly white, but it's perfect for her.

Her eyes go round as she stares at it. "A pearl?"

"A natural pearl—as rare and beautiful as you are," I explain. "And as precious as you are to me."

Smiling, she leans in for a kiss. "I love it. I love *you!*"

"I love you too," I murmur before stealing another kiss.

A Note From Cara

Thank you for reading *A Second Glance*! If you enjoyed reading it as much as I enjoyed writing it, I hope you'll consider taking a moment to leave a review and share your thoughts. Reviews are magic fairy dust readers use to help good books fly. Your review could help other readers decide to read I Kinda Do and the other stories in the Tarnished Hearts series.

My newsletter is a great way to stay up-to-date with the newest releases. If you haven't already signed up, you can do so on my website, caradsmith.com. You'll get a free short story about the day Ronni, Fern, and Mason met when you sign up, and there are sure to be more short stories made available to subscribers along the way!

Acknowledgments

This page is always harder than writing entire books. I'd need a book to properly thank everyone involved in this effort. Especially since, in so many ways, this one feels like the end of something to me. It's not, of course, but a year ago this was the end of this particular road for me. I thought I'd be sitting at a T in the road right now, trying to decide between right and left, one series I've already completed and another, but now the middle is an option.

Thank you to my Misters for your patience when I tell you I'm almost done and stare blankly at the screen for another hour. It seems like it should be so easy to just walk away and leave whatever I'm doing for later, but I'll leave half of my brain at the keyboard if I do. We made it, though, and I couldn't have done it without either of you. And I learned my lesson. I'll never commit to that many books in a year again. At least not without having them all written in advance. Steven, you told me once that I should write a book, and I told you I couldn't. Damn it, I was wrong.

To the usual suspects, Kelsey, Shannon, and Katie, for the usual madness. The random messages claiming I can't do this when we all know I can; I only need someone to whack me over the head with a truth bomb. And, of course, the endless well of support and input, even when I'm whining. For seeing it through from the bare-bones first draft to the fully fleshed out final product. I know it seems like nothing to you, but it's everything to me. Especially since I know you all have a lot going on in your lives right now. And you don't have to do any of it, but you choose to. Thank you from the bottom of my heart.

Jen, you're new to the team, such as it is, but your help is invaluable. I was far too shy to do what you do. I'm getting better, but I still second-guess myself. Thank you for all of your hard work.

May, I don't know how you take my half-assed description of the picture I see in my head and turn it into a masterpiece, but I'm so glad you do. I told you once that I trust your judgment, and that holds true. Thank you for giving my words a face.

Dawn and Nancy, I've learned so much from both of you. From the outside looking in, your job probably seems easy. I know better, though. You take the flawed stories I send and polish them, all while staying true to the voices of my characters—something I struggle to do at times and the voices are in my head. Thank you for all that you do!

Dear reader, thank YOU. Doubly so if you're still reading this. I released my first book with a hope and a prayer that it would maybe, maybe, attract ten readers a month. Thank you for showing me that I'm not reaching high enough. And an extra thank you to the fans who go out of their way to tell me that they're already ready for the next one. You know who you are, but the list is too long to put here.

Thank you to my family, blood or not, who don't make things weird when I see you out in the wild. You know what I mean. No one ever expected those scenes from me. Side note, y'all are the original reason for that special warning page at the beginning. Now, I keep it because it's funny. I apologize; there are simply too many of you to list.

As ever, last but not least, thank you to my mom and dad for your unfailing support. For telling me from a young age that I can be whatever I want to be and having my back while I find my way to where I'm meant to be. It was a long, winding road, but you told me once that knowledge can never be taken away from me. I like to think that everything I've done until now contributes to my stories in some way.

Follow Cara

My website:
www.caradsmith.com

Facebook:
www.facebook.com/CaraSmithAuthor

Instagram:
www.instagram.com/caradsmith

Also By Cara

Tarnished Hearts:
*Hired—Newsletter bonus short story
I Kinda Do—Mason and Fern
*Surprise!—Deleted Epilogue
Right By You—Gabe and Tara
Dare To Love—Austin and Jamaica
(TBD)Tarnished Hearts 3.5—Noel and Colton
It's Not You—Ryan and Trista
A Second Glance—Chris and Heidi
(TBD)Tarnished Hearts 6—Madi and Logan

Each book in the Tarnished Hearts series is a stand-alone, meaning each story is self-contained and they can be read in any order. Some jokes, conversations, and references might make a little more sense if you read them in the order in which they were written, but it is not necessary. Each story has a guaranteed HEA.

*Find these on my website.

Tarnished Hearts doesn't end here! Stay tuned for Madi's story.

www.ingramcontent.com/pod-product-compliance
Lightning Source LLC
LaVergne TN
LVHW041628060526
838200LV00040B/1480